# DEATH OF AN ADEPT

# DEATH OF AN ADEPT

## A Novel of The Adept

## KATHERINE KURTZ
## DEBORAH TURNER HARRIS

ACE BOOKS, NEW YORK

DEATH OF AN ADEPT

An Ace Book
Published by The Berkley Publishing Group
200 Madison Avenue, New York, NY 10016

The Putnam Berkley World Wide Web site address is
http://www.berkley.com/berkley

Make sure to check out *PB Plug*, the
science fiction/fantasy newletter, at
http://www.pbplug.com

First Edition: December 1996

Library of Congress Cataloging-in-Publication Data

  Kurtz, Katherine.
    Death of an adept / Katherine Kurtz and Deborah Turner
Harris. — 1st ed.
      p.  cm. — (The adept series ; 5)
    ISBN 0-441-00367-2
    I. Harris, Deborah Turner.  II. Title.  III. Series: Kurtz,
Katherine.  Adept ; [bk. 5].
PS3561.U69D4   1996
813' .54—dc20                        96-881
                                        CIP

Printed in the United States of America

10  9  8  7  6  5  4  3  2  1

*To David and Ursala Winder,*
*Just because . . .*

# ACKNOWLEDGMENTS

Once again, we are indebted to a number of people for their valuable technical advice and assistance, among them:

Dr. David P. Winder, MD, ChB, FRCA, Consultant Anaesthetist, Hull Royal Infirmary, who graciously allowed himself to be drafted as consultant anaesthetist for this project, and who was *not* the model for the slimy Dr. Mallory;

Inspector Ian MacPherson, Highlands and Islands Police, Stornoway, for guidance on policing procedures on the Isle of Lewis, Outer Hebrides, who hardly batted an eye when informed that we were bringing crime to his island;

First Officer Bob McLellan, Loganair, for allowing us to pick his brain about island-hopping and civil aviation procedures at Stornoway Aerodrome;

Sgt. Frank Urban, Strathclyde Police, Motherwell, for telling us where the bodies go;

Margaret Carter, for sleuthing out the corridors of UCSF-Mount Zion Medical Center in San Francisco;

Peter Morwood, for again providing technical background on helicopters and the SAS.

To these and all the others who assisted our development of the background for this story, our most sincere thanks.

# PROLOGUE

SOMEWHAT unusually for mid-December, Paisley-town lay under a dusting of winter-white. The citified blend of building heat and traffic fumes that kept the snow from lying in the streets of Glasgow, ten miles away, did not prevent a thin layer of powder from settling on the crow-stepped gables of a tall Victorian house that stood in stately seclusion behind a high stone wall at the southern edge of the town. The bells of a nearby church were striking eleven o'clock when a steel-grey Lancia sporting the logo of one of Scotland's leading press agencies nosed into the upper end of the street, creeping along to halt outside the front gate of the house.

The dark-haired woman who emerged from the driver's door in a swirl of silver fox conveyed an immediate impression of expensive cologne and couturier fashions, but the artfully made-up eyes behind the designer sunglasses she removed and tossed onto the dash were hard, the red-painted lips set in an expression of taut annoyance as she stalked up to the gate in a brittle tattoo of high-heeled leather boots.

The gate swung back with a discordant screech, and she scowled as she continued up the steps to the white-painted door, impatiently tugging off black leather gloves. The ring on the hand she raised to the ornate brass door-knocker flashed blood-red in the grey daylight—a carved carnelian caught in a modernist setting of heavy gold. Adorning the oval stone was the incised design of a lynx's tufted head, its mouth agape in a feral snarl.

The dark-eyed Spanish houseboy who answered the door backed off· immediately at the sight of the ring, glancing aside with a deferential murmur. Emerging from behind a newspaper, a somewhat older man in olive-drab military sweater and khakis unfolded himself from a wing chair just inside the entry hall, a lazy grin splitting his well-tanned face as he laid the paper aside.

"Morning, Miz Fitzgerald," he said, tugging the bottom of his sweater over his trousers—and the bulge of an automatic pistol in his waistband—as his gaze swept from well-coifed head to leather-booted toe. "My, my, the newspaper business must be good."

Angela Fitzgerald, one of Scotland's more highly paid gossip columnists, flung a sharp glance over her shoulder at the otherwise empty street and pushed past the houseboy.

"Save your American sarcasm, Barclay," she muttered. "You know I don't like coming here. And have that gate oiled. Where is he?"

"Upstairs in the library. Jorge will show you. My, but we *are* testy today, aren't we?" he added under his breath, continuing to smile as she jammed her gloves into a coat pocket and headed up the stairs, shedding her furs to reveal a smart ensemble of emerald-green. The cowed Jorge scurried after her to take the coat, only barely overtaking her to knock at a gothic-arched door at the top of the stair.

"What is it?" a voice from within demanded.

"Señora Fitzgerald to see you, *jefe*," the houseboy ventured.

"Come in, Angela," the voice replied.

The room beyond displayed the flamboyant neo-gothic style made popular by such arbiters of Victorian taste as Pugin and Burges. Above the fireplace, Minton tiles in shades of red and gold depicted a colorful scene from Chaucer's "Nun's Priest's Tale," and the handsome mahogany bookcase gracing the south wall bore the design signature of Philip Webb.

The dominant presence in the room, however, belonged to the fair-haired man seated behind the desk in the wide bay window, his willowy frame clad in a dark wool suit of impeccable cut.

"How good of you to come," he said, rising gracefully from the leather-upholstered depths of his chair. His smile was slow and lazy, dangerous. "Welcome to my humble abode."

Angela ignored both the irony and the veiled menace in his greeting as she flounced into the room, the houseboy withdrawing with alacrity to close the door behind him.

"This had better be important," she said. "By your own account, it isn't safe for any of us to be seen together, here or anywhere else."

Francis Raeburn elevated a blond eyebrow in mild irritation as he waved her to one of the three lyre-backed chairs opposite the desk and resumed his own seat.

"We aren't exactly going to be *seen* together," he answered, settling back to steeple his fingers before him. "And the house is of sufficient architectural interest that, as a reporter, you can certainly claim a legitimate reason for being here. Besides that, there are sufficient safeguards in place that I think you need not worry about being discovered in my company."

"You mean Barclay, with his ridiculous pistol?" she retorted.

"You are well aware that Mr. Barclay has other talents at his disposal. The pistol is the least of our defenses, though it and he would serve their purpose, if required. But as long as you are under this roof, I promise that you are in no danger of discovery."

"I certainly hope not," she muttered. "I don't want to end up like Kavanagh, with a headline for an obituary: 'Suspected terrorist found dead in prison: Police report no leads.'"

Raeburn began idly rearranging some of the items on the desktop before him. Fluid and precise, his movements called attention to the handsome carnelian lynx ring that he, too, was wearing.

"Kavanagh was a competent operative, but he had a somewhat inflated notion of his own abilities," he said coolly. "He was warned that a Hunting Lodge might try to interfere. When they showed up, he should have known better than to try and cross swords with them single-handed."

"So he made an error in judgement. Was that any reason

to leave him where Dorje's operatives would have no trouble finding him?''

''And what would you have had me do?'' Raeburn asked. ''Stage a jailbreak on his behalf? You know as well as I do, that would have left a trail so conspicuous that even those witless clods who pass for ordinary policemen might have been able to track us down. No, I had the welfare of the rest of us to consider—a fact for which I should think you would be grateful!''

The Kavanagh to whom they were referring had been arrested the previous spring during an attempt to salvage a Nazi treasure trove from a submarine left hidden in a sea cave on the northwest coast of Ireland. While the trove had included a sizeable cache of diamonds, their immense worth had been negligible compared to the accompanying chest of manuscripts on Tibetan black magic.

Recovery of the items had been commissioned by a man called Dorje, shadowy superior of an obscure Buddhist monastery tucked deep in the Swiss Alps, whose inner cadre of initiates recognized him as the current incarnation of an infamous black Adept known to Tibetan legend as the Man with Green Gloves. Born Siegfried Hasselkuss, the product of Nazi selective breeding, Dorje's esoteric resources seemed to support that claim; and recovery of the knowledge contained in the manuscripts, called *Terma* or ''treasure texts,'' would have redoubled his already formidable powers.

Raeburn himself was no novice in such matters; but neither was he a match for Dorje. Drafted by Dorje to undertake the salvage operation—and in expiation for a previous venture gone wrong—Raeburn had reluctantly agreed to accept a share in the diamonds as payment for his services, fully intending to appropriate the *Terma* texts for himself if a suitable opportunity arose.

But the recovery operation had been thwarted by agents of a secret enforcement organization known as the Hunting Lodge, themselves practitioners of esoteric disciplines no less potent than those of Raeburn or Dorje. Raeburn had narrowly escaped with a share of the diamonds, but only at the expense of betraying his Tibetan handlers, abandoning the manuscripts, and leaving the luckless Kavanagh to be arrested by conventional law enforcement authorities on charges of terrorism.

Nor had Kavanagh languished long in jail before being found dead in his cell, of causes yet to be explained by medical science but which Raeburn had no doubt could be laid at the feet of the vengeful Dorje. Lacking the occult resources to combat his former employer on equal terms, at least for the present, Raeburn had temporarily dispersed his own followers and gone into hiding, leaving his associates to find what safety they could while he himself went searching for the means to shift the balance of power in his favor.

Angela's expression was stormy as she contemplated a well-manicured thumbnail.

"No doubt I am meant to be *reassured* by the knowledge that you threw Kavanagh to the wolves," she said coldly. "All that tells me is that you wouldn't hesitate to dispense with me or Barclay or anyone else in this organization, if it suited your purposes at the moment."

"Then take comfort from the assurance that I value your talents far too much to dispense with them for any trifling reason," Raeburn said drily. "Why else do you think I forbade you to employ your occult abilities until further notice, if not to ensure that you didn't betray yourself to our enemies?"

"Don't you mean *your* enemies?" she said archly.

"I doubt very much that Dorje would make that distinction," Raeburn said, "and neither should you, if you want to survive."

"If survival is all you care about," said Angela, "perhaps you should think about resigning as Lynx-Master. A change of leadership might do this organization a world of good."

"Are you proposing to replace me? Don't even think about it," Raeburn warned with a chilly smile. "Not unless you really believe you're up to taking on Barclay and Richter as well as me. And even if, by some miracle, you did succeed in bringing me down," he continued, "do you suppose for one moment that would pacify Dorje?"

"You could consider giving him back his diamonds, by way of a peace offering," she ventured.

Raeburn dismissed this suggestion with a snort of bitter laughter.

"If I had ten times the value of that chest to give him, Dorje would still consider me in his debt for letting his precious *Terma* fall into the hands of the Hunting Lodge," he replied. "Besides that, I *earned* those diamonds. As it is, I remain Dorje's principal target. Remove me, and you merely add insult to injury by cheating him out of the chance to wreak his revenge on me. And the only ultimate beneficiaries are Adam Sinclair and his Hunting Lodge."

The mention of Adam Sinclair brought a grimace of malevolent dislike to Angela's carefully tinted face. In the social circles in which she moved professionally, Sir Adam Sinclair was regarded as one of Scotland's most eligible bachelors. Angela herself had been dazzled by his dark good looks, even as she connived at his death a few years before. Titled and accomplished, with a comfortable independent income and a gracious country house just north of Edinburgh, not only was Sinclair a patron of the arts and a much respected amateur antiquarian, but his professional reputation as a psychiatric physician was matched by few others in Great Britain.

What the world at large never suspected was that he was also a powerful agent of the Law—not as that Law was represented by conventional police authority (though he did work regularly as a police consultant), but in its transcendent expression as the ruling principle of Divine Order, enforced by groups of dedicated individuals formed into Hunting Lodges on the Inner Planes. Scotland's Hunting Lodge regarded him as their Chief, Master of the Hunt. As adversaries of the Hunting Lodge, ironically, Raeburn and his reluctant guest knew far more about Sinclair's secret vocation than did the innocent and unsuspecting public he and his so diligently served.

"Sinclair!" Angela hissed under her breath. "Damn him and all the rest of his ilk. What I wouldn't give for a chance to wipe the smug smiles from their sanctimonious faces!"

"That opportunity may be closer than you think," Raeburn said blandly. "I believe I've finally found a way to repair our broken fortunes."

Before Angela could demand a fuller explanation, a knock at the door heralded the arrival of Barclay, who ushered in a blue-suited man of similarly compact build, with a dense blond crewcut and square, steel-framed glasses. As Barclay closed the door behind them and continued into the room, the newcomer drew himself up with a snap reminiscent of a military salute.

"*Guten Morgen, Herr Raeburn,*" he said, reverting then to accented but otherwise flawless English. "I trust I am in good time for this meeting?"

"Punctual as always," Raeburn agreed pleasantly. "I believe you remember Angela?"

Klaus Richter accorded her a cool nod of his head. Like the other three present, he was wearing a lynx ring. Angela eyed him up and down with no trace of commendation, not stirring from her chair.

"Mr. Richter," she said stiffly.

"I believe we'll have some refreshment before we proceed to the reason for this meeting," Raeburn said with a faint smile, waving Richter and Barclay to two remaining chairs. "But I can assure you that what I have to say will be well worth the risk all of you took to come here."

A tug at the antique bell pull next to the desk recalled Jorge, this time carrying a china tea service on a heavy silver tray. Setting it on a corner of Raeburn's desk, the little valet stayed long enough to distribute a round of tea before retiring from the room with timorous alacrity. Raeburn sipped at the delicate Queen Anne blend with the thoughtful appreciation of the connoisseur. Then, abruptly, he bent his pale, steely gaze upon the expectant faces of his subordinates.

"I think I need not tell you that these past five months have seen a sad decline in our affairs," he began dispassionately, setting aside his cup and saucer. "Suffice it to say that being sought by two enemies at once has left us in an unprecedented state of disarray. With Dorje on the one hand and Sinclair on the other, we've been forced to abandon a whole range of promising enterprises and divert all our energies to the necessary but not exactly exalted pursuit of retaining our lives and our liberty. That situation is about to be changed, however—and the instrument of change is in my possession.''

With this dramatic announcement, he opened the desk drawer and withdrew a long, narrow bundle wrapped in undyed silk, which he placed before him on the blotter. As his three associates leaned forward with varying degrees of expectation, he plucked aside the wrappings to expose an ancient-looking dagger.

It was an ugly thing, forged out of iron, its blade pitted with age and corrosion. The stubby hilt surmounting the blade was overlaid with grotesque zoomorphic traceries reminiscent of the interlocking figures occasionally to be found on Pictish standing stones. Obviously an object of great antiquity, the dagger had about it a subtle aura of crude violence. Its decorative designs, dark and sinuous, drew the eye like a magnet, exerting a fearful fascination.

Richter licked his lips, his pale face alight with hungry admiration. ''It is *herrlich*—magnificent,'' he breathed. ''Where did you get it?''

''It was a legacy,'' Raeburn said. ''From the Head-Master.''

The significance of the name was not lost on his three listeners, though only Barclay had been present with Raeburn at the bequeathal. The individual so-named had once been a powerful member of Hitler's inner circle, before private ambition or perhaps mental instability had impelled him to decamp to Britain. By means known only to himself, the Head-Master had survived the war, secured his freedom, and subsequently contrived to establish a base for himself in the mountains of central Scotland.

There he had remained until two years ago, quietly working his dark intentions, until the Hunting Lodge led by Adam Sinclair had taken his scent and run him to ground. He had perished amid the ruins of his Highland fortress, but his malign influence was still making itself felt, and would continue to do so for a long time yet to come.

Angela was among those who retained a clear recollection of the Head-Master himself, though she had not been present at his demise.

''He would have valued such an important artifact,'' she

said. "How did you convince him to part with it?"

Raeburn showed his teeth. "Arguments from me were superfluous, with the Hunting Lodge threatening to knock down the walls around our ears. Suffice it to say that neither of us saw any virtue in allowing it to fall into the hands of Adam Sinclair."

"Why haven't you told me about this before now?"

"There was little of substance to tell," Raeburn said. "Only now, at the end of two years' study, do I find myself in a position to expound reliably on the secrets of its origin and its esoteric associations."

He steepled his long fingers before him with the air of a university professor about to deliver a lecture.

"To digress briefly," he went on, "and primarily for Mr. Richter's benefit. Those of you who had the distinction of serving under the Head-Master will remember that among his most prized possessions was an ancient relic which he referred to as the Soulis torc. As the name implies, the torc had come to be associated with one William Lord Soulis, an infamous Scottish mage of the fourteenth century—though the torc itself was already ancient by the time it passed into his possession. It was a product of Pictish workmanship, embodying its makers' rapport with the powers of the elements."

"Why don't you cut to the chase, Francis?" Angela said sharply. "We all know that the torc was destroyed, partly thanks to Sinclair. What does it have to do with the dagger?"

"Your impatience begins to wear thin, my dear," Raeburn replied. "To continue, I have been able to establish, to my satisfaction, that this dagger belongs to the same period as the torc, and may even be the product of the same craftsman.

"The connection between the two is to be found in various common features of the workmanship and design. Like the torc, the dagger is fashioned of meteoric iron, and shows evidence of having been made by a similar process of smelting and forging. Certain ogham inscriptions on the blade are likewise closely akin to those on the torc, containing idiosyncratic elements I have not encountered anywhere else."

"Which means what?" Richter ventured.

A faint smile stirred Raeburn's lips, though his eyes remained cold. ''The Head-Master used the Soulis torc as the focus for invoking Taranis, hailed by the ancient Picts as the lord of air and darkness and, especially, storm. In exchange for promises of service and sacrifice, he received the power to call down lightning from the realm of eternal tempest— which authority he delegated to me, though only as it related to the torc.''

''Which was destroyed,'' Angela reminded him.

''I have already conceded that point, Angela dear,'' Raeburn said evenly. ''Fortunately, I now have every reason to hope that, properly manipulated, this dagger will provide a similar focus for re-establishing contact with the Thunderer. If I am correct in my expectations, we may soon find ourselves in a position to reclaim the power of the storm and direct it toward Dorje, or Sinclair, or anyone else who thinks he has a right to meddle in our affairs.''

The silence that briefly fell upon his listeners was pregnant with speculation.

''You say 'properly manipulated,' '' Richter mused, after a thoughtful silence. ''Perhaps you would care to instruct us regarding what, specifically, will be required of us.''

Raeburn inclined his head in graceful acquiescence.

''It is a basic axiom of esoteric practice that objects intended for ritual use must first be consecrated to that purpose and empowered. The dagger is no exception. If we wish to make it actively responsive, in the same degree and to the same purpose as the Soulis torc, it follows that we must determine what rituals were applied in the first instance, and repeat them in conjunction with the dagger, with whatever modifications can be deemed appropriate in the light of our present circumstances.''

''Just where are you planning to get your information?'' Angela inquired, much of her former waspishness dissipated in light of the facts Raeburn had just presented. ''Our latter-day grasp of Pictish culture is sketchy at best—and I expect that the priests of Taranis would have guarded their mysteries as jealously as any modern occultist. Unless the inscriptions you mentioned a moment ago supply the necessary details.''

Raeburn shook his head patiently. ''The inscriptions have some bearing on the case, but they convey a series of cryptic clues rather than a set of explicit instructions. I've no doubt that a dedicated scholar might eventually unravel the conundrums, but we can't afford that kind of time. That's why I've taken the liberty of calling in a specialist whose resources in these matters far exceed my own.''

Even Barclay looked somewhat askance at this announcement.

''What kind of specialist?'' Richter asked, with an uneasy glance toward the windows. ''You said nothing about outsiders.''

''His name is Taliere,'' Raeburn replied, ''and he isn't exactly an outsider. He was an associate of my father's.''

This disclosure silenced Richter and elicited a grave nod from Barclay, for those in Raeburn's inner circle were well aware that their chief had been born the son of one David Tudor-Jones, a powerful Welsh Adept whose esoteric interests and activities had spanned a wide variety of subjects, many of them decidedly dark in focus. Only Angela seemed unsatisfied by Raeburn's explanation.

''An associate of your father's? That could mean anything,'' she muttered. ''I'm a public figure, Francis. Before I agree to make this person privy to any secrets of mine, I'm going to need to know a bit more about him.''

''As you wish.''

Reaching into the left-hand drawer of his desk, Raeburn produced a black and white snapshot and flipped it across the desk in front of Angela. She captured it and turned it right-side up, tilting it to accommodate Richter as he also leaned closer to inspect it.

The man in the photograph was elderly and majestic of mien, with luxuriant white hair to his shoulders and a long white walrus moustache. He appeared to be wearing theatrical costume—a fantastic headdress featuring bird's wings, and a mantle of dark fur clasped over a long white robe. Dependent from a broad leather belt cinching the robe were a drawstring pouch and a small, sickle-bladed knife. His left hand grasped a gnarly staff surmounted by the skull and antlers of a stag.

''What is he, an actor?'' Angela inquired somewhat incredulously.

"A Druid," Raeburn corrected. "And not just a modern pretender, either. Taliere is an ardent and discerning follower of the old ways. You may take it from me that his knowledge of his tradition reaches far into the distant past."

"That sounds almost like high praise," Angela said.

"I always like to give a man his due," Raeburn replied. "In this instance, I believe he is precisely the one to assist us in divining what we need to do."

"When do we meet him?"

"As soon as I can arrange a safe rendezvous—which, with the help of Mr. Richter, should be in a few days' time."

"I am prepared to assist," Richter said, "but also I have questions. Why should this Taliere be interested in helping us? What does he have to gain?"

"A measure of revenge, among other things," Raeburn replied. "Besides sharing some of the same aims, we also share at least one common enemy."

"Meaning Adam Sinclair," Angela declared, more a statement than a question. When Raeburn did not deny it, she added, "How *are* we going to prevent our peerless baronet from poking his long nose into this affair?"

"By moving quickly, before he has time to rally his forces," Raeburn said, wrapping up the dagger again. "Thanks to our own recent spate of inactivity, I doubt he suspects I'm in Scotland. I've also been careful to stay clear of the Edinburgh area. With any luck at all, we'll be able to achieve our objective before he's any the wiser."

Angela made a face. "I wouldn't count on that."

"Wouldn't you?" Raeburn's solicitude carried a hint of malice. "Then you'll be pleased to know that I've already taken the precaution of having Sinclair watched, along with those members of his organization we've been able to identify. If any of them should show signs of becoming a problem, we shall take steps to eliminate the offending party."

# CHAPTER ONE

A DAM Sinclair was a regular at the Royal Scots Club in Edinburgh. He never visited its premises in Abercrombie Place without remembering his late father, Sir Iain, who had been a member of the club since his regimental days—and his father, before him. On this frosty afternoon in mid-December, with the early winter dusk crowding in low over the castellated rooftops of the city, the club's brightly lit windows seemed to beckon with the bidding warmth of a blazing coal fire.

Bracing himself against a biting wind, Adam hunched deeper into the shelter of topcoat and scarf and dashed the last few yards to the front door to ring the bell, with the easy air of a man paying a call on an old friend. The porter who came in answer was quick to recognize the patrician features of the tall, dark-haired man at the top of the steps, and opened the door with a welcoming smile.

"Sir Adam, come in out of the cold," he exclaimed. "A very happy Christmas to you and yours!"

"Thank you, Hamish, and a very happy Christmas to you," Adam replied, as he came into the foyer and let the porter relieve him of coat and scarf. "Inspector McLeod and Mr. Lovat were supposed to be meeting me here. Have they arrived yet?"

"Aye, sir, they have. You'll find the pair of them waiting for you in the lounge bar."

The lounge was a cozy panelled room at the front of the building, redolent of port, pipe smoke, and leather uphol-stery. Not yet crowded with the evening clientele, it had the comfortably lived-in look of a favorite pair of old slippers. A venerable silver-haired gentleman, who had known Adam's father, was smoking a pipe in an armchair near the fireplace, placidly poring over the pages of *The Scotsman*, and raised his pipe in amiable greeting as Adam approached.

"Evening, Adam."

"Good evening, Colonel. You're looking very fit."

"Not bad for an old-timer," the old man allowed. "Your friends are over there."

He gestured with his pipe to where Adam had already spotted two familiar figures at a table in one of the window bays—the elder of the pair clad in a dark tweed jacket with white shirt and knit tie, the bespectacled younger man stylishly informal in grey flannel trousers and a turtleneck pullover of the same shade. Murmuring his thanks, Adam clasped the colonel's shoulder in affection before moving on toward them.

Judging by appearances alone, the two might have seemed an unlikely pair. A twenty-year veteran of the Lothian and Borders Police, Detective Chief Inspector Noel McLeod was craggy and solid as a block of Highland granite, with a thatch of grizzled hair and a bristly military moustache bracketing gold-rimmed aviator spectacles. Youthfully slight by contrast, with hair like cornsilk and candidly observant hazel eyes, Peregrine Lovat was gaining a widespread reputation as a portrait artist and was in increasingly well-paid demand for his talents. Though a casual observer might wonder what the two men could possibly have in common, Adam was in a position to appreciate the complementary nature of their differences.

McLeod was the first to notice Adam's arrival, sitting with his back to the wall and a clear view of the room and its entrance, in instinctive adherence to good police procedure. Alerted by the sudden shift in McLeod's attention, Peregrine half turned in his chair to grin and wave as he, too, spotted Adam.

Returning the salute, Adam made his way over to join them. The two had whisky glasses on the table in front of them, with an untasted third glass set before the one remaining chair.

"I'm glad to see that you two haven't been shy about making yourselves at home," Adam remarked. "Is that extra measure of the MacAllan spoken for yet?"

"We've been keeping an eye on it for you," Peregrine said.

"Aye," McLeod agreed with a twinkle. "But it won't go to waste, if you'd prefer an alternative."

"Not at all!" Adam said. "Nothing else would do justice to the company."

He folded himself gracefully into the vacant seat and appropriated the glass in question, lifting it briefly in salute before tasting. As he rolled the whisky's peaty savor to the back of his tongue and swallowed, his gaze lighted upon the colorful assemblage of parcels piled on the floor beside Peregrine's chair. Protruding from the top of one large carrier bag marked Jenners Department Store was a child's costume kit that included a horned helmet, a circular shield, and a large plastic battle-axe.

Amusement tugged at the corners of Adam's expressive mouth as he set down his glass.

"Who's the aspiring Viking in your life?" he asked.

The young artist grinned. "Alexandra Houston," he replied, naming the younger daughter of a clergyman colleague of theirs. "Christopher's been reading her stories from Norse mythology. She's decided she wants to become a shield maiden when she grows up. Or failing that, an opera singer."

Adam chuckled. "There's a noble ambition for you. I'm sorry I won't be here to share in the fun on Christmas morning."

"So am I," Peregrine said, "but I expect your regrets will evaporate pretty quickly, once you get to the States."

"Once he gets past his medical symposium in Houston," McLeod corrected gruffly.

"You make it sound as if I'm going there to fight a dragon, not deliver a paper," Adam said.

"Even if you were," said Peregrine, "it would take more than a titan among all dragons to keep you away from that fair lady of yours. What time is your flight tomorrow?"

"Seven A.M. Once at Heathrow, I've got nearly four hours to kill before the Houston flight—but this time of year, anything less leaves too slender a margin for comfort. And I don't relish the holiday rush.''

This observation was attended by a grimace. Flying visits to the States had become an increasingly frequent occurrence for Adam over the past eighteen months, and more than once his travel arrangements had been disrupted by missed connections.

The lure that kept drawing him back to the opposite side of the Atlantic was Dr. Ximena Lockhart, an American surgeon turned trauma specialist, whom he had met two years before whilst undergoing treatment in the otherwise unromantic confines of the emergency room at Edinburgh Royal Infirmary. The mutual interest kindled by that initial encounter had subsequently blossomed into a bright flame.

That flame had remained constant despite the separation forced upon them when Ximena learned that her father had fallen victim to a terminal illness. Though she had gone home to San Francisco to care for him, the strains of time and distance had failed to dampen the ardor of the relationship still growing between her and Adam. In this instance, an invitation to address a gathering of American medical colleagues was providing Adam with a professional excuse for being absent from his Edinburgh practice in order to spend the Christmas holidays with Ximena.

"In some respects, it's going to be an awkward visit," he admitted to Peregrine and McLeod. "I'll finally get to meet Ximena's family, but her father isn't doing well at all."

"What *is* the latest word on his condition?" Peregrine asked quietly.

"No better than it's ever likely to be, I'm afraid," Adam replied. "Given the original prognosis, it's nothing short of miraculous that he's lasted this long."

"Aye, and one has to wonder whether that's really a mercy," McLeod murmured. "That form of cancer is pretty painful, isn't it?"

"I'm afraid it is," Adam replied. "And he's already lasted six months beyond what his doctors ever expected. Ximena can't even talk about it. I can only imagine that he must have some very powerful, private reasons for wanting to cling to life. I'll be in a better position to form an opinion once we've met face to face.''

''I'm frankly surprised that Ximena hasn't introduced the two of you before now,'' Peregrine said.

Adam shrugged. ''I expect it's a reflection of the help-lessness she feels as a physician—not being able to help her father when she thinks he needs her most. If I meet him, she has to deal with that helplessness.''

''Is that why you've always met elsewhere?'' McLeod asked.

Adam nodded. ''This is the first time she's consented to let me fly all the way out to the West Coast. I'm given to understand,'' he added lightly, ''that it would be bad form on her part to let me make *all* the travel concessions—hence, our metropolitan tour of the East Coast.''

The list of cities they had visited together in recent months included Atlanta, Boston, and New York. Adam had not dis-puted the choice of venues, knowing that these were places where Ximena could escape, however briefly, from the cares and responsibilities that burdened her at home. For that very reason, her invitation to meet this time in San Francisco gave him cause for no small concern. If she was now afraid to leave her father's side—and ready to face her own helpless-ness—the end must truly be in sight.

''That reminds me,'' Peregrine said, breaking in upon Adam's reflections. ''I've got something here for you—if only I can find the right bag.''

With these words, he ducked partially from view below the level of the table. The sound of energetic rummaging shortly gave way to an exclamation of triumph. When Per-egrine re-emerged, he was holding a parcel gaily wrapped in Christmas paper.

''Your real present will be waiting for you when you get back,'' he told Adam with a puckish grin. ''This, on the other hand, is for opening now—sort of a bon voyage present. It may come in handy if you should accidentally get separated from your friendly native guide.''

''Why, Peregrine, this feels like a book,'' Adam said with a pleased smile, as he began stripping off the paper. ''Surely you haven't forgotten that I already *have* a book?''

"You don't have this one!" Peregrine said gleefully as Adam pulled free a copy of Fodor's pocket-companion to San Francisco.

"Indeed, I don't, and I thank you very much," Adam said with a grin, as he flipped through a few pages. "The Baedeker I have back at the house must be a quarter century out of date. My mother brought it back from a trip she took when I was in my teens."

"So I discovered, the last time you left me alone in your library," Peregrine said drily. "This one should keep you *au fait* with the attractions of the present day. Use it in good health."

"So I shall," Adam promised, bending to set it on the floor beside his chair. "And what about your Christmas plans?" he asked, adroitly diverting the conversation from himself. "Will you and Julia be getting away at all for the holidays?"

Peregrine made a wry face and shook his head. "We can't go anywhere before Christmas Day. Julia got roped into a concert on Christmas Eve—Hebridean carols. It's at St. Margaret's in Dunfermline, where we were married, so when Father Lawrence told her that all proceeds would be earmarked for the church roofing fund, she couldn't very well say no."

"Indeed, not," Adam agreed. "I'll be sorry to miss it."

"She'll be sorry, too," Peregrine replied. "As for me, I've still got quite a bit of work to do on that group portrait that Sir Gordon's Masonic Lodge commissioned for their centenary. If I can at least get all the facial studies finished, I'll feel justified in taking the week off between Christmas and the new year. In that event, we'll probably head up to Aviemore to check out the prospects for a few days' skiing."

"Lucky you," McLeod grunted. "It's going to be business as usual at police headquarters. All too many of our local ne'er-do-wells think of Christmas as the season for taking, rather than giving. Only yesterday, four blokes in workmen's coveralls hijacked a removal van carrying a baby-grand piano."

"A valuable historical piece, I take it?" Adam said.

"So one would think, based on the furor the theft has

caused,'' McLeod replied sourly. "No, this one was new. According to the inventory, it was painted pearl-pink, with rhinestone inlay.''

Peregrine's reaction proclaimed a startled mixture of disbelief and artistic affront.

"Someone's having you on!" he declared. "Why on earth would anyone even want to *make* a thing like that, let alone *steal* it?''

McLeod shrugged, his blue eyes lighting with the humor of the affair. "I'm afraid the report is legit. The piano was being delivered to a new American-style nightclub that's just getting ready to open down at the foot of the Grassmarket. The transport company is one that usually specializes in household removals. I expect the thieves thought they were making off with a load of furniture and small appliances. Are they going to be surprised!''

At McLeod's grin, Peregrine's eyes rolled behind his gold-framed spectacles.

"Talk about a waste of police resources . . .''

"Aye, but believe me, I'm quite content to chase burglars for a change, given what sometimes gets dished up to us. If things stay quiet—as I dearly hope they'll do, with Adam away—Jane and I might sneak away to a hotel for a few nights, so my daughter can have the house to herself and her university friends over Hogmanay. And I may take a few extra shifts, to give some of the younger lads extra time with their families. Otherwise, I'll be at home, trying to dissuade the cats from stealing the baubles off the Christmas tree.''

"Surrounded by thieves and robbers!" Adam said with a laugh, picking up his glass. "Perhaps it's time we had a toast. Noel, will you go first?''

The inspector knit his brow briefly, rubbing at his moustache, then lifted his glass. "All right, here's one my grandfather favored:

> *"Lang life and happy days,*
> *Plenty meat and plenty claes;*
> *A haggis and a horn spune,*
> *And aye a tattie when the ither's dune.''*

"Your grandfather was a practical man!" Peregrine said with a chuckle, when the toast had been duly solemnized.

"He certainly knew what was really worth having out of life," McLeod replied, and cocked an eye at the young artist. "How about it, laddie? Have *you* any pearls of wisdom you'd like to contribute on this festive occasion?"

"I might," Peregrine said. He thought a moment, then recited:

> *"Lang o' purse,*
> *And licht o' heart.*
> *Health tae thee,*
> *In every part."*

Once again the three friends lifted glasses to their lips.

"I think this makes it your turn, Adam," Peregrine said, as he set down his glass.

"Very well," Adam said. "Since I'm off to the West, I have in mind a Gaelic blessing. Somehow it seems appropriate:

> *"May the road rise to meet you.*
> *May the wind be always at your back.*
> *May the sun shine warm upon your face.*
> *May the rains fall softly upon your fields until we*
> *    meet again.*
> *May God hold you in the hollow of his hand."*

Breaking off, he smiled at his companions. "It's going to be up to you to keep the peace while I'm away. But I know you're equal to the task. *Slainte var!*"

"*Slainte var!*" the two of them repeated, as they drank the ancient toast.

It was still dark the following morning when Adam set out for the airport, driven by his faithful valet-butler, Humphrey. An overnight drop in the temperature, with the attendant promise of ice on the roads, made the steel-blue Range Rover, with its four-wheel drive, the only choice of vehicle. As they nosed out of the stable mews, high-performance tires crunching on a white carpet of frost, the windscreen wipers only barely kept at bay a moist ground-fog that was verging on a drizzle. Looking back over his shoulder as they crawled down the drive, Adam could see the turrets and gables of Strathmourne silhouetted against a crystalline backdrop of morning stars. The windows in the kitchen wing showed a scattering of lights where Mrs. Gilchrist, his cook and house-keeper, was clearing up the remains of a frugal breakfast.

The avenue leading to the gates passed between sentinel ranks of copper beech trees, their branches black and bare against the pre-dawn sky. Off to his left, through the pas-senger window, Adam glimpsed another cluster of lights marking the location of a stout, stone-built steading held by one of his tenant farmers. A gentle bend in the road brought them abreast of the gate lodge, its darkened windows con-firming that Peregrine and Julia, his bride of seven months, were still asleep.

Hunching down contentedly in his topcoat, Adam let his thoughts touch fondly on the couple as Humphrey eased the big car quietly past their front door and swung onto the main road. Peregrine had been still a bachelor when he first ac-cepted Adam's invitation to take up residence in the gate lodge, in exchange for what Adam quaintly termed a "pep-percorn rent." The fair Julia had come to share her husband's affection for the little house, and considered Adam to be the most agreeable and charming of landlords, but both Lovats eventually realized that they were going to need more room if they ever intended to have a family.

Toward that end, with Adam's help and encouragement, the pair had recently purchased a decommissioned chapel, but a few miles away, and had happily begun working on plans for its conversion into a residence. That alone might take upwards of a year, sandwiched in between Peregrine's portrait commissions; and Adam guessed that completion of the work might take another year or even two.

Even so, the Lovats would ultimately be moving—not far, but Adam still would be sorry to see them go. Quite apart from the convenience of having another member of the Hunt-ing Lodge so close at hand, Peregrine had taken on aspects of close friend, star-pupil, favorite nephew, the younger brother Adam had never had, and the son he wished one day to father.

The wistful notion of a son of his own, a child of his body as well as his heart and soul, turned his thoughts to the woman he hoped could be persuaded to share his life and bear that child. Thus preoccupied, and still lulled by the early hour, he failed to notice a flicker of movement among the shadows clustering under the trees outside the gates—and Humphrey was focused on road conditions. As the Range Rover carefully picked up speed, its tail-lamps receding in the wet, pre-dawn darkness, a black-clad figure rose from cover behind a stand of broad oak trees and raised a wrist-strapped micro-com to the mouth-opening of a black ski mask. The wearer's report was rendered in a clipped under-tone, after which he settled back to resume his surveillance of the gates and the lodge beyond.

Some five miles ahead, at a wooded junction where the narrow country back road to Strathmourne connected with the A-route to Edinburgh, a head-scarfed woman in a dark grey Volvo set aside a similar comlink and sat up straighter, peering through the screen of trees that hid the car from the road. Only when the blue Range Rover had whispered past did she smile a mirthless smile in the darkness, reaching down to start the engine and then pulling quietly onto the road to follow.

The ground fog had mostly dissipated by the time Humphrey pulled the Range Rover onto the M90. Local traffic was light at first, but increased steadily as they headed south toward Edinburgh. Content to leave the driving to Humphrey, and made somewhat drowsy by the rhythmic hiss of tires on pavement and the hypnotic sweep of the windscreen wipers, Adam leaned back against the headrest and lost himself in fond reflections of the woman he was on his way to see, letting himself drift, searching for Ximena wherever she was to be found amid memories of past joys and parting sorrows.

With an ease born of habitual longing, his mind's eye lit upon Ximena as he first had seen her. In that hospital setting, kitted out in surgical green, she had been all brisk, well-scrubbed efficiency, as supple and well-honed as a steel blade, with a wit to match and a keen sense of humor that gently teased but never mocked. It cost him a pang to recall how that bright resilience had later melted under the reverent caress of his hands and lips, revealing a warm responsiveness of flesh vibrant with laughter and desire.

The memory brought a wistful smile to his lips. With almost painful immediacy he found himself recalling the way her dark, unbound hair spilled like silk through his fingers, the porcelain quality of her skin, smoothly drawn over the finely chiselled bones of her face. Of all the women he had ever known, she alone seemed to have the power to release him from the convoluted toils of his own intellect, to set him free to enjoy the simplicity of the present moment. In exchange for such a gift, he was willing to offer everything he himself had to give. But he was by no means certain that she would find it in herself to take it. And while her father lived, Adam's conscience would not allow him to argue his own case.

His mood of introspection did not go unnoticed by Humphrey, though the older man was well accustomed to his employer's silences and had learned not to let his own vigilance be distracted. Trained in the driving techniques necessary for executive protection, as well as the skills that made him an outstanding butler and valet, Humphrey made automatic note of the dark grey Volvo keeping pace with them along the M90; but any real concern evaporated when the vehicle in question turned off at the exit for Dunfermline and Kincardine.

Relaxing a little, he concentrated thereafter on minding the traffic along the approach to the Forth Road Bridge. When a black Edinburgh taxi nosed in behind them in the queue for the bridge tollbooth, its appearance was so commonplace that Humphrey hardly spared it a second glance.

They arrived at the airport just as a big Aer Lingus jet was coming in for a landing. Bypassing the short-term car park, Humphrey made for the terminal building and pulled into a space reserved for limousines outside the main concourse. Adam roused as the car came to a halt, and vouchsafed his faithful valet an apologetic smile as he undid his seat belt and reached behind for the briefcase on the back seat.

"Sorry to be such a poor companion, Humphrey. As Mrs. Gilchrist would say, I'm 'awa' wi' the fairies' this morning."

"I trust nothing is wrong, sir?"

"No, not at all. Everything is very right—or as right as it can be, under the circumstances. And I promise to keep my feet firmly on the ground from here on out—at least until my flight is airborne."

A faint smile played at the corners of Humphrey's mouth as he glanced at the steering wheel between his gloved hands, then essayed a glance at his employer.

"If I may say so, sir, I hope that when you reach San Francisco, you'll not bother too much with keeping your feet on the ground. I—would regard it as a great favor if you were to convey my particular greetings to Dr. Lockhart."

"I shall certainly do that," Adam said quietly, well aware of Humphrey's hopes that Ximena might become the next Lady Sinclair. "But it's a difficult situation, as you know."

"I do, sir," Humphrey murmured. "And she and her father are in my prayers."

"Then they have a powerful advocate. Thank you." Adam sighed heavily, then glanced at his luggage in the back of the car and reached for the door handle. "Well, if you'll see to the luggage and get me checked in, I'll meet you at the Air UK desk. If the news agents are open yet, I believe I have time to pick up a copy of *The Scotsman* before boarding."

"You do, indeed, sir. I'll take care of the bags."

Alighting from the car, Adam shrugged out of his overcoat and slung it across his arm, then headed into the terminal, making for the nearest news kiosk. Five minutes later, as he approached the Air UK check-in, he found Humphrey just turning away from the counter, replacing a handful of travel documents in their paper folder.

"Here we are, sir," Humphrey murmured, as they moved a few paces away from the desk and Adam set down his briefcase between his feet. "Here are your tickets, your passport, and your boarding card. The bags are checked through to Houston, and you have a bulkhead seat for this flight, with plenty of leg room. Your seat on the Houston flight is pre-assigned.''

"Humphrey, you are indispensable," Adam replied with a smile, tucking the tickets into an inside pocket. "I'll check back with you from time to time to see how things are going. I've left a full itinerary back at the house, if anyone should need to reach me."

"Very good, sir. Have a safe trip."

He handed Adam his briefcase and raised a hand in farewell as his employer headed off toward the gate, watching until he had disappeared through the security checkpoint before turning away to return to the car.

Across the departures hall, a nondescript-looking man in a dark suit gazed after Humphrey from behind a newspaper, then furled it under his arm and strolled casually in the direction of the security checkpoint, glancing at his watch and then at the monitor that announced imminent departures. When the London flight had disappeared from the display and his quarry did not emerge, he turned and headed purposefully toward the Air UK desk, discarding his paper in a convenient refuse barrel and then elbowing past a queue of passengers waiting to check in.

"I'm Dr. Travis," he announced to the pretty ticket agent tagging a bag on the scale beneath her counter. "I do beg your pardon, madam," he said, turning briefly to address the passenger he had shoved aside. "Did a Dr. Sinclair get on your London flight that just left?"

A male agent one position down looked over with interest.

"Sir Adam Sinclair? I believe he did, sir. Is there some problem?"

Feigning dismay, "Dr. Travis" glanced at his watch, then back at both agents in more urgent appeal.

"Oh, dear, I'd hoped to catch up with him before he got away. It's rather an emergency. Do you know if London was his final destination? If so, I might be able to track him down there. His nurse only said he was on his way to the airport. Fortunately, there aren't too many flights this early."

As the two ticket agents exchanged bewildered glances, their inquisitor lifted both palms in entreaty.

"Please, I need to know where to reach him," he insisted. "It may be a matter of life and death."

"What did you say your name was?"

"Travis. Dr. Edward Travis. I'm a colleague of Dr. Sinclair."

Won over by his urgency and apparent authority, the male agent quickly called up Adam Sinclair's flight details on his computer terminal. Ten minutes later, "Dr. Travis" was ringing his employer from a pay phone in another part of the airport terminal.

A little over a hundred miles away, in a secluded Victorian house in Paisley, Francis Raeburn's Spanish-born valet took the call, then strode to the dining room.

"Señor Richter, you are wanted on the telephone," he announced, as Klaus Richter was just sitting down to an early breakfast. "It is Mr. Toynbee."

Richter took the call in the seclusion of the adjoining study. Through a burst of background noise, he could hear a voice relaying information over a public address system.

"Richter here. What is it?"

"I'm at the airport in Edinburgh," came the voice from the other end of the line. "There's been an interesting development."

"Yes?"

"The chief subject you're interested in has just boarded a flight to Heathrow," his informant reported, above the din of another flight announcement. "From there he flies on to the United States, with a two-day stopover in Houston and then an onward connection to San Francisco. How long he intends to stay there is anybody's guess, but he checked two bags. That suggests more than an overnight visit. The return ticket is open-ended."

"Open-ended, you say? That may be worth knowing. Well done," Richter acknowledged. "Will you be able to confirm that he makes that Houston flight?"

"We can hack into the system to confirm that he checks in for it, and that his bags are en route. We can also flag the system to alert us when he books his flight back."

"Excellent. As soon you are certain he is on the Houston

flight, you will transfer your attentions to the other individuals on your list. In the meantime, an appropriate compensation for your services will be deposited in your account, as usual. Thank you very much, Mr. Toynbee.''

Raeburn appeared at the door of the study just as Richter was cradling the phone.

"That was one of my men checking in," Richter announced with a thin smile. "Sinclair is leaving the country. And there is evidence to suggest that he may be planning to be gone for some time."

When Richter had recited the particulars he himself had just received, Raeburn gave a satisfied nod.

"I sense a matter of personal importance," he observed. "I hope it's nothing trifling. The longer Sinclair stays away, the better. But in any event, I propose to take full advantage of his absence."

# CHAPTER TWO

"SCHOLARS !" Jasper Taliere said with a derisive snort. "What know they? Their reliance on the tools of so-called science has made them deaf and blind to the promptings of their own intuition. They treat the past as if it were naught but a quarry, to be mined without discrimination or respect. Is it any wonder that the greater truths forever elude them?"

The old man's deep voice carried across the library with theatrical resonance, reminding Raeburn of the actor Richard Burton at the height of his form.

"Not everyone can boast your particular sense of historical perspective, *Taoiseach*," Raeburn said mildly, "especially with regard to the ancient mysteries of our native isle."

Raeburn had used the Gaelic title meaning "Head," an apt honorific. Accepting it as his due, Taliere turned restlessly from the window bay, where he had been gazing out at a flight of snow geese silhouetted against the wintry sky.

Despite his age, Taliere was a hale figure of a man, broad across the shoulders and gnarled as a mature oak tree, with shaggy, beetling white brows and lush moustaches lending eccentric character to a lean, sharp-nosed face. A receding hairline had endowed him with a natural tonsure approximating those shown in lithographs of ancient Druids, hairless across the top of his head from ear to ear, with the rest of his hair swept back in a silvery mane. Though clad unalarmingly in baggy tweeds and a nondescript pullover, out at the elbows, the overall effect was that of an ageing and unpredictable lion—an aspect that grew more pronounced as he studied his host through yellow-green eyes.

"You need not exert yourself to flatter me, Francis," he growled. "I have already agreed to do what you desire."

"On terms of your own dictating," Raeburn pointed out drily. "Mind you, I'm not complaining," he continued when the older man showed signs of bridling. "Knowledge never comes without a price. But don't pretend that you're lending me your assistance purely out of the goodness of your heart. You stand to profit as much from this experiment as I do."

"I doubt that," Taliere said bluntly. "You have your father's propensity for seeing that the scales are weighted in your favor. But I did not come here to quibble. Where is this dagger you wish to show me?"

"One of my initiates is fetching it from the safe," Raeburn said. "He should be here momentarily."

As if on cue, there was a knock at the door. At Raeburn's acknowledgement, Barclay came in with a small wooden casket under one arm. He accorded Taliere an unabashedly curious glance as he crossed to set the casket on the desk before his superior.

"Here you are, Mr. Raeburn. Do you want me to wait, so I can put it back in the safe, or shall I just leave it here?"

"I'll call you when I'm ready for it to go back," Raeburn said. "For now, why don't you and Mr. Richter make certain the wards are secure?"

With a nod, Barclay retired from the room. As the door closed behind him, Taliere pulled a scowl and ensconced himself into one of the chairs opposite Raeburn.

"That man of yours is far too inquisitive for one of his degree and station," he observed disapprovingly. "What prompted you to take an American into your service?"

He pronounced the word "American" as if it were an epithet. Raeburn shrugged.

"He's an excellent pilot."

"But you described him as an initiate."

"The two functions are not mutually exclusive."

Taliere's response was a disgruntled snort.

"I dislike Colonials," he informed Raeburn. "They have too much regard for their own self-worth. That kind of arrogance fosters an unbecomingly cavalier attitude toward authority. I would not recommend you trust this Barclay too far.''

''I know just how far he's to be trusted,'' Raeburn said blandly. ''He is equally clear on what to expect from me, should he ever consider violating his articles of service. On that understanding, we contrive to get along quite well. Mr. Barclay may be a rough diamond, but he has incidental facets to his character that are sufficiently brilliant to outweigh many a shortcoming in his deportment. As you will discover, if matters progress as we both would wish.''

With these words he indicated the casket in front of him. ''Here is the dagger. Will you or will you not examine it?''

''That is not the question,'' Taliere said grimly. ''The question is, Are you fit to share any revelations I may encounter?''

Raeburn professed shock and reproach. ''How can you doubt it? Am I not my father's son?''

''In many respects,'' Taliere allowed. ''But not all.'' He subjected Raeburn to a penetrating glare. ''Do you know what sets Britain apart from her sister-nations on the Continent? It is more—much more—than any intervening body of water. No, of all the estates of Europe, Britain alone still preserves intact the living spirit of her ancient past, the spirit which has always safeguarded her identity. That spirit was given to her by the old gods in the days before the coming of the White Christ. It has endured patiently over the centuries, sustained by those few of us who still remember the gift and revere the Givers. But if we should ever fail in our charge, that spirit would wither and die, and the land would be empty again—a body without a soul.''

He leaned back in his chair and studied Raeburn down his long nose. ''Your father had a proper reverence for the old gods,'' he went on. ''Had he not, I would never have given him the benefit of my assistance. Before we proceed with this venture, I must know what your position is. What exactly do you want from the old gods, and what are you prepared to give them in return?''

''What I want,'' Raeburn said simply, ''is power. As to what I intend to offer . . .''

He let the sentence hang a moment before going on. ''I will be frank with you. As matters stand at the moment, I am caught between two enemies. One of them is a foreign sorcerer, a scion of the self-proclaimed master race which tried to overrun this island—and, indeed, the world—fifty years ago. The other is native-born, but a traitor to his birthright—an Adept who has forsaken the ancient paths for the sake of the White Christ. Each, in his own way, would like to see the old gods driven out of this corner of the world in order to make room for the patron that he serves. In providing me with the means to defend myself, the old gods would be giving me the means to protect their own interests as well.''

''You have yet to mention where your own service lies pledged,'' Taliere said.

''All my former alliances were terminated when the Head-Master's citadel was destroyed by those who claim to champion the New Light,'' Raeburn said. ''As of now, any principle of power which aids me will find me appropriately grateful.''

''I hope, for your sake, that there is no guile in your words,'' Taliere muttered. ''The old gods are not to be mocked. If you are lying, they will not countenance your profiting from their indulgence. And I warn you now, they have ways of taking revenge against those who abuse their trust.''

''The old gods have already seen my willingness to serve,'' Raeburn replied, a trifle sharply. ''Two years ago, when the lord Taranis permitted me to wear his torc and bear his lightnings, I showed my gratitude by giving him many holocausts. I would be prepared to do the same again, in return for a similar loan of power. What I require is a focus for communicating the terms of the bargain.''

''If all of this is true,'' Taliere said, ''then I hope that this dagger is all you claim it to be.''

''By all means, see for yourself,'' Raeburn replied, opening a hand toward the casket before him.

Making no secret of his reservations, Taliere rose and approached the casket from his side of the desk. As soon as his fingers touched it, however, his face underwent a marked change of expression. Leaving the casket unopened, he stroked questing fingers over the lid, his touch as perceptive and knowledgeable as that of a blind man reading an inscription in Braille.

"There is, indeed, considerable power represented here," he said softly, glancing at Raeburn in wonder. "The resonance it generates is sensible even at one remove. Whether the blade itself will consent to speak with me regarding its affinities is another matter. But we shall know soon enough."

Gingerly, he opened the box. The dagger lay visible within, pillowed on layers of silk. Taliere drew breath sharply, then let it out again in a gusty sigh.

"If I am to commune with this object, it must be in the spirit of its own time," he said, not taking his eyes from the dagger. "I can return there by passing through the sacred grove, but may I rely upon you to stand ready as an anchor-line to the present?"

Raeburn smiled thinly. "Have no fears on that account, *Taoiseach*. With so much at stake, I would be foolish to let you lose yourself among the shadows of the past."

Taliere signified his acceptance with a nod. After further silent contemplation of the dagger, he struck a formal posture of invocation, feet braced apart and gnarled hands upraised above his head. When he opened his mouth to speak, it was in a long-dead tongue that Raeburn only belatedly recognized from rare encounters with its graven form.

At once adamant and oddly liquid, the words spilled from the old man's lips like angry waters rushing down a cataract, an ancient formula to set the stage. At the conclusion of his utterance, he abruptly dropped his arms and brought his hands together in an intricate sign of warding. Only then did he venture to pluck the dagger from its nest of silk, clasping both hands around its hilt and carrying it to his breast, its point toward the ceiling.

"I am ready to set out," he announced, as he closed his eyes in an attitude of stiff composure.

"And I am ready to guide and guard you," Raeburn said.

He rose smoothly and came around to stand next to Taliere, lifting his left hand to rest lightly on the older man's right shoulder. At once Taliere's rate of respiration quickened.

After a moment, the old man drew a deep breath, held it a moment, then released it in an explosive gust of expelled air. With his next deep intake of breath, his face went momentarily blank. Then he began to mutter to himself, stringing words together in a singsong, semi-metrical chant.

> *"I have been the blind striving*
> *Of a worm turning in the earth.*
>
> *I have been the racing of the blood*
> *In the heart of the running deer.*
>
> *I have been the captive silence*
> *Of a trout in the singing brook.*
>
> *I have been the rooted strength*
> *Of the oak tree in its prime."*

The chant trailed off and he began to sway, but Raeburn's hand on his shoulder steadied him.

"Tell me where you are now," Raeburn murmured, after a long pause.

Taliere's face took on a look of fierce exultancy.

"Home," he murmured. "Among the trees, before the Burning Time."

His voice lifted again in bardic song.

> *"Tall and green were the sacred groves,*
> *when the sky rained fire from heaven.*
> *Then did we take up our sickles of gold,*
> *venturing into the fields by night*
> *to reap a harvest of fallen stars."*

With these words he broke off, his hands tightening around the dagger's hilt while he cocked his head, as if listening for some approaching sound.

"Yes . . . Yes . . ." he murmured.

*"The iron speaks with a creaking voice.*
*It cries aloud in the tumult of the storm.*
*I hear its clamor in the hollows of the hills.*
*I hear the echoes in the chasms of the sky."*

Raeburn stared more intently at the old man, his eyes pale and bright.

"Tell me what the iron is saying," he instructed softly.

A look of consternation passed over Taliere's lined face.

"The speech it employs is not that of the wood," he breathed. "The sense is there, but not the words. . . ." He struggled a moment longer, as if trying to fix an elusive impression.

"The Thunderer speaks, but only in riddles," he muttered at last. "One must be found with the skill to interpret. The storm-wind waits to carry him aloft. Let him harness the tempest and make his ascent—"

A sudden seizure gripped Taliere, choking off anything more he might have said. As the dagger fell from his palsied fingers, a violent shudder sent him caroming against a lyrebacked chair, which overturned despite Raeburn's attempted intervention. As the old man collapsed twitching to the carpet, a white foam frothing at his mouth, Raeburn was only partially able to break his fall.

"Barclay, get in here!" Raeburn shouted.

Barclay answered the summons on the run, bursting through the library door to find his employer kneeling over the thrashing Taliere, forcing the spine of a paperback book between his teeth.

"Give me a hand here, damn it, before he does himself damage!" Raeburn barked.

Between them they managed to restrain the old Druid until the fit showed signs of subsiding. As the final paroxysms trailed off, Raeburn cautiously eased the tooth-marked paperback from Taliere's jaws and looked around him. The dagger was lying under the overturned chair. Drawing a deep breath, he retrieved the dagger, set the chair right-side up, and laid the artifact back in its casket. As he turned back to Barclay and the supine Taliere, he saw that his aide had one hand clasped to the Druid's scrawny wrist.

"His pulse is hammering like a freight train," Barclay said. "Is he going to be all right?"

"He'll need someplace dark and quiet to rest for a while," Raeburn replied, "but I doubt there's any harm done. The ancients sometimes called this the 'divine madness.' In this case, it's a sign that he probably made a genuine contact."

"Do you think Dr. Mallory should have a look at him?" Barclay asked.

"Aye. When Mallory arrives, send him up to check him over. Meanwhile, get Jorge to help you carry him up to one of the spare bedrooms. He can rest there until he feels sufficiently recovered to rejoin us."

Taliere was already showing signs of regaining consciousness by the time Jorge arrived. Once the old Druid had been safely installed in his room, Barclay returned to the library to report on his condition. Raeburn was seated behind his desk again, turning the dagger thoughtfully in long fingers.

"He's looking a bit better, but he still seems disoriented," Barclay told his employer. "When I left him, he was muttering to himself in some strange language of his own. If he doesn't manage to pull himself together, there won't be much point in going through with this afternoon's meeting. Do you think maybe you'd better put it off until tomorrow?"

Raeburn shook his head. "Don't underestimate Master Taliere's powers of recovery. I'm quite confident he will be back in full possession of his faculties by the time the rest of the party arrives."

"Guess you've been acquainted with him long enough to know, Mr. Raeburn," Barclay said with a philosophic shrug. "He sure doesn't waste much time trying to make himself easy to live with, though. Does he really have the authority he claims to have, or is it all just attitude?"

Raeburn permitted himself a tight smile and replaced the dagger in its casket.

"Taliere is a Druid of the old school," he told his aide. "He sees himself as one of the last bastions of Britain's ancient mysteries, charged with the responsibility of keeping those mysteries alive. If he seems a trifle fanatical, that's because he is. His inner life is rooted in the soil of Anglesey."

"Anglesey?"

"The holy island of Druid Britain," Raeburn explained. "Only a narrow strait separates it from Wales. It was the nerve center of the Druid religion, in much the same way that the Vatican represents the heart of Catholic Christendom. Following the Roman occupation, Anglesey became a pocket of native resistance, and in A.D. 64, Agricola gave orders that the community there should be destroyed.

"Taliere's past memories stretch back to the days when the Roman legionnaires invaded the island, slaughtered its priestly inhabitants, and put the sacred groves to the torch. It would be safe to say that a part of him has never left that time and place."

"How does that make him useful to us?" Barclay asked.

"As a vehicle of knowledge," Raeburn replied. "The Druids, like the followers of Taranis, recognized and venerated the cardinal powers of the elements. Although separated geographically, both cults were active in Britain at roughly the same time. Both shared an affinity for the gifts of prophecy. That the two traditions were closely akin to one another is reflected in such artifacts as the famous Gundestrup cauldron, which pictures a figure of Taranis side by side with that of Cernunnos, the horned god of the wood. If anybody can determine what we need to do to recover our link with Taranis," he concluded, "Jasper Taliere is the one."

Shortly before three o'clock, Raeburn assembled his chosen lieutenants for the appointed briefing. Of the three people summoned to the previous meeting, Angela Fitzgerald was absent, having already been given a separate assignment to fulfill. Her place for this occasion had been taken by a well-built young man with smoldering eyes and extravagant pretensions toward fashion, whose dark-haired good looks were somewhat marred by early signs of self-indulgence. With the addition of Taliere, who now seemed fully recovered after his seizure, those present constituted a company of five.

Directing the others to chairs set around the library table, Raeburn took his place at the table's head and prefaced his opening remarks with a round of brief introductions for Taliere's benefit.

"You and Mr. Barclay have already met. Now let me present Klaus Richter, my chief advisor on matters of security, and Dr. Derek Mallory, one of our most promising associates."

Mallory preened slightly at the compliment, already aware of his brief to examine Taliere after the meeting was concluded. Ambitious, and apparently without moral scruples, he had begun his career with the Lodge of the Lynx while still an intern, augmenting his burgeoning medical expertise with impressive psychic ability as his competence in both disciplines progressed. Now a qualified anaesthetist, he had recently secured a residency at the Royal Edinburgh Hospital, which listed Dr. Adam Sinclair among its senior psychiatric consultants. Mallory's promotion to Raeburn's inner circle, replacing another physician who had failed in his duties, not only restored that facet of functioning to the Lodge of the Lynx, but Mallory's particular situation gave him an ideal opportunity to keep an eye on Sinclair's movements and interests.

Richter was the first person called upon to report. An attentive silence reigned as he delivered an updated account of what his surveillance agents had observed in the course of the two days since Adam Sinclair's departure from Scotland.

"My operatives in the States have been able to confirm that Sinclair is in Houston, attending a medical symposium. Of the nine telephone calls that have gone out from his hotel room, five have been directed to a number in San Francisco, which is listed to a Dr. X. Lockhart. A computer search of Dr. Lockhart's personal records identifies her as the physician who attended Sinclair two years ago, and with whom he has since formed a romantic liaison. All the evidence so far accumulated suggests that he intends to remain in the United States for the duration of the Christmas holidays. This leaves us free to concentrate our attentions on his known associates."

From the black leather briefcase he had brought with him Richter produced a selection of black-and-white photos. The first set of pictures to be circulated showed a head-and-shoulders shot of a grizzle-haired man whose craggy features were offset by a bristling military moustache and a pair of metal-rimmed aviator spectacles.

"This man, as most of you will know, is Detective Chief Inspector Noel Gordon McLeod, of the Lothian and Borders Police," Richter noted coolly. "Though it is never officially acknowledged in police circles, he is the officer always detailed to deal with cases involving any esoteric or occult element. He is particularly adroit at misdirecting the attentions of the press—for which we can be as grateful as our opposite numbers."

As Taliere slowly nodded, Richter continued.

"Besides being a Master Mason, McLeod is also known to be a member of the Hunting Lodge. There is strong evidence to suggest that he ranks as Sinclair's second-in-command. So far, all his recent movements have been routine and accountable, but my operatives will be alert for any changes. His near dependents—if I may refer you to the other photos you have before you—include his wife, Jane Ellen, and one daughter, Kate Elizabeth, who is in her fourth year of studies at the University of Aberdeen. We are keeping all three of these subjects under surveillance, and will continue to do so until further notice."

The next photograph to be circulated was that of a much younger man, also bespectacled, but fair-haired and clean-shaven, with features that might have been chiselled by Della Robbia.

"This man is Peregrine Andrew Lovat, a portrait artist whose reputation has soared since he was first taken under Sinclair's patronage about two years ago. The full spectrum of his talents has yet to be determined, but it would seem that his artistic abilities are augmented by some form of extrasensory perception that allows him to see and record resonances of the past. He has been significantly involved in a number of police investigations in which Sinclair and McLeod have likewise been factors. There can be little doubt that he is a Huntsman, and since the visionary nature of his talents makes him a particular danger to us, we shall be watching him very closely, indeed.

"His wife's involvement is, at present, unknown," Richter went on, tossing out a fifth set of photos. "They were only married last spring, but Sinclair seems to have introduced them, or at least encouraged the match. Her name is Julia.''

''Very nice,'' Mallory murmured, allowing himself a broad grin as he scanned up and down a publicity photo of Julia posed beside one of her harps. ''Any time your people get tired of watching her, I'd be delighted to lend a hand.''

''Sadly for you, Doctor, your talents are likely to be required elsewhere,'' Raeburn said, on a crisp note that wiped the smile from the younger man's face. ''Mr. Richter, I think we've spent enough time acquainting Master Taliere with the principal opposition players. With Sinclair temporarily out of the picture, I don't think we need worry overmuch about the others.

''The reason I've called you all here,'' he went on, ''is to hear from Taliere himself regarding our coming operations. Earlier today, he took time to examine the dagger I obtained from the Head-Master. After reflection, he has some recommendations to make regarding its future empowerment. *Taoiseach?*''

The old Druid set his fingertips together in a narrow triangle, regarding them with eyes the color of peridots.

''Each of the Lords Elemental has his own realm and his own tongue,'' he began, with ponderous dignity. ''As a servant of the Wood, I have little grasp of the language of fire. Nevertheless, at the behest of your chief, I sought audience with the lord Taranis and was granted it after a fashion. No words passed between us, but I have been given to understand that the Great One is willing to look with favor on the prospect of renewing your former alliance.''

This announcement drew murmurs of approval from his listeners.

''What must we do to secure this alliance?'' Richter asked.

''Lord Taranis will dictate his terms directly to those desiring to take part in the bargain,'' Taliere declared. ''In so doing, he will set his seal upon them, so that thereafter they may understand and obey his commands. To receive his instructions, the ancient methods of divination must be employed, as prescribed by the Druids in ancient times. The eve of the Winter Solstice shall be the appointed time, some four days hence. Listen closely, for this is what must be done.''

# CHAPTER THREE

"I'M taking you back to my apartment first," Ximena murmured, as she and Adam embraced at the USAir gate in San Francisco after his late-morning arrival. "I want some time for *us* before I share you with my family."

She did not mention her father as they walked arm-in-arm to the baggage-claim area, chattering a little too single-mindedly about heavy traffic on the way in and the expected ordeal of trying to retrieve Adam's luggage amid the pre-Christmas crowds. It was only as they made their way out to the airport car park that she even skirted the unspoken question that lay between them.

"Oh, Adam, if I've learned nothing else during these past months, it's how much I miss your company," she blurted, as they wheeled his luggage trolley out of one of the car-park elevators. "I'm so glad you're here."

The glance she directed his way spoke volumes, as did the taut caress of her hand against his, just before she gestured down the next aisle in the car park. Feeling the tension, and all too aware of his own long-banked yearnings, Adam only smiled and said, "So am I."

Her manner turned brisk again as she directed him toward a black Honda Prelude neatly inserted in a space between two larger vehicles.

"Well, this is my current bus," she said, as she opened the trunk to accommodate his bags. "It isn't a Morgan, but it's never let me down."

One of the things Ximena had left behind her in Scotland was a yellow Morgan sports car, presently collecting spider webs under a dust-sheet in one of Adam's stableyard garages. Watching her buckle up, he was obscurely glad she hadn't had the heart to get rid of it. As they pulled out of the car park and headed northward on the freeway from the airport, it was clear that she had lost nothing of her flair for driving.

"Thanks for not asking questions that I'm not ready to answer," she said over her shoulder, as she overtook a pickup truck pulling a sailboat on a trailer. "I'll make sure you don't regret this. Just promise me something."

"What's that?"

"Promise me that for the next few hours you won't speak of anything that doesn't apply directly to *us*. There's time enough for—the other."

He could not see her eyes behind the sunglasses she had donned before taking to the road, but her grip on the steering wheel was stronger than it needed to be.

"I promise," he agreed, and simply reached across to touch a hand to her knee before subsiding into companionable silence for the duration of the drive to her apartment.

By common consent, neither of them allowed any shadow of the future to intrude upon their lovemaking. Initially wary of giving full rein to his passions, Adam had been moved beyond words to find himself courted with a fervor equal to his own. Sheer physical delight, long denied by their separation, washed over him in a dazzling torrent. Temporarily bereft of all intellectual reservation, he surrendered blindly to their shared ardor, finding in that union a rare moment of release.

The intensity of that pleasure left behind a lingering glow of profound well-being, but precious as that sensation was, Adam would willingly have exchanged it for the burden of care he knew Ximena must shortly resume. Time was moving on, and there was nothing he could do about it. But if he could not keep her from the grief that lay ahead, perhaps he could still offer her a prospect of happiness beyond.

Possibly to hold her own thoughts at bay, Ximena had set some music playing in the next room before she went off to shower. Adam let the music wash over him without particular awareness, fresh from his own shower and a change of clothes as he settled on the couch in her little sitting room and put his feet up, curling his palms contentedly around a steaming mug of Earl Grey tea.

Her apartment occupied the top floor of a newly renovated town house near San Francisco's Golden Gate Park. The view of the neighborhood, seen from the living room windows, embraced a vivacious fin-de-siècle collection of gables, cupolas, and widow's walks decorated in gingerbread woodwork. On a clear day it was possible—so Adam had been told—to catch a fugitive glimpse of the Golden Gate Bridge beyond the dark green feathering of trees that marked the intervening presence of the Presidio. Today, however, both the park and the bridge were shrouded under a silvery haze of the dense fog for which the city was famous.

Relaxed and beginning to feel gently jet-lagged, Adam withdrew his gaze from the neighboring skyline to contemplate the more intimate features of the apartment's interior, sipping distractedly at his tea.

Ximena's rented flat in Edinburgh had been comfortably suited to her needs, especially for a busy ER physician who frankly spent little time there, but it had come already furnished, leaving her little or nothing to say regarding the decor. This place, by contrast, had started off empty, giving her ample scope for indulging a more personalized expression of taste. Adam expected that much of the furniture had been handed down from her parents or bought second-hand during her student days, but most of the appointments seemed to bear what he was beginning to recognize as Ximena's distinctive style. Left to his own devices while she showered, Adam found it instructive as well as pleasant to contemplate the effects of her self-expression.

The room was sparely appointed, in keeping with the clean, sunlit expanse of wide windows and stripped woodwork. The variegated tones of wood, tile, and stonework contrasted elegantly with the thick, cream-colored plushness of the fitted carpet. The sofa upon which Adam was sitting was a luxuriously comfortable design piece executed in brick-red Cordovan leather.

That terra-cotta hue was reflected several times over in the selection of prints by Diego Rivera and Joaquin Torres-Garcia that were scattered across the walls. Among the original objets d'art in the room were a stained-glass depiction of a smiling Madonna done in rich blues and golds, an *art naif* oil painting of three jaguars, and a lively bronze casting of two dogs dancing that recalled examples of Calima statuary Adam had once seen in an exhibition of pre-Columbian art. He was touched to see a blue glass votive candle he had given her, set beneath the portrait of the Madonna.

The overall effect was one of discriminating eclecticism. That effect was all the more commendable since Alan Lockhart's progressively worsening condition had left his daughter with little opportunity for shopping—or indeed anything else—in the months since her return.

Despite Ximena's earlier protestations that she would not allow her concerns to intrude on their time together, she had finally updated Adam on her father's condition before sending him off for his shower, huddled miserably in the circle of his arm while she recited the essentials in detached clinical phrasing that left little doubt of her growing sense of helplessness.

Though Lockhart's attending physicians initially had been able to arrange his medication to permit relative comfort and alertness during the daylight hours, steadily mounting levels of pain had eaten into that schedule until now he was left with only two narrow windows of lucidity each day: a few hours early in the morning and a similar period late in the afternoon. By structuring their own activities to take advantage of his periods of alertness, Lockhart's wife and family had managed to achieve a fragile semblance of routine. But there was no hiding the fact that Ximena's father was rapidly approaching the point where conventional medicine could offer him nothing more than a choice between agony and oblivion.

Adam had in mind a third alternative—though whether Ximena's father would be receptive to the idea could only be determined at first hand. Formal introductions were to take place later that afternoon, when Lockhart would be awake and all the other members of Ximena's family would be present.

In the meantime, there had been this precious interlude. Adam finished his tea and set aside his mug with a sigh, cocking an ear toward the bedroom as awareness of a different piece of music drew his attention back to more pleasurable contemplations.

Passionate and precise, the rippling string-notes of a *vihuela* provided intricate accompaniment to a woman's clear contralto. From the formal structures of counterpoint, Adam was willing to guess an origin in Renaissance Spain. After a while, Ximena's own voice floated in from the direction of the bathroom, matching that of the recording artist, note for note:

> *"Yo me soy la morenica . . .*
>
> *Soy la sin espina rosa*
> *Que Salomon canta y glosa . . .*
>
> *Yo soy la mata inflamada*
> *Ardiendo sin ser quemada. . . . "*

I am the dark girl . . . I am the rose without thorns, that Solomon sings of. I am the bush in flames, burning without being burnt. . . .

Ximena's accent was virtually flawless. But then, Adam reminded himself, her mother was a native-born Spaniard. Teresa Constanza Morales and Alan David Lockhart had met thirty-six years ago in Granada, where Lockhart, then a student of architecture, had come to study the designs which glorified the memory of the Nasrid empire. They had married the following year, thereby setting in motion the stars of fates other than their own.

Still humming along with the music, Ximena appeared at the door to the bedroom hallway, wearing a casual suit of forest green. Pausing in the doorway, she cocked her head first one way and then the other as she fitted on a pair of gold-and-jade earrings in the form of Aztec totem frogs. Adam watched her with a smile playing over his lips.

"*Morenica,*" he said aloud.

Ximena looked up. "I beg your pardon?"

"You are the dark girl, *morenica cuerpo garrida.*"

Ximena wrinkled her forehead at him. " 'The dark girl

with the handsome body'? Don't let my parents hear you call me that before they get a chance to know you better.''

Adam chuckled. ''I wouldn't dream of it,'' he assured her. ''What time are we meant to be there?''

Coming forward, Ximena leaned down and kissed him on the mouth. ''In about as long as it takes to drive from here to there,'' she said with a smile. ''Are you ready?''

''I will be, as soon as I've put on a tie,'' Adam said, stretching to retrieve the one he had draped across the back of the couch. ''Your parents are expecting a Scottish laird. I'd better look the part.''

Laughing, she took the tie from him and looped it around his neck, pulling him closer for another kiss.

''I'm content with *el señor de corazon,* the lord of my heart,'' she told him happily, pulling him to his feet.

It was another five minutes before they reluctantly left the apartment.

UCSF-Mount Zion Medical Center lay to the north of Golden Gate Park, between Post and Sutter Streets. With the onset of visiting hours, the hospital car park was crowded, but Ximena swung in through the emergency room entrance and tucked the Honda into one of the spaces reserved for members of the staff.

''Lucky for us you have some rank to pull here,'' Adam remarked lightly as Ximena turned off the engine and set the handbrake.

''Lucky, indeed!'' Ximena agreed with a rueful grimace. ''My old supervisor must have pulled a dozen strings to get me reinstated. I'm going to owe a lot of favors when this is over and done with.''

They entered the hospital through the door adjoining the ambulance bay. Inside, Ximena paused to trade greetings with admiring members of the nursing staff and several of her colleagues, though she kept moving the two of them in the direction of the elevators. Adam could sense her pleasure in her co-workers' reaction as she introduced him—he was long accustomed to turning female heads, and not a few male ones—but her manner was brisk as they made their way together into the heart of the hospital complex.

It was only when they came within sight of the doors

leading into the concentrated care unit that her composure showed signs of wavering. The indications were subtle, but Adam was instantly aware of them.

"Are you all right?" he asked.

Ximena squared her shoulders, not looking at him. "I will be," she murmured. "Let's go in."

Adam stepped in front of her long enough to open one of the double doors. Once past the threshold, they carried on along a carpeted corridor, Ximena nodding to several nurses as she passed. At the nurses' station halfway down the corridor, a slim, erect woman in a bright red jacket and black skirt was conversing with one of the nurses.

The woman was similar in height and build to Ximena, with smooth dark hair, densely threaded with silver, caught up in a chignon at the back of her neck. When she turned her head, her profile had the attenuated elegance of a study by El Greco. Mentally matching up images, Adam knew that the woman could only be Ximena's mother.

His conviction was confirmed a moment later when the sound of their footsteps caused the woman to look around. Her thin, sensitively molded face lit up at the sight of Ximena.

"Oh, there you are, *mi corazon!*" she exclaimed. "I was hoping I might catch you as you came in. Your father is having a chat with Mrs. Jenny. It seemed a good time for me to slip out and stretch my legs—and to exercise my maternal curiosity."

Before Ximena could speak, her mother's liquid dark eyes transferred their gaze to Adam, and the smile grew warmer still.

"There can be no doubt that you are the dashing Scottish gentleman of whom our daughter has spoken at such length. It is a great pleasure at last to be meeting you, Dr. Sinclair."

Her voice was deeper than Ximena's, her English overlaid with the stately accents of her Andalusian homeland. Taking the slender hand she held out to him, Adam raised it to his lips in courtly salute.

"The pleasure is mine, Señora. And no one regrets the delay more than I do."

"Ah, I perceive that you have the manners of a *grandee*,

Dr. Sinclair. But I hope that will not prevent you from addressing me as Teresa,'' she said with a bit of a twinkle in her eye.

"Only if you agree to call me Adam,'' he replied, releasing her hand.

"That I will do,'' she agreed, shifting to draw Ximena into a fond hug, though her twinkle quickly faded as they drew apart. "But we must not keep your father waiting. He has waited a very long time for this moment.''

Alan Lockhart had been installed in a private room not far from the nurses' station. His visitors arrived to find the door standing partly open. A petite, dark-haired young woman in a neat grey suit and clerical collar was standing just inside the doorway, jotting down entries in the notebook she carried in the crook of one arm.

"I'm glad you remembered that one,'' Adam heard her say. "It's always been one of my favorites. Did you have anyone in mind for a soloist, or will you trust me to find someone? I've got more than a few contacts over at the university music school—some lovely voices.''

An indistinct murmur came from within the room. Adam could make out nothing of the words, but the woman paused to write down something more in her notebook.

"I'll see what I can do,'' she promised. "I'll make some phone calls and get back to you in the next few days. In the meantime, I'd better say goodbye. I'm due over at the Student Mission Center at four, and I've got a couple of other people to see before I leave.''

Turning, she pulled up short as she became aware of Teresa Lockhart and her companions.

"You mustn't go *just* yet, Jenny,'' Teresa said with a smile, motioning her to come into the corridor. "Here is Ximena, and a gentleman from Scotland whom we both would very much like you to meet. His name is Dr. Adam Sinclair, and I am told he ranks as an expert consultant in the field of psychiatric medicine. Dr. Sinclair, allow me to present the Reverend Jenny Carstairs, one of our hospital chaplains.''

"For my sins!'' Jenny Carstairs directed an ironic glance toward the ceiling, then extended a firm hand and a pixie-like smile. "Nice to meet you, Dr. Sinclair. I understand you just flew in this morning."

"I did," Adam replied. "I was addressing a medical symposium in Houston, and I was delighted to escape."

"Well, I'm sure everyone is delighted that you did," she said. "I've heard very nice things about you."

"Probably greatly exaggerated," Adam protested, with an amused glance at both Ximena and her mother.

"Jenny has been a great comfort to all of us," Teresa said, her smile still in place but shading into sadness. "Sometimes I don't know what we would have done without her, especially these past few months."

"Now, Teresa, that's giving me far more credit than I deserve," the chaplain answered robustly. "You and the rest of your family have been the real workhorses."

"Speaking of which, where's Austen?" Ximena asked. "I thought he and Laurel were going to hold the fort until I got here."

Jenny Carstairs gave her hand a pat. "Your father had a few things he wanted to discuss with me in private, so your brother volunteered to make a run down to the cafe in search of coffee. Laurel and Emma have gone down to Mrs. Chang's room so that Emma can show off her costume for the Christmas play."

"My granddaughter is a gregarious soul," Teresa explained wryly. "She has made friends with several of the other patients here. Mrs. Chang is a particular favorite. She can make animals out of folded paper. As far as Emma is concerned, origami might as well be magic."

"Maybe it is," Adam said with a smile, thinking of McLeod. "I have a friend with a similar interest. I'm not sure there isn't some magic in the way he gets his results."

"Well, I told Laurel I'd let her know as soon as we were finished here," the chaplain said. "Dr. Sinclair, I'm happy to have met you, but I'd better be on my way. Goodbye for now, and I hope I'll be seeing you again. Teresa, Ximena— I'll check back with you in the morning."

With a farewell wave, she headed off down the hall. As her footsteps receded, Ximena drew herself up and summoned an air of determined calm.

"Time to make our entrance," she observed aside to Adam. And pushed the door open wide.

Tall enough to see over her head, Adam found his gaze drawn immediately to the bed that dominated the room. The gaunt figure under the sheets was lying very still, eyes shut, jaw set in an attitude of grim endurance. An image came to Adam's mind of a cadaverous tomb effigy left behind as a *memento mori* by a medieval bishop of Arles. It seemed hard to credit that the ravaged frame of Alan Lockhart could still harbor a living spirit.

"Hello, Daddy, I'm back," Ximena said as she headed toward him. "I've brought someone to meet you."

Lockhart roused himself with visible effort, his face a sunken mask from which all color had long ago fled. Only his eyes were still alive, burning with a preternatural intensity fuelled by the spirit within.

"*Bene ça, niña.*" He greeted her with the merest flicker of a smile. "How is your Flying Scotsman?"

His voice was roughened by suffering. Advancing to the bedside, Ximena reached down and lifted her father's wasted hand to her lips.

"Why don't I let him tell you himself? Adam, come and be introduced. This is my father, Alan Lockhart."

Joining her beside the bed, Adam found himself subjected to searching scrutiny. Returning that regard, he received a vivid impression of the man Alan Lockhart had been in his prime—tall, vital, and vigorous, as stalwart and individualistic as the buildings he had designed during his working lifetime. To see so much that had once been fine and strong now reduced so spitefully to ruin gave Adam a pang of grief he had experienced all too often in his career as a physician. It was like seeing a noble cathedral wantonly levelled by the ravages of war.

A war of insurrection. To be a victim of cancer run rampant was to have one's own body rebel against itself in pitiless self-destruction. Adam still intended to read Alan Lockhart's case notes when he got a chance, but those notes, he knew, could go only so far in detailing the course of devastation. The human effect was much, much worse.

Their mutual scrutiny lasted but a few heartbeats. Blinking, Lockhart extended a hand that was nothing but bones and tightly stretched skin. Adam took it with careful firmness, wincing inwardly at the insubstantial fragility of the long fingers.

"Forgive me if I don't get up," said the man in the bed, in a labored display of humor. "I'm very much the prisoner of my condition these days. Jenny Carstairs has been helping me plan my escape. But I've one or two pieces of unfinished business yet to attend to, before I can make good on those arrangements."

His words were painfully measured, but the force of the soul behind them reached out to Adam in an almost palpable appeal. Nor did the man seem inclined to release Adam's hand.

"Sometimes it's good to let someone else take on some of the burdens of responsibility," Adam said. "Under the circumstances, perhaps you ought to consider appointing a deputy."

"Maybe so," Lockhart conceded, his eyes never leaving Adam's. "The difficulty lies in finding the right man for the job."

His transparent lids drooped, and for a moment he seemed to fold in upon himself. Adam waited steadfastly, Lockhart's hand still in his, until the other man drew a sighing breath and re-opened his eyes.

"You've come a long way to visit my daughter. I'd like to know more about you—in your words, not hers. Pull up a chair and tell me about your house."

Though the request seemed a trifle odd on the surface, Adam sensed that it was not the non sequitur it appeared to be.

"What would you like to know?" he asked, releasing Lockhart's hand and moving a chair closer to the head of the bed to sit.

Lockhart's chest rose and fell. "Anything and everything," he said with a faint smile.

"Don't be silly, Daddy," Ximena murmured, interposing uneasily. "The rules to your game won't apply here. Strathmourne has been the Sinclairs' family residence for several generations. Knowing about the house won't tell you very much about Adam himself.''

"Let me be the judge of that," Lockhart told her, with a flash of his former strength. Directing his gaze toward Adam, he said, "Humor me."

As Adam scooted his chair closer, prepared to oblige, he felt Ximena's hand on his shoulder.

"As an architect, Daddy has always maintained that you can tell a great deal about a person's character from the kind of house he lives in," she warned.

"I see nothing amiss in that," Adam said, with a reassuring smile. "On the contrary, I expect an architect would find Strathmourne of great interest."

While Lockhart lay back and listened, and Ximena and her mother drew up chairs on the other side of the bed, Adam began describing the house, from its Palladian façade and gothic windows to the allocation of space in the kitchen wing. More and more, however, he found himself digressing to talk about Templemor, the seventeenth-century tower house elsewhere on the Strathmourne estate. Once a ruin, Templemor had been undergoing extensive renovation during the past two years. Most of the structural repairs were now complete, and Adam was starting to consider plans for the interior refurbishments which would eventually make the old tower habitable again.

Almost without being aware of it, he found himself pouring out his enthusiasm for the project with a fullness he had rarely shared with anyone outside the ranks of the Hunting Lodge. Lost in contemplating the image in his mind's eye, he only belatedly became aware that Alan Lockhart was smiling up at him with genuine warmth. He stopped himself with a self-deprecating grin.

"You'll have to pardon my misplaced fervor. Restoring Templemor has been an ambition of mine since childhood."

Lockhart's smile remained in place, his voice firm when he spoke, even if weak. "Sounds as if you're not only a traditionalist, but a romantic as well," he said softly.

Adam gave the architect a quizzical look. "Is that good or bad?"

"Either way," said Lockhart, "it makes you a man after my own heart."

A sudden commotion from the direction of the hall put an end to any further discussion. An instant later, a small figure came bursting into the room in a diaphanous flutter of white robes, *papier-mâché* wings, and a tinsel halo atop titian curls. This cherubic apparition was closely pursued by a taller figure in royal blue, who scooped up her quarry with maternal single-mindedness.

"Easy, Emma!" she admonished. "This is a hospital, not a circus tent."

Laurel Lockhart had fiery-red hair and the springy fitness of a natural athlete. Her freckled cheeks were flushed with the chase, and she grinned good-naturedly over her daughter's somewhat tousled head as she noticed Adam.

"Excuse me if I seem to have my hands too full to offer any other form of greeting, but I'm Laurel Lockhart," she said. "You must be Adam. There couldn't possibly be a second man fitting the descriptions we've had from Ximena."

A diversion from Emma spared Adam the necessity of framing a response. Wriggling loose, she darted over to the bed to stretch on tiptoe, flourishing a slightly crumpled construction in silver paper.

"Look, Grandpa!" she urged. "See what Mrs. Chang made me!"

Lockhart retained strength enough to feign ignorance. "Is it a goose?"

"No, silly, it's an angel!" Emma crowed triumphantly. "Mrs. Chang says it's supposed to be me."

"That was very complimentary of her," said a joking male voice from the doorway. "It's a good thing Mrs. Chang doesn't know you like we do, eh, pumpkin?"

Emma whirled away from the bedside. "Daddy!" she exclaimed happily, and hurled herself at the newcomer with puppy-like abandon. Clearly Ximena's brother, he bore a close resemblance to what their father must have looked like in his youth.

"I'm Austen," the man said, staggering under the impact of his daughter's embrace around his knees. "You must be

Adam. It's a pity we couldn't have met sooner. Now that you're here, I hope you'll be staying long enough for us to get better acquainted.''

"I hope so, too," Adam said, turning a physician's eye on the elder Lockhart. "In the meantime, though, perhaps we'd all better adjourn to the lobby. Your father looks as if he's needing a rest."

Even as he spoke, a nurse appeared at the door.

"Sorry to interrupt," she apologized, "but it's time for Mr. Lockhart's medication."

"That's all right. We were just getting ready to leave," Austen said. "We'll see you tomorrow, Dad. And we'll take pictures of the angel for you—if monsters disguised as angels register on film!"

So saying, he scooped up his daughter, being careful not to crush her wings, and carried her giggling into the corridor, followed by Laurel, Ximena, and Adam, leaving Teresa to sit with her husband as he drifted off into drug-induced oblivion. Adam watched briefly from the doorway before turning to join Ximena and her brother, while Laurel attempted to straighten little Emma's halo.

"This play of Emma's starts in just over an hour," Austen was saying to Ximena, "and we still have to grab a bite to eat. I don't suppose you and Adam would care to join us at McDonald's?"

"That sounds fine to me," Adam said, before Ximena could decline. "I'm game, if you are," he told her.

"Play and all?"

"Play and all," Adam agreed without a quaver. He cocked an eyebrow at Ximena and added, "You can regard it as a test of my devotion."

"More like a trial of courage," Ximena murmured, "but you did volunteer."

"Obviously he doesn't know the difference between courage and foolhardiness," Austen said with a laugh. "But never mind, Adam: The experience may one day stand you in good stead."

# CHAPTER FOUR

**E**ASTWARD across a continent and an ocean, on the northernmost island of the Outer Hebrides, less angelic forces were gathering to enact far darker drama than a play to celebrate the birth of a God of Light. Francis Raeburn had set the night's agenda, and took particular satisfaction in the knowledge that one of the more troublesome champions of that Light, Adam Sinclair, was at least temporarily occupied many thousand miles away.

The ancient site selected by Raeburn's associate, Taliere, was well suited to the night's work. Sprawled across a wind-scoured flatland beside a sea loch thrusting deep into the western coast of the Isle of Lewis, the standing stones of Callanish loomed stark and ever mysterious under a frosty, moonless sky, in grandeur second only to Stonehenge in all the British Isles.

The heart of Callanish centered on a ring of thirteen rough-hewn stones, almost all of which were taller than a man. At the foot of a slender, even taller stone in the center of the circle, the remains of a small chambered tomb-cairn lay half-hidden under a frost-scorched mound of peaty grass and a light powdering of snow.

A broadening avenue of lesser stones stretched northward from the circle for nearly a hundred yards, with shorter single lines of stones radiating east, west, and south. The overall pattern greatly resembled a slightly skewed Celtic cross, though its unknown builders had laid it out nearly three thousand years before the coming of the Child whose birth was about to be celebrated in Christian lands, and whose adherents had appropriated cruciform shapes to symbolize a new faith.

The stones themselves were known by more than one name amongst the Gaelic-speaking people of the island. Some called the stones *an Fir-Bhreige Chalanois*—''The Deceitful Men''—recalling obscure legends of a band of forsworn outlaws changed into stone by an enchanter. Indeed, in Victorian times, clearance of encroaching peat from a height of four to five feet around the bases of the stones had left a bleached effect on the lower halves that inspired one illustrator to depict the color difference as the clothing of the ''deceitful men,'' with a skeleton emerging from the newly uncovered tomb-cairn and winged spirit-forms cavorting in the air above the stones.

That Callanish had long possessed associations with the supernatural was undoubted. Another name for the site was *Tursachen*, betokening a place of pilgrimage and mourning where, in bygone days, it had been customary for courting couples to come and make their marriage vows. Some few would recall how this local tradition was rooted in a far more distant past, when other seekers had come to Callanish to bind themselves with darker oaths in the brooding presence of powers ancient even when the stones themselves were new.

The folk who lived within sight of the Callanish Ring had long ago come to terms with its presence. By day, especially in summer, when the tourists had retreated to accommodations in the island's main town of Stornoway, some fifteen miles to the east and north, it was not uncommon to find local children playing among the stones. By night, however, all and sundry tended to keep well clear, content to leave the ancient ring to guard its own secrets. This was especially true in the dead of winter, when the northern darkness closed in early and the bone-numbing chill of the near-Arctic dusk drove people indoors by mid-afternoon, there to huddle gratefully around the warmth of their own hearths as the cold winds blew, with no desire to venture out again.

On the twenty-first of December, the ice-blue clarity of the lowering twilight promised a night of bitter cold. By five o'clock, the temperature had plummeted past the freezing point. By suppertime, the open ground between the houses was aglitter with traces of gathering frost. Shortly after ten, the last of the village lights winked out.

Not long thereafter, a small black Mini Cooper bearing four men ghosted quietly through Callanish Village from the north, dousing its lights as it entered the unpaved car park far at the south end of the village. Beyond the wire fence at the edge of the car park, the distant stones of Callanish glistened under crystalline starlight bright enough to cast shadows.

At that same moment, a compact recreational vehicle was backing into a construction site behind the rocky outcropping known as Cnoc an Tursa, several hundred yards to the other side of the stones, where work had been suspended for the winter on what was scheduled to become a National Trust visitor center for the site. The RV's weathered paint and air of gentle decrepitude suggested nothing of any dark intent on the part of its occupants as its driver doused the headlights and killed the engine.

In the car park, silent under the winter stars, the passenger door of the Mini Cooper opened to disgorge two male figures kitted out in snow-camouflage coveralls, ski masks, and infrared night-goggles. Though their brief was to prevent any untoward interruption of what their employer had planned, hopefully by ensuring that no one became aware of anything amiss, both carried long-barrelled pistols loaded with anaesthetic darts—and both were prepared to use the silenced Lugers they wore holstered as backup, if lesser force failed.

As the second man quietly pressed the car door closed and the Mini Cooper moved off silently along a single-track road, quickly disappearing from sight, his partner was already melting into the shadows near the end of the thatched cottage fronting the car park. With a glance in that direction to mark the location, the second man vaulted a closed gate in the fence and positioned himself behind one of the larger stones marking the northern avenue. When he had settled, he whispered briefly into the slender curve of a miniature microphone close beside his mouth.

Back at the construction site, inside the darkened RV, Klaus Richter pressed a headset to his ear, nodding as he whispered a brief reply, then turned to his employer, who was sitting in the front passenger seat beside Barclay. Like the men he had just spoken to, all of them wore snow-camouflage.

"Erich and Gunther are in position at the upper car park," he said quietly. "The Mini is taking up position at the bottom of the road to meet the horse-box when it arrives. Otto will drive it in."

"Excellent," Raeburn replied. "Then we'll begin securing the site. Barclay, why don't you give him a hand?"

As Barclay headed aft between the two front seats and Richter opened the RV's side door, Derek Mallory swivelled his chair and moved his medical bag aside to let Richter pull out two zippered duffel bags, one of which he handed to Barclay before the two of them disappeared up a path leading around the dark outcropping that was Cnoc an Tursa.

Behind Mallory, the white-robed Taliere was seated on the long couch that stretched across the back of the RV, head bowed in the shelter of the robe's hood. He did not stir as Raeburn donned a headset and then came aft to pull on a similar white robe over his heavy winter clothing. When Raeburn had returned to his seat, silently gazing out at the road where the horse-box was expected, Mallory also drew on a white robe, settling less patiently into the growing chill to wait.

After perhaps five minutes of this, when Taliere stirred enough to smother a slight cough, Mallory glanced at his watch, then back at the old Druid.

"It's getting late," he murmured. "If those rustic colleagues of yours have gotten lost . . ."

Taliere's expression could not be read in the darkness, but his voice was sharp with disdain.

"They know the island," he muttered. "They will be here."

Before Mallory could frame a reply, Raeburn held up a hand and hissed for silence, listening intently to his headset.

"The horse-box is on its way up," he whispered, laying the headset aside. "We'd best be ready to greet our honored guest."

He and Taliere were waiting in front of the RV as a battered white Land Rover towing a horse-box slowed and stopped a few yards past the entrance to the construction area, followed by the Mini. After a slight pause, the Rover reversed the dark bulk of the horse-box neatly into the space to the left of the RV, with the noses of the two vehicles lined up. One of Richter's men was at the wheel, and alighted from the driver's side as soon as he had killed the engine and set the brake.

As the Mini tucked in neatly ahead of him, also disgorging its driver, the Rover's two other occupants disembarked rather more tentatively, though they let themselves be guided to the rear of the horse-box by the Mini's driver. They were brawny specimens, already attired in the capacious white woollen robes deemed proper for the night's work, and looked palpably relieved when Taliere appeared from between the two vehicles. Inside the horse-box, something large and heavy shifted restlessly in the confinement of the narrow space, churning straw underfoot.

"Let us waste no time," Taliere whispered, touching each man's arm in reassurance. "You know what to do."

He stood aside to watch as they folded down the tailgate of the horse-box, bidding one of Richter's henchmen assist in spreading a quilted rug on the ramp to muffle the sound of hooves. The animal attached to the hooves was a fine black Angus bull, its eyes rolling white in the surrounding darkness as its handlers entered the compartment and backed it down the ramp, clinging to its halter and a ring through its nose.

While they gentled the bull, its snorting breath pluming in the cold, Taliere fetched a crown woven of holly and mistletoe from the RV. This he fastened around the bull's horns, attaching it with two twists of wire and then blowing softly into the bull's nostrils as he crooned a low-voiced charm. The animal immediately became docile.

"You know the path to the stones," Taliere said to his men, ignoring Raeburn's expression of bemusement. "Await our coming, outside the circle."

As Taliere withdrew to the RV to finish robing, Raeburn signalled Mallory to accompany the men with the bull, himself returning to the RV to fetch the casket containing the

Pictish dagger. This he tucked possessively under one arm while he turned to watch Taliere complete his preparations by the light of a single candle.

"That was a rather impressive trick with the bull," he said mildly, as Taliere fastened on a silver necklet incised with ogham figures. The old Druid had already bound a cincture of braided horsehair around his waist, from which hung a tooled-leather bottle and a small sickle of burnished bronze, its blade edge honed to no less a sharpness than the gaze he turned to Raeburn's darkling reflection in the mirror.

"It was no trick," he said in a low voice. "And you had better have no trick in mind when we enter the sacred circle. I hope you realize what you are doing."

Raeburn lifted an innocent eyebrow. "Doing? Why, my objective is entirely straightforward, dear Taliere: I wish to renew my alliance with the lord Taranis."

"I do not question your aim," Taliere replied, sullenly shouldering a cope-like mantle woven with many-colored feathers. "I do have grave reservations about your methods."

"So you have told me, repeatedly," Raeburn coolly acknowledged. "Nevertheless, we shall proceed according to my instructions."

Snuffling disapproval, the old Druid donned a feathered headdress in the form of a speckled bird with volant wings, scowling at his reflection as he adjusted it to his liking.

"If you persist in departing from the old ways, you are inviting trouble," he warned. "The rituals I have specified were instituted long ago, when men hearkened more closely to the dictates of nature. To permit—even encourage—interference from modern science is to commit a breach of faith. And by doing so, you risk compromising the results."

"It is a risk I am prepared to take," Raeburn said softly.

"Would that the risk were yours alone!" Taliere retorted, turning to take up a stout staff of peeled ash wood, its height trimmed to match his own. "The diligence with which a suppliant is prepared to execute his charge reflects the purity of his intentions. As your mediator in this transaction, I am less than eager to see myself implicated in what might well be perceived as a violation of respect."

"You take too much upon yourself," Raeburn said. "In

the final analysis, it will be for the lord Taranis to decide whether or not the bargain I offer him is acceptable—and it is I who offer it, not you! Come. We have important work to do.''

With these words he blew out the candle and stepped outside, the dagger casket still cradled under one arm. Taliere alighted after him, his back stiff with disapproval, but made no further argument, though he moved as if his limbs were weighted with lead as the two of them trudged along the trail that led to the stones of Callanish.

They saw the stones as they crested Cnoc an Tursa, stretched before them in the windswept moonlight like an inverted cross, with the sleeping village of Callanish silent in the distance. As they drew nearer, a faint shadow as of ground fog seemed to obscure their view of the central circle of the stones.

The black bulk of the bull waiting just outside the circle was all but invisible behind the white robes of those attending it. Barclay had robed after arriving at the circle, though his weathered face was set and uncharacteristically pale in the starlight. Mallory had his medical bag tucked under one arm. Richter stood between two of the stones with a wand of birch wood in one hand, surmounted by a fragment of rock crystal.

''*Lynxmeister*, I give you charge of the circle,'' he said in a low voice, offering the wand to Raeburn with a brisk dip of his chin. ''*Taoiseach*, the nemeton is prepared.''

Bowing, Raeburn handed off the casket to Barclay, then took the wand from Richter and stepped aside, back pressed against one of the stones. He could feel familiar power stirring in his hand as he held the birch wand aloft and the others fell into processional order behind Taliere: first the two assistants flanking the still docile bull, then Barclay and Mallory, and finally Richter, bringing up the rear. When all were in position, Taliere thrice struck the ground between the two stones with the butt of his staff, then lifted his eyes toward the icy stars as he clasped the staff with both hands.

''This is the hour appointed,'' he whispered, in a tone both hushed and resonant, ''the hour of darkness that belongs neither to the sun nor to the moon. This is the hour of blood and prophecy. Let all who hunger come forth from the darkness and be present at the feast!''

The light wind seemed to die, giving way to an expectant hush. The winter stars shone out with sudden, fierce brightness, as if the intervening air had been thinned and rarefied by an abrupt shift in altitude. As the hush lengthened, Taliere drew himself up and stepped through the gap into the compass of the ring.

Those behind him followed, the bull snuffling in mild protest, for where the air outside the circle had been dark and clear, here within the perimeter it was luridly brightened by the glare of oil lamps set at the four quarters. Once all the members of the procession had passed within, Raeburn stepped inside the circle and scribed his wand three times across the gap between the two stones, then laid it across the threshold in final sealing. Content for the moment to let Taliere take center stage, Raeburn positioned himself beside Barclay, standing with his back to one of the stones, and nodded his readiness for Taliere to continue.

The old Druid moved to the center stone, between it and the darker depression of the ruined cairn, and halted to bend at the waist in profound obeisance. For a moment he remained thus, silent and with head bowed, gnarled hands knotted together around the neck of his staff. Then slowly he straightened and solemnly began to chant.

The language he used was not Scots Gaelic, but an ancient Celtic dialect called up out of the distant past. Soft at first, his voice accumulated pitch and force, sending dissonant echoes ricocheting eerily around the circle from stone to stone, though Raeburn knew that the sound could no more pass outside than the light of the lanterns could. The chant peaked to a crescendo, then ceased. In the heavy silence that followed, as Taliere turned to regard his fellow celebrants, his gaze took on an otherworldly sharpness, as did his voice.

''Know ye that this is the place of oath-fasting, sacred to the Lords Elemental. Know that these stones were erected to honor Them; nor will They abandon this site for so long as the stones themselves retain their memory.

''To quicken that memory, I invoke Earth in the presence of Cailleach, Mother of All,'' he continued, raising his staff, "and Fire in the person of Gruagach, the Long-haired One. Water I invoke in the presence of Shoney, Lord of the Western Seas. But it is to Taranis, the Thunderer, Lord of the Air, that I stand ready to offer sacrifice. May he be pleased to accept our oblation, and look with favor upon the petitions that we bring!"

On cue, his two assistants led the bull forward into the shadow of the monolith. Barclay accompanied them at Raeburn's signal, opening the ash-wood box to offer it in oblation.

Laying aside his staff, the old Druid reverently drew out the ancient meteoric dagger, cold and deadly in the starlight. Pivoting to face the standing stone, he elevated the dagger before him in both hands.

"Here is the instrument of sacrifice!" he announced. "Be present, Lord Taranis, in this blade, born of a stone which fell from the sky. Taste and savor the blood we offer in token of our devotion."

With this invocation, Taliere turned again and advanced on the bull. Hitherto docile, the big animal flung up its crowned head in sudden uneasiness, snorting in wall-eyed alarm, and it took the combined strivings of both handlers to steady the animal until Taliere could again work his charm.

But then the bull stood unflinching, hooves planted wide as Taliere moved a step sideways and drew back his arm. And as one of the handlers seized the animal by its nose-ring and wrenched its head upward, a darkling glimmer seemed to shiver along the ancient dagger, lending it life of its own.

"*Taranis!*" Taliere cried, as a stunning surge of strength drove his arm down and then up in a deadly arc, the blade rending the vulnerable throat and piercing deep into the brain.

With a hoarse bellow, the bull started back, but it was already dying. Nonetheless, the violence of its recoil tore the dagger loose—for Taliere would not relinquish it—widening the wound and sending a dark fountain of blood spraying outward from severed arteries.

But the big animal was already sinking ponderously to its knees, its crowned head weaving. As Taliere stepped clear, his attendants moved in to steady the dying beast. At the same time, the old Druid raised a blood-drenched arm to point the dagger at Mallory in a summons not to be denied.

Mallory was ready, though he had not expected the compulsion that accompanied the gesture. Almost without volition, he found himself scurrying closer to press a large stainless-steel basin under the bull's streaming throat, watching it fill as the animal bled out its life.

He did not remember returning to his place beside Barclay, though the bowl of blood steaming at his feet testified that he had done so. Taliere had shed his feathered mantle and was watching the bull's final agonies, the handlers drawing back as it slowly rolled onto its side and was still.

But Taliere was not finished. Bidding the handlers stand back with another imperious gesture of the ancient dagger, he approached the bull again and, in another display of uncommon strength, bent over the bull's still-twitching carcass to plunge the blade into the belly, ripping open the body cavity with a single stroke.

A tangle of entrails spilled onto the ground in a noisome effusion of blood and digestive juices, steam softly rising above the body opening. Back at Mallory's side, Barclay went a little pale, but Raeburn only moved a half step closer to observe.

Crouching closer beside the bull, Taliere breathed in the reek of blood and bile as he examined the exposed mass of the bull's internal organs, poking at some of them with the tip of the dagger, muttering under his breath as he lightly shook his head. After a moment, Raeburn moved impatiently closer to crouch beside him.

"Well?" he prompted. "What do the signs portend?"

The old Druid rocked back on his haunches, gazing almost stupidly at the dagger in his hand—suddenly only a dagger—then lifted his gaze to Raeburn's, his expression one of consternation.

"I find the auguries less than favorable," he said uncertainly. "This bull you have offered, while outwardly unblemished, possesses a number of hidden imperfections. The heart is slightly enlarged and I have observed a scattering of lesions on the liver.

"Such anomalies may point to unforeseen complications which have not yet manifested themselves. Or they may indicate that your own motives in making this offering are less pure than you profess. Either way, I would not advise that we continue this night's work."

"Why not?"

Raeburn's voice was calm, but contained a hint of underlying menace. Taliere set his jaw.

"To be wholly acceptable as a sacrifice, the animal in question must be completely without flaw," he replied. "Whatever the implications of the signs I have noted, there is a very real possibility that the lord Taranis will spurn the offering as unworthy. If you persist under these circumstances, I cannot be answerable for the consequences."

"I see." Glancing around the circle, Raeburn considered for a moment, then shook his head.

"I am not frightened by your caveats," he said quietly. "I require information—and suspension of our quest for that information is not an option, having committed ourselves thus far. As you yourself pointed out earlier, you are our mediator. If the lord Taranis is disposed to be overly dainty in his requirements, I rely upon you to smooth over any difficulties."

# CHAPTER FIVE

**D**ESPITE Taliere's grave misgivings, Raeburn remained adamant in his determination to carry on. When it became clear that he would not be moved, the old Druid grudgingly agreed to continue. His assistants appeared less than pleased, but dutifully bent to the task of stripping the bull's hide from its still-warm carcass—a heavy, messy task that left both men mired with gore.

While they were busy plying their knives, Taliere took the basin of blood that Mallory had collected and began tracing bloody symbols on the inner faces of the stones that circumscribed the circle, chanting a sibilant singsong under his breath as he did so. From there he returned to the base of the central monolith and proceeded to mark out the perimeter of a smaller circle between it and the sunken depression of the tomb-cairn, with bloody *S* runes radiating outward from the center, like the broken spokes of a wheel.

While Raeburn observed these preliminaries, his three remaining henchmen were making their own preparations. Moving into the lee of one of the larger stones, Barclay cast off his robe to reveal himself stripped to the buff beneath, shivering as he hastily rewrapped himself in the warmth of a goosedown sleeping bag which Richter shook out and draped around his shoulders. At Mallory's direction, he hunkered down and then sat at the base of the stone, suffering the physician to apply a blood pressure cuff and stethoscope while Richter rolled up the discarded robe and laid it atop the now empty duffel bags. After a moment, Raeburn drifted back to glance questioningly at Mallory.

"He's ready for you," Mallory said, pulling off the blood pressure cuff and returning it to his bag, though he left his stethoscope clamped around his neck as he rose and backed off.

Huddled motionless under the sleeping bag, Barclay sat with forehead bowed on folded arms atop his knees. He lifted his head as he sensed Raeburn taking Mallory's place beside him, but his eyes had already taken on a glazed, faraway look, and his breathing was shallow and slow.

"No last-minute reservations, I hope?" Raeburn asked.

Barclay bestirred himself enough to shake his head dreamily. "No, sir."

"I knew you would not disappoint me," Raeburn murmured. "This will be your greatest challenge, but also your finest commission. So long as your nerve holds, I foresee no difficulties."

Three days of rigid fasting had sharpened the planes of Barclay's already lean face and drained him of some of his usual vitality, but the flash of wry grin he offered his employer reaffirmed his customary good humor.

"Just promise me I'll get that big, juicy steak I've been dreaming about, Mr. Raeburn. And a huge baked potato with lots of sour cream and butter. And plenty of cold beer to wash 'em down."

"I expect that can be arranged," Raeburn replied softly, smiling as he laid a hand lightly on one of Barclay's. "Settle yourself now. You've important work to do."

Barclay put his forehead back on his knees and closed his eyes in passive anticipation, slipping effortlessly into trance at a few further words from Raeburn. Mallory stood by watching, his expression one of cynical attention, and moved a few steps apart with Raeburn when the latter rose.

"A man of rather ordinary appetites," he observed. "Are you sure he's the right man for this job?"

"Have no doubts in that regard," Raeburn returned frostily. "Whatever his social shortcomings, Mr. Barclay's talents as a medium are second to none."

"But to play host to one of the Patrons—"

"Will constitute a laudable triumph," Raeburn said.

"Help Richter bring him over to Master Taliere. I believe he's ready for him."

The old Druid was standing impassively beside the bloody bull's hide, now spread hair-side down beside the rune-marked circle he had earlier inscribed. Half a dozen narrow, bloody strips of bull's hide dangled from his bloody fingers as he bade Mallory and Richter guide the now somnambulant Barclay to a recumbent position in the center of the hide. The discarded sleeping bag Raeburn wadded under his head for a pillow.

Without speaking, Taliere crouched to bind rawhide ligatures tightly around Barclay's ankles, wrists, and upper arms—restriction of blood-flow to subtly shift Barclay's body chemistry and enhance his altered state. Then he passed a longer strip beneath Barclay's torso to hold in place the dagger, still bloodied from its kill, which he positioned on Barclay's chest with the point against his throat.

Finally, at Taliere's nod, his assistants moved in to wrap the gory sides of the bull hide close around Barclay's naked form, one stretching the bloody edges to meet while the other began sewing him tightly into the hide with laces of bloody sinew, starting at his neck and working toward his feet. Barclay seemed to take no note of any physical discomfort, even though his rigid body rocked with the force of each stitch through the tough bull hide.

After a moment, Raeburn knelt at Barclay's head and bent to whisper in the pilot's ear, fingertips tracing a symbol on his forehead and then continuing to stroke the weathered brow.

"Hear me, Barclay, and know this for your mission. The dagger at your breast is the key which will unlock the door to the elemental planes. Once past the threshold, you are to seek out the lord Taranis with this message: *Your votaries languish for want of your empowerments, O Mighty One. Return to us and renew our strength. Defend us by your lightnings from our enemies, and we will honor you with offerings of blood and sacrifice.* Repeat what I have just said."

Barclay repeated the message three times before Raeburn was satisfied. Each recitation added to the tension building within the circle, but by the third recitation, Taliere's now thoroughly be-gored assistants had finished their grisly work. When Taliere had pronounced himself satisfied, he directed the pair to shift the cocooned Barclay onto the sleeping bag which Richter and Mallory now spread atop the blood-runes beside the central monolith. When they had zipped him into it, Raeburn crouched at his head and administered a further prompting that sent Barclay plunging even deeper into trance.

Meanwhile, Taliere had instructed his associates to withdraw to the other side of the circle, where the central monolith blocked much of their view. Richter shifted closer to watch them. When the two had settled, side by side with backs against one of the stones, the old Druid donned his feathered mantle again and crouched opposite Raeburn to anoint Barclay's forehead with bull's blood, muttering a charm under his breath. But when he removed the leathern bottle from his belt, Raeburn thrust a restraining hand against his wrist.

"I told you to save your potions," he said to Taliere. "We have more reliable means for liberating the psyche."

The old Druid stiffened. "Tradition requires that the emissary be given a draught of mistletoe to speed his spirit on its inward journey."

"I've no doubt that such herbals once had their uses," Raeburn replied. "But it's been my experience that modern psychotropic equivalents act more predictably, and with fewer unexpected side effects. Dr. Mallory?"

Moving forward from beside Richter, Mallory blandly displayed a capped hypodermic syringe. With an explosive exclamation, Taliere sprang to his feet and planted himself indignantly between Mallory and their subject.

"This is entirely unacceptable!" he protested over his shoulder to Raeburn. "Let me remind you once again that the lord Taranis is one of the higher powers of nature. How can you possibly hope to win his favor when you continue to demonstrate this kind of contempt for the natural world?"

His face was flushed with barely controlled anger, his fists clenched at his sides. Behind him, watching from the sidelines, Klaus Richter drew himself up, muscles tensing as he prepared to step in. Raeburn, however, signalled with a glance for the German to hold his position.

"Your objection is not without merit, *Taoiseach*," he acknowledged formally. "Very well. For the sake of tradition, I will agree to a small dose of this mistletoe brew of yours—in addition to my own methods. But make it no more than a sip. I shouldn't want to risk another chemical interfering with the effects of Dr. Mallory's drug."

Grudgingly Taliere accepted the compromise. Returning to Barclay's side, he bent to tip a small measure of mistletoe liquor into the pilot's mouth, then corked the leathern bottle and rose again to lift his arms above his head in a gesture of invitation.

"Mighty Lord Taranis!" he called out in a loud voice. "Here is one who offers himself as a consecrated vessel. Descend, we implore you, upon this, your servant, and speak to us through his mouth."

Mallory, meanwhile, had dropped to one knee at Raeburn's signal and was scrubbing an alcohol swab over an area just below Barclay's left ear. Pulling the cap from the hypo with his teeth, he held the barrel briefly to the light of the nearest lamp, then injected its contents directly into the jugular. He had finished almost before Taliere realized what was happening, capping the hypo and dropping it into his open bag as he moved back beside Richter.

The drug worked quickly, given thus. A shuddering sigh escaped Barclay's slack lips. An instant later, his eyes flew wide, their dilated gaze shifting sightlessly across the starry firmament overhead. He took a hoarse, choking breath. Then all at once he began to tremble.

"Seize him, Taranis!" Taliere whispered, sinking to his knees to watch avidly.

The tremors increased in violence and intensity. Mallory glanced anxiously at Raeburn, but the latter's gaze was glued to Barclay's face. Within a matter of seconds, the pilot's whole body was twitching and jerking uncontrollably, as if caught in a surge of electrical current, his visage contorted in an expression of mingled anguish and ecstasy. Only the confinement of the hide wrappings prevented him from rolling out of the circle painted on the ground.

"*Take him, Taranis!*" Taliere whispered fiercely, fists clenched at his chest.

Barclay's eyes bulged in their sockets as an even stronger convulsion seized him. His jaw gaped, tongue protruding from his mouth like that of a hanged man, and strangled noises began to issue from his throat.

"He's in trouble!" Mallory muttered, starting forward with his medical bag.

"*Be still, you fool!*"

Taliere's vehement command stopped Mallory in his tracks no less than Raeburn's urgent gesture to forbear. Before the young doctor could even consider disobeying, a torrent of garbled speech began pouring from Barclay's writhing lips.

"Can you make out what he's saying?" Raeburn whispered to Taliere.

The old Druid shook his head. Suddenly Barclay gave a rending shriek, then began to rant in a harsh, rolling voice that patently was not his own.

"Cowards! Traitors!" he howled. "How *dare* you presume to venture here, thinking with mere words and token oblations to win the ear of the lord Taranis? A curse upon you, false son of Thunder, and a curse upon all who aid you! The Prince of Storms is not to be cozened by oath-breakers such as you! So long as I retain a tongue to speak, you will never gain a hearing in his presence!"

The tirade degenerated into incoherent ravings, but not before Raeburn began to discern an eerie note of familiarity in the harsh timbre of the voice. Stiffening, he placed it: the embittered accents of the man he himself had once hailed as the Head-Master.

Even as the unwelcome implications of that discovery began to dawn on him, the voice renewed its rantings through the foam-flecked lips of its medium.

"Vilest of ingrates! Betrayers of Taranis! May his lightnings scourge the flesh from your bones! May the fury of his storms consume your very souls! May your spirits be raked across the plains of desolation on the talons of the wind! May you never more know rest or resolution!"

With these words, the voice broke off with another anguished howl. A violent convulsion racked Barclay's bound form from head to foot. For a moment it seemed as if he must surely either burst his bonds or break his limbs. Then all at once the paroxysm ceased and he went limp.

The silence that suddenly descended was almost physical. Raeburn was the first to recover. Scrambling closer on hands and knees, he set one hand on Barclay's forehead and thrust the other hard against the side of his neck, searching for a pulse as Mallory also dashed to their patient's side and thumped to his knees, himself checking Barclay's pulse and then frantically rummaging in his medical bag for another pre-loaded syringe. Barclay was still breathing, but his face was ashen and his heartbeat erratic.

"Let's get him out of this!" Raeburn barked, tearing at the sleeping bag's zipper and at the same time summoning Richter, who was already on his way.

"It can't have been the drug," Mallory protested, as he found what he was looking for and injected Barclay in the neck again.

Richter produced a Swiss Army knife and began cutting Barclay free of his bull bindings, and once the ancient dagger had been freed, Raeburn used it to assist Richter. Meanwhile, Mallory jammed his stethoscope into his ears and thrust its bell into the growing opening over Barclay's chest, relaxing a little at what he heard; and Taliere at last bestirred himself to take up the sickle at his belt and use its sharpened blade to cut the ligatures binding Barclay's arms and ankles. By the time they had the pilot completely freed, both Mallory and his patient had begun to breathe more easily.

"I thought for a minute we were going to lose him," Mallory murmured, as he and Richter lifted Barclay's limp and blood-smeared body free of the remnants of the bull hide and laid it on the white robe Raeburn had stripped off and spread beside it. "If we don't get him warm pretty quick, we may yet lose him."

As they wrapped Barclay in the robe and Mallory stood long enough to strip off his own, adding it to the first, Richter ran to fetch the robe Barclay had discarded earlier. This, too, was bundled around the hapless pilot. As Mallory wound his blood pressure cuff around Barclay's slack arm and pumped it up, Richter lifted a corner of the bloody sleeping bag.

"Do you want this, too?" he asked.

"No, it'll be clammy from all the blood," Raeburn replied. He snapped his fingers at Taliere's two assistants, who had scrambled apprehensively to their feet during the crisis. "You men, give him your robes. Derek, how's he doing?"

Nodding, the physician released the pressure on the cuff and bent briefly to peer under one of his patient's eyelids, then slipped his stethoscope from his ears and breathed out a cautious sigh.

"He's still shocky, but I think we're past the worst of it. We need to get him back to the RV. I want to put him on oxygen."

"Right," Raeburn said, getting to his feet. "You men, help carry him," he said to Taliere's assistants. "Richter, open the circle and go with them, and recall your men. Taliere and I will finish up here and join you shortly."

Richter nodded acknowledgement, his pale eyes unreadable in the lantern-glare as he retrieved the birch wand and cut a doorway between the two nearest stones. Before stepping outside, he laid the wand on the grass beside the closest lantern, pointing at the opening.

Taliere's assistants meanwhile had folded the discarded sleeping bag with the bloodiest surface inside and zipped it shut, forming a narrow, makeshift stretcher onto which they shifted the unconscious Barclay before lifting it by both ends. As they carried him carefully after Richter, Mallory closed his medical bag and followed along at his patient's side.

Taliere watched in stony silence as the party receded against the darker mass of Cnoc an Tursa, turning only when Raeburn brushed past him, the dagger in one hand and Taliere's staff in the other, to lay the staff beside the open gateway that Richter had left. The old Druid said nothing as he watched the younger man replace the dagger in its casket, which he then slipped into one of the duffel bags lying there.

"When you proposed sending this servant of yours to seek audience with the lord Taranis," Taliere said softly, as Raeburn bent to pick up the nearest lantern, "why did you neglect to mention that another—an adversary, moreover—would be there ahead of us to dispute the way?"

Raeburn had been anticipating a question along those lines, and decided that truth would serve as an answer for now.

"Why? Because before now, I knew nothing about it myself," he replied, lifting the lantern to blow it out. "I assure you, I was as much surprised as you were to encounter such violent opposition."

Taliere glared at him sourly, following as Raeburn picked up a second lantern, extinguished it, and pressed the handles of both into the old man's hands.

"I find that hard to believe," Taliere retorted, "given that our contact's animosity seemed to be directed principally toward you. Have you any idea who he might be, that he sees reason to heap curses upon your head?"

Raeburn picked up the third lantern and favored the Druid with a calculating glance.

"What would you say if I told you that it was none other than the Head-Master?"

Just before he extinguished the lantern, he was gratified to see that this announcement had reduced Taliere momentarily to stunned silence.

"When the Hunting Lodge overran his stronghold in the Cairngorms," Raeburn went on, moving to pick up the fourth lantern, "I urged him to flee, but he refused. The citadel was levelled soon after, and I assumed that he perished in its fall.

"I see now that he must have been caught up, body and spirit, into the realm of eternal storm. The translation," he finished, with a puff of breath to blow out the last light, "does not appear to have improved his sanity."

Digesting this information as Raeburn pressed the last two lanterns into his hands, Taliere turned his gaze distractedly in the direction of the bull's carcass, now discernible only as a glistening mound under the starlight.

"I warned you that the auguries in this matter were unfavorable," he whispered. "You ought to have listened to me. As it is, we have squandered valuable time and resources to no good purpose."

Behind him, Raeburn bent to pick up the birch wand from where Richter had left it pointing to the circle's gateway.

"On the contrary," he said, "we have gained a revelation which will be of considerable value to us the next time."

Taliere stiffened, hardly noticing as Raeburn lifted the wand and turned a full circle counterclockwise, murmuring the words to dispel the illusion that had cloaked their work.

"Next time?" the old Druid repeated blankly. "There will not *be* a next time."

"Of course there will be a next time," Raeburn replied softly, taking Taliere's arm. "Surely you don't think I would let this one temporary setback stand in my way. If we cannot contact the lord Taranis by one method, we shall simply have to find another."

As he led Taliere from the circle, the two guards who had been stationed at the upper car park were waiting to take the lanterns Taliere still held, hurriedly packing them away in the remaining duffel bag. Each man shouldered one of the bags as they fell in behind Raeburn and Taliere, one of them pausing to retrieve the old Druid's staff while the other spoke briefly into his microphone. Speechless, Taliere allowed himself to be escorted nearly back to the waiting vehicles before he found words to express his displeasure.

"Francis, this cannot continue," he whispered, as they approached the RV. "You may do as you like—you always have—but if you intend to persist in this rash course of action, then you will have to do it without my help. I have already been persuaded to compromise my principles, by assisting you thus far. I cannot allow my integrity to be further eroded by continuing this association."

Shaking his head, Raeburn glanced casually back at the men following them, then ahead to where a faint glow spilled from the open side door of the RV, between it and the Land Rover. The darker silhouette of the Mini Cooper was just visible beyond the Rover, positioned to lead out. The driver of the Mini was half-sitting against the RV's near front bumper, but he came to his feet and moved a little closer as Raeburn and Taliere approached. Of Taliere's two assistants there was no sign.

"I'm sorry you feel that way, *Taoiseach*," Raeburn said softly, as they passed between the horse-box and the rear of the RV. "I suppose you speak for your associates as well."

"I do," Taliere said stiffly.

"A pity."

Even as Raeburn's hand tightened on Taliere's elbow, a soft call from inside the RV summoned the Mini's driver to the open door to reach in and take the booted feet of a slack, burly form. Taliere gasped as the rest of the form emerged, the head and shoulders of one of Taliere's assistants supported by Richter, but heavy hands on his own shoulders from behind warned the Druid not to cry out.

"Dear God, what have they done to him?" he said, his voice breaking in a muffled sob as he watched Richter and his man drag their dead or unconscious charge toward the front of the Land Rover. He turned his gaze to the face of the man who suddenly had become his captor. Raeburn's smile was as cold as a shark's.

"My dear Taliere," Raeburn purred, "I should have thought it would be obvious. Your associates were always expendable, but tonight's little setback has sealed their fate."

"But—"

"Think about it: After what happened tonight, did you really think I could risk having my involvement discovered through some accident of indiscretion? As you cannot have failed to notice, I already have more than my share of powerful enemies looking for me; I don't need the civil authorities as well. Sometimes, for the greater strategy of the game, a few pawns must be sacrificed."

"Are they dead?" Taliere asked numbly.

"No, but they *will* have to die," Raeburn replied, not unkindly, as Richter returned to direct the removal of Taliere's second associate from the RV. "If it's any consolation, Dr. Mallory tells me the preparation will have been relatively painless. It always amazes me what can be done with a couple of bottles of cheap whisky, a funnel, and a few feet of rubber tubing in the hands of someone medically trained—and with a whiff or two of chloroform to ease the inevitable resistance. I believe Mr. Richter has an accident in mind: alas, too much drink before driving an altogether too treacherous road."

While Raeburn spoke, Taliere's second assistant was carried away, and the men accompanying Raeburn and the

Druid had stowed the duffel bags and Taliere's staff in the RV. As Richter returned to fetch two fresh liquor bottles, lifting them to the old man in ironic salute before heading back toward the Land Rover, Raeburn gently removed Taliere's headdress and feathered mantle and handed them off to one of Richter's men to stow. Taliere did not resist as Raeburn took him by the elbow and guided him to the door of the RV, but he shook off the other's grip and mounted the step himself.

Inside, Mallory was adjusting an oxygen mask on the still unconscious Barclay, who was stretched out on the couch across the back of the cabin and wrapped in a bright silver thermal blanket. The physician turned as Raeburn and Taliere entered, picking up a loaded hypodermic syringe while Raeburn pushed his captive into one of the padded swivel chairs toward the front. Outside, the engines of the Mini Cooper and then the Land Rover rumbled to life, the two vehicles pulling out just before Richter and one of his men entered the RV and closed the door.

"Time to settle in for a long ride, *Taoiseach*," Raeburn said softly, as Richter's man went forward and Richter himself came to hold the old man for Mallory's ministrations. "Dr. Mallory is going to give you something to relax you."

Taliere turned his face away as the deed was done, not resisting, his eyes dull with incomprehension. When Mallory had returned to his other patient, turning out the interior lights in favor of a small pocket flashlight, and Richter had retreated to the front passenger seat, Raeburn slid into the chair beside Taliere, carefully buckling the old man's seat belt.

"Why do you not just kill me and be done with it?" the Druid asked, as the RV's engine turned over with a muffled purr. "Why should I be spared, when my associates must die? They trusted me, Francis, and you have betrayed that trust."

"Why do I spare you?" Raeburn said, himself buckling up. "Why, I entertain the fond notion that you may still prove useful to me. At very least, you have provided me with an abundance of red herrings to confound those who would try to interfere with my plans. Why do you think I didn't bother cleaning up the physical evidence at the circle? Investigating it will give the police something to occupy their time, but they haven't the resources to learn much from it. And if, by chance, tonight's work should come to the attention of some higher investigative authority, the signature of power is yours, not mine.''

As the RV pulled quietly onto the road and began its slow progress back toward Stornoway, Taliere turned his face away and closed his eyes, not bothering to fight as Mallory's sedative dragged him gently into oblivion.

# CHAPTER SIX

"I can't claim to be an experienced judge of such matters," Adam said the next morning, over breakfast with Ximena, "but in my humble estimation, your niece's nativity play went extremely well."

"Yes, it did, didn't it?" Ximena agreed, pausing to spread wild blackberry jam on a bite of warm croissant. "I hope your memory is in good working order. Dad is going to want a full account."

"I thought that's why you and Laurel took so many photographs," Adam said, amused.

"The photos are just the starting point," Ximena replied. "They don't cover the backstage details—which, as far as Dad's concerned, is where the meat of the entertainment lies. More coffee?"

"Please!" Adam said with feeling. "If only to hone my faculties as a drama critic."

They were breakfasting together in the small dining area adjoining Ximena's kitchen, both wrapped in terry-cloth robes. It was early yet, and the sun was shining diaphanously through tattered mist outside the windows. Watching as Ximena deftly replenished his cup from a glass *cafetière*, Adam marvelled anew at the unstudied grace that seemed to invest her every move. Even at rest, she had the lissom poise of a gypsy dancer.

"You make me think of scenes from the court paintings of Goya," he remarked fondly. "It takes very little effort to imagine you in a lace mantilla."

"Ever the romantic!" Ximena laughed. She returned the

*cafetière* to its place on the starched damask tablecloth, then glanced at her watch.

"Good heavens, is that the time?"

"Why, are we late?"

"Not yet," she conceded. "But we can only afford the luxury of lingering over our fancies for another quarter of an hour. After that, I have to start getting ready to cut a professional figure in the eyes of the workaday world."

At nine o'clock Ximena was scheduled to deliver a lecture on triage procedures for the benefit of new trainees on staff. Following the lecture, Teresa Lockhart would be meeting them at the hospital so that they could all be in attendance together during her husband's morning period of wakefulness. Provisional plans had been made for Ximena and Adam to break away for lunch together out on Fisherman's Wharf, but Adam was well aware how those plans might have to be rewritten at a moment's notice.

While he was finishing his second cup of coffee, Ximena went and fetched the collection of Polaroid photographs from the night before. A whimsical smile played about her lips as she flicked through the stack.

"A penny for your thoughts?" Adam offered, noticing her expression.

"I suppose I was just . . . remembering," she said wistfully, jogging the stack of photos into an orderly pile. "Christmas is such a special time for children."

"I know what you mean," Adam agreed. "You may remember that my friend Christopher has two young daughters—incorrigible charmers, the pair of them. I've promised myself the pleasure of shopping for something really special to bring back for them. Something out of the ordinary that wouldn't be available in any of the toy shops back in Scotland."

"I can recommend a good place for you to start," Ximena said. "There's a little shop in the Mission District that does handcrafted wooden toys. I'll be sure to take you there."

"You sound as if you know the place well," Adam said.

"I suppose I do," Ximena said with a small laugh. "Browsing in toy shops has always been a favorite pastime of mine. Having a four-year old niece is a good excuse to indulge in it.''

Adam debated with himself a moment, then decided to speak his mind. ''Having children of your own is an even better excuse,'' he pointed out softly.

Ximena avoided meeting his eyes.

''Yes,'' she agreed. ''I seem to recall my dad saying much the same thing.''

She stopped and bit her lip. When she found her voice again, it had the air of one determined to change the subject.

''What was the best Christmas present you ever received as a child?'' she asked.

Adam thought before answering. ''I'd have to say it was my first pony,'' he told her. ''She was a lovely little dapple-grey who went by the name of Felicity. She was ten years old—twice my age at the time—and my father said she was sensible enough for both of us. The following summer she carried me to my first-ever pony club victory. I still have that rosette somewhere. I suppose it's one of my most treasured childhood mementoes.''

He set his cup aside and smiled. ''What about you?''

Ximena straightened up in her seat, her gaze reminiscent.

''I think it would have to be the doll's house my father made for me when I was eight. It wasn't just a house, it was a palace. Dad modelled it on one of the Moorish castles he visited in southern Spain. It had arches, and turrets, and trellises—even a facsimile of a fountain in the central courtyard. Needless to say, I was completely enraptured. It wasn't until much later, when I grew up, that I came to understand what a labor of love it was.''

''What became of it?'' Adam asked. ''Is it still in your parents' house?''

Ximena nodded. ''Mother's looking after it until Emma's old enough to appreciate it.''

Adam cocked an eyebrow at her. ''You don't think you might one day have a daughter of your own to pass it on to?''

This time Ximena met his gaze squarely. ''I won't deny I haven't fantasized about it now and then,'' she told him. ''But that belongs to a future I can't begin to plan as long as my father needs me. God knows, he devoted himself to my brothers and me when we were small. The least I can do is be here for him now, doing whatever I can to make what life he has left a blessing, not a curse.''

The silence that followed was painfully brittle. Ximena drew a deep breath before continuing, her voice suddenly trembling under the stress of her emotions.

''Adam, this may be heresy,'' she said quietly, ''but I can't help asking what my father ever did to deserve a fate like this. He's always been a good and upright man, a man of principle and integrity. Surely he deserved better than to end his life like this . . . suffering so.''

The slight catch in her voice was like the first crack to appear in a dike. It bespoke a crisis of faith that had been many months in the building. But Adam had seen enough of human grief, in his personal life as well as his professional experience, to recognize the thorny issue that lay at the heart of the matter.

''What you really want to know,'' he amended quietly, ''is, 'Why do bad things happen to good people?' Or, if you prefer, 'How can any God worthy of the name permit such a blatant miscarriage of Divine justice?' You're hardly the first to ask such questions, and you certainly won't be the last. I pondered the problem long and hard myself when my own father passed away.''

''And what conclusions, if any, did you come to?''

To answer obliquely, Adam realized, would be tantamount to condescension. Nothing less than total honesty would do.

''Let me see if I can articulate this without sounding like a psychiatrist,'' he said. ''First of all, I've come to understand that suffering is not to be seen as Divine retribution for some past unatoned sin. On the contrary, it's simply one of the dangers inherent in being the mortal creatures that we are.

''Human beings appear to be unique amid the whole of creation, for having both a spiritual and a physical aspect to their existence,'' he went on. ''As physical creatures, we're subject to the same natural laws that govern the rest of material creation. Nothing stands still in the material world; everything is caught up in a complex pattern of cause and effect. If these overlapping patterns of change now and then give rise to some destructive natural event in our vicinity—say, an earthquake, or an accident, or the encroachment of some deadly disease—we're compelled by our physical nature to suffer the consequences.''

"I understand that much," Ximena said. "What I don't understand is, If God is as loving and benevolent as Scripture claims, why doesn't this God intervene and stop us from becoming victims of these natural disasters?"

"Because such intervention would violate the conditions that enable man to operate according to his own free will."

"How does that follow?" she asked.

"A fair enough question. One of the proofs that we have a spiritual, as well as a physical, side to our makeup is our ability to override natural instincts to control our own behavior. In other words, we are free to make conscious, evaluative choices regarding what we do and how we do it. In order for us to exercise that freedom of choice, however, the surrounding world in which we operate has got to be coherent and consistent. Do away with these governing principles, and you're left with nothing but chaos—a chaos as devoid of meaning as it is of morality.''

"You're saying that God can't set aside His own law?" she asked.

"Of course He can," Adam replied, "since, by definition, God is omnipotent. But He doesn't; nor should He. If God were to suspend every process that might have destructive consequences, the effect would be to undo creation itself. A world governed by natural laws, therefore, is the only world possible. If, in the process, the physical body falls victim to the operation of those natural laws, that is the price we pay for spiritual immortality—the voluntary ability to seek and find union with God.''

"I suppose this is meant to give me comfort," Ximena said miserably.

"It is," he replied softly. "Because this much is also true: that when the physical body fails, God is on hand to guide the spirit home.''

She gazed at him for a long moment, then said softly, "You really believe that, don't you?"

"I *know* it," he corrected.

Sighing, Ximena set her hand on his.

"I wish I had your faith," she said. "Maybe you could spare me some."

"It's been my experience," Adam said, "that those who want faith are given it—and from a source that flows far stronger and clearer than my own."

Ximena had little to say while they dressed and made their way to the hospital. It was plain from her expression that she was deep in thought. What the outcome of her musings would be, Adam could not begin to predict. He could only hope that he had succeeded in pointing her toward some resolution.

While she was off giving her presentation, he made his way up to the floor where her father was in residence. Alan Lockhart was still asleep—if his drug-induced state of temporary oblivion could rightly be called that. After reintroducing himself to the nursing staff and acquainting them with his credentials, Adam took advantage of Ximena's absence to read over her father's medical records in careful detail. He was pondering the results of his reading when Lockhart's attending physician arrived for morning rounds.

Dr. Andrew Saloa was a big, hearty man whose smooth, coffee-brown skin and almond eyes proclaimed his Polynesian background. Once Adam had identified himself both as a physician and friend of the family, Saloa proved more than happy to discuss the case. Adam could see from the outset that his colleague had a lively sympathy and liking for his patient—qualities which Adam regarded as essential under the circumstances. He was further encouraged by the fact that Saloa made no secret of the fact that he was at a loss to account for the lengthy duration of Lockhart's illness.

"Why do some cancer patients succumb within a few weeks or months, while others manage to hold out long past what anyone might expect?" he observed to Adam with a genial shrug. "If I could come up with an explanation for that, I'd be well on my way to a Nobel prize. What we do know is that those who have some strong reason to live tend to hold out far longer than those who simply give up. But then, as a psychiatrist, you probably know far more than I do about the power of mind over matter.''

Adam could only agree that Lockhart must have some powerful motivation for hanging on, though he could hazard no guesses, based on so short an acquaintance.

''Well, he's hanging on, for whatever the reason,'' Saloa said. ''I can't but admire his fortitude, but I have to tell you that I'm not at all satisfied with his pain management.''

''I believe young Austen intends to speak to you about increasing his father's medication,'' Adam offered.

''Believe me, I'd love to,'' Saloa replied. ''Unfortunately, Alan is a very stubborn man. I tried him on patient-controlled analgesia, but he wouldn't use it often enough. He contends that the level of painkiller he really needs leaves him too muddle-headed to make the most of the time he has left. I respect that decision, but I know it periodically makes his existence a living hell. I wish there were an alternative.''

''Perhaps there is,'' Adam said. ''Has anyone suggested trying hypnosis?''

''Funny you should ask that,'' Saloa replied. ''Only yesterday, I was reading a *Lancet* article about using hypnosis as an alternative—or at least an adjunct—to drug analgesia. But I've no experience with hypno-technique, and don't know anyone on the staff here who does. Unless you might possibly have some expertise in that area?'' he added, with a shrewd glance at Adam.

Adam smiled. ''As luck would have it, it's rather a specialty of mine. I'd be more than happy to offer my services, if you think your patient might benefit.''

''I'm certainly willing to give it a try,'' Saloa said. ''But the deciding vote will have to come from Alan himself, of course.''

''Then, if you have no objection, I'll put the suggestion to him at the first likely opportunity.''

''You do that,'' Saloa replied. ''I'll leave you to choose your moment.''

Adam accepted the other doctor's cordial invitation to be present during his morning visitation. Lockhart was just rousing when they entered his room. A night's rest had brought the sick man a fragile measure of restoration, but the sunshine streaming in through the window only served to high-light the parchment-like transparency of his skin.

Lockhart greeted both doctors warmly, though his expression indicated some surprise at seeing Adam in the absence of his family. Saloa conducted his routine examination with relaxed efficiency, his medical inquiries deftly intermingled with bantering small-talk. When he was finished, he bade his patient goodbye and absented himself in a show of breezy good humor. Left alone with Adam, Lockhart quirked an ironic eyebrow.

"I gather you've been powwowing with Saloa," he observed. "He's a good man. You've also managed to give my daughter the slip. What brings you back here all on your own?"

Adam smiled. "She's busy teaching just now. Besides that, I got the distinct impression you wanted to speak with me further. I thought you might find the conversation less tiring if there were just the two of us present."

Lockhart's gaze conveyed full appreciation for what Adam was suggesting. "You're very perceptive," he said. "Pull up a chair. Now, where were we, when we were so rudely interrupted by my obstreperous granddaughter?"

"I seem to recall being encouraged to go on at length about my pet restoration project," Adam said, settling into a chair close beside the head of Lockhart's bed.

"The tower-house, yes," Lockhart murmured. "Ximena tells me that the property itself has been in your family for many generations. It must be very satisfying to see this monument to your family's history brought back to life."

"My workmen and I have met with our share of obstacles along the way," Adam said, "not least of which is the problem of how to incorporate such modern-day necessities as electricity, plumbing, and heating, without doing violence to the structural design. But we're making progress. One day I hope to be able to take up residence there, at least for part of the year. Your daughter has been gracious enough to indulge my bit of whimsy."

This observation drew a wan grin from his listener.

"Hardly whimsy, where my daughter is concerned," Lockhart replied. "She has a lively interest in history. Even as a child, she was fascinated by ruins. When she was twelve, we took her with us on a trip down to Chichén Itzá. The expression on her face when we arrived at the city was something I've never forgotten.''

Adam listened with complete attention as Lockhart reminisced about this and other trips he had taken with his wife and children. The recollections helped Adam begin to build a comprehensive picture of the relationship the older man shared with his daughter. Lockhart was manifestly proud of Ximena's personal and professional achievements, but it troubled him that, for all her talents and abilities, she had yet to find a place to anchor her affections.

''She's always been in love with a challenge,'' Lockhart mused, almost as if he were thinking out loud. ''When she was little, I thought I was doing the right thing by encouraging her to exercise her intellectual curiosity. Now I begin to wonder if I pushed her too far in that direction. In nurturing her academic development, did I also, unwittingly, encourage her to neglect her emotional growth and satisfaction?

''You haven't been a father—yet,'' he continued, ''so I'm going to tell you something about parenthood that you may not realize. You'll want your children to have everything you never had, everything you ever had, and then some. You'll want them to partake in full measure of all the joys, wonders, and pleasures you've ever tasted in this life. And so far, Ximena's only halfway there.''

''What do you feel she's in danger of missing?'' Adam asked quietly.

''A family of her own,'' Lockhart said bluntly. ''What my daughter needs now, more than anything else in her life, is a reason to look beyond the day after tomorrow. Having a husband and children would give her that change in perspective. Responsibilities like these would encourage her to shift her sights toward a future greater and more far-ranging than her next career move.''

''Do you regret her professional success?'' Adam asked.

''Good heavens, no! That's just the point. She's woman enough to have it all. I *want* her to have it all. But she has to find it for herself. And I'm not sure she's looking in the right places—or if she is, she's blinding herself to what's staring her in the face.''

As the older man paused to gather his strength, Adam wisely said nothing, for he sensed that Lockhart was building up to some point in particular. That suspicion was confirmed when Ximena's father spoke again.

"Adam, I have to tell you something. I've always been a man of my word, and I know enough not to give that lightly. Upholding one's word is, after all, a matter of personal honor. I've never made a promise I didn't mean to keep, and I've always done my best to follow through. And that puts me in a very difficult position now.''

Adam raised an eyebrow in inquiry but did not speak.

"Ximena probably doesn't remember this,'' Lockhart continued, "but when she was eight she made me promise I would come to her wedding. I gave that promise solemnly, in good faith. And it goes hard with me now that I may not be able to keep it.''

"I see.'' An inkling of the reason for Lockhart's continued survival suddenly became clear to Adam. "Does that mean you wish you hadn't made it?''

Lockhart gave a gasp of laughter. "God, no! But that's one reason why I've been looking forward to your visit— wanting to see what kind of man you are. I've been hoping you'd be the one my daughter's been looking for all her life. Are you?''

Adam did not allow his gaze to waver, for Lockhart deserved an honest answer.

"I don't know,'' he told the other man truthfully. "For my own part, I think she's what *I've* been looking for—and we've certainly talked about marriage, if mainly in the abstract. But so far, she hasn't seemed disposed to commit herself.''

After an uncomfortable pause, Lockhart whispered, "It's because of me, isn't it?''

"If so,'' Adam said quietly, "you may be sure it was only out of love.''

"Dear God,'' Lockhart said, almost inaudibly—for, like Adam, he now was forced to consider the ironic possibility that, by postponing all decisions regarding love and marriage, Ximena might unwittingly have made him feel impelled to cling to life long past all reason—and thereby sentenced him to needless suffering.

"Adam," he said softly, "maybe it's time to talk to my daughter again."

"Does this mean I have your official permission to renew my suit?" Adam asked.

A ghost of a smile touched Lockhart's ashen lips. "Of course you do—and I won't ask you to promise me anything. But if you're even half the man I think you are, and my daughter has even half the sense I give her credit for, the two of you ought to be able to come to some understanding."

"I'll do my best to justify your faith in me," Adam said, smiling. "And here's my hand on it."

He reached down, enfolding Lockhart's skeletal fingers in a firm, light hold that was more than a handshake. Recognizing the grip of a Master Mason, Lockhart shot Adam a look suddenly luminous with pleasure and surprise.

"You . . ." he breathed.

Adam nodded, meeting the older man's gaze with steady reassurance. "Yes, I am your brother, sworn in faith. As your brother—and I hope as your friend—I swear that I will do everything in my power to safeguard the welfare and happiness of the daughter you love."

Lockhart's frail hand returned the clasp, tears welling in his eyes, beyond the need to speak. For a long moment, the two men remained thus, in silent affirmation of their common bond.

Then the sound of the door latch broke the spell. Their hands parted only seconds before Ximena and her mother entered the room. Adam rose easily to his feet.

"Oh, there you are, Adam," Ximena said, as she and her mother came to greet her father. "Good morning, Dad. Did you have a good night?"

"Actually, a bit better than most," he assured her with a smile. "Teresita, did you bring me the pictures from Emma's play?"

"I did," Teresa replied, "and I can assure you that our granddaughter performed exactly like an angel!"

While she sat down at her husband's bedside to share the

photos, Ximena slipped an arm through Adam's and casually drew him aside.

"It looks as if you and Dad have been finding plenty to talk about," she remarked.

"We continue to discover how much we have in common," Adam said. "He's a fine man. Tell me, is there someplace we can go, away from here? A chapel, maybe?"

Ximena looked at him slightly askance. "There's a meditation room downstairs."

"Then let's excuse ourselves, shall we?" Adam said. "I'd like a few words with you in private."

# CHAPTER SEVEN

THE meditation room was a tiny, intimate retreat tucked away on the ground floor at the far end of the lobby. Perhaps eight feet by ten, it housed two small pews capable of seating three to four people, a lectern against the far wall, and a stained-glass panel suspended in front of a floor-to-ceiling ivory curtain that filtered the light from a window beyond. The panel, done in blues and rich jewel-tones of gold and crimson, read: *The Lord bless thee and keep thee.* At the rear of the room, a small shelf held a vase of dried flowers and copies of the Bible and the Torah.

"Good, there's no one here," Ximena said, leading Adam inside and closing the door. "Now, what on earth did my father say to you that made you want to bring me all the way down here to tell me about it?"

Given the tragic ironies of the situation, Adam knew he was going to have to tread delicately. Smiling gently, he drew Ximena to sit beside him in the rear pew.

"He said very little on his own account," he told her. "Mostly, we talked about you. It won't come as any surprise to you to hear that he loves you very much. What you may not realize is the scope of the many aspirations he cherishes on your behalf."

A small, puzzled furrow appeared between Ximena's winged eyebrows.

"I know he's always wanted me to be happy and successful," she said. After a moment's hesitation, she added, "Have I somehow failed to satisfy him on those accounts?"

Adam mentally drew a deep breath. "Let us say that his

satisfaction in life won't be complete until he feels that yours is.''

Ximena's perplexity deepened. ''I'm not sure I understand.''

''Then let me see if I can help,'' Adam said, choosing his words carefully. ''Forgive me if, for a moment, I sound like a psychiatrist again.

''Everyone has some notion of what it would take to make him or her perfectly happy. Happiness is frequently defined as that state of contentment which an individual experiences when he or she has satisfied a significant number of personal goals. It's a sense that one's life is in balance—an awareness of personal harmony that comes from living out one's highest aspirations and promises. In short, it's the conscious attainment of wholeness which thereafter becomes the rock upon which the rest of life can confidently be founded. 'Fulfillment' might be an apt one-word descriptor.''

He broke off, his dark eyes earnestly searching hers, but she turned her gaze away.

''What are you trying to tell me?'' she asked.

''If you feel your life is already complete as it is, then your father needs to be assured of the fact,'' he replied. ''If not, it might set his mind at ease to know that you're at least aware of what you truly want, and have some notion how to go about getting it.''

He paused to give Ximena a chance to offer comment. When she remained mute, only lowering her eyes, he forced himself to continue.

''Ximena, yesterday you asked me to promise to think only of the present, and I agreed,'' he reminded her. ''Now I'd like to ask you to change that perspective. I'd like you to overleap all thoughts of the present and think about the future.''

''How far into the future?'' Ximena asked. Her face was pale and her voice strained, and she would not meet his eyes.

''Far enough to put yourself beyond any of the grief you're no doubt anticipating,'' Adam said. ''Maybe five years from now. If you could shape that future any way you wanted, where would you like to be, and what would you like to be doing?''

Ximena plucked at a fold of her skirt, still not looking at him. "You'll have to give me a minute or two to think about that," she murmured. "You've got to understand that for over a year I've been teaching myself to take things one day at a time."

"I understand completely," Adam said. "Take as long as you want."

He settled down to wait, one arm resting along the back of the pew but not daring to touch her. After a moment, she buried her face in her hands and was motionless for a very long time. When she raised her head at last, she had recovered some measure of her usual composure. She spoke softly, and with great deliberation, as she redirected her attention to Adam's watchful face.

"My father used to say that building a future for yourself is a bit like designing a house," she said. "You draw up the plans to meet your expectations, then start in on the construction. Sometimes there are builders' strikes or shortages of materials, and sometimes you have to modify the plans, but you go on as and when you can.

"The way it looks right now, my future has more than its share of empty rooms," she said more firmly. "But I know what I'd like to put in them, if I were allowed to have my way."

"Please go on," Adam said softly, as she glanced at him for reassurance.

She nodded, her gaze shifting unfocused to a point on the back of the pew before them.

"My career will always be important to me," she said, "but it isn't everything and it certainly isn't enough. Above and beyond the satisfactions of being a doctor, I want to love and be loved in return. I want children to cherish and nurture in celebration of that union. I want the joy of growing old in fond companionship. In other words," she finished on a softer note, looking up at him beseechingly, "I want *you.*"

Adam's heart swelled within him, and his hand shifted to her shoulder. But before he could say anything, Ximena laid a silencing finger tenderly across his lips.

"No, let me finish, darling. This isn't easy to say, and I don't want to lose my nerve. I know I've caused you no end of frustration in the last year or so, with all my dithering and indecision. At the same time, I guess the fact that you're here means you don't intend to hold that against me. With all you've put yourself through on my account, you deserve to hear me say that there isn't anything I wouldn't do to redress the balance—that is, if you think you're still willing to have me.''

Their eyes met. Ximena's were bright beyond all shadow of remaining doubt, and answered whatever hesitation Adam himself might have entertained. Only barely containing his joy, he took her hand and turning her palm up, kissed it with a tenderness approaching reverence.

''This is not the setting I imagined,'' he told her gravely. ''Certainly not the one this moment deserves—but it will have to do.''

In a single fluid movement, he left the bench and sank down on one knee before her, keeping her hand in his.

''We've talked about marriage before, but never come directly to the sticking point,'' he continued. ''Well, I'm coming to the point now. I would give you the sun, the moon, and the stars thrown in, if that would make you happy. Will you marry me?''

Ximena was wavering between laughter and tears. With her free hand she dashed the wetness from her eyes.

''Adam, you dear fool, of course I will!'' she exclaimed. ''Just tell me when and where.''

Although Dr. Philippa Sinclair was American born and bred, and currently residing in New Hampshire, she had spent more than half of her life in Scotland as the wife of a Scottish laird. Among the British customs she had adopted in the course of her marriage was the time-honored ritual of afternoon tea.

That custom had been introduced as a regular feature at the private psychiatric clinic at which Philippa was chief consultant. On the twenty-second of December, she was taking tea in the parlor with senior members of staff when one of the secretaries poked her head into the room.

''Dr. Sinclair, I have your son on the line. He says he's ringing from San Francisco.''

"It's Adam? Good heavens. Put it through to my office, please, Janine."

She had known, of course, that Adam was stateside. He had rung her from his hotel in Houston, primarily to advise her of his safe arrival, but they had also spent some time discussing the situation he expected to encounter when he joined Ximena on the West Coast. En route to her office, as she calculated the time difference between California and New Hampshire, she concluded that something significant must have occurred to warrant Adam's phoning in the middle of the day.

Her first thought—that Adam was calling to report the death of Ximena's father—was put to flight the moment she heard her son's voice, buoyed up with a strange note of excitement that conveyed a wide range of emotion.

"Philippa," he said, "are you sitting down?"

"No," his mother said astringently. "Should I be?"

She thought she detected the suppression of a chuckle.

"Quite possibly. I've got a fairly important announcement to make."

"I see," Philippa said, groping behind her for her chair. "All right, I'm ready. Now, what's your news?"

"I think you'll find it to your liking," Adam said with a laugh. "Will you mind terribly if I bring a new Lady Sinclair home to Strathmourne?"

"What? Do you mean—"

"That's right. Ximena and I are getting married."

Philippa restrained an undignified impulse to squeal.

"Oh, thank heavens!" she exclaimed. "And about time, too! Have you set a date?"

"Ah. That's partly why I thought I'd better call you as quickly as possible," Adam replied, on a note of apology. "Do you think you could get out here for Christmas Eve?"

"*This* Christmas Eve?" Philippa blurted, then made haste to recover herself. "Probably not without a minor miracle," she allowed, "but this being a good and worthy cause, I daresay I could probably conjure one up."

"I know. I'm sorry. I know this must seem a bit sudden."

He sounded like a guilty schoolboy—which gave Philippa an absurd twinge of delight.

"Oh, I don't know," she said airily. "I've seen it coming for at least the last year. So far as I can see, the only mystery involved is what took you so long. That having been said, I hope you'll forgive me for asking why you're going ahead so precipitously now?"

Adam's voice took on a more serious note.

"I'm afraid the rush isn't intended for our benefit. It seems that, many years ago, Alan Lockhart promised his daughter that he would attend her wedding—and Ximena and I would like to make that possible. He's already waited far longer than he should have done."

Philippa's agile mind was quick to seize the unspoken implications of this disclosure, but she made herself move on to practicalities.

"I see. Holiday air schedules aside, have you considered other important logistics?" she asked. "Blood tests shouldn't be a problem for two doctors, but this close to Christmas, the license might be."

"We've already decided not to worry about that for now," Adam replied. "We haven't the time. *Alan Lockhart* hasn't the time. We'll have a second ceremony when we get back to Scotland. Besides, Christopher will be crushed if he doesn't get to officiate."

"Quite so," Philippa agreed, somewhat taken aback.

"Meanwhile, we're making arrangements for a small, very intimate ceremony in Alan's hospital room," Adam went on. "The chaplain who's been working with the family has agreed to preside, and to offer a Eucharist, and she's in full agreement with our reasons for rushing things through and waiving the legalities. Even if the wedding isn't technically legal, it will be sacramentally valid."

"Very sensible, under the circumstances," Philippa concurred, "though that still leaves a great many loose ends to tie up. Professionally speaking, is Ximena quite resigned to giving up her job there in San Francisco?"

"It wasn't her job that brought her back to San Francisco," Adam reminded his mother quietly, "though she wouldn't be human if she didn't have a few regrets. Fortunately, with her qualifications, she'll never have any shortage of job offers. I was pleased to learn that she's kept up her contacts with her old colleagues at the Edinburgh Royal Infirmary. Apparently most of them would be delighted to have her back, including the head of section. But even if that doesn't work out, she assures me that she's still committed to returning to Scotland, once her responsibilities here in San Francisco are discharged.''

"You seem to have the larger issues well in hand," Philippa said, deciding not to pursue the lingering questions centered around Ximena's father. "Just to give you more to think about, I wonder if you've thought about your own obligations back in Scotland. Social obligations, if nothing else. I know you've thought about the others."

"Social obligations?" Adam said, puzzled.

Philippa clucked her tongue. "Adam, Adam—getting married ought to be one of life's most memorable experiences, not only for the bride and groom, but also for those who are closest to them," she pointed out. "You needn't make any decisions just yet, but speaking as the most senior surviving member of the Sinclair family, I would like to see you celebrate the event in a style worthy of your station and equal to a mother's fondest ambitions."

This declaration earned her a chuckle from her son's end of the line.

"I see what you're getting at," he said. "Did you think I'd make Ximena settle for a registry office wedding?"

"Well, hardly that. You did mention having Christopher preside, and he'll insist on bells and smells, even if you'd prefer to run away to Gretna Green. Just remember that most little girls dream of a fairy-tale wedding to a handsome prince. If that's Ximena's dream, you wouldn't want to deprive her of it."

"It's my fondest wish never to deprive her of anything," Adam replied with a chuckle, "but I'm afraid she *will* have to settle for a baronet rather than a prince. But never fear: Ximena deserves nothing but the best—and whether she knows it or not, I intend to see that our 'official' wedding is no exception. Since we've got to go through the forms a second time in any case, we might as well make the most of the occasion."

"Then, there *will* be a splendid party! Excellent!" Philippa exclaimed. "I shall look forward to helping the two of you plan the details. Incidentally, have you given any thought to a ring?"

"Not yet," Adam admitted.

"Then don't," Philippa said. "Unless, of course, you think Ximena would be averse to wearing the sapphire that belonged to my mother."

"The Rhodes sapphire?" Adam was obviously taken with the idea. "Mother, you have me at a loss for words. Thank you. I'll ask her, but I imagine she'd be delighted to wear it."

"Then I'll be sure to bring it with me," Philippa said crisply. "Being a surgeon, she'll probably want a plain gold band to go with it, but we can sort that out later. At least you've left me twenty-four hours' grace to get it out of the safe deposit box."

"I gather this means you approve of the match," Adam said wryly.

"Have you forgotten who you're talking to?" Philippa countered, and smiled to herself. "If your stars have been slow on the ascendant, my dear, their impending conjunction presages as bright a future as any two people could ever wish for."

# CHAPTER EIGHT

THE Lothian and Borders branch of the Scottish police had its Edinburgh headquarters in a large office block on Fettes Avenue. Despite the seasonal garnishes of tinsel and holly scattered throughout the building, Detective Chief Inspector Noel McLeod was not in a particularly festive mood, thanks to an eight-hour shift spent trying to reduce an accumulated backlog of paperwork. He had nearly cleared his desk and was thinking fondly of going home when there was a sudden, unwelcome knock at his office door. Stifling an inward groan of misgiving, he barked, "Come!"

The door opened, admitting Sergeant Donald Cochrane, one of McLeod's most promising investigative aides. The younger man was brandishing a piece of fax flimsy in one hand.

"Glad I caught you before you left, sir," he said. "You remember that tarted-up pink piano that went missing last week?"

Cochrane's expression indicated that he might just have found it.

"Aye," McLeod said apprehensively.

"Well, I've just taken a call from Sergeant McGuinness over in North Berwick. He thinks he's found it."

"He *thinks*?" McLeod muttered testily. "Hell's teeth, Donald, there couldn't be two like that! Where is the damned thing?"

"The van turned up in a derelict warehouse," Cochrane said. "A watchman stumbled on it more or less by accident, and notified the police. When they went to check it out, they found the piano in the back. McGuinness just faxed through the report.''

Rolling his eyes heavenward, McLeod put out his hand.

''I know—crime of the century,'' Cochrane said, as McLeod skimmed the details. ''But McGuinness thinks it might tie in with some heavy-duty burglaries in another part of his patch, and he and his lads have locked down the warehouse until the lab can get someone over there to dust for prints. I can handle it, if you want to get on home,'' he added, noting his superior's sour grimace.

Shaking his head, McLeod rose and retrieved his jacket from the back of his chair.

''No, I'll go. I've been cooped up here all day. Besides, you have a pretty young wife at home, and a baby daughter about to experience her first Christmas. You shouldn't miss that.''

''You're sure?''

''Aye, off with you. I'll scare up a print man and get over there as soon as I can—and call Jane to let her know I'll be late for dinner. Just ring McGuinness before you leave, and tell him he'd better be at the warehouse when we arrive, or I'll sign it off and he can whistle for his prints. That club owner has been on my back three times a day since the blessed thing was stolen. With any luck, he may just be able to have it ready for his Christmas Eve opening after all.''

''Will do, Inspector. Thanks. I'll see you tomorrow.''

It was after eight o'clock by the time McLeod returned from North Berwick. Back in his office, he was just putting the finishing touches on his report when the telephone rang. This time McLeod did not scruple to curse out loud as he reached for the receiver. But his initial irritation soon lost its edge when the caller introduced himself.

''Inspector McLeod? This is Detective Sergeant Hugh Chisholm, ringing from Stornoway, Isle of Lewis.'' Chisholm's voice held the soft lilt of the Western Isles. ''We've not had occasion to speak before, but I believe you've worked with my wife's nephew, Sergeant Callum Kirkpatrick, who works out of Blairgowrie.''

McLeod's stomach did a slow, queasy turn, for Blairgowrie recalled the ritualistic murder of a member of the Hunting Lodge—though that connection had never come to light during the investigation following its discovery. What *had* emerged was a well-orchestrated campaign to destroy prominent Freemasons, masterminded by a cult of black magicians operating from a secret base in the Cairngorm Mountains. Though Kirkpatrick, himself a Mason, had never learned the full truth behind the murders, he remained high on McLeod's list of approved contacts. Which meant that Chisholm also was likely to be more than a casual contact.

"Callum Kirkpatrick," McLeod repeated slowly. "Yes, indeed. I remember him well. He's a good man, and a fine police officer. I was impressed with his handling of that Blairgowrie case." He paused a beat. "I hope you aren't ringing to tell me you've got another one like it?"

"Not exactly," Chisholm allowed. "But there are some creepy similarities."

"Are we talking about a murder, Mr. Chisholm?"

"No, no—or at least I don't think so, though we're still checking on the human angle. But there certainly appears to have been some kind of ritual sacrifice involving a bull."

"I think you'd better give me all the details," McLeod said, reaching for a pen and notepad.

"Right. I don't suppose you know the stone circle at Callanish?"

McLeod had never been to Lewis, but he had read about the Callanish Ring and seen photos.

"Not directly," he replied, "though it strikes me as a hell of a place for nasty doings."

"Well, your instincts are dead accurate where *that's* concerned."

Quickly Chisholm outlined the case, stressing his own inexperience with such matters.

"We figure it must have happened late last night," he said thoughtfully. "We can account for at least three vehicles, plus a trailer or horse-box to transport the bull, and maybe six or eight perpetrators. You'd think someone in the village would've seen or heard something, but no one's talking, if they did. You know how local superstition can run in a place like this—and apparently for good reason, in this case. Besides, folk aren't apt to poke their noses out of doors much past about seven o'clock, this time of year—and the snow and wind would have muffled most sound anyway. The perps sure left an unholy mess, though. There was blood everywhere.''

''Yes, you mentioned something about a ritual sacrifice,'' McLeod said, trying to shake off mental images of another secluded, snow-shrouded location drenched in blood, two years before, and a friend and colleague lying dead in the snow. ''Mind telling me exactly what you found?''

A heavy sigh issued from the receiver. ''Well, the bull had had its throat cut and its entrails pulled out, and then someone had flayed off the hide, quite expertly. We also found remnants of what looks like a crown of mistletoe and holly. And like I said, there was blood everywhere: daubed on the stones, painted on the ground—''

''Sounds like some kind of divination ceremony,'' McLeod said, praying that was all it had been. ''What makes you think there might be a murder involved, as well?''

''Well, we found a sleeping bag near the scene, literally saturated with blood,'' Chisholm replied. ''When we examined the bull hide, it showed signs of somebody maybe having been sewn up inside it, so we're hoping it's bull's blood on the sleeping bag, but we just don't know yet. We had a man fly the bag over to Grampian Labs in Aberdeen this afternoon, but we won't have the results until sometime tomorrow. It'd be just our luck to find that some wretched camper has been done in.''

McLeod had been busy jotting down the details as Chisholm relayed them. Now he paused, pen in hand, and scowled at the page before him.

''We'll hope it doesn't come to that,'' he observed. ''Who made the initial discovery?''

''A young chap, name of Iolo MacFarlane. He's a bit of an eccentric, but reliable enough. I've known him since he was a wee tad. He's got a New Age sort of group who style themselves latter-day Druids, and they occasionally stage ceremonies up at the circle—all quite harmless, we thought, at least until now.''

''Any chance he could have reported the incident to cover his own group's activities?'' McLeod asked.

"Iolo? Not a chance. Like I said, I know him; hell, I know most of his lot. They were slated to do a Winter Solstice ceremony at noon today. Needless to say, that had to be cancelled. No, he went up to the site just after sunrise, planning to start setting up, and immediately roused one of the neighboring villagers—who phoned the station officer up at Carloway, who phoned me in Stornoway when he'd had a look. The rest you know."

Chisholm sounded anything but happy about it, and the inspector couldn't blame him.

"How are the press reacting?" McLeod asked. "I assume that's at least part of the reason you called me."

"Aye, they've been sniffing around all day. The Solstice 'do' would've brought them out in any case, and this was just an added bonus, where they were concerned. It's hard to keep something like this under wraps on an island this small. I've got a man out at the site tonight, but I didn't want to dismantle too much until I'd talked to you."

McLeod could sense the incipient request to come in person, but he decided to forestall it for as long as possible.

"How about your neo-Druids?" he asked. "Are they apt to talk, if some reporter buttonholes one of them?"

"I doubt it," Chisholm replied. "Any publicity connected with this case is apt to be bad, so they'll want no part of it. They've worked hard to keep up a a good public image. I can't guarantee their silence, of course, but I expect they'll have the sense to keep their mouths shut."

McLeod shunted aside the question of press curiosity for the moment in order to focus on more practical matters. "How about the bull?" he asked. "Have you been able to find out where it came from?"

"Not yet," Chisholm replied, "though I've got a man checking that angle. We've mostly sheep here on the island, but there are a few farmers who raise cattle, mostly for dairy herds. They'd know who has bulls, but someone could easily have brought one in for last night's piece of work. Horse-boxes come and go all the time, and no one would notice if a bull was in one."

"And no one's reported a stolen bull?"

"Not on the island—though it's early on. Farmers don't

always check their fields every day. I'd hate to think any of our local men might be mixed up in something like this, but the evidence—or rather the lack of evidence—seems to be pointing that way. Unless you have a better suggestion, I intend to press on with this line of inquiry until I get an answer.''

The only alternatives McLeod could think of demanded the exercise of talents beyond the scope of an otherwise competent investigator. Chisholm, meanwhile, was worrying out loud.

''Legally, we're on uncertain ground here, even if we do find the perps,'' he went on. ''Unless that turns out to be human blood on the sleeping bag, we've only got offenses relating to the defacement of a public monument and violations of various public health statutes. You should have seen the carrion crows flocking around the site by the time we got there.

''At the same time, I don't like to think of some weird cult setting up operations here in my patch. There's a degree of depravity at the back of this affair that really puts my hackles up. I know it's a long way from Edinburgh up to the Hebrides,'' Chisholm finished, ''and I know it's a terrible time of year to ask this, but I'd really feel easier in my mind if you could manage to fly up here and examine the site for yourself—and maybe help me deal with the press.''

It was the appeal McLeod had known would be forthcoming—and if the Stornoway officer's instincts were correct, then the sooner a full investigation could be implemented— McLeod mentally emphasized ''full''—the better the chances for arresting the evil before it could spread. Chisholm, meanwhile, was still talking.

''I know you can't get up here tonight,'' he said, ''but how about tomorrow? I feel *really* out of my depth, Inspector.''

''I'll see what I can do,'' McLeod told Chisholm. ''Leave me a phone number where you can be reached, and I'll get back to you as soon as I've managed to sort out the necessary travel arrangements. I'm going to have to call in a few favors.''

''I do appreciate this, Inspector,'' Chisholm said, sounding greatly relieved. "I'll wait to hear from you."

The Stornoway policeman rang off with a promise to fax McLeod a copy of the incident report. Returning his telephone receiver to its cradle, McLeod mentally reviewed his assignments for the following day and decided there was nothing on his agenda so urgent that it couldn't be either delegated or left to lie fallow for a day or two.

Chisholm's report was waiting for him out in the fax room by the time he finished jotting off a note to Cochrane to cover for him the next day. He read it through once, clipped it to Cochrane's memo, then ran a finger down his address file to check a number. If Harry Nimmo was available, he was the perfect man for the job. And Peregrine Lovat's talents would be useful, as well.

The harp notes drifting in from the adjoining room had the light, bell-like clarity of music-box chimes. Pausing to listen, Peregrine recognized the hauntingly beautiful melody of the Hebridean carol known in English as "The Christ Child's Cradle Song."

It was one of several pieces Julia had been practicing all week in preparation for her Christmas Eve concert, now only two days away. Peregrine was privately of the opinion that his wife could hardly hope to improve her already-perfect performance, but he was always happy to listen whenever she played.

Shortly after coming to live at the gate lodge, he had converted the smaller of the two upstairs bedrooms into a studio. It was here that he still did most of his painting in the daytime. Whenever he had any additional work to do in the evening, however, especially research, he preferred to do it downstairs in the sitting room, where he could enjoy simultaneously the glowing warmth of an old-fashioned fireplace and the pleasure of his wife's company.

Just now he was ensconced in one of the armchairs by the hearth with a notebook on his knee and a stack of art history books on the table at his elbow. The local chapter of the Saltire Society had invited him to give a lecture on the history of Scottish portraiture, and having agreed to do it, he was now reviewing the subject by way of advance preparation. His efforts at note-taking were being somewhat hampered by the latest addition to the household, a roly-poly black and white kitten whom Julia had christened Hero. Having had his pencil knocked twice from his hand, Peregrine was attempting to fend off yet another spirited mock attack when the telephone rang.

"I'll get it!" he called through to Julia.

Surrendering his pencil to Hero, he reached for the receiver. The caller was McLeod.

"What's your schedule like tomorrow?" the inspector wanted to know.

Peregrine's intuition went instantly on the alert. "I've heard that line before," he said. "What's up?"

"Something that warrants our attention," came the gruff response from the other end of the line. "There's been an incident up at the Callanish Ring on the Isle of Lewis. A police colleague has paid me the dubious compliment of asking my opinion—at the scene. He's related by marriage to Callum Kirkpatrick, up at Blairgowrie."

The mention of Kirkpatrick and Blairgowrie instantly brought back to Peregrine chill recall of the horror they had discovered when called out on another cold winter night to investigate a case. He was already familiar with the stone circle at Callanish, having sketched it during his university days in conjunction with a survey course on Scottish archaeology. When McLeod related how the site had been desecrated, the young artist experienced a mingled pang of distaste and foreboding.

"If you think I can be of service, of course I'll come," he told the inspector. "What are the arrangements?"

"I've got some pull with a chap who's got a private plane," McLeod replied. "Weather permitting, he's agreed to fly us up at first light."

"Well, fortunately, that isn't nearly as early as it might be, other times of the year," Peregrine said, retrieving his pencil from Hero to jot down notes. "About half past eight, then?"

"Aye. Meet us at the airport, and don't forget your kit."

"Will do. Have you any idea when we'll be getting back?"

"None," McLeod said succinctly.

"That's what I like about working with you, Noel: everything's always so well-planned," Peregrine said drily. "Anything else?"

"Nothing I can think of. See you tomorrow morning. Cheery-bye."

The inspector rang off. Peregrine cradled the receiver, grimacing at McLeod's ironic farewell, then realized that Julia was standing in the doorway.

"That was Noel McLeod, wasn't it?" she observed. "Is there some kind of trouble afoot?"

"I don't know yet," Peregrine said. "Hopefully, just a bit of a mystery."

Julia scooped up the kitten. Cradling the purring bundle on her shoulder as she sat, she asked, "Are you allowed to tell me about it? Or does this fall under the Unofficial Secrets Act?"

Peregrine gave his wife a sharp look. "The *Un*official Secrets Act?"

"That's what I call it, anyway," Julia said with a smile. "You know what I'm talking about: the Statute of Confidentiality. The Code of Professional Conduct for Psychic Investigators. Whatever system of ethics sets the rules of the game when you and Noel and Adam have an investigation under way. The sort of thing you do on the quiet so the newspapers won't find out about it."

Julia's manner was composed, her blue eyes disconcertingly bright as she waited for his response. Peregrine shifted uncomfortably, toying with his pencil.

"You make it sound very hole-in-the-corner," he protested.

"That's what makes it so exciting," she said. "Are you going to tell me about it or not? I know you may not be able to tell me *everything*, but—"

It was not the first time Peregrine had found himself caught out by his wife's discernment. With an inward sigh, he asked, "How much have you heard already?"

"Your half of the conversation," Julia said. "Which was, shall we say, less than complete."

Peregrine hesitated, not quite certain how to begin. "The facts aren't very savory," he warned.

His wife arched an eyebrow. "Worse than finding a body on our honeymoon?"

"No. Not nearly as bad as that, thank God."

The body had been that of an Irish Fisheries officer washed up on the west coast of Scotland, initially believed merely to have been lost at sea. But eventually the body had tied in with a far more sinister set of circumstances that had taken the resources of both the Scottish and Irish Hunting Lodges to resolve. As at Blairgowrie, the trail had led back to one Francis Raeburn, a powerful black magician as dedicated to the pursuit of illegitimate power as the members of the Hunting Lodge were dedicated to the service of the Light. Though Raeburn again had managed to elude justice, at least his intentions had been thwarted—but not before Peregrine had been obliged to make some telling disclosures to his new wife about his secondary line of work as a psychic investigator.

"Are you going to tell me nor not?" Julia said quietly, still stroking the kitten. "You needn't be coy. If you can take it, so can I."

Still prey to some misgivings, Peregrine repeated the broad facts of the case as McLeod had reported it to him.

"This may turn out to be nothing more than a crass and ugly prank," he told her at the end of his recital. "On the other hand, there might be something far more serious at stake. Either way, since Adam's in America, it's up to Noel and me to look into the matter."

Julia absent-mindedly scratched the kitten's furry ears as she mulled over what Peregrine had told her.

"What exactly are you going to be looking for?" she asked. "I mean, I know you don't see things as other people do—or rather, that you see things that aren't apparent to the rest of us. But since psychic impressions aren't exactly admissible as evidence in a court of law, I'm not sure what practical purpose your efforts serve."

"It all depends on what area of jurisdiction you're talking about," Peregrine replied. "I'm less concerned about satisfying the requirements of the law than I am with upholding Justice.''

"It sounds like you're talking about some kind of justice on a higher plane," she ventured.

He paused a moment, nodding as he continued. "I suppose I am. But actually, you might think of Noel and me—and Adam—as being the psychic equivalents of government health inspectors. Where conventional public health officials are charged with the task of identifying environmental health hazards, we look for evidence of psychic pollution.''

"*Psychic* pollution?''

"Precisely," Peregrine went on more eagerly. "You see, evil, like goodness, is an active force in the world. It involves traceable expenditures of energy—psychic energy as well as physical exertion. That expenditure of psychic energy leaves behind residual evidence in the form of psychic resonances. Those resonances can be as tangible in their own way as a bad smell or a dissonant jangle of noise—or images, in my case. If you're psychically attuned to the right frequency, you can sense what is wholesome and what isn't.''

Julia considered this explanation, finally nodding comprehension. "I see. And if you and Noel find something unwholesome in this instance, what will you do about it?''

"Extend the investigation, and hope it will get us to the root of the problem, so we can resolve it.''

"But health inspectors don't have enforcement authority,'' Julia pointed out. "What if the problem turns out to be more than you can handle?''

"Then we call in more help," Peregrine said. "And we do have enforcement authority." He smiled at his wife reassuringly.

"Noel and Adam and I aren't alone in this venture, Julia. I don't know all the other people involved in our vocation, but I do know this: We stand united in opposing evil wherever it rears its head. It isn't easy work—and I won't lie to you and tell you it's always safe. But if one of us should ever be seriously in need of help, there are no lengths the rest wouldn't go to in order to render aid.''

# CHAPTER NINE

A forty-mile stretch of open water separates the Isle of Lewis from the Scottish mainland. Skimming half a mile above the foam-flecked waves in their twin-engine Cessna, Peregrine pressed his forehead against the window glass and watched the shadow of the plane sweep before them like a dark hound leading the hunt. He hoped there was nothing but poetic allusion in the comparison. With the nature of the case confronting them yet to be determined, he preferred not to encounter any ill omens at this early stage of their investigation.

The flight itself had been uneventful, apart from some expected wintry turbulence over the Grampians. Fortunately their pilot, one Harry Nimmo, was no stranger to flying in adverse conditions. Indeed, he was no stranger to their work. McLeod had briefed Peregrine about Harry while they watched him fuel the plane, though only later had he disclosed the most important piece of information about Harry Nimmo.

By then, Peregrine had learned that Harry was a former major in the SAS, who had flown Harrier jump-jets in the Falklands War before taking up a highly successful career in the law. In the years since, though his considerable legal talents had earned him the coveted apanage of Queen's Counsel, Harry had continued to indulge his love of flying, not only retaining active flying status with the reserve RAF, but also making occasional guest appearances at air shows as a pilot of vintage aircraft. Harry had flown everything from Spitfires, Lancasters, and Hawker Hurricanes to the even more exotic aircraft of the biplane era—Tiger Moths and Sopwith Camels, the latter so named for the distinctive humpbacked outline of the fuselage and made famous by the flying exploits of Charles Schulz's Snoopy and the Red Baron.

McLeod's matter-of-fact recitation of Harry's flying credits had sparked fond memories of some of Peregrine's favorite boyhood reading—of Biggles, the fictional British flying ace whose dashing escapades had made him the hero of many an English schoolboy. On finally meeting Harry, Peregrine had found himself picturing the pilot-cum-barrister in the leather flying jacket, goggles and helmet, jodhpurs, and boots affected by Biggles and other pioneers of aviation. Indeed, with his lean, lightweight build and self-assured good looks, Harry Nimmo might easily have served as Biggles' prototype.

Not that anything in Harry's present attire or even his manner suggested much of a Biggles parallel. As he'd led them out the Cessna parked on the general aviation apron, Harry was togged out like his two passengers in a serviceable, close-knit sweater over collar and tie, with hard-wearing woollen trousers and stout winter boots—sensible, professional-looking winter-wear for assisting in a police investigation, whether as police officer, artist, or senior barrister. Only his military-issue sunglasses lent a touch of the exotic—though the dark lenses were more a necessity than an image statement against the harsh glare of snow glittering beside the parking apron.

The anomaly between reality and reputation had persisted as Harry unlocked the plane's cabin and directed them inside, himself ducking under a wing to make a final pre-flight inspection. As Peregrine clambered into one of the Cessna's rear seats and stowed his sketch box in front of the seat beside him, leaning out then to take the coats that McLeod handed up, he had begun to wonder if perhaps he had been too quick to draw the parallel between Harry Nimmo and the dashing Biggles.

Except that as Harry came around the aircraft, removing his sunglasses as he ran a hand along the near wing, Peregrine caught a glimpse of an eagle-keen blue gaze—just before Harry produced a navy baseball cap from a hip pocket and donned it with a flourish. The cap bore the logo of the *Starship Enterprise*. Simultaneously, Peregrine realized he had just dumped his and McLeod's coats atop an old-fashioned brown leather flying jacket, fleece-lined and with an embroidered set of RAF wings sewn above the left breast. A creamy-white silk scarf spilled from one of the pockets.

"If the jacket looks familiar," McLeod had said over the back of his seat, "it's because you may have seen it a couple of years ago. Harry flew one of the helicopters on the Cairngorm mission."

Now more than an hour into the present mission, Peregrine glanced wistfully at his sketch box, set on the floor behind the pilot's seat, half-tempted to try some trial sketches to see what would show up—for McLeod's attitude toward Harry had soon made it clear he was far more than a crack barrister and sometime Biggles clone, and that the Cairngorm mission was but one of many in which Harry had placed himself and his talents at the service of the Hunt. Listening to the drift of their conversation, filtered through the headsets that all of them wore to communicate above the drone of the twin engines, Peregrine inferred that the pilot was one of those individuals he had sometimes heard described as a Hunt Follower.

The realization gave him pause, for hitherto, he had always understood a Hunt Follower to be someone with no particular psychic gifts, who was nonetheless associated with the Hunting Lodge. Whether that association was familial, marital, or professional, Peregrine had further understood that whatever aid a Hunt Follower might be prepared to render, such an individual could never be allowed to know the full scope of the work of the Hunting Lodge itself. The principle of "need to know" was for the mutual protection of all concerned, since what a Follower did not know, he or she could not be induced to betray.

Yet McLeod had been more than usually candid while briefing Harry on the case, once they were airborne, and allowed himself to be drawn out on rather specific possible esoteric implications. Granted, Harry was trained to ask probing questions, but the exchange made Peregrine wonder whether the role of Hunt Follower might be subject to fewer restrictions than he had hitherto supposed.

Confronted with this possibility, the young artist found himself examining his earlier assumptions. Perhaps the role of Hunt Follower was to be interpreted more flexibly, as dictated by the relative strengths and proclivities of the individuals concerned. It certainly made sense that, just as Adept talents varied from individual to individual, some Followers would have a greater capacity for knowledge and understanding than others—and judging from McLeod's display of confidence, Harry was more capable than most. Even without the esoteric dimensions of their present assignment, it was clear that Harry Nimmo would be a good man to have behind them in any crisis, if any real trouble was looming ahead.

Contemplating the form such trouble might take, as the Isle of Lewis itself loomed ahead, Peregrine found himself cupping a hand over the slight bulge of his Adept ring in a trouser pocket. Very shortly, Harry's voice jarred him back to the present, a little tinny-sounding in the headphones.

"We're about to start our descent into Stornoway. Anything else I should know, before I get involved in tower chitchat?"

"Nothing I can think of," McLeod replied. "Just keep your eyes open. If anything at all strikes you as odd, don't hesitate to point it out. Just be careful what you say in Chisholm's hearing. He's a good man, but he can't be expected to think like one of us."

"Roger that," Harry replied, reaching for the radio. "Let's take her down, then."

The next few minutes passed in a buzz of landing preparations and tower chatter as Peregrine considered McLeod's phrase, *one of us*. The ride down was bumpy, and the artist braced himself as the ground came rushing up to meet them, idly noting a Loganair commuter plane parked on the apron beside a very small terminal building. The lightweight Cessna jibbed briefly under the force of a random crosswind and snow flurries, but Harry set the little craft down with the effortless precision of a man placing an egg in a basket. After taxiing to an area apparently reserved for light aircraft, he shut down the engines and McLeod opened the door to a blast of wind and cold. A patrol car in the white and blue livery of the Highlands and Islands Police was waiting just beyond the chain-link perimeter fence, and the driver's door opened as McLeod poked his head out and raised a hand in acknowledgement.

"That'll be Chisholm, I expect," he muttered, as all of them put on their coats.

Chisholm joined them as they were lashing down the wings to tie-downs set into the tarmac—a lanky, pink-cheeked figure in a policeman's cap and a dark-blue parka zipped to his chin against the cutting wind. When he and McLeod's party had traded introductions and handshakes all around, the island officer ushered them out through a gate in the chain-link fence.

"I figured I'd better collect you myself," Chisholm said to his visitors as they piled into the police car, McLeod in the passenger seat beside him and Peregrine and Harry behind. "Fortunately, the weather isn't too bad today, but it's about fifteen miles across the island to Callanish—and you'll love the road."

He buckled up his seat belt before starting the engine, then pulled a manila folder from between the two front seats and handed it to McLeod.

"That's the production file thus far," he said, putting the car into gear. "I sent you the incident report, but there are some photos that might tell you a lot. Incidentally, the blood on the sleeping bag *was* bull's blood, thank God. But that still doesn't explain what was going on."

As McLeod opened the file and started to leaf through the notes accompanying the incident report, Chisholm fell silent, whipping the car out of the parking area and past the adjacent RAF station, then winding through the fringes of Stornoway itself. McLeod had gotten to the photographs by the time they were speeding south and westward along the snow-edged A859—a stretch of road that traversed some of the bleakest highland landscape Peregrine had ever seen.

"We've had a clean-up crew in this morning to remove the carcass and offal," Chisholm said, as McLeod shook his head over one of the photos, "but those will give you some notion of the state the place was in when our first witness discovered it. He was pretty upset, and I can't say I blame him. This was as grisly a mess as I've ever seen outside a slaughterhouse.''

McLeod shuffled through the set of pictures, pausing now and then to consider one at an alternate angle. When he was finished, he passed the folder back to his companions. Perusing the photos in his turn, with Harry looking on, Peregrine was inclined to agree with their guide's assessment. He was glad the pictures were in black-and-white.

''I'll tell you, Inspector, I've been fifteen years a policeman on this island, and I've never seen anything like this before,'' Chisholm said, slowing momentarily as they passed through a tiny village. ''I'm not saying we haven't had our share of eccentric visitors—these prehistoric stone circles seem to attract nutter types—but all the ones I've encountered up till now have been essentially harmless. I guess what worries me is the thought of what might come next. Based on your experience, *is* this what you would call black magic?''

Sighing, McLeod took the file Harry passed forward and tucked it back between the seats, letting his gaze range over the winter terrain flashing by.

''Not necessarily,'' he said, though without much conviction. ''The formal aspects of the bull-sacrifice—the mistletoe crown, the method of slaughter—are certainly in accordance with some forms of Druid ceremonial magic. And the arrangement of the entrails certainly suggests some kind of divination procedure. In order to qualify as *black* magic, however, such a ritual would have to be specifically dedicated to an evil purpose by people seeking to interface with the powers of darkness. But photographs alone don't yield sufficient evidence to make such an assessment.''

''What about the black bull?'' Chisholm asked. ''Does that have any significance?''

''Well, the traditional color was white,'' McLeod allowed, ''but black might have been all they could get. I'd prefer to reserve judgement until I've had a chance to go over the ground at the scene.''

''Well, you'll soon get that chance,'' Chisholm replied,

hardly slowing as the snow-crusted road narrowed to a single lane with passing places.

A row of cottages briefly relieved the winter landscape as they sped on, domestic tendrils of chimney smoke snaking lazily upward against a grey sky threatening more snow. Here and there sheep huddled in the lee of wall or fence or stunted tree, masquerading as rocks, and snow lay in shallow drifts among tussocks of winter-burned grass.

Very shortly they were winding through the outskirts of Callanish Village, creeping past a long, thatched cottage to nose into a muddy car park at the far end of the main street. Beyond a barbed-wire fence, a broad avenue of standing stones pointed the way to the Callanish Ring itself. The webs of bright yellow police tape strung among the ancient stones seemed jarringly out of place—an ugly reminder of the criminal present, as intrusive as scrawls of spray-painted graffiti.

Two police cars and a rainbow-painted minivan were among the half dozen vehicles already drawn up around the edges of the car park. As Chisholm pulled in between the two police cars and cut the ignition, McLeod indicated the van with a jerk of his chin.

"Would that belong to your neo-Druids?" he asked.

"Aye, Iolo must be around here somewhere," Chisholm replied. "I think I told you he was the first one to report the incident. I asked him to meet us here, in case you had any questions you wanted to put to him. And there's a second site beyond that rise, where the suspect vehicles apparently parked. I'll take you there on foot. That's where we found the sleeping bag."

As the four of them began to alight, Peregrine gazed narrowly across the distant ring of monoliths, pausing with one hand on a door handle. Even at this remove, he could see there was something amiss. The entire area defined by the stones appeared slightly beclouded to his sight, as if the stones themselves had been treated to a coating of dirty grease.

Recalling his purpose, he tucked his sketch box under his arm and followed after Chisholm and McLeod, noting that the latter unobtrusively took his Adept ring from a pocket and slipped it onto his finger before pulling on his gloves.

Peregrine did the same, trying not to draw attention to the gesture, though Harry clearly noticed. As they passed through a gate bearing the logo of the National Trust for Scotland and began trudging up the muddy pathway toward the main standing stones, Peregrine found himself oddly reassured to have the enigmatic Harry bringing up the rear.

Closer to the lines of tape, two uniformed policemen had been assigned to perimeter security. One was crouched down talking to a handful of children who had come to gawk, and the other was engaged in a rather more emphatic conversation with two adult civilians—reporters, judging by their persistence. As Chisholm and his companions approached, the officer dealing with the children sent them off and came over.

"Morning, McIver," Chisholm said. "This is DCI McLeod, up from Edinburgh. McIver normally runs the one-man station up at Carloway, Inspector, but he was first officer on the scene yesterday."

He went on to complete the introductions. By then, the two civilians had accepted their rebuff from McIver's partner and were trudging back toward the car park. From beyond the tapes on the other side of the circle, another man, with a camera and telephoto lens, was trying to frame a shot of the central cairn chamber, but McIver's partner was already on his way to deal with the situation. Chisholm's mouth tightened as he returned his attention to McIver.

"Press been giving you trouble?" he asked.

McIver gave a stolid shake of the head and blew on his gloved hands to warm them. "Not much, sir. This morning, there isn't much to see. Those two chaps have been most persistent, but it looks like they've given up. There might be a couple of stragglers still nosing around the village in search of an angle, but I don't think they'll get very far. The locals seem to be sticking to their original statements that no one saw or heard anything worth reporting."

"They never do," Chisholm said with a grimace. "See if Maxwell needs a hand with that photographer, would you? I want to give Inspector McLeod a quick tour of the site before he talks to our witness."

"Aye, sir."

The wind up by the stones was sharp. When Peregrine had

ducked under the tape that Chisholm held up for them, he turned up the collar of his duffel coat with a shiver. McLeod seemed impervious to the vicissitudes of the weather, as did Harry. Frost crunched under their feet as they made their way toward the center of the circle, now seen to mark where the stone avenue and three single lines of stones converged in a rude Celtic cross design.

The details inside the stone circle were much more foreboding. An icy slick of reddish-brown still darkened an open space beside the central stone—obvious location of the bull's demise—and looking more closely, Peregrine could see where blood had been used to trace the outline of a smaller circle on the short wintry turf between the central stone and the irregular depression of an open tomb cairn. More blood still marked the insides of all the stones defining the circle—which he had seen in the photographs, of course, and with the bloody carcass of the bull still in place.

But somehow the reality was far more disturbing, even after the first attempts at clean-up. As Peregrine tried to make some sense of what he was seeing, a sudden flood of psychic impressions rose to meet him, beating against the barriers of his inner Sight with an urgency that was almost irresistible.

"Inspector," he said, as casually as he could, "if you don't mind, I'm going to pull off to one side and start making some sketches. This seems as good a place to start as any."

"Please yourself," McLeod muttered. "You know what we need. Harry, why don't you give him a hand?"

Harry merely inclined his head and gestured for Peregrine to lead the way. Chisholm, meanwhile, drew McLeod aside to point out what looked like a scorch mark at the base of one of the central stones, where the wintry turf showed pale and withered.

"What do you make of that?" he asked. "There are three more like it."

Crouching down on his hunkers, McLeod prodded at the mark with the end of a pen, then glanced around the circle and located the three other marks, obviously marking the cardinal points of the compass.

"At a guess, I'd say they were made by lights of some

kind—kerosene lanterns, maybe, or oil lamps, or possibly votive lights.''

''That was my thought, too,'' Chisholm agreed. ''But you'd think someone would have noticed. There wasn't even any moon that night.''

McLeod shrugged as he rose, all too aware how a sufficiently powerful Adept might contrive to screen his doings behind a veil of obscurity, especially if he harnessed the power of the moon at full wane. Such practice did not necessarily betoken dark intentions, but neither did it bode for good, coupled with the sacrifice of a black bull. But all he said was, ''If they were shielded lanterns, and set at the right angles behind the stones, they might not have been visible from the village. And given that this apparently occurred well after dark, on a cold and windy night . . .''

''Aye, you're probably right.''

Chisholm went on to show McLeod the symbols which had been painted in bull's blood on the standing stones of the circle. Though McLeod readily identified them as Druidical signs of warding, he did not mention to Chisholm that the symbols had been fortified by signature flourishes of unusual potency. Pausing to copy them into the small notebook he always carried with him, McLeod became conscious of a foreboding prickle at the base of his skull. Though the residual power of the stones themselves appeared to be neutral, it was becoming increasingly clear that the individuals who had carried out this work on Solstice Eve were anything but novices.

''I think it's time I went and had a word with that witness of yours,'' he said, snapping his notebook shut and turning briefly toward Peregrine and Harry. ''I'll be back in a bit,'' he called.

The witness in question was sheltering in the lee of the furthermost stone in the south arm of the Celtic cross described by the stones. Enveloped in a heavy grey wool cloak instead of a coat, he had been almost invisible until he rose at their approach, pushing back the cloak's hood from long reddish hair plaited into braids on either side of his face.

He was a lanky young man, perhaps a bit younger than Peregrine, with a straight mouth, a bushy moustache, and a pair of earnestly frowning eyebrows that almost met across the bridge of his nose. Beneath the cloak, which was fastened at one shoulder with a bronze penannular brooch, he was wearing faded blue jeans, knee-high sheepskin-lined boots, and a mossy-green medieval-style woollen tunic, the latter girt at the waist by a broad leather belt with a buckle of handcrafted bronze. Cradled in the crook of one arm was a tall ash-wood staff surmounted by a shard of rock crystal.

He drew himself erect, like a prince receiving petitioners, as Chisholm led McLeod into his presence, taking the staff in hand and planting it firmly in front of him. Despite the hint of challenge in his manner, his dark eyes betrayed no trace of guilt or evasion.

"This is Iolo MacFarlane," Chisholm said to the inspector. "Iolo, this is Detective Chief Inspector Noel McLeod."

MacFarlane looked minutely relieved, but retained his guarded stance. "A DCI? I hope this means someone is going to take this case seriously."

His voice was a light, ringing tenor, not as confident in tone as his manner had suggested. Adopting a less aggressive approach than first intended, McLeod removed his aviator spectacles to polish them casually with a pocket handkerchief.

"Mr. MacFarlane, my associates and I flew up from Edinburgh this morning at Mr. Chisholm's request. You may take that as an indication that we are all interested in getting to the bottom of this affair. I'm hoping you can help us."

"Oh." MacFarlane seemed to unbend slightly. "You really came all the way from Edinburgh?"

"Aye."

"Well—thank you. Ah, how can I help?"

"I read over the case report and saw the photographs before I came," McLeod replied, "but obviously they don't tell the whole story." He put his spectacles back on. "Judging by the signs, this would appear to have been a Druid sacrifice, but there are elements here that don't add up. So I'd like to go back over your impressions, beginning when you first arrived on the scene."

"My impressions?" MacFarlane retorted. "How would you feel if you turned up for church on Sunday morning and found that somebody'd left a dead sheep on the floor in front of the sanctuary?''

"I'd be pretty thoroughly outraged," McLeod said with blunt candor. "And I'd bloody well want to find out who did it." He cocked an eye at the younger man. "Mr. Chisholm says you're a practicing Druid yourself. I know a bit about that, and I know this isn't how it's meant to be." He gestured back toward the site. "Suppose you tell us what you can surmise about the people who did this."

MacFarlane drew a deep breath, then inclined his head in guarded assent. "They certainly seem to have known their history. Sacrificing bulls *was* a regular practice amongst the later Druids, as was divination from the entrails. And they knew enough to carry it out in the traditional manner. But no true followers of the Druid way would have left such a mess behind. That's sacrilege. This is holy ground. And they used it like the floor of a slaughterhouse!"

He stopped short, his eyes blazing, and McLeod gave a sympathetic nod.

"Your anger and resentment are fully justified," he said quietly. "We'll try to wind up the technical part of this investigation as soon as possible, so you and your people can come in and do what's necessary to cleanse the site."

This statement earned McLeod a look of mingled surprise and gratitude.

"We'd be very much obliged," MacFarlane said.

"I'm the one who's obliged," McLeod replied. He took one of his cards from his pocket and presented it. "If you come across anything *you* regard as unusual in the clean-up process, I'd appreciate your giving me a call. I need to know, if we're to find who did this."

MacFarlane took the card, fingering it thoughtfully. "I'll do that," he promised.

"Thank you," McLeod said, and then turned to Chisholm. "Now I'd like a look at where you said you think the vehicles parked."

Meanwhile, Peregrine had set about his own work, preparing to settle in while McLeod and Chisholm inspected the stones and then moved off to find Iolo MacFarlane. Before he could even begin to draw, his initial task was to isolate the impressions of immediate relevance from the surging background sea of historical images. At such an ancient site, it would not be easy.

Moving outside the circle of stones, Peregrine withdrew along the western arm of the cross until he could find an angle that gave him an overall view of the central circle. Taking shelter in the lee of one of the stones, he pulled off his right glove and opened his sketch box long enough to remove a sketch pad and pencil, then gave the box into Harry's keeping while he turned his attention to the circle stretched before him.

A slowly drawn breath eased him into trance with a smoothness born of practice as he set himself to filter out all the other resonances, layer by layer, until he at last was left focused on a stratum of dark images from the immediate past. Under cover of blowing on his fingers to warm them, he set the stone of his Adept ring briefly to his lips, commending himself to the guidance and protection of the Light, then set pencil to paper and let the dark images channel through his drawing hand. Wholly absorbed in his work, Peregrine soon ceased to be aware of anything else.

He worked thus for perhaps half an hour, changing location several times, filling half a dozen pages of his sketchbook with impressions. Harry observed the process with interest at first, but Peregrine's concentration clearly did not invite comment or conversation. Growing fidgety after a while, Harry circulated around the site on his own, making his own observations, increasingly restless but always drawn back to the young artist's side to see what was taking shape beneath his flying pencil, especially when Peregrine changed locations.

Peregrine had moved into the center of the circle to sketch, now sitting on his sketch box, which he'd retrieved from Harry. He was deep in a study of the dark stain where the bull had lain when Harry again returned to his side. This time, as he peered over Peregrine's shoulder, he found the other man's pencil strokes blurring in front of him like the ghost-image of a spinning propeller-blade, almost drawing him into the sketch.

Removing his sunglasses, Harry knuckled at his eyes and

turned away. As he did so, his gaze lighted upon a blackened curl of something that looked like a small black snake lying on the ground beside the central monolith, just inside the blood-traced circle.

Curious, he moved closer to crouch in the lee of the monolith, prodding whatever it was with one earpiece of the glasses and then lifting it for a closer look. It was not a snake. He was just considering whether the object might be a narrow strip of bull's hide when it slid down the earpiece and onto his hand. Its touch triggered a startling and overwhelming cascade of alien images that set him reeling back to sit hard in the snow.

Harry's strangled exclamation jolted Peregrine from his sketching trance. Looking up sharply, he saw the barrister crumpling dazedly against the central monolith, eyes unseeing and fists clenched hard against his chest. Jamming his pencil through the spiral binding at the top of the sketch pad, Peregrine thrust the pad under his arm and sprang to Harry's aid.

"Harry!" he whispered urgently, seizing the man's arm and at the same time trying to block him from view by anyone who might be watching. "Harry, what's the matter?"

Both the scrap of hide and Harry's sunglasses had fallen from his fingers as he sat, and he shook his head in dazed bewilderment as he regained awareness of his surroundings—and his wet posterior.

"Christ!" he murmured under his breath, bracing himself against Peregrine and scrambling back to a crouch, brushing vainly at the seat of his trousers.

"What happened?" Peregrine demanded, giving Harry's arm a shake when he did not immediately respond. "Harry, are you all right?"

"Yeah, I—I'm fine." Harry groped automatically for his sunglasses, folding them clumsily into a breast pocket of his flying jacket, then stiffened as he saw the curled scrap he had dropped. His finger began trembling as he pointed it out to Peregrine.

"Do you see that?" he whispered.

"Yes."

"The damned thing—*bit* me!" he said, for want of a better descriptor—though Peregrine had a sudden inkling of what he meant. "Fetch McLeod, would you?"

McLeod was out in the long avenue that led back to the car park, conferring with the two police constables as they gestured around the location and the nearest cottages, apparently discussing who might or might not have been able to see anything. Chisholm was back in the police car, talking on the radio. Heading partway back to McLeod and the two constables, Peregrine raised his sketch pad to catch McLeod's eye.

"Inspector, can I see you a minute?"

McLeod excused himself immediately and came to join the young artist, his brow furrowing at the look on Peregrine's face.

"What is it?"

"I dunno. Something just happened to Harry. He seems to be all right now, but he said that something 'bit' him. I think he meant psychically. It looked like a fragment of bull hide."

"Did he touch it?"

"I think so."

McLeod nodded and headed in Harry's direction.

"That's one of the reasons I brought him along. I expected that something like this might happen, if I just gave him time and opportunity. I do believe our Harry may have made a personal breakthrough."

Harry had struggled to his feet during Peregrine's brief absence, and was leaning heavily against the central monolith on the side away from the others, folding something into a pocket handkerchief.

"I didn't touch it a second time," he said in a low voice, as McLeod came close beside him. "Didn't mean to touch it the first time, but it sort of slid onto my hand when I was trying to scoop it up with one of the stems of my sunglasses. It's in here," he added, handing the folded handkerchief to McLeod and immediately wiping his hands against the legs of his trousers, as if to divest himself of something unpleasant.

Very carefully McLeod opened the handkerchief enough to see what was inside, nodding as he glanced back at Harry.

"Care to tell us about what happened, Counsellor?"

Harry swallowed audibly and managed a sickly grin. "Tell me this, first. Would there have been a reason to sew somebody inside the skin of that bull?"

McLeod nodded carefully.

"And some kind of binding in addition to that?" Harry persisted. "Some kind of ligatures around the wrists, the upper arms, the ankles?"

Again McLeod nodded, refolding the handkerchief over its contents and slipping the bundle into an inner coat pocket.

"Restricting the movement of a subject is a form of sensory deprivation," the inspector explained. "It can enhance states of altered consciousness. And the ligatures would restrict blood flow to the limbs—and hence concentrate blood flow to the brain—also enhancing psychic activity. Psychotropic drugs are sometimes given for the same reason. What did you see, Harry?"

Harry glanced at the remnants of the circle outlined in blood, hugging his arms across his chest to suppress a shiver.

"Something really dark," he whispered. "And for just a few seconds, I seemed to be part of it."

"Tell me," McLeod said quietly.

Harry swallowed and nodded. "I was lying in the center of that circle of blood. I was sewn tight into that damned bull hide with my arms strapped to my sides, stark naked inside. I couldn't move, I could hardly breathe; my feet and hands were numb."

"Go on."

"There were—a couple of men were bending over me," Harry continued, blue eyes going unfocused as he remembered. "One of them was old, with white hair and some kind of crown on his head—I'd know him if I saw him again. The crown wasn't metal, or even leaves. It had wings like a bird, but—close to the head. Not Viking or anything like that."

"Did he say or do anything?" McLeod asked.

"Aye. He—put a flask to my lips and tipped something into my mouth. I can almost taste it, even now—odd, aromatic . . . And then things *really* began to get weird. . . ."

He paused and gulped for breath. Peregrine had an odd

look on his face, but McLeod only nodded slowly.

"I don't suppose this man had a name?"

Harry closed his eyes, wrestling with a memory just at the edge of retrieval. "He did. It wasn't said, but somehow I knew who he was. Something—something beginning with a *T*. Tal—Toller, maybe? No, more like Talley . . . but longer. Tallier. That's not quite it. Tallier . . . No—Taliere. Yes, that's it. Taliere."

"Taliere." McLeod tasted the four syllables, then shook his head. "It doesn't ring any bells. What happened then?"

Harry shuddered and shook his head. "I can't remember exactly. Things got very dark. I—can only describe my feeling as one of dread. My head felt like it was about to explode, like there was something in there, trying to get out— or something outside, trying to get in. . . ." He shuddered again. "I can't remember anything more, but it was awful." He swallowed with difficulty and finally looked at McLeod again. "What—what does it mean?"

"It means, my friend, that you seem to have experienced a rather potent flash of psychometry, almost certainly triggered by contact with that bit of ligature," McLeod said casually, laying a gloved hand on Harry's forearm in reassurance. "I've been half expecting it for some time, though I didn't anticipate anything quite this dramatic, first time out."

Harry's jaw had dropped during McLeod's explanation, and now his face went pale beneath its tan.

"I'm not sure I want to hear this," he whispered. "You know I haven't any psychic talents."

"So you've always claimed," McLeod said with a faint smile. "However, I've suspected otherwise for some time. The ability to pick up psychic impressions from physical objects is one of the more useful and better-documented types of psychic sensitivity."

"I know what psychometry is!" Harry snapped, then raised both hands to rub at his temples distractedly, shaking his head in denial. "God, I don't believe this. Couldn't this just have been imagination run rampant?"

McLeod smiled thinly. "Counsellor, I would never venture to describe you as a fanciful man."

"And even if you were," Peregrine said quietly, "I think I can produce some rather compelling independent evidence."

He turned to one of the newly filled pages of his sketchbook and held it out for Harry to see: a sketch-portrait of an elderly white-haired man garbed in the costume of a pagan priest, crowned with a winged headdress in the form of a speckled bird.

"Is this anything like the man you saw?" Peregrine asked.

Harry stared at the drawing. His jaw dropped slightly, his face growing paler still under its healthy sheen of outdoor tan.

"Dear God, that's him exactly!" he whispered, suddenly weaving a little on his feet. "That's him, right down to the last detail."

Casually pulling off his right glove, McLeod turned the stone of his Adept ring inward and lightly clasped the back of Harry's neck, making certain the stone made contact.

"Steady, old son. Just close your eyes for a minute and take a deep breath," he directed with calm authority. "Now let it all the way out. You're perfectly all right. There's absolutely nothing wrong with you. Quite the contrary, in fact. Psychometry's a very useful talent. We'll talk more about this later. In the meantime, just relax and take another deep breath . . . Now another . . . You'll be fine in a few seconds."

Harry did as McLeod instructed, trembling beneath the inspector's hand. After a moment or two, his breathing steadied and his face started to regain its normal color. After another few seconds, McLeod slid his hand down Harry's shoulder and gave it a reassuring squeeze.

"Better now?" he asked, as Harry sheepishly opened his eyes.

The counsellor nodded and took a deep breath, letting it out with a whoosh.

"You'll have to excuse the attack of funk," he murmured to his companions, suddenly self-conscious. "I never thought anything like this would happen to me. Maybe proximity to you people triggers this kind of thing, Noel. Or maybe it's just that one is more inclined to believe, having seen you work."

*Or it could be that the time is ripe for you to come into possession of your own talents,* Peregrine reflected. He certainly had no trouble remembering how alarmed and confused he had been when his own talent first had begun to manifest itself, not so very long ago.

But before he could offer Harry any words of reassurance, the sound of hurried footsteps on frosty ground heralded Chisholm's return. He was shaking his head, looking grim.

"I'm afraid I'm going to have to leave you on your own," he announced. "If you'll let McIver know when you're ready to head back to Stornoway, he or Maxwell will run you in."

"Trouble?" McLeod asked.

"Aye, but only the usual sort, thank God—not that the poor bastards involved will know the difference," Chisholm replied. "We've got a vehicle over the side on a really bad stretch of road, down toward Harris. It looks like two dead—local chaps. A recovery team is on the way, and I've said I'll meet them there."

McLeod raised an inquiring eyebrow. "I don't suppose there's any chance of a connection with this?"

Chisholm shrugged, but he looked unconvinced. "I suppose it's possible," he allowed. "Dispatch said it's a Land Rover—which is certainly capable of pulling a horse-box with a bull in it. But it's far more likely that the two incidents are unrelated. This time of year, people drink far more than they should and then try to drive. It's probably just poor judgement and bad luck."

"But you'll let me know if you find anything to change your mind," McLeod insisted.

Chisholm cocked his head quizzically. "Do you know something you're not telling me?"

"No. Just ring me if anything seems odd. I tend to mistrust coincidences, when dealing with something like this."

"All right. And ring *me* if you come to any conclusions about all of this."

"I will, that."

After Chisholm had taken his leave, McLeod and his companions walked the outside boundary of the circle a final time before seeking out PC McIver for the promised lift back to Stornoway. Their departure was noted with what appeared to be only casual interest by a man loading photo equipment into the passenger seat of a grey Toyota, but he lifted a long telephoto lens to observe as the police car pulled away and disappeared down the single track leading back to the main road.

When he had stowed the camera in a fitted case and closed the passenger door, he produced a small cellular phone from a breast pocket of his anorak and, as he walked around to the driver's side, punched in a Glasgow telephone number.

# CHAPTER TEN

IN Francis Raeburn's library, Angela Fitzgerald cradled the telephone receiver with a brittle click, then turned to Raeburn with a peevish grimace that contained no mirth whatsoever.

"That was one of *my* people checking in," she informed him tartly.

Raeburn was ensconced in a chair by the library hearth, feet on a footstool, meditatively nursing a measure of fine brandy. Pausing to take a sip, he eyed Angela over the crystalline rim of his snifter. "And?"

"*And* it seems your little piece of playacting up at Callanish has already drawn some of the very attention we hoped to avoid. The cops on Lewis are more savvy than you gave them credit for. They called in McLeod."

Raeburn's lip curled in slight vexation at the news, but his Second's sarcasm left him unmoved. "I would have been surprised if he *hadn't* shown up," he observed with a shrug. "Let him snoop all he wants. He won't find anything worth his time."

"I wish I could be so confident," Angela said. "Or don't you care that McLeod had his little pet artist in tow? I think we can safely assume they didn't leave entirely empty-handed."

Raeburn looked mildly pained. "*Do* try to have a little faith," he admonished. "Klaus and I took every precaution to ensure that we were shielded throughout. Talented as Lovat is, he won't have been able to penetrate any of Klaus's bulwarks."

"You've been wrong before," Angela reminded him. "You were wrong about Taliere. You might be wrong about Lovat, too."

"Taliere was equal to the task as we originally envisioned it," Raeburn said patiently. "Who could have foreseen the intervention of the Head-Master?"

"That's precisely my point," Angela said. "You don't know what other tricks the Hunting Lodge may have in reserve."

Raeburn sighed, setting aside his drink. "What would you have me do? Sit on my hands and do nothing, simply out of fear that the Hunting Lodge may have acquired a new secret weapon? Since when did cowardice ever achieve anything? If it's safety you want, Angela dear, perhaps you ought to get out of this business."

"Don't lecture me about the virtue of taking risks," she snapped. "It's your penchant for adventuring that's largely to blame for our present predicament."

She darted a look across the room at Barclay, who was sitting huddled beside a radiator in an overstuffed chair, an afghan around his shoulders and both hands shakily wrapped around a mug of hot soup. The pilot had slept around the clock following his Callanish ordeal, but he was still ashen and hollow-eyed from the aftereffects.

"Look at him!" she whispered fiercely. "You're lucky he isn't dead, after the way you let Mallory push him to the brink the other night!"

"I didn't know you cared," Raeburn remarked drily.

Angela just missed stamping her foot. "I hate to see a good tool misused, that's all! If I were you, I'd keep a closer eye on our young doctor. He's too ambitious by far. He wants results, and he doesn't care how he gets them."

Raeburn shrugged. "A streak of ruthlessness is, on the whole, no bad thing in our vocation."

"He'll turn it against you, if you don't watch out," Angela warned, and gave a fastidious shiver. "Nasty little toad, he makes my skin creep. He probably started out by pulling the wings off flies when he was a boy! I hate to think what he gets up to on his own, in the middle of the night."

"He can do what he likes, as long as he continues to obey my orders," Raeburn said mildly.

Angela gave an unlady-like snort. "Some day you may rue that remark. What happens now?"

Before Raeburn could answer, there was a knock at the door. At Raeburn's query, Mallory entered, looking irritable.

Raeburn arched an eyebrow. "Why, Derek, what *is* the matter?"

The young physician made a petulant gesture of disclaimer. "It's Taliere. He came round about half an hour ago, and he's been making a right nuisance of himself ever since. He's demanding to be allowed to speak with you, and says if you don't consent to see him, he'll start sending up fireworks on the astral."

"Is that a fact?" Raeburn smothered a heavy-lidded yawn. "Then I suggest you put him back under sedation. And keep him that way until I tell you to do otherwise."

"I'll need some help."

"Then go borrow two of Mr. Richter's men. Restraining people is part of their vocation."

Raeburn went back to contemplating the fire on the hearth, retrieving his brandy with a gesture on the edge of boredom. Realizing that he had been dismissed, Mallory turned on his heel and strode out. As the door shut behind him, Angela directed a glare at the back of Raeburn's head.

"That's another point where we differ," she said. "The old man is becoming an increasing liability. Why don't you do us all a favor and get rid of him?"

"Because," Raeburn responded, "he's our shield."

"Our shield?"

"Indeed. Why else do you suppose I ordered the Callanish site to be left as it was, rather than cleaning it up? Why else would I allow Taliere to play the dominant role in the ritual itself, if not to ensure that it was his presence, not mine, which was stamped on every blade of grass within the inner circle. Who among our enemies is likely to waste valuable time looking for us when there's so clear and obvious a trail leading off in another direction entirely?"

"I wish I had your confidence in this enterprise," Angela remarked. "Has it occurred to you that this new alliance you contemplate may not be any more successful than the last?''

"Are you questioning my decisions?'' Raeburn showed his teeth. ''The party in question is hardly likely to take umbrage at being offered a chance to escape from limbo. I anticipate no difficulty in reaching an accommodation.''

As he spoke, the fax machine on a table in the corner came suddenly to life. As the message came chittering through, Raeburn left his chair and crossed the room to retrieve it.

"It's from Klaus,'' he reported over his shoulder. ''I hope you'll be pleased to hear that he has managed to assemble all the properties necessary for us to go ahead with our plans for the thirty-first.''

Later that afternoon, the winter dusk was settling in by the time Harry Nimmo brought the Cessna in for a landing at Edinburgh Airport. McLeod had made a brief telephone call before leaving Stornoway, and would have taken Harry along to the meeting he had just arranged, but the counsellor was already late to pick up his son at the train station. Young Rory was at Eton; and since Harry was a widower, he and the boy usually spent the Christmas holidays with Harry's parents in Perth.

"Fair enough, then,'' McLeod said, as the three men headed for their respective cars, back in the airport car park adjoining general aviation. ''Have a happy Christmas, Harry. We'll try not to need you in the next few days.''

"No problem,'' Harry returned cheerily.

Accordingly, only Peregrine followed McLeod as he led the way back to Edinburgh and an Edwardian town house in the New Town district. There, over hot coffee and sandwiches, the two of them shared the day's findings with Lady Julian Brodie, the oldest member of the Hunting Lodge, and Senior in Adam's absence.

"Have a piece of fruitcake,'' she urged, as Peregrine hesitated over a stacked plate. ''It sounds like the pair of you have earned your treats for the day.''

Though over seventy, and physically so frail that she had been confined to a wheelchair for nearly a decade, Julian retained her full vigor of spirit and intellect, as well as a penetrating curiosity. An accomplished amateur goldsmith,

she still turned out the occasional special commission for
friends. Several members of the Hunting Lodge wore rings
of her crafting; and Peregrine's had belonged to her late husband.

Wrapped tonight in a festive shawl of silk paisley, her
silver hair soft around her face, she followed McLeod's report with unwavering attention before shifting her regard to
the sketches Peregrine dealt out like oversized cards on the
table they had cleared of the remains of their meal. The bit
of bull's hide wrapped in Harry Nimmo's handkerchief also
came under her careful scrutiny. Only after she had examined
each item did Julian at last venture an opinion.

"An interesting proposition," she said thoughtfully. "On
the surface, at least, this does appear to be a classic Druid
divination ritual of the old school. All the elements are there,
as Peregrine's drawings clearly show. The bull was crowned
with mistletoe and then sacrificed by having its throat cut,
after which the auguries would have been read from its death
struggles and the flow of blood and examination of the entrails. The Romans called the practice 'haruspicy,' from the
Etruscan *haruspex*, which was the name given to priests who
performed this kind of divination; and in earlier times, the
sacrificial victim would have been a man.

"Fortunately, our unknown perpetrators proceeded along
less drastic and probably more efficient lines. The bull was
flayed and a designated subject bound up in the animal's
hide, probably with ligatures tied at wrists and ankles and
upper arms, as Noel has suggested, to restrict blood flow and
facilitate an altered state of consciousness. From what you
say Harry reported, it appears that the subject was also given
some hallucinogenic substance—probably something containing mistletoe, if they continued to follow traditional procedures. The man supervising all of this would appear to be
wearing the accoutrements of an arch-Druid."

She singled out a detailed study of a hale, elderly man
with luxuriant moustaches, a winged headdress in the form
of a speckled bird, set above a high, domed forehead, and
craggy features fixed in an expression of austere exultation.
Peregrine's skill had endowed the portrait with the clarity of
a photograph.

"That's the chap Harry called Taliere—if that's his real name," McLeod said. "His looks are distinctive enough. If he's got a police record, we shouldn't have much trouble coming up with a match."

Peregrine picked up a wider-angled drawing showing several white-robed and hooded figures crouched around a circle traced on the ground. The elderly Druid had his arms upraised in a posture of invocation above an anonymous form lying swaddled in bull hide on the ground at his feet, within the circle. The figure's head was turned away from the artist's point of view, but even if it hadn't been, that area of the sketch had the appearance of being somehow unfinished.

"Let's get back to the man in the bull skin," Peregrine said, tapping his finger on the figure. "He was Harry's contact, apparently through this piece of bull skin." He indicated the scrap of dried hide in the handkerchief. "If it *is* part of a ligature such as you've both described—and Harry's talent is triggered by physical contact—I suppose it's no wonder he got such a psychic jolt when he touched it.

"Unfortunately, this one sketch is the only view I was able to get of this man," Peregrine went on. "And even this one didn't show me his face. I kept trying, but something seemed to be obscuring it—almost like a veil being lowered between me and what I was trying to see."

"Probably some shadowy emanation of whatever was speaking through him," Julian observed. "And from Harry's impression, it would appear that the possession was rather more forceful than the subject was expecting."

"Aye, 'terrified' was the word Harry used to describe the feeling," McLeod said.

"There was probably good reason," Julian replied. "I would venture to guess, from the reaction, that the contact may not even have been human—or at least no longer human."

Peregrine shivered, and McLeod pulled a scowl.

"But there are several other points about what we've pieced together that give me cause for concern," Julian went on, moving several of Peregrine's drawings side by side, depicting successive stages in the ritual. "First is the use of a black bull instead of a white one. As Noel rightly noted, this may simply reflect the unavailability of a white bull; but it could also indicate an intention to connect with the darker aspects of one of the old gods.''

"That symbolism seems a little obvious to me,'' McLeod muttered. ''These people clearly had a pretty good idea what they were doing, and why they were doing it. I keep wondering why they took themselves off without making any effort to tidy up after themselves. It's almost as if they were *inviting* an inquiry.''

"Why would they want to do that?'' Peregrine asked.

"Maybe for the chance to make a statement of some kind,'' McLeod replied. ''If some sort of cult is behind this, they may be out to glorify themselves in the eyes of the world—rather like some terrorist organizations who revel in media coverage because it highlights the importance of their activities. The phenomenon is well known in criminal psychology. Maybe this bunch is drumming up publicity in preparation for promoting their own particular political agenda. Modern Druidism has given rise to its share of schisms and fringe organizations, both here and in America.''

"Somehow I don't think it's that prosaic,'' Peregrine murmured, almost to himself. He paused, recollected himself, and started again. ''Noel, could we perhaps be dealing with a group of copycats?'' he asked. ''You know, like one criminal using another criminal's methods as camouflage for his own activities? I'm thinking of Randall Stewart's murder, two years ago,'' he added. ''Every time I look over these drawings, I get a sense of *déjà vu*—and it isn't just that both incidents happened in the snow.''

Julian went a little taut, and McLeod looked at her sharply before picking up one of Peregrine's sketches.

"There *are* surface similarities,'' the inspector conceded, not really wanting to consider a closer connection. ''The white robes, the careful adherence to known Druidical practices, the confinement of the sacrifice in a magic circle of blood. But there are also notable differences, not the least of which is the sacrifice of a bull rather than a human being.''

"How do we know they didn't also sacrifice the man in the bull skin?'' Peregrine asked. ''Just because it wasn't human blood on the sleeping bag doesn't mean he didn't die.''

"I think it's far more likely that his role was that of a medium, rather than a sacrifice," Julian said fairly confidently. "And to function as a medium, he was almost certainly a willing subject. As Noel can tell you, it takes years for a good medium to come to his or her full potential; one doesn't lightly throw away such talents."

Peregrine nodded, but he was still unconvinced.

"Maybe it was something besides murder, then," he muttered. "Maybe something worse than murder. It was certainly more than mere theatrical posturing to re-enact a historical procedure. There was—*betrayal* here. Of whom, I have no idea."

"Perhaps there was," McLeod allowed. "But it takes time, resources, and energy to conduct a ritual as complex as this one. Anyone knowledgeable enough to organize the ceremony in the first place would know better than to perform it under false pretenses—or should know better."

"Indeed," Julian agreed, and added grimly, "If the events surrounding Randall's death proved nothing else, they served to demonstrate that the old elemental powers are still a force to be reckoned with, and are ill-disposed to being exploited."

Peregrine nodded, slowly beginning to gather up his sketches.

"I suppose you're right," he said. "All the same, I feel that there's something here we're overlooking—something right under our noses." He shook his head as he continued. "It connects with my sketches somehow. It's funny, but all the while I was drawing, I had the feeling that I wasn't Seeing the whole company."

McLeod picked up two of the sketches and looked at them more closely, then held them out to Julian.

"You know, I think he's onto something," he said. "Look at these two. Notice anything unusual about them?"

Julian cast her eyes over the two pages, and nodded. "I do believe you're right. He's drawn almost every figure so that you can't see the face. The only exceptions are these two men holding the bull—and the Taliere figure."

As Peregrine himself came around to look at the sketches again, an odd expression stole over his face. "Now that you mention it, there's something else odd. That Taliere fellow may have been running the ceremony, but I had the sense that there was someone else present who never appeared in my Sight, someone shadowy and aloof. I made several attempts to focus in on him, but nothing ever came of it. Each time I tried, some other person or thing always seemed to get in my way.''

McLeod eyed him up and down. ''You never mentioned this before.''

Peregrine grimaced. ''I'm not sure I even really noticed until I started trying to pin down why I'm still so uneasy about this whole thing. I'm still not sure whether it was worth mentioning.''

His elders traded glances. ''It's still possible that the fogginess can be ascribed to whatever entity they were trying to contact,'' Julian suggested.

''Aye, or it could have been someone's attempt to set us up for a wild goose chase,'' McLeod said grimly. ''God, I don't want to even think about possibilities like that, especially with Adam away!''

''Do you think we ought to give him a call?'' Peregrine asked, owl-eyed behind his spectacles.

An odd smile quirked at the corners of Julian's mouth.

''Actually, no,'' she said. ''He's otherwise engaged.''

McLeod glanced at her sharply.

''What is that supposed to mean?''

''It means,'' she said, ''that Adam is engaged. He's going to marry Ximena tomorrow night. Philippa rang me a few hours before you arrived.''

''But, why didn't you tell us?'' Peregrine blurted, a huge grin creasing his face as McLeod's stunned first reaction gave way to a similarly delighted smile.

''I *am* telling you—and I didn't want your analysis of the situation at Callanish to be clouded by distractions. Since we're all agreed that we don't really know anything yet, I think it's safe to delay bothering Adam until we do know something.''

''That rascal!'' McLeod muttered, still smiling. ''He couldn't wait to do it here, in proper style—''

''Oh, they're still going to do it here,'' Julian assured him. ''Christopher would never speak to him again if they didn't.

Tomorrow night's ceremony will be a very small, private one—and there's no time for licenses and the like, so it won't even be legal—but Alan Lockhart's dying wish is to see his daughter married. Apparently Adam doesn't expect him to last much beyond the ceremony.''

Sorrow shadowed Peregrine's sensitive face.

''That's going to be hard,'' he murmured. ''I know it's for the best, but—''

''I don't think there's any question of intruding at a time like this,'' McLeod said quietly. ''We can handle this for now—and we'll certainly keep alert for traps and red herrings. Meanwhile, I'll start running inquiries first thing in the morning about our mysterious Taliere—though getting the results back may take a bit longer than usual. Most of the relevant agencies will be shutting down early for the holiday weekend. I don't think we can expect to hear anything before Tuesday.''

''Then we'll definitely wait before worrying Adam,'' Julian replied with a smile. ''And mum's the word, until you're told otherwise. Let him enjoy his Christmas while he can.''

# CHAPTER ELEVEN

IN a hospital room in San Francisco, Adam leaned down to plug in the lights on a tiny Christmas tree set on a bedside locker, then took a seat beside the man propped up in the bed.

"I've had a chance to review your case notes, Alan," he said casually. "I also managed a few minutes with Andy Saloa, after I read them. I wanted to talk to him about your pain management."

Alan Lockhart's wasted face tightened in a grimace. "It's *my* pain. My waking hours are short enough as it is. I don't want to spend what's left of my life in a narcotic stupor—especially not now."

Scarcely twenty hours had passed since a laughing yet tearful Ximena had told him of accepting Adam's proposal of marriage, with a small, intimate ceremony to be held in her father's hospital room on Christmas Eve. Lockhart's response had been one of heartfelt relief, his tears no less joyful than his daughter's; and the other members of the Lockhart family had welcomed the announcement with delight. Ximena's younger brother, Vance, an astronomer, was already scheduled to arrive at midnight, flying in from his research post in the Hawaiian Islands. Philippa would be joining the party later that afternoon, having contrived to secure a flight from Boston in spite of the holiday rush.

The attendant flurry of activity, added to the usual pre-Christmas bustle, had taken Ximena off with her mother this morning to order flowers and a wedding cake, leaving Adam to keep Lockhart company in their absence. That absence now offered Adam the opportunity he had been seeking since his conversation with Dr. Saloa.

"I can certainly appreciate your desire to be clear-headed," he told Lockhart. "I wonder if you're aware, however, that narcotics are not the only option for pain management."

The older man stirred restlessly, his discomfort all too apparent in the lines of strain about his face.

"What else is there, for a man in my condition?" he asked bleakly.

"Dr. Saloa was wondering much the same thing," Adam said. "I suggested that hypnosis might be the alternative both of you have been looking for."

"Hypnosis?" Lockhart said.

"Yes. In fact, it was one of the first options that occurred to me. I use it regularly in my psychiatric practice, but there are medical applications as well as psychological ones. It can be especially useful in the control of pain, particularly when teamed with drug analgesia. When I mentioned the possibility to Dr. Saloa, he was quite open to the idea. If you'd like to give it a try, I'd be more than happy to direct the experiment."

"Hypnosis, you say?"

As Lockhart considered, a light knock at the door heralded the arrival of a dark-haired nurse with a medication tray.

"Sorry to disturb you, Dr. Sinclair, but I have Mr. Lockhart's medication."

"Not now!" Lockhart blurted, turning to Adam in appeal. "Adam—I think I'd like to try that experiment."

"Very well." Adam glanced at the nurse and smiled. "I think we can take it that Mr. Lockhart consents to Dr. Saloa's alternative orders," he said. "Alan, I'd like to have you let Mrs. Hanna give you half your usual medication, just to take the edge off your discomfort and help you relax."

Lockhart's jaw tightened, pain and a little uncertainty in the gaze he darted toward Nurse Hanna. After a labored swallow, his gaze flicked back to Adam.

"Could you give it to me?" he whispered.

"I could, of course," Adam said with a faint smile, "but

you wouldn't want to get Mrs. Hanna into trouble, would you?''

''No, but—''

As Lockhart turned plaintive eyes on the nurse, she moved closer to extend the medication tray to Adam.

''If you don't mind me observing while you administer the medication, Dr. Sinclair—and sign his chart, of course—I'm sure there won't be any problem. Dr. Saloa did authorize the lower dose.''

''Alan, will that be all right?'' Adam asked.

Closing his eyes gratefully, Lockhart nodded, stirring to watch somewhat apprehensively as Adam injected half the contents of the syringe into a port in his IV line and then busied himself with signing the necessary paperwork. By the time Adam closed the door behind Nurse Hanna, with instructions that they were not to be disturbed, Lockhart was looking somewhat less tight around the lips, though he was still obviously uncomfortable.

''What now?'' he asked, as Adam returned to sit in the chair at his bedside. ''Watch the watch?''

''Something like that,'' Adam said with a smile.

From the side pocket of his waistcoat, he produced the antique silver pocket watch that had been left him by his father.

''I was being facetious,'' Lockhart murmured. ''I didn't think you'd really pull out a pocket watch.''

Adam's smile deepened as he detached the matching silver chain and fob from his buttonhole. ''Actually, just about anything can be used as a focus. But as you've noted yourself, I'm a traditionalist by nature—and you obviously were expecting a pocket watch. Are you reasonably comfortable?''

''I s'pose so.''

''Good. Try to relax, then, while I tell you a little about hypnosis,'' Adam continued easily, letting the watch begin to twirl at the end of its chain. ''I don't know how much you've heard or read, but I can assure you it has nothing to do with what old radio shows like *The Shadow* used to refer to as 'the power to cloud men's minds.' You yourself may choose to cloud certain perceptions—and this can be a blessing, just as release from pain is a blessing.

"But contrary to what the old B movies might have you believe, no individual, however deeply entranced, can ever be compelled to act against his or her will. The role of the hypnotist is simply that of guide and companion, and the trance state experienced by the subject can best be described as a directed daydream—and daydreams can be very, very real, as we all know. The suggestions themselves come from without, but any and all *powers* of suggestion come from within, from the depths of the subject's own psyche."

Lockhart was already predisposed to accept Adam's direction; and this disquisition, delivered in tones of quiet reassurance, only served to enhance the desired response. As Adam slowly lifted his hand holding the gently twirling watch, Lockhart's eyes tracked with it.

"Relax and breathe deeply, then," Adam instructed softly. "You're already far more relaxed than you were . . . and you can become even more relaxed. Every time you exhale, feel yourself breathing out a little more of the pain, ridding yourself of a little more anxiety, becoming more and more relaxed, more and more comfortable, more and more at ease. . . .

"You're doing just fine," he continued, as Lockhart's eyelids began to flutter. "As you become more relaxed, you may find that your eyelids are growing heavy, but try to keep your gaze on the watch. See how it catches the light, like ripples on the surface of a pool—shifting, changing . . . If watching becomes too much effort, you can let your eyelids close, because you'll still hear every word I say—and hear *only* my words, as you float in a calm, warm, sun-dappled pool— very quiet, very peaceful, floating in the comfort. You can experience the water like a cradle, gently rocking you to sleep, gently washing away the pain. . . ."

Under the lulling influence of Adam's voice, Lockhart's eyes soon closed and he settled more heavily into trance. As his breathing eased, the taut facial muscles lost their habit of tension, and a slight flush touched the parchment-like cheeks. Adam continued to take him down, putting away his watch and taking his Adept ring from a coat pocket, watching as the telltale flicker of eye-movement beneath Lockhart's closed lids continued to indicate an ever-deepening trance-state. Satisfied that his patient had achieved a reasonably pain-free state, Adam turned now to the more far-reaching question that he hoped to address.

"Rest easy for a while now, Alan," he murmured, slipping his Adept ring onto the third finger of his right hand. "Rest in the Light, and when I touch your wrist, go twice as deep as you are now, letting nothing disturb you until I call you by name and touch your forehead."

His touch to the emaciated wrist elicited a faint sigh and a further settling of his patient. Now satisfied that Lockhart was adequately prepared for the work that lay before them, Adam turned his thoughts to the next part of his own work.

The question of Lockhart's pain had several dimensions. Most immediate was the pain itself—now suppressed, but this was only a temporary respite. Adam thought he could help Lockhart hold the pain at bay for a few more days or even weeks—certainly long enough to keep his promise and see his daughter wed—but beyond that point, simple human compassion questioned what purpose was served by Lockhart's continued suffering, in a condition beyond all hope of recovery or respite or quality of life.

But perhaps Lockhart had some other purpose beyond his promise to his daughter. Or perhaps some higher purpose was being served. Or perhaps there was no further purpose, and Lockhart simply needed permission to let go, having fought the good fight. It was not Adam's place to give that permission; but he perhaps had access to counsel in how best to guide Lockhart, who must himself choose how and when to endure or to abandon.

Clasping his hands before him, elbows resting on the rail of Lockhart's bed and his left hand cupped over the sapphire of his Adept ring, Adam drew a deep breath and closed his eyes and ears to the room around him, turning inward as he retired in spirit to the deep-seated threshold of the Inner Planes. Mentally assuming the sapphire-blue vestments of his higher calling, he stretched forth a spirit-hand to open the way between the sensory world and the transcendental realms that lay beyond, at the same time breathing forth the Word that proclaimed his right to access. The veil parted before him, and he stepped through it onto the outermost rim of a far-flung galaxy of stars.

The galaxy took the form of a luminous spiral, turning inward on an axis of fire. Suns and comets whirled past him in a scintillating dance, bound for the center of the galactic cluster. With his ring now blazing like a blue dwarf star, he let the cosmic wind of their passage pick him up and sweep him along a shimmering corridor of light, toward the distant center point which was the origin of all bright Mystery.

The music of the Inner Spheres sang in his ears. Constellations streamed past him, reduced to hurtling streaks of white radiance. His momentum catapulted him forward through nebular clouds of lambent light. Then the clouds parted, and he found himself approaching the Center itself.

His speed slackened. Before him, like a volcanic island emerging from the waves, rose a towering atoll of incandescent flame. Brighter than any refiner's fire, the mountain drew him like a magnet. As he entered the blazing envelope of its corona, he became aware of a great temple crowning its summit, its myriad spires coruscating like solar flares.

His soul-flight carried him to the foot of the temple mound, where his bare feet grounded on the bottommost step of a wide-sweeping stairway. Mounting the stairs, he arrived at the base of a pair of mighty doors, where he touched his ring to his brow with a graceful obeisance and signed the right-hand door with the Sign by which he was known to those in authority over him.

Bands of hieroglyphic inscriptions came to life at his touch, twined like a fiery caduceus around the doorposts and across the lintel. The language was that of the angelic realm, simultaneously the root of all human speech and yet in itself too subtle for the human tongue to utter save by a dispensation of grace. Having long ago been granted that dispensation as a mark of his appointed office, Adam spoke the Word aloud as it was here and now revealed to him anew. With the speaking of that Word, the great doors parted and slowly swung open.

What lay beyond was an airy plateau, ringed round about with translucent textures of golden light. The light was leafed and gathered like the convoluted petals of a great golden flower. A gentle breeze blew across the plateau, bringing Adam the Orient perfume of frankincense. He breathed it in deeply, aware that he had been granted leave to enter into the audience chamber of Gabriel, the angelic minister of all Divine mysteries of healing.

He advanced across the threshold and felt the fragrance of incense enfold him like a welcoming benison. The great archangel was nowhere coherently visible, but everywhere immanently present. At the center of the plateau stood twelve slender columns of alabaster arrayed in a circle around a raised altar of the same flawless purity. As Adam approached, the pillar nearest him came to life in a coruscating shimmer of rainbow fire, and he heard himself addressed in tones of familiar greeting by one whose presence he had come to recognize as the Master.

*Welcome, Master of the Hunt. We have been awaiting your arrival.*

Crossing his arms in front of his chest, Adam bowed low in deference to his superiors. "Is my reason for coming likewise foreknown to you?" he asked.

*You have the appearance of one bearing a heavy weight of care on his shoulders,* came the lightly ironic response. *Why else have you brought that burden with you into our presence, if you do not seek the means to be rid of it?*

Adam understood that he was being invited to explain himself more clearly.

"The matter in question exceeds the scope of my judgement," he began. "It concerns a patient only recently come into my care—one Alan Lockhart. He is suffering acutely from a cancer of the bone which has all but devoured him. Despite the torment of his condition, he clings to life in what has seemed a defiance of all necessity.

"I now believe the necessity to be one of his own choosing," Adam went on, "but since it comes of love, it is not my place to gainsay it. Still, his suffering brings heartache to his family as well.

"If this burden of pain has been ordained to serve some higher purpose, then I will do what I can to help him and them bear it for as long as his spirit remains fettered to his body. But if his suffering serves no further purpose, then

Alan Lockhart needs to be given assurance of that fact. For I am convinced that only then will he consent to allow himself to pass into the Mercy.''

Having delivered this appeal, Adam fell silent, watching with wonder as the Master's radiant form took on a gentler glow.

*Your compassion has guided you aright in this matter,* the melodic voice affirmed softly. *Alan Lockhart has already suffered far more than was ever to be required of him, and we are aware of his reasons. If you will bring him before us, we will render the assurance he craves in a form which he will not mistake for anything but a vehicle of truth.*

# CHAPTER TWELVE

THE plateau melted away. In a flickering shift of imagery, the golden light of the presence chamber yielded to illumination of another kind as Adam found himself standing over a figure stretched out upon a burning funeral pyre. The gaunt face upturned toward the sky was that of Alan Lockhart.

Lockhart was struggling feebly, mouth agape in a silent moan, but a ponderous array of iron chains held him fast-fettered to the pyre. The flames licked up from the edges of the pyre, and the chains glowed cherry-red in the firelight, hot enough to brand the cringing flesh, but Lockhart's body itself remained unconsumed. In a flash of intuitive insight, Adam realized that he was seeing Lockhart's condition translated into dream terms.

He realized further that in order to bring about any change in that condition, he himself would have to enter Lockhart's dream. Such personal intercession carried its own share of risks, but Adam was no stranger to confronting such dangers. Touching his ring to his lips, he commended himself and his work to the Light and, with that prayer still resonant at the back of his mind, spread his arms above Alan Lockhart's body.

Lockhart's moans became audible as Adam bent nearer. Drawing a deep breath, he reached down among the embers and seized one of the binding lengths of chain. The iron was blistering hot to the touch, but Adam bit back on a gasp of pain and tightened his grip, giving the chain a sharp, rending tug.

The chain snapped and fell away. Teeth clenched hard, Adam reached for another length. As he continued to break his way through the other man's chains, the pyre-flames began to die out and Lockhart's struggles diminished. By the time Adam had severed the final length, the embers were all but dead.

Though himself unharmed, Adam's pulse was pounding with the effort as he drew back. Lockhart's unmoving body now wore a robe of pristine white. As Adam turned his gaze heavenward, he at last became aware that the ground on which he stood was situated halfway up the side of a rocky mountain. High on the summit could be seen the outline of a mighty temple built of hewn stone—clearly their intended destination.

Returning his gaze to Lockhart, he called his name aloud. Lockhart's eyelids flickered back in wonder and surprise. Smiling gentle reassurance, Adam held out his hand.

"You can get up now," he told him. "Rise and come with me."

With Adam's assistance, Lockhart eased himself down off the pyre. Mutely he allowed Adam to guide him up the rugged slope. The very act of climbing, paradoxically, seemed to restore to him a measure of strength. Before long he was able to relinquish the support of Adam's arm and proceed unaided.

Their ascent took them through a shallow gorge which bore signs of having been used as a stone quarry. As they emerged on the other side, Lockhart uttered a muffled exclamation of discovery and hastened forward. The cause of his excitement was a small sapling rooted in a bed of loose earth among a nest of small boulders.

"Acacia!" Lockhart exclaimed softly.

The word brought Adam enlightenment. Acacia was revered among Freemasons, and Lockhart was an ardent Freemason. According to Masonic legend, it was an acacia sprig that had marked out the hidden grave of Hiram Abiff, the master-architect of the temple of Jerusalem and the father of Masonic tradition.

As Lockhart reached out with trembling hands to pluck the sprig from the earth, Adam smiled—for he now knew the general structure that Lockhart's encounter with the Master would take. The older man clasped the sprig to his heart as he hurried on toward the temple above with renewed speed.

The temple was a great domed edifice surrounded on all four sides by a colonnaded porch. Lockhart made his way as if by instinct to a lofty portal in the west façade, where the frieze above was enriched with colored marble and semiprecious stones arranged in a complex pattern of geometric designs. Shining pillars flanked the portal, cast in bronze and polished to the lustre of burnished gold.

At Lockhart's word and touch, the doors parted. Adam followed him through, for he, too, had the Mason's Word. An aisle paved like a chequerboard stretched toward the central crossing, where a dais elevated the high altar beneath the soaring vault of a golden dome. Waiting before the altar stood a tall figure majestically garbed in the white-and-red vestments of a Masonic Templar of the highest degree. When Lockhart would have faltered to a standstill, the figure lifted a white-gauntleted hand and beckoned both men closer with a gesture both of welcome and command.

Adam accompanied Lockhart to the foot of the dais, where the Templar Master accorded them a solemn bow of greeting before accepting Lockhart's acacia sprig and conducting him forward to the altar. From that altar the Templar Master took a furled scroll bound with a tasselled golden cord, reverently setting the acacia sprig in its place between the altar's two tall candles before presenting the scroll to Lockhart with a gentle smile.

The look on Lockhart's face was one of awe, but encouraged by a sign from the Master, he slipped the golden bindings from the scroll and carefully unfurled it. The inscription within was limned in letters of fiery gold, clearly decipherable to Adam from where he stood:

*Well done, good and faithful servant. Enter thou into the joy of thy lord.*

Lockhart gazed at the scroll in tearful wonder, looking up as the Templar Master addressed him by name.

*Alan David Lockhart, with honor and love have you discharged all your appointed tasks—and more than was ever asked. Take to your heart these words of immortal favor, knowing that you have been faithful to the last. The battle has been well-fought, and the victory won. Nothing now remains but for you to return Home.*

Lockhart's hands trembled as he reverently cradled the scroll to his chest, but a faint shadow disturbed his look of joy.

"Reverend Master, I am awed and humbled to hear such words of grace," he said meekly, "but I think I must not come before I fulfill a promise sworn years ago to one whose love I would never, ever betray. I have lived by my honor, and by the honor of God. To be forsworn at my life's end would set all my life's previous honor at naught, and would do no honor to Him whom I have served."

*What promise have you left unfulfilled?* the Master inquired.

Lockhart's face took on a sad, wistful expression as he lowered his gaze.

"When my daughter was eight, I promised that on her wedding day I would place her hand in that of her chosen beloved," he said softly. "She—tells me she loves the man who stands beside me, and he has vowed that he loves her." Lockhart lifted his gaze boldly to the Master's. "If this match is not meant to be, then I have no wish to precipitate an action that will make them both unhappy, merely to satisfy a dying man's last wish. But if he is prepared to cherish her as I have done, then I—would see them wed before I die. Do I ask too much?"

"I think he does not," Adam interposed quietly, "for I have some inkling of the love that lies between Alan Lockhart and his daughter—and of its reflection, in the love that she and I share."

*His body is spent,* the Master replied, turning his gaze on Adam. *Would you condemn him to further suffering?*

"It is he who chooses thus," Adam replied, "and only out of love. For my own part, I have already undertaken to unburden him of such suffering, insofar as I am able, so that the time remaining to him will be no heavy penance. If Alan is determined to honor his promise, despite the cost in pain, is this so great a favor to ask, from so good and faithful a servant?''

The Master's stern gaze softened, the majestic head inclining slightly.

*You plead eloquently, Master Healer. Very well, so be it.* Then his attention returned to Lockhart. *Your daughter's intended spouse is well worthy of her. Go now in peace, Alan Lockhart, and may that peace abide with you until you come to claim the place which has long been prepared for you.*

Lockhart closed his eyes and bowed his head in reverent acceptance of this decree. As he did so, the temple and its environs dissolved in a ripple of light. Adam experienced a familiar moment of disorientation as his spirit and Lockhart's were left momentarily adrift.

Then his mind's eye sought and found the twin silver cords that were their lifelines, and he drew a deep breath as, still in trance, he opened his eyes and gently laid a hand on Lockhart's shoulder.

''Alan, it's time to begin settling back into your body now,'' he said aloud. ''I'm here with you. When you wake, your conscious mind will not remember what has passed here, but your inner self will retain full knowledge of the revelations you have gained, and give you guidance in the times to come. Come back when you're ready, feeling comfortable and at peace, free from care and pain. That peace and comfort will remain with you from this moment onward, until you loose the silver cord and set out on the journey Home.''

Closing his eyes again, Adam drew the other soul with him along the silver cords. Together they passed through the gateway that stood between the Inner Planes and the outer world. The transition marked the end of their directly experienced rapport, but Adam slid his hand down to Lockhart's wrist and remained lightly in contact, feeling his patient's pulse steady beneath his fingers, sensing his breathing light and easy. Satisfied that both he and his subject had achieved their desired objective, Adam allowed himself the luxury of a few moments' private reflection and meditation, pondering the loving and courageous soul who was Alan Lockhart.

A short while later, a knock at the door recalled Adam

from his contemplation. Rousing himself, he looked around and released Lockhart's wrist as Ximena and her mother entered the room, their arms filled with parcels. Teresa started to speak, then stopped short, her dark eyes widening in sudden alarm as she stared at her husband's still form.

"It's all right, he's only asleep," Adam hastened to tell her.

Teresa recovered herself and forced a brittle smile. "I'm sorry. It's just that he looks so relaxed. I thought, for a moment . . ."

"I've been using hypnosis to help him bring the pain under control," Adam explained. "It's been my experience that the benefits of this kind of therapy are often enhanced by the laying on of hands. As you can see, your husband proved an excellent subject. When he comes back to us, you should see a significant improvement."

This prediction proved true. When Lockhart roused a short while later, he declared himself to be feeling better than he had in months.

"You'll still need some medication from one day to the next," Adam advised his patient, "but not so much as to cloud your senses. It isn't a cure, of course, but I think you can at least look forward to seeing the rest of your life through clear eyes."

Lockhart reached out and fondly patted his daughter's hand. "Just let me see you safely through your wedding, my girl," he told her with a smile. "That's the only thing that matters now."

"Hush!" Teresa reproved. "That's no way for you to talk."

But there were tears welling in her eyes. Adam could see she had guessed the truth—that her husband had just numbered his remaining span of days.

Well into the afternoon, toward the time when Adam and Ximena must head for the airport to collect Philippa, Alan Lockhart was still bearing up well, reminiscing animatedly with Teresa and Ximena. Dr. Saloa came to check in, and was astonished to observe his patient's good spirits and apparent lack of pain.

"He's still hanging on by a thread, but now I know why," Adam confided, when Saloa drew him aside to inquire about the morning's experiment with hypnosis. "He promised Ximena he'd be at her wedding. She was eight at the time."

Saloa blew out softly through pursed lips. "I knew he was stubborn," he murmured. "I guess it took a psychiatrist to get it out of him. The question is, Can he hold on for another thirty-six hours?"

"I think so," Adam replied, "though you'll want to continue his previous medication at about half the dose. And you *are* planning to attend the wedding, aren't you? I know it's Christmas Eve, and that's family time, but it would mean a great deal to this family. Alan thinks very highly of you, and he hasn't got long."

"Do you think he'll see the new year?" Saloa asked quietly.

"No. I don't think he'll see Christmas morning."

Saloa sighed, shaking his head. "A tough call. But it will be a mercy."

"Aye, it will. For all concerned."

"Right," Saloa said with another sigh. "I'll see to that change of medication on his orders. I expect you and Ximena ought to be heading for the airport."

The pair of them met Philippa's plane at San Francisco Airport, where holiday congestion only amplified the usual stir that accompanied Adam's mother when she travelled. Philippa embraced Ximena warmly, even before greeting Adam, holding her in a comforting hug for a long moment; and though they would have taken her back to the hospital to meet Ximena's family straightaway, she elected to retire early instead.

"We'll all be more rested in the morning," she said, firmly bidding them good night at the door to her hotel room. "Ximena, ring your mother from the lobby and tell her I'm exhausted from jet lag. See if she can join us for breakfast tomorrow, and then the two of you take some time for yourselves tonight."

"I adore your mother," Ximena said as they returned to the hotel car park. "When it comes to making a grand entrance, she'd put the likes of Cleopatra to shame.''

Adam acknowledged Ximena's tribute with a chuckle. At seventy-seven, Philippa Sinclair had lost none of her ability to command attention wherever she went. On this occasion, she had been the cause of a minor stir when one helpful gentleman had collided with another whilst vying for the privilege of retrieving one of her suitcases from the baggage carousel.

'' 'Age cannot wither her, nor custom stale her infinite variety,' '' he quoted lightly. ''My father was fond of saying that he was glad duelling had gone out of fashion by the time he met Philippa Rhodes, else he would never have had a moment's peace in his life. Do you like the ring?'' His mother had handed him the red morocco-leather ring box once the three of them were settled in Ximena's car.

''Like it?'' she exclaimed. ''It's magnificent!—though you do realize that I'm also going to have to have a plain gold band to wear when I'm working.''

''She told me you'd say that,'' Adam said happily. ''Will you mind waiting until after we get back to Scotland? I don't think there will be time tomorrow.''

''You can marry me with the Rhodes sapphire,'' she replied, hooking her arm through his. ''And then I'll wear that as my engagement ring. Meanwhile, there was some talk of that Fisherman's Wharf expedition we missed yesterday, if you don't think it will be too cold.''

Adam grinned and gave a snort. ''This is San Francisco, my dear, not tropical Scotland.''

She laughed with delight as they got into the car.

A light breeze was blowing steadily off the ocean as they made their tour of the many open-air establishments for which the Wharf was famous, dining on fried clams and chips and then indulging in gourmet ice cream at Ghirardelli Square. Though Adam thoroughly enjoyed the experience, he couldn't help noticing that Ximena's mood had darkened with the coming of sunset.

''Not having second thoughts, are you?'' he asked, as they paused to gaze out at the lights on Alcatraz Island. ''About the wedding, I mean?''

Ximena looked slightly startled at the suggestion. ''Good

heavens, no!'' she exclaimed. ''What makes you ask?''

Adam shrugged lightly. ''You've been rather silent since we stopped to watch the sun go down. I was wondering what was on your mind.''

''Nothing of any consequence,'' Ximena said, not looking at him. ''It's just that—''

She paused, her brow furrowing pensively. ''Adam, this all seems so . . . rushed. There's so much to do, and so little time to do it in.'' She shook her head. ''When I phoned Edinburgh Royal Infirmary to ask about the possibility of getting my old job back, the last thing I expected was to be told to show up for work in ten days' time. Much as I appreciate being considered a unique asset, you have to admit that's cutting things a bit fine at this end.''

''You don't *have* to go back to ERI,'' Adam said. ''There are bound to be other jobs.''

Ximena pulled a slightly crooked grin. ''But I like that one. After all, I helped set up the program. No, this is nothing short of a gift from heaven, and I'd be a fool not to take it. At the same time, though, the prospect of actually going means that—''

She stopped short and glanced away furtively. ''I'm sorry,'' she whispered. ''Whenever I let myself start thinking about the future, I automatically think about—''

''Just keep reminding yourself that there *will* be an end to it all,'' Adam said gently, well aware of the double meaning in his words.

Ximena swallowed audibly, not lifting her head.

''Adam,'' she said in a small voice, ''you see a lot farther than most people. Do you know how much time my father has left?''

The question was accompanied by a searching look that Adam chose not to meet.

''That's crediting me with an omniscience I don't possess,'' he replied.

''It isn't long now, is it?'' she persisted.

Adam could recall only too vividly Lockhart's brief exchange with the Master.

''No,'' he acknowledged. ''A matter of days, I would guess. No more.''

Ximena lowered her eyes. "I'm glad," she murmured—then shivered as if chilled by her own words. "Is it wrong of me to want it over and done with?"

Adam gathered her hands in his. "No," he told her gently. "I'd say it was only natural."

Lost in her own thoughts, Ximena hardly seemed to hear him.

"I feel as if I've been saying goodbye to him for months," she continued bleakly. "This whole city is full of memories from my childhood. Everywhere I go, I find myself thinking, *This is where Dad used to buy us ice cream,* or *This is where we used to come for picnics,* or *This is where he used to take my brothers and me on Saturday afternoons.* It's hard to think of all that coming to an end."

"Then perhaps it would be better to start thinking of it as a beginning," Adam said quietly. "We are made for eternity," he went on. "There are no limits to what we can aspire to become—only limits to how much we're able to see at any given time. The caterpillar enters the chrysalis knowing nothing about what it's like to have wings, but during that entombment it becomes transformed into a creature of flight.

"Everything we experience in this lifetime helps to prepare us for transformations yet to come," he continued. "And if we make a conscious effort to prepare ourselves well, the approach to death brings with it a shift in perspective that enables us to catch glimpses of the wonders that lie ahead. Saint Paul put it rather well. He said: 'For now we see through a glass, darkly; but then face to face. Now I know in part; but then shall I know even as also I am known.' "

Ximena eyed him quizzically. "Anyone listening to you would think you'd made this journey often enough to be familiar with the route. But then, I suppose you've done enough counselling in this area to make you an expert by association."

Adam thought it wisest not to comment, for there were still untold truths about himself that Ximena was not yet ready to hear, especially not now.

"Bereavement counselling *does* give one a somewhat different perspective on life,'' he allowed. ''But that makes it no less true that your father's death is part of your own life's experience. He would want you to use it to good purpose— not as a source of grief, but as a foundation for new hope.''

Ximena sighed as if suddenly weary, slipping her arms around Adam's waist to rest her head against his chest.

''I can see that you believe what you're saying,'' she whispered. ''Just stay close by my side, and see me through to the end.''

''You know I will, my darling,'' he murmured, tenderly stroking her hair.

# CHAPTER THIRTEEN

MID-MORNING of Christmas Eve saw all members of the wedding party engaged in last-minute arrangements save for the bride, who was on duty until six in the Emergency Room. The two mothers had met over breakfast in the hospital dining room, and had now retired to a couch in the lobby, where they were happily engaged in ticking off items on a final list of things to be done. Most of the tasks had been assigned.

Austen Lockhart had already collected the flowers. The boxes were stacked outside Alan Lockhart's room, waiting for the ministrations of his womenfolk, and Laurel had been dispatched to fetch several family heirlooms to be used in transforming Lockhart's room into a wedding chapel. The Lockharts' younger son, Vance, had arrived from Honolulu late the night before, completing the Lockhart family circle, and would collect the wedding cake and champagne before noon.

Adam, for his part, had little to do besides show up at the appointed time, once he had seen the two mothers ensconced, so he made it his morning's task to see to the comfort of his bride's father. As he joined Dr. Saloa for his morning visit to Lockhart's bedside, it became immediately apparent that Lockhart's pain was breaking through.

"I'd like you to get some sleep, Alan," Saloa said, after noting that Lockhart had spent a restless night and declined his morning medication. "Will you please let me order you a sedative? Just to hold you through the afternoon."

Lockhart slowly shook his head on the pillow, the effort obviously costing him considerably.

"I've got plenty of time to sleep, after my girl is married, Andy," he whispered. "I don't want to risk being muddle-headed."

"How about if *I* put you to sleep, the way I did yesterday?" Adam said, glancing at Saloa. "I promise you won't be muddle-headed; but I *will* ask that you let Dr. Saloa give you another half-dose of your usual pain medication, to make my work easier. Would that be all right?"

Wearily Lockhart nodded, his eyes heavy-lidded with pain only barely held at bay. Signalling with a glance that Saloa should fetch the indicated medication, Adam settled beside Lockhart's bed, gently taking his hand as the other doctor slipped quietly from the room.

"I think you've made a wise decision, Alan," Adam murmured, gently stroking the back of Lockhart's hand. "Close your eyes now, and let yourself go back to that place of peace and comfort you found yesterday. Take a deep breath and let it out, and feel the pain draining away as you float and drift. . . ."

Lockhart was deeply asleep by the time Saloa returned, relaxing even more profoundly when the medication had been administered. Saloa watched in something of amazement as Adam bent to murmur final instructions in Lockhart's ear, though he did not speak until they had left the room and closed the door.

"Does hypnosis usually work that well?" he asked, jotting a notation on Lockhart's chart.

"It depends on the patient—and the hypnotist," Adam said with a faint smile. "Anyone can learn the basics. I suggest that you might find hypnosis useful in your practice, if you're prepared to put a bit of effort into it."

"I may just do that," Saloa replied. "I may just."

Adam headed down to Emergency after that, stopping en route to alert Philippa regarding what he had done with Lockhart. Then, after joining Ximena for coffee, he set out to brave San Francisco traffic to pick up the champagne and glasses before the stores began closing for Christmas Eve; Vance had gotten tied up fetching the wedding cake.

Meanwhile, following a quick lunch, the two mothers repaired to Lockhart's room and settled into the happy task of arranging the floral decorations for the coming wedding ceremony. Lest their bustling disturb the sleeping Lockhart, Teresa drew the curtain around his bed—though Philippa assured her that he would not stir, and checked on him from time to time, in case Adam's instructions needed reinforcement. In honor of the season—and also to minimize too close a concentration of floral scent that might overpower the room's fragile occupant—much of the greenery consisted of holiday garlands of holly, ivy, and evergreen fronds to supplement the tiny tree at Lockhart's bedside.

The floor nurses looked in from time to time to admire the decor and offer help, but Teresa declined, sweetly but firmly. Slowly the illusion grew. But midway through the afternoon, when Philippa returned from speaking to one of the hospital porters about bringing in chairs, she found Teresa softly singing a Spanish lullaby to her husband, tears all but blinding her as she fastened a garland of evergreen across the foot of his bed with love knots of red and white satin ribbon.

Philippa tactfully withdrew before she could be noticed, taking care to make more noise when she returned a few minutes later, this time pushing a small wheeled table.

"Teresa, I think this might do for an altar," she said, calling to the other woman as she rattled the table into place against a side wall. "Anything bigger, and we'll have no room for the wedding guests."

"I'll be there in a moment to take a look," Teresa replied, from behind the curtain.

When she emerged a few minutes later, Philippa was busily engaged in covering the table with a white sheet appropriated from the linen room, careful to make no reference to Teresa's swollen eyes.

"I believe you said you have a proper cloth to go over this," Philippa said brightly, giving the other woman a sympathetic smile.

"Yes, Laurel and Austen are bringing it, along with some other things," Teresa said. "They should be here very shortly."

As if on cue, the door swung back to admit Teresa's older

son and his titian-haired wife, both of them still clad in jeans and sweatshirts. Austen was carrying a cardboard carton, and gave an admiring whistle as he glanced around at the garlands swagged around the window and above the door.

"Wow, now it *really* looks like Christmas!" he exclaimed with a grin. "You two have worked wonders in the time we've been gone."

"Were you able to find everything?" Teresa asked, a shade anxiously.

"Sure did," Laurel assured her. "Your directions were better than a treasure map. I also put some red votive lights in the box. I thought they might look nice on the window-sill."

While she spoke, Austen had been lowering his box to an empty chair. As Teresa came to look, Laurel began to unpack its contents. First out of the box was a finely woven table-cloth of snow-white damask, its patterning as delicate as lacework.

"Ah, *sí,*" Teresa breathed. "This belonged to my mother," she explained to Philippa, as she took the cloth from Laurel. "It was made by the nuns at the convent school she attended outside Barcelona, and she and her sister were allowed to do a little of the stitching on the hem. I had it on the altar for my wedding, and Austen and Laurel had it for theirs, and I always promised Ximena it would be hers one day, to grace the altar at *her* wedding—and maybe be passed on to *her* daughter."

The cloth was accompanied by a pair of bronze candlesticks, lovingly polished, and a pair of tissue-wrapped wedding candles. Last to emerge was a carefully swathed bundle the size and shape of a large book.

"This is one of my dearest treasures," Teresa whispered, as she removed its wrappings.

What came to light was not a book but an iconographic painting of the Good Shepherd, executed on wood in egg tempera. The style of the painting, like the gilt-wood frame surrounding it, proclaimed its Spanish origin. Gazing down at the sensitively modeled features of the Christ-figure, as Teresa shyly laid it in her hands, Philippa silently commended the creative artistry of its maker, who had endowed the work with a tenderness and compassion that transcended any denominational labels.

"Teresa, it's beautiful," she murmured, shaking her head in wonder.

"Gotta run, Mom," Laurel broke in, before Teresa could comment. "Do you need anything else, or can Austen and I head out? We've got to pick up Emma from the day-care center and see that she gets changed into her party dress. I don't think she'd ever forgive us if we brought her to her Auntie Mena's wedding in a paint-splattered track suit."

Laughing softly, Teresa gave her daughter-in-law a fond hug.

"Oh, *sí*, my darling. Go! Every woman, even the littlest, must be allowed her indulgence of vanity, especially on such a night! By all means, go and get changed—as Philippa and I must do, as soon as we have finished here. And assure my granddaughter that we will be looking forward to admiring her loveliest frock!"

Following Austen's and Laurel's departure, the two mothers set about dressing the altar, laying the damask cloth in place and then nesting the candlesticks amid arrangements of evergreen and white Christmas roses at either side. When Philippa had straightened the wedding candles in their holders, Teresa carefully placed the icon-painting on an easel at the back of the altar and then stood back to let Philippa make a final, minute adjustment to the drape of the white damask cloth.

"It is perfect," she said to Philippa, nodding to herself. "Thank you so much for all your help."

"It was my pleasure," Philippa said warmly, with a glance at her watch. "We've some time to spare yet before we get changed; and your husband shouldn't stir until Adam gets back. I expect he's showering and changing just about now. Shall we go and get a cup of coffee?"

"You go ahead, Philippa *amiga*," Teresa said. "I shall join you presently. I find my thoughts are scattered, and it is in my mind to remain here for yet a little while until I am able to collect them."

Her dark eyes reverted to the image on the altar, their expression suddenly sorrowful. Attuned to the sudden shift in the other woman's mood, Philippa cancelled any thought of leaving.

"I'll leave you if you like, Teresa—but I'd like to stay. The icon—did you bring it with you from Spain?"

Teresa nodded without looking around. "It was a wedding present from Father Olivero, who was our parish priest when I was a girl. Two years after my marriage, he entered the missions, and even now serves among the native peoples of Ecuador. I have written him a letter to tell him of this wedding. There is no knowing when it will find him, but when it does, he will be as pleased as Alan to know that our Ximena is at last to be wed to the man of her choice."

This disclosure gave Philippa pause for a moment's thought. "You must have been raised a Catholic. Was there opposition when you wished to marry outside the Church?"

Teresa smiled wryly. "It was far more complicated than that. But I knew there was never going to be anyone else for me but Alan, and so I told both my fathers."

She tilted her head reminiscently. "Had Alan not already been a Mason when we met, perhaps there might have been some room for compromise. But as you probably know, the Church does not approve of Masons, and Alan could not retire from his Order without committing a serious breach of his word.

"My father understood and accepted this, for he, too, was a man of honor. And Father Olivero was more understanding than many, for he had come to know Alan personally and believed in his integrity. But there were others of our family who did not know Alan as my father and Father Olivero did, and there was much bitterness toward my father that he did not takes steps to forbid the marriage. It was years before many of those old wounds were healed. I am glad my daughter will have the loving blessing of both our families from the start."

Smiling, she lifted her gaze to meet Philippa's. "You have a son greatly to be proud of, Philippa *amiga*! For all the strength I see in him, he is a man of gentleness and fine sensibility. I could ask no better match for my Ximena. I am confident that he will make her as happy as Alan has made me."

She held out her arms to Philippa, who returned the embrace with unfeigned affection.

"You've been very lucky to have a man like Alan," Philippa murmured. "One of my few regrets in this life is that Adam's father could not be at my side tonight."

"Your husband is dead, then?"

"Yes, many years ago," Philippa replied, drawing back to gaze at Teresa.

The other woman nodded gravely. "Then I am lucky, indeed, that my husband has been permitted to live to see this day," she said. "When it is over, I know he will be content to die whenever our Lord sees fit to call him. My heart tells me that it may well be this very night. If that is true, so be it: I would not for all the world see him suffer any longer, and I am confident that the hosts of Heaven will receive him kindly."

Toward seven o'clock, with all preparations complete, the wedding party began to assemble. The bride had not yet arrived. Adam stationed himself outside the door of Lockhart's room with his mother and Ximena's to greet their guests, a white rose boutonniere pinned to the lapel of his grey three-piece suit. Shortly, Jenny Carstairs joined them, vested in a white chasuble and stole for the coming nuptial celebration. The celestial sounds of Gregorian chant drifted into the corridor through the open doorway, along with the gentle murmur of conversation.

Adam could see the guests if he turned to look—only a select few at short notice, and limited by space. Austen and Laurel sat to the left of the elder Lockhart's bed with little Emma, who was turned out in a frilly pink party dress and patent leather shoes. Teresa had gone inside to wait, and stood on the other side of the bed, holding her husband's hand and looking strained. Saloa, one of his interns, and several nurses were gathered behind Teresa, adjacent to the Christmas tree.

Seen mostly by candlelight, and with the altar set up along the wall with the window, the room had, indeed, taken on something of the aspect of a chapel. The room's overhead lights had been switched off, leaving only the soft night light above the head of Lockhart's bed, the tree lights, the altar candles, and a row of red votives lined up along the windowsill above, with the lights of San Francisco spread like a sparkling net beyond. In a corner of the room, with the aid of a small flashlight, Vance Lockhart tended the CD-player providing the music.

After a few minutes, Teresa Lockhart came out to peer searchingly down the corridor toward the distant elevators. Sneaking another look at his watch, Adam noted that it was nearly eight o'clock. Word had come half an hour earlier that Ximena was just finishing an emergency surgery but would be there as soon as she showered and changed. Teresa was getting anxious. As Adam pocketed his watch, Philippa slipped an arm through his and leaned up to kiss his cheek.

"You're fidgeting, darling," she murmured, pretending to adjust his boutonniere. "She'll be here as soon as she can."

He nodded without comment, casting his gaze restlessly up the corridor to the nurses' station, where a white-draped table held a small wedding cake, paper plates and napkins, plastic forks, and champagne glasses. Beneath the table, the champagne was chilling in several ice chests—half a dozen bottles, for the modest wedding reception would be shared with the entire staff on the floor. Beside him, his future mother-in-law adjusted the tortoise-shell comb that held her black lace mantilla—dramatic contrast to her Christmas-red suit. Philippa wore royal blue, with a sprig of holly pinned in her platinum hair.

Just then, a flurry of motion at the far end of the corridor heralded the emergence of two white-coated women from one of the elevators, carefully screening a third as she followed them out.

"There she is," Teresa murmured, breaking into a relieved smile as she stooped to pick up a wreath of red and white roses from their box on the floor.

At the same time, Jenny Carstairs set a hand under Adam's elbow and began drawing him toward the doorway.

"Time for us to make our escape," she said to Adam with an elfin grin. "You aren't supposed to see your bride until she's ready."

Smiling faintly, Adam let himself be led inside, moving

with Jenny to the left of Lockhart's bed. The head of the bed was slightly elevated to give Ximena's father a better vantage point, and a festive garland of holly had been twined around his IV stand. The attached line trailed from the hand he held out to Adam in greeting, and the coils of a pale green oxygen tube snaked from his nostrils to a control panel above his head, but his grip was firm as Adam clasped his hand and bent to embrace him, even though his eyes were fever-bright. Someone had pinned a boutonniere like Adam's to his hospital gown.

"She'll be here very soon, Alan," Adam whispered. "How are you doing?"

"I'm hanging in there," Lockhart replied, though weakly.

"Good man," Adam murmured. "Let's see if we can do a bit better than that. Take a deep breath for me, and let it all the way out, along with any pain," he said, delving into a coat pocket for his Adept ring. He slipped it onto the little finger of Lockhart's right hand and turned the stone inside.

"Alan, I want you to wear this for me," he said, closing the hand to keep the ring in place. "Consider it a kind of good luck charm—or maybe like a security blanket. Any time the pain should start to break through, I want you to rub your thumb on the stone and take another deep breath. As you let that breath out, the pain will recede. Can you do that for me?"

Lockhart did not question the instructions, only nodded acceptance, his eyes now alight with single-minded eagerness—and pain-free. He was one of the best subjects Adam had ever worked with. As Adam released his hand, glancing reassurance at Saloa as he straightened to stand beside Jenny, the older man smiled and, with Adam, turned his gaze to the open doorway in anticipation.

"Daddy, is Auntie Mena coming?" Emma demanded, from Adam's other side, clutching her small bouquet of red carnations and squirming with ill-concealed excitement. "I want to see her dress!"

This announcement, delivered with the stentorian effect of a stage whisper, drew amused chuckles from the other guests, but Austen only bent down indulgently to ruffle his daughter's curls.

"Quiet, pumpkin," he murmured fondly. "That's Mena just coming now."

Instead, one of the women accompanying Ximena slipped into the room with an apologetic smile and set a blue glass votive candle on the altar in front of the icon. A faint smile touched Adam's lips as he watched her light it, for it was the one he had given Ximena.

Meanwhile, out in the corridor, Philippa's blue-clad form blocked much view of the two white-coated figures beyond, but Adam still managed to catch a glimpse of Ximena as she bent down to receive the wreath her mother laid on her dark hair, which was loose on her shoulders. She glanced past Philippa as she straightened, the color high in her cheeks, and caught Adam's eye before stepping deliberately into better view and shrugging off her lab coat.

Underneath, she was wearing a creamy cowl-necked sweater and a matching calf-length skirt that struck a familiar chord. As she handed her coat to her friend and then caught up the bouquet of red and white roses that Philippa pressed into her hands, never taking her eyes from Adam's, he remembered where he had seen the outfit before.

She had worn it on her first visit to Strathmourne, during another Christmas season, two years before. Her initiative that day in making a totally unexpected but welcome "house call" had given him rare pleasure, which only deepened as they came to know one another better. But even more powerful than those memories was the promise in her eyes at this present moment.

"I think we're nearly ready to begin," Jenny said quietly, nodding to Vance as Ximena's second friend came in to join Saloa. And as Philippa quietly entered to stand beside Adam as his witness, the strains of Gregorian chant faded away, to be replaced by a poignant orchestral piece that Adam instantly recognized.

It was the love theme from *El Cid*, the film that had inspired Teresa Lockhart to name her daughter for the wife of Spain's great national hero. Hearing it, Ximena smiled and slipped her arm through her mother's, tears glistening in her eyes. Together the two of them came slowly into the room, pausing briefly to bow their heads before the icon. When they moved on to places at the right side of her father's bed, Ximena bent down to kiss him and receive his kiss. The music faded to silence as she straightened to gaze across the bed at Adam, who had almost forgotten to breathe as he watched her enter.

"Dear friends," Jenny Carstairs said quietly, gathering their attention and embracing the room with the warmth of her smile, "it is both my privilege and my pleasure to welcome you on behalf of Ximena and Adam, who have come before us on this most holy night to be joined together in the estate of holy matrimony. Following the wedding itself, we will celebrate Holy Communion according to the Anglican Rite, but I invite all men and women of good will to share in this Feast of Love, regardless of denomination. For the Light that entered into the world on this night of nights was born for the salvation of all humankind, and those who partake of this sacred mystery become partners with Christ in the work of that redemption."

So saying, she opened the prayer book clasped to her breast and began to read.

"Dearly beloved: We have come together in the presence of God to witness and bless the joining together of this man and this woman in Holy Matrimony. The bond and covenant of marriage was established by God in creation, and our Lord Jesus Christ adorned this manner of life by His presence and first miracle at a wedding in Cana of Galilee. . . ."

Adam had attended many a wedding in his lifetime. Even so, as Jenny Carstairs delivered the familiar opening words of the wedding ceremony, it was suddenly as if he were hearing them for the first time. Whole phrases leapt to his attention with the dazzling suddenness of a lightning flash, infused with new and intimate meaning.

He knew a moment's mental pang when Jenny made the required inquiry regarding the lawfulness of the marriage, for there had been no time for the legal paperwork that would have made possible a valid civil marriage; but glancing at the woman standing across the bed from him, Adam could entertain no doubts that the covenant about to be sealed between the two of them was a sacred one.

"Will you, Ximena Maria Sophia Lockhart, have this man

to be your wedded husband,'' Jenny asked, ''to live together according to God's law in the holy estate of Matrimony? Will you promise to love him, comfort him, honor him, and keep him, in sickness and in health, and forsaking all others, remain faithful to him alone, so long as you both shall live?''

''I will,'' Ximena said, never taking her eyes from Adam's.

''And will you, Adam Iain Geoffrey Sinclair, have this woman to be your wedded wife, to live together according to God's law in the holy estate of Matrimony? Will you promise to love her, comfort her, honor her, and keep her, in sickness and in health, and forsaking all others, remain faithful to her alone, so long as you both shall live?''

''I will,'' Adam said. Ximena's face was luminous in the candlelight. Never had she seemed more beautiful.

''And will all of you witnessing these promises do all in your power to uphold these two persons in their marriage?'' Jenny inquired.

''We will!'' came the heartfelt response of everyone present.

''Who presents this woman to be married to this man?''

All eyes turned to the man lying in the hospital bed, and Ximena leaned down to take his hand and give him a kiss. As she straightened, her hand in his, Lockhart reached out with his other hand to take Adam's, drawing them closer and joining their two hands with more strength than anyone but Adam would have believed possible.

''Take care of my girl, Adam,'' he whispered. ''And Ximena, you take care of him. You've got yourself a good man.''

''I know, Daddy,'' she mouthed almost silently, tears in her eyes.

Smiling, his eyes bright with tears of his own, Lockhart released their hands and took his wife's, shifting his fond gaze to the white-clad priest.

''Her mother and I present her, Reverend. Go on now, *querida,* scoot,'' he concluded, making a faint shooing motion for Ximena to move to the other side of the bed and stand beside her betrothed.

Buoyed up by the intensity of his emotion, tears running down his cheeks unheeded, Lockhart followed the subsequent Scripture readings with avid attention, holding his wife's hand tightly and silently mouthing the words as his daughter and her intended then exchanged their wedding vows. Smiling, he shared the whispered sigh that rippled among the rest of the company as Adam produced his grandmother's sapphire and reverently placed it on his wife's ring finger.

"Ximena, I give you this ring as a symbol of my vow," Adam said, seeing only her, "and with all that I am and all that I have, I honor you. In the name of the Father, and of the Son, and of the Holy Spirit. Amen."

Adam might have seen only his bride, but as Jenny Carstairs pronounced them husband and wife, and Adam then bent to receive from his wife's lips their first wedded kiss— to a spatter of light applause from the watching witnesses— Philippa had a brief impression that the room grew suddenly and unaccountably brighter.

In that same instant she was drawn into remembrance of her own wedding day, so many years ago, and the happiness she had known with Adam's father. Coupled with the emotion of the present moment, the memory brought tears to her eyes—and then the fleeting sensation of invisible arms tenderly enfolding her from behind, and the feather-brush of a kiss soft against her cheek . . . and the sure and certain knowledge that Iain Sinclair somehow was present at their son's wedding, and approved.

Jenny Carstairs, moving to the altar to receive the offerings of bread and wine from the bride and groom, was likewise aware of a subtle change in the atmosphere, as if the air itself had suddenly been charged with fresh and vibrant energy. That aura of freshness remained, heady as incense, throughout the ensuing Communion service, nuptial celebration sliding easily into the proper liturgy for Christmas Eve.

As the bride and groom gave one another Communion and then the wedding guests came forward, one by one, to share the sacramental bread and drink the wine of gladness, a profound sense of peace settled over the company, made the more poignant when Jenny came to give Communion to the weakening Lockhart. Conveyed without words to all who shared this Eucharistic banquet was the surety that the bond between heaven and earth stood once again affirmed by the coming of the Light of the World—an affirmation reinforced by the words of the final collect Jenny had chosen.

"O God, you have caused this holy night to shine with the brightness of the true Light," she prayed, lifting her hands in orison. "Grant that we, who have known the mystery of that Light on earth, may also enjoy Him perfectly in heaven, where with You and the Holy Spirit He lives and reigns, one God, in glory everlasting. Amen."

Following these words, and at a murmured request from Ximena, Jenny Carstairs invited everyone to sing "Silent Night," with little Emma to start them off. Emma's piping voice made itself heard among the others like a flute among violins, clear and sweet and tremulous. Somewhere in the midst of the singing, Alan Lockhart quietly surrendered to his weakness and allowed his eyes to close.

Adam was the first to notice, his eye caught by the glint of his Adept ring as Lockhart's hand opened atop the blankets draped across his chest. Ximena saw her new husband's glance and turned with a soft intake of breath, even as her mother gasped and pressed Lockhart's other hand to her lips.

"Dear God!" Teresa whispered.

Adam was already moving closer to press his fingers to the side of Lockhart's throat, feeling for a pulse. Saloa, too, had started forward, but Ximena shook her head emphatically, seizing her father's free hand to bathe it with her silent tears as her brothers crowded closer to the foot of the bed. Philippa was comforting Laurel, and one of the nurses had taken Emma by the hand and was leading her from the room.

Adam could sense the fragile balance still binding Lockhart to his wasted body, but the pulse was a mere flutter beneath his fingertips, his breathing very shallow.

"He's going," Adam murmured, laying his other hand on the failing man's brow and bending closer to his ear. "Alan, we're here," he whispered, gently stroking the forehead. "No pain, Alan. No pain—only the Light. Embrace the Light, Alan. It's all right to let go now. It's time to go home. Ximena, tell him it's all right to let go. Teresa, tell him it's all right."

"It's all right," Teresa breathed through her tears, softly

repeating it over and over. "It's all right, *querido*. It's all right. *Vaya con Dios, mi corazon. . . .*"

And Ximena, pressing her lips to her father's slack hand, also whispered, "It's all right, Daddy. I love you. It's all right. It's all right. . . ."

At the touch of her lips a brief flicker of movement stirred Lockhart's closed eyelids. The merest ghost of a smile passed over his face, then departed with a sigh.

He did not draw breath again. Nor was any attempt made to resuscitate him. When Dr. Saloa had confirmed his passing, and Ximena numbly pressed herself into the comforting circle of Adam's arm, Adam gently retrieved his ring and slipped it into a pocket while the other members of Lockhart's family paid their final respects one by one and left the room, until only Adam, Ximena, and her mother remained. Someone had started the CD-player again, and Gregorian chant once more whispered in the background.

"I would like a moment," Teresa said softly, still sitting by her husband's side with his hand in hers.

Nodding wordlessly, Ximena removed her bridal wreath and laid it tenderly on her father's chest, then retrieved her bouquet from the altar and set it in the wreath's circle, bending to kiss his forehead a final time in farewell. Only then did she allow Adam to lead her from the room, closing the door behind them.

Outside, Vance was weeping in the embrace of Jenny Carstairs, and Philippa was comforting Austen and Laurel. One of the nurses had drawn little Emma aside and was plying her with a can of soda. As Adam and Ximena emerged from the room, Dr. Saloa left the solemn knot of his medical colleagues to come over to them.

"Is your mother all right?" he asked Ximena. "Would you like me to get her a sedative?"

"No." Ximena shook her head numbly. "She'll be all right. She's just saying goodbye. Thank you for everything, Andy. I—can't believe it's finally over."

Emma, meanwhile, was becoming increasingly frustrated that more refreshments were not forthcoming.

"Daddy, I think Grandpa fell asleep at the wedding," she

piped. "Shouldn't somebody wake him up? He's going to miss the party and the cake."

In her innocence, she did not comprehend the irony in what she said, but her words gave Adam sudden inspiration. Taking both Ximena and Saloa by the elbows, he bore them over to the reception table, beckoning for the others to gather around.

"Emma," he called, ducking briefly to pull two bottles of champagne from one of the ice chests, "no one's going to miss the party. Your Auntie Mena is going to cut you a piece of cake, and Dr. Saloa is going to help me pour the champagne. Andy, your surgical skills do extend to opening a bottle of champagne, don't they?" he asked, handing a bottle to Saloa and twisting at the foil-wrapped wire that held the cork on his own. "I should like to propose a toast to an absent friend."

All conversation had ceased as he began to speak. But as his intentions became clear, Saloa began energetically attacking his bottle and Philippa slipped deftly to Ximena's side to help her cut a small piece of cake for Emma. The pop of the champagne corks seemed to free the rest from their stunned silence and draw them close around the table, there to take up glasses and extend them for filling. Little Emma, with her slice of cake and a towel pinned around her neck to protect her party dress, settled herself in a chair against the wall. There she began happily forking butter creme frosting into her rosy mouth, while several more nurses from the floor gathered around as word of Lockhart's passing began to spread.

As Adam checked to make sure that everyone had champagne, Ximena whispered in his ear and then went back into her father's room for a moment, soon emerging with her mother, once again wearing her bridal wreath. Taking up two glasses, Adam made his way over to them, kissing first one and then the other on the cheek before giving each a glass and turning to face the assembled company. Philippa had followed with two more glasses, and pressed one into her son's hand before taking a place at his side.

"Dear friends and family," Adam said quietly, "I ask you to lift your glasses in honor of my father-in-law, Alan David

Lockhart. Though we met in person only a few days ago, I have come to know and love him in the brief time we spent together, preparing for this day—not only because of the love I bear his daughter, but for his own sake. Men like Alan Lockhart come along all too seldom in this world.

"I salute him, then, as a man of stainless integrity. I honor him for his example of peerless courage. And on this most holy night especially, I thank him for entrusting me with his beloved Ximena, who has become my wife. With my fondest good wishes and, I am sure, with the love of all present, I offer this toast: To Alan—May flights of angels sing him to his rest, and may his memory live forever in our hearts."

"To Alan!" Philippa responded.

Glasses were raised with hushed murmurs of agreement as everyone drank the toast, after which Teresa firmly insisted that Ximena and Adam should make a proper cutting of the cake.

"Your father and I did not buy this beautiful cake to see it go to waste!" she scolded, when Ximena would have demurred. "This is the bridal feast he dreamed of—and Christmas Eve as well! He would wish us to share this sweetness with our dear friends—especially since some of them have yet many hours to work before they may go home to their own families!"

With that she marched the pair of them over to the cake to make the traditional first cut, with Philippa then taking over to serve individual portions. In the wake of Teresa's pronouncement, the guests made a valiant effort to do justice to the cake—and Ximena and Adam dutifully fed one another the requisite morsels—but neither happiness for the bridal couple nor the spirit of Christmas could overcome the sadness of Alan Lockhart's passing, even if tempered by relief that his ordeal was over.

With the fragile festivity of the occasion thus irretrievably muted, the guests soon began to disperse, Jenny Carstairs bidding one and all a good night and a peaceful Christmas, and the medical personnel headed back to their duty stations. As a somewhat recovered Vance helped Laurel gather up the sleeping Emma to take her down to a car, and Austen conferred with his mother and Philippa, Adam set aside his champagne glass and turned to Ximena.

"What about you?" he asked. "Are you all right?"

Ximena nodded somewhat numbly. "I think so. At least I will be. I feel a little punchy, but—it isn't nearly as bad as I thought it might be. I guess it's partly because we'd already taken so long to say goodbye. . . ."

"Think of it as an *au revoir*, not a goodbye," Adam said quietly. "A casting-off of a worn-out garment. You *will* see one another again, someday."

"Yes, I believe that now," she replied. "I'll miss him— and I'm sad for that—but I know it's for the best. And wherever he is now, I know he's going to be fine. I have a clear sense that some part of him continues. You said faith would come to me. I guess you knew what you were talking about."

Philippa joined them as they were speaking, and slipped an arm around Ximena's waist to hug her.

"Dr. Saloa is going to see to the arrangements here at the hospital," she informed them. "And Alan apparently left very detailed instructions with Jenny Carstairs, so she'll handle the rest—but not until everyone's had a good night's sleep. Austen and Laurel are taking Teresa and Vance on home with Emma. They've brought two cars, so they've offered to drop me off at my hotel on the way. So there's nothing to stop you two from taking yourselves off. It's your wedding night, after all."

"Thank you, Philippa," Ximena murmured, wearily resting her head for a moment on her mother-in-law's shoulder.

After making sure the remnants of the reception would be cleared away, Philippa accompanied the newlyweds down to Ximena's car, fending off several well-wishers en route. When Adam had handed Ximena into the passenger seat and closed her door, he turned back to bid his mother good night.

"Good night, darling," Philippa murmured, returning his embrace. "You take good care of my new daughter. She's a very special young woman, but she wants holding just now. It *is* your wedding night, but I wouldn't expect too much."

Adam smiled faintly and kissed her on the cheek. "I expect to spend the rest of my life with her, Mother," he whispered. "Ximena and I have all the time in the world now."

# CHAPTER FOURTEEN

ALAN Lockhart's funeral was held on the day after
Christmas, at the small Episcopal church in the Mission
District where he and his family had worshipped for more
than thirty years. Despite the season, the service was well-
attended, with many of the Lockharts' friends and former
clients on hand to bid him farewell. Indeed, the church itself
was something of a memorial to the deceased, for over the
years Alan Lockhart had given generously of his time and
professional expertise to restore and maintain the building.
In accordance with his wishes, the service was conducted
jointly by the local rector and Jenny Carstairs.

Adam and Philippa sat with the Lockharts at the service,
lending their prayers and support to all the members of the
family. Under the circumstances, it had been decided not to
announce Ximena and Adam's marriage until after the formal
public ceremony in Scotland; but at the reception which followed the funeral, Adam was introduced as Ximena's fiancé,
and all interested well-wishers outside the immediate family
were given to understand that the couple had become officially engaged on Christmas Eve, with Alan Lockhart's
blessing. The news did much to brighten the mood of the
occasion.

"At least Alan got to meet your young man," one of
Ximena's paternal aunts confided to Ximena, as she was at
the point of leaving. "I only wish he could have lived to
walk you down the aisle. But your ring is gorgeous, my dear.
Diamonds and a sapphire—how very Old World. I'm sure
he must have been very proud."

"He was, Aunt Ellie," Ximena whispered, with tears in her eyes as she returned the older woman's embrace.

On the following morning, while Ximena and Adam set about winding up Ximena's affairs in San Francisco, Philippa flew back to her home in New Hampshire—though only for long enough to make arrangements for an indefinite leave of absence before travelling on to Scotland. She set out on the evening of the twenty-eighth, fortified with luggage enough for an extended stay, arriving at Glasgow's Prestwick Airport early on the morning of the twenty-ninth. The redoubtable Humphrey was there to meet her, instantly familiar in his dark suit and black chauffeur's cap.

"Welcome home, Lady Sinclair," he said, as she came through into the arrivals hall, beckoning to the adoring attendant pushing her luggage trolley.

"Hello, Humphrey. What a relief to find you here waiting," she said, extending her hand in greeting. "Whenever I have to travel at short notice, I always worry that there'll be some last-minute glitch. How are you keeping?"

"Very well, indeed, milady," he told her, taking over the trolley and heading toward the exit. "It's good to have you back. Permit me to be the first to congratulate you on the happy turn of recent events."

Philippa acknowledged this oblique comment with a warm smile, for the faithful Humphrey belonged to the select handful of individuals on this side of the Atlantic who had been entrusted with the whole truth. The very soul of discretion, Humphrey had long ago perfected the art of presenting a stolid exterior to the world—though Philippa knew he was not nearly so impassive as he took pains to appear, particularly where his beloved employer's welfare was concerned. On this occasion, there was an unmistakable twinkle in his eyes that belied the sobriety of his outward manner.

"Thank you, Humphrey," she said. "And thank you for your circumspection. I shouldn't want any rumor of our little secret to leak out prematurely. On the contrary, I intend to avail myself of a few days' peace and quiet between now and Hogmanay. With any luck, our two lovebirds will be joining us in time to see in the new year."

Always noticeable by virtue of her willowy elegance and imperious bearing—and visually striking this morning in a crimson coat and hat—Philippa attracted not a few admiring and speculative glances as she and Humphrey sailed out of the terminal building. Adam's blue Bentley was parked just outside, in honor of her arrival. After handing the lady into the roomy comfort of the rear passenger seat, Humphrey proceeded to stow what he could of her luggage in the inadequate boot, stashing the rest in the back beside Philippa and in the front passenger seat.

Amongst those who took notice of this operation was a burly young man seated in one of the vehicles waiting at the adjoining taxi stand. As the Bentley pulled away from the curb, the young man shucked aside the magazine he had been pretending to read and pulled out of the taxi queue, transmitting a brief message over the radio on a frequency that was not normally within the broadcast capabilities of a taxicab operator.

The message, briskly relayed through trusted intermediary channels, was not slow in reaching the ears of its intended recipients.

"Sinclair's mother!" Angela Fitzgerald exclaimed, when she heard the news of Philippa's arrival. "What the devil is *she* doing back in Scotland?"

This question was addressed to Richter and Mallory. The three of them had been summoned to Raeburn's library for an updated briefing session, but Raeburn himself had not yet made an appearance. In the interim, Richter had provided the others with folders containing annotated reports on the movements of all suspected associates of the Hunting Lodge, including the McLeods, the Lovats, and the members of Adam Sinclair's domestic staff. It had been judged too risky to tap into the telephone system at Strathmourne itself, but Humphrey's early morning departure in the Bentley had alerted Richter's operatives that something of note was afoot; and an intercepted conversation on the car's mobile phone had confirmed Humphrey's intended destination as Prestwick Airport, to meet an incoming flight from Boston. With that information, it had been a simple task to have an operative stake out the airport, confirming the arrival of Philippa Sinclair.

"We don't yet know about the plans of Sinclair himself," Angela reminded her companions, "but doesn't it strike you as a trifle odd that this meddlesome old she-cat should be paying a visit to the family manor while her son is still absent in America? It makes me wonder if McLeod and Lovat might have stumbled onto something up at Callanish to arouse the suspicions of the Hunting Lodge. If Sinclair couldn't come himself, it makes sense that he might send her."

Richter's bland expression remained unchanged. "Then we shall have to watch her as closely as we are watching Sinclair's other associates."

"And just hope to get lucky?" Angela asked.

Mallory had been considering his own reflection, captured at various angles in the mirror-like polished glass of the surrounding bookcases.

"I can't say the surveillance reports have made very interesting reading up to now," he observed over his shoulder. "*I* certainly haven't seen anything in them worth worrying about."

"Oh, really?" Angela countered scornfully. "And what would *you* know?"

"I know how to get more fun out of life than these self-sanctified Huntsmen do," Mallory replied. He picked up one of the folders Richter had distributed earlier and threw it open. "Just listen," he said derisively. "This is the entry for Christmas Day."

He struck an attitude and began to read, adopting for the purpose a parody of Richter's clipped German accent.

"*At 0942, Mr. and Mrs. Peregrine Lovat were observed leaving Strathmourne Lodge. They got into their car and drove to Kinross, where they attended Christmas Day services at the Episcopal Church of St. Peter and St. Paul. Following the worship service, they repaired to Rose Cottage, the home of the Reverend and Mrs. Christopher Houston. The Lovats lunched at the cottage and stayed to socialize for several hours thereafter. At 1613 they took leave of the Houstons and drove back to Strathmourne Lodge, where they remained for the rest of the day.*"

He broke off with a gesture of dismissive. "Not *my* idea of a good time, I can tell you. But I guess that's the best you can do when you won't allow yourself the luxury of a few honest vices. I could almost feel sorry for them, knowing they've got nothing to add spice to their lives. Or almost nothing," he amended as his gaze lighted upon one of the photographs attached to the report.

The photo showed Julia Lovat seated at her harp. She was dressed in an Empire-style gown of white organdy, with a softly flared skirt and leg o'mutton sleeves. Her red-gold hair was caught up into a knot at the back of her head and pinned in place with a spray of white Christmas roses. In the background, slightly out of focus, could be seen the candlelit outline of a stained-glass window.

Mallory ran a caressing forefinger over the image in the photo. "How positively angelic!" he sighed expansively. "She might almost tempt me to set foot in a church myself one day."

Angela snatched the file away, photo and all, and tossed it on the table.

"Save it, Derek. We've more important things to do than listen to you indulge in crude adolescent fantasies."

Mallory bridled at her tone, but before he could reply, a languid voice intruded on the conversation.

"What seems to be the trouble, children?"

The three of them turned to see Raeburn lounging in the doorway, hands in the pockets of a navy blazer, looking somewhat underslept. Barclay shadowed him half a pace behind, mostly restored to his normal resiliency by a week's rest and recuperation, though dark smudges still stained the hollows of his eyes, giving him a haunted look. He followed as Raeburn made his way over to the desk and unhurriedly took his seat.

Mallory gave a Byronic toss of his head and moved a straight chair closer to the desk. "Our dear Angela has been expressing some concern over the news that Philippa Sinclair was seen arriving at Prestwick Airport less than two hours ago," he announced.

Raeburn raised a blond eyebrow, apparently no more troubled than a senior financial officer advised of some trivial bookkeeping problem.

"Indeed," he said mildly. "And why should that necessarily cause us concern? Sir Iain Sinclair's widow still has friends and family living over here. It *is* possible that this could be nothing more than a social call."

"With Adam Sinclair out of the country, and Christmas already past?" Angela retorted. "I think it far more likely that she's here at the behest of the other members of the Hunting Lodge, to help them look into the Callanish affair."

Mallory directed an arch glance in Angela's direction. "They must be in bad form, if they need assistance from a woman old enough to be my grandmother."

"That old woman," Angela said evenly, "is as much a Huntsman as any of them. And all of us would do well not to forget that."

"No one is forgetting," Raeburn said patiently, "but it seems I must keep reminding *you* that the Hunting Lodge have nothing of substance to go on. Such evidence as does exist points only to Taliere—and as long as we have him under wraps, that evidence won't get them very far. So let them keep spinning their wheels by attempting to track him down. By the time we're finished with him, he'll be of no further use to anybody. Do I make myself understood? Good. Then let's get down to the business at hand."

The others had moved closer while Barclay arranged more chairs in a semicircle in front of the desk, and Raeburn gestured for them to be seated.

"Now," he began, "the operation at Callanish was always a calculated gamble. Though that gamble failed to pay off, we have by no means exhausted our potential for success. On the contrary, Callanish was only the opening gambit of the game. I have been reviewing our position, and have come up with an alternative strategy which promises to yield even higher returns than our original plan."

"It had better," Richter said. "We are playing for very high stakes."

"I'm well aware of that," Raeburn agreed. "But we've come too long a way to waste our energies thus far—and I believe we can build on what we *have* achieved.

"Our error at Callanish was in trying to make direct contact with the lord Taranis. Taliere was not equal to the challenge, and the intermediary he brought through was less than helpful—which is no fault of Mr. Barclay's," he added, with a nod at the pilot. "The problem was compounded by the fact that Taliere and I differed from the outset in our notions of how the procedure should be approached; and the compromise we reached proved less than satisfactory. I will not compromise again."

"Can you explain how the Head-Master came to be involved in the operation?" Richter asked neutrally.

"No, I cannot. He'd become very unbalanced just before his death, but he *was* the last person to harness the power of the Soulis torc—and the last wielder of the dagger before myself. I would venture to guess that the dagger drew him to our working—which tends to confirm that it can be made to function as the torc did. As to his tirade during our ritual, I can only attribute it to the demented ravings of a tormented soul. He was quite mad by the time Taranis took him to his own."

"Mad or not," Richter replied, "he still possessed the ability to focus the power of the torc—and presumably the dagger. How do you propose to gain his cooperation?"

"I don't," Raeburn said simply. "I know of another who was able to do what the Head-Master was able to do, and that is the same Lord Soulis whose name came to be associated with both the dagger and the destroyed torc. Indeed, the Head-Master claimed to have derived his knowledge from Soulis."

"Ah." Richter's eyes had narrowed as Raeburn spoke. "Perhaps you should further acquaint us with this Lord Soulis."

Raeburn inclined his head in assent. "Certainly. I should tell you, first of all, that in his day, William Lord Soulis was known as 'the wickedest man in all Scotland'—though that sobriquet was bestowed by his enemies, who did not understand his work. He had his seat at Hermitage Castle, down in Liddesdale, and accounts surviving from his own lifetime relate how he used the cellars of the castle as a temple to his magical arts. Personally, I would draw the line at sacrificing young children—or at least torturing them—but Soulis apparently exercised no such restraint. Or perhaps his demon familiars demanded such oblations, and Soulis was willing to pay that price for their favors.

"One of his familiars is said to have used its powers to render Soulis invulnerable to the weapons of his enemies, who otherwise would have brought him to justice. It was known as Redcap Sly or Robin Redcap, so-called from its practice of dyeing its cap in the blood of its victims."

"What does this have to do with the torc and the dagger?" Mallory asked. "Calling on familiars is all very well and good—*I* can do that—but Taranis is no mere familiar like Redcap; he's an elemental lord."

"And Soulis was a sorcerer of immense power," Raeburn replied. "It is a matter of record that he was able to bind and control a number of infernal spirits, and we know that he had control of the torc and the dagger. Since we also know that Soulis was the source of the Head-Master's knowledge of how to invoke Taranis, it occurred to me to wonder whether Soulis himself might have been able to go that one step further."

Angela stiffened—apparently first to seize upon the significance of what Raeburn was implying.

"Are you saying," she said, "that you think Soulis might have found a way not simply to invoke Taranis, but to *bind* him?"

"I think there's a fair chance of that," Raeburn replied. "And at very least, Soulis was able to invoke Taranis in the same way the Head-Master did, and induce him to channel *his* power through the torc. I *know* that power, Angela; I've tasted it. And oh, it is *sweet!*"

"Power is always sweet," Richter murmured. "What if it cannot be channelled through the dagger?"

"I feel confident that it can," Raeburn replied. "We have already begun potentializing the dagger by using it in the bull sacrifice. I remind you that the torc was activated by the lifeblood of human sacrifice. If anything, the dagger should prove an even more potent focus, since it is the direct instrument of sacrifice."

"That assumes that we can contact Soulis," Angela said.

"And that he will agree to share his knowledge."

"We can contact him," Raeburn said confidently. "Our Derek is acquainted with the basic methodology."

Mallory went a little pale. "I only assisted," he whispered. "It was Geddes who summoned Michael Scot."

"I'm quite aware of that," Raeburn replied. "And I shall require your assistance in a like manner for this operation. I mention the incident only to underline that we do have experience in summoning the dead. In the case of Soulis, we shall use a wizard to summon a wizard. Master Taliere will serve very well in that capacity, and you, my dear Derek, will ensure that he cooperates."

Mallory breathed out a relieved sigh and nodded slowly.

"Suppose Soulis is currently incarnate?" Angela asked. "You can't have forgotten the problems with Scot."

"No, and it wouldn't have been a problem, if not for Sinclair's meddling," Raeburn snapped. "In fact, Michael Scot would have been my first choice for this operation, but Sinclair put him beyond our reach by placing his protection on Scot's current incarnation."

"*Was ist das?*" Richter murmured, raising a startled eyebrow in inquiry.

"A schoolgirl named Gillian Talbot," Raeburn murmured, with a dismissive wave of his hand. "She'd be about fourteen by now. We'll retrieve her one day. But for now, we'll have to settle for Soulis."

"What *about* Soulis?" Angela said. "You never answered my question fully. Even if we can contact him, what makes you think he'd agree to help us?"

"Because I can offer him the one thing he desires more than any other thing," Raeburn said, smiling thinly. "I can offer him his liberty."

"His liberty?" Richter repeated. "Are we to understand that this Soulis is somehow a prisoner?"

"In a manner of speaking," Raeburn said somewhat smugly. "In the past few days I've engaged in some covert investigation of my own. It seems that Soulis' spirit presently languishes in a state of limbo, to which he was exiled at the time of his death by an edict of banishment which prevents him from ever again reincarnating."

The cavernous pause elicited by this revelation was at last broken by Richter's perplexed sigh.

"If Soulis was as powerful as you claim," he said tentatively, "how could he have allowed himself to be bound in that way?"

A pained smile flickered across Raeburn's face, almost a grimace.

"Perhaps I should acquaint you with the manner of his passing. As the years went by and his excesses became more outrageous and more blatant, Soulis apparently became overconfident in his own abilities and allowed his defenses to slip. Outrage and anger had been growing among the folk around Liddesdale, and he also appears to have come to the notice of a Hunting Lodge of the time.

"I have no details on what *they* did," Raeburn went on, amid looks of indignation from his listeners, "but I *can* tell you that his tenants eventually rose up in a body, attacked the castle, and took him prisoner. Somehow his occult powers were nullified, or at least suppressed. Laden with iron chains, and wrapped in a sheet of lead, he was taken from Hermitage Castle to a site now known as the Nine Stane Rig and there boiled alive in oil in his own brazen cauldron. His body was burned thereafter and his ashes scattered on the wind. His soul . . ."

"Bound by a Hunting Lodge," Mallory muttered through clenched teeth.

Raeburn shrugged. "Save your indignation for the Hunting Lodge *we* must deal with, Derek. Suffice it to say that I've analyzed the spell that bars Soulis from the Wheel of Reincarnation. For all its potency, it appears none too complicated. *He* can't unlock it—but I can."

"Oh?" Angela said, a note of challenge in her tone.

"The real challenge will be in locating Soulis," Raeburn continued, ignoring the jibe. "Since he is presently adrift among the Inner Planes, it will be necessary to conjure him back to the material world in such a manner as will allow us to acquaint him with our proposal. It will not be pleasant for him, since I plan to use the circumstances of his death to structure our summoning.

"Given his situation, I would be very surprised if he de-

clined to cooperate with us. After all, what other prospect
has he got? It may be centuries before anyone else is inclined
to make him a better offer.''

''You make it sound so straightforward,'' Angela said.
''Has it occurred to you that, given the chance to speak,
Soulis might try to take advantage of the moment by calling
one or more of his erstwhile familiars to his aid?''

''It did occur to me,'' Raeburn said drily. ''That's why
the ritual I've devised will have some very specific controls
built into it from the outset. Since the turning of the year is
an auspicious time for beginning new endeavors, I propose
that we summon Soulis to his old haunt of Hermitage Castle
in two days' time. I fancy it will be a fitting way to usher
out the dying year.''

A hundred miles away, just north of Edinburgh, Philippa
Sinclair was inspecting an invitation to quite another kind of
affair to mark the turning of the year.

''As you requested, milady, I telephoned Sir Matthew and
Lady Fraser as soon as you informed me you were coming,''
Humphrey said, as he poured her tea in the library, ''so they
sent along an invitation to their annual Hogmanay party. Of
course I made no mention of Sir Adam's news.''

''No, that's to be a delicious surprise,'' Philippa said,
helping herself to sugar and milk. ''I'm not certain whether
Janet will be delighted to find that Adam is about to lose his
bachelor status or annoyed that she didn't make the match.
She does like Ximena, though—everyone does. I can't tell
you how happy I am that he's finally found the right woman,
Humphrey. If things take their natural course, you'll soon be
serving your third generation of Sinclairs.''

''It will be my privilege and pleasure, milady,'' Humphrey
said with an uncharacteristic smile. ''Will there be anything
else, or shall I see to your luggage? I had Mrs. Gilchrist
prepare your room.''

''No, go ahead, Humphrey. I want to make a few telephone calls before I head upstairs for a nap. I don't handle
jet lag as well as I used to.''

''Very good, milady.''

Sighing, Philippa settled herself comfortably into one of

the wing chairs by the fireside, clasping the warmth of her teacup between both hands as she gave herself over to the nostalgic comfort of coming home. By habit, her gaze reverted to the framed photograph on the mantelpiece, showing her late husband in his regimental uniform, and she rendered his likeness a fond salute with her teacup.

"I hope he'll be happy, Iain," she said with a wistful smile. "He deserves to be happy. It isn't an easy life he's chosen for himself."

By the time she had finished her tea, Philippa was feeling sufficiently restored to repair to Adam's desk and make her phone calls. The first was to her clinic back in New Hampshire, where she left a message notifying the staff of her safe arrival. The second was to Lady Julian Brodie.

"Pippa, dear, I can't tell you how glad I am to hear your voice!" Julian exclaimed by way of greeting. "How did it go, on Christmas Eve? I've only told Noel and Peregrine and the Houstons, but we're all so delighted!"

"Well, it won't be official until after the public wedding," Philippa reminded her with a laugh. "For now, they're simply engaged. I'll tell you about it when I see you. In the meantime, before I sally forth into my new role as mother of the groom, I thought I'd better apply to you for an update on local current events."

The request carried several levels of meaning, and Philippa was somewhat surprised at the slight pause on the other end of the line before Julian replied.

"Yes, indeed. Always happy to oblige. Perhaps you'd like to come and join me for tea tomorrow—say, between three and four? I'll invite a few other friends as well."

Philippa was quick to catch what was *not* said in Julian's seemingly innocent comment—and the meaning implicit in her inclusion of "a few other friends."

"I can come sooner, if you like," she said.

"No, no, tomorrow will be fine," Julian replied. "I'm eager to see you, but there's no urgency until you've recovered from your travels. We're neither of us getting any younger."

With this reassurance—and increasingly aware of her jet lag—Philippa rang off with the promise to join Julian on the morrow. She spent the remainder of the day napping and unpacking, and retired early after a light supper.

The next day dawned windy and changeable, with patches of brilliant sunshine interspersed with fragmentary bands of snow cloud. Philippa breakfasted in the front parlor, then puttered the morning away. The house seemed very empty with Adam absent. Shortly after two, out of deference to the uncertainty of the weather, she had Humphrey bring the Range Rover around instead of the Bentley. Soon they were cruising southward toward Edinburgh, Philippa contentedly ensconced in the back seat with a tartan rug tucked over the lap of her emerald-green suit.

Already alerted by the tone of Julian's invitation, she was not surprised to find Peregrine Lovat's familiar green Morris Minor parked at the curb a few yards down from the front gate of Bonnybank House. Nor was she surprised, upon being shown into Julian's cozy sitting room, to discover that Noel McLeod and Father Christopher Houston had been included in the invitation.

"How wonderful to see you all!" she exclaimed, as she exchanged hugs all around. "A belated happy Christmas to you. I can't tell you how good it is to be back, and with such news!"

Initial conversation revolved entirely around the subject of Adam's marriage, as Julian presided over a silver tea service and Peregrine helped distribute plates of cakes and scones. Prompted by their eager questions, Philippa took the opportunity to furnish the other members of the Hunting Lodge with a full report of the wedding at the hospital.

"It was so moving, on so many levels," she finished wistfully. "The timing of Alan's passing was a little difficult, of course, but I think it was a relatively easy transition for him, especially after being in so much pain for so long. I know it meant a lot to him to see Ximena married; and the people he loved most were there with him, at the end. Adam had done an incredible job of preparing the way, so there was no question that everyone was ready to let Alan go."

Julian dashed tears from her cheek with the back of one frail hand, and Christopher bowed his head. Philippa sniffled back her own tears and put on a fragile smile.

"In any case," she went on, "I have no doubt that it's a marriage of hearts and souls. Christopher, I'm sure I can trust you to help Adam sort out the appropriate legalities at this end. He's very keen to have you perform the formal ceremony here, and apologizes for jumping the gun without you, as it were. But I see nothing to prevent us from throwing our hearts into a wedding celebration worthy of them both—and a splendid reception at Strathmourne, though it will be difficult to top yours and Julia's, Peregrine."

Though Philippa's shift back to the more pleasurable prospect of Adam's wedding had somewhat banished the sobriety surrounding the account of Alan Lockhart's death, the company's mingled looks of pleasure and uneasiness caused her to set aside her cup and cast her gaze over the lot of them appraisingly.

"Very well," she said briskly. "It's clear there's more on the agenda than what happened in San Francisco. But you did indicate that it wasn't urgent, Julian."

"Not—urgent," Julian allowed. "But a bit worrisome, nonetheless." She glanced appraisingly at McLeod. "Noel, perhaps you'd care to do the honors?"

McLeod nodded and set aside his teacup. "Just about a week ago I got a call from a fellow copper up in Stornoway, name of Chisholm. There'd been a ritual bull-slaying up at at the Callanish stone circle, and he wanted to ask my advice."

In as few words as possible he went on to render an account of the investigation.

"Since Adam was off on his first holiday in some time," McLeod concluded, "there didn't seem any point in reporting the incident to him right away—especially when there was nothing any of us could do that couldn't be done equally well by the Island police.

"Since then, however, further information has come to light that suggests the Hunting Lodge ought to become more actively involved in the case. Peregrine and I were just getting ready to leave the crime scene at Callanish when Chisholm got called away to investigate a seemingly unrelated incident—a car gone off the road, with two dead.

"Chisholm got back to me the next day with further details. That was Christmas Eve—which is why this information didn't figure in our decision not to bother you or Adam when we'd evaluated the case the night before. Chisholm had assumed, as did the first officers on the scene, that the incident was drink-related. Empty whisky bottles were found in the wreckage of the car with the bodies of two dead men, and the medical examiner's report confirmed that both victims had high levels of alcohol in their blood.

"Problem is that Chisholm knows most of the regulars on the island, and the driver was practically a teetotaller—name of Macaulay. The barman at his local had never served him anything stronger than a shandy, and then never more than one. Chisholm checked with the victim's GP, who confirmed that Macaulay had a chronic liver ailment that effectively deterred him from heavy drinking."

"A holiday lapse?" Christopher queried.

McLeod shook his head. "I doubt it. The other man in the car was Macaulay's nephew, a chap named Treen. When Chisholm checked into his background, he found out that some years ago, Treen had been a student of veterinary medicine at the University of Aberdeen before getting thrown out for poor performance. No one seemed to know much about his drinking habits, but when Chisholm's men paid a visit to his farm, one of the things they found was an old horse-box with cattle droppings scattered all over the floor. More to the point, amongst the livestock papers stuffed away in Treen's desk were the registration documents and vaccination certificates for a two-year-old Black Angus bull. The animal in question was nowhere to be found on the premises, and in the absence of any bill of sale, it seemed reasonable to suspect that this was the beast slaughtered at Callanish.

"All of which circumstantial evidence," he went on, "prompted Chisholm to order some forensic work done on the bodies. When traces of bull's blood turned up on the men's shoes and under their fingernails, no one was much surprised. It seems pretty obvious now that these two individuals were directly involved in the Callanish incident. It seems equally obvious that somebody else wanted to ensure they didn't talk about it afterwards."

"Which suggests very strongly that the situation warrants our looking into it," Julian said.

Philippa nodded thoughtfully. "Let's go back to that name your Mr. Nimmo picked up," she suggested. "What was it again—Taliere?"

"Aye," said McLeod. "I ran the name through our files and came up empty. Whoever this Taliere may be, he doesn't seem to have a police record—at least not in Lothian and Borders or Strathclyde Departments, and not under that name. Of course, we've got six other jurisdictions in Scotland, and I've started inquiries in all of them; but without a central database to work from, it could be weeks before we get any useful results. That's assuming, of course, that Taliere is a real name, and not a pseudonym, and that he's come to police attention in the past."

"It sounds like we wait, then, and see what further you can turn up," Philippa said. "Adam will be back in two days' time. Maybe by then, we'll know something more."

# CHAPTER FIFTEEN

ARRIVING at London Heathrow at mid-morning on New Year's Eve, Adam and his bride of a week caught the first available connecting flight to Edinburgh. As the Air UK shuttle began its descent, just past one o'clock, he was profoundly relieved to see the familiar sprawl of Edinburgh taking shape off the starboard wing, with the snow-capped ridge of Arthur's Seat rising like an iceberg above the historic tangle of the city center. Though both he and Ximena had managed to doze during the nine-hour trans-Atlantic flight, the added strain of the preceding week had taken its toll. Ximena was heavily asleep in the seat beside him. As the Fasten Seatbelts sign came on, he turned to lay a gentle hand on her shoulder.

"Wake up, *querida*," he murmured fondly.

Ximena roused with a start and glanced at her watch.

"Good heavens, is that really the time? I only meant to rest my eyes."

"You obviously needed the sleep," Adam said with a smile, brushing a fingertip lightly down one cheek. "You haven't missed anything important. How do you feel?"

Smiling drowsily, she let her gaze shift out the window beyond Adam, at the broadening vista of the city and its surrounding hills, white with snow. A contented sigh escaped her lips.

"I feel like it's good to be home again," she said, resting her head on his shoulder and slipping her arm through his.

Humphrey was waiting for them in the domestic baggage claim area, holding a large bouquet of mingled roses, lilies, and forget-me-nots. As soon as they emerged from Arrivals, he stepped forward and presented it to Ximena.

"Welcome back to Scotland, Dr. Lockhart," he said, with a courtly little bow. "It's a pleasure to have you back with us."

"Why, thank you, Humphrey, these are gorgeous!" she exclaimed delightedly. "Adam says you always think of everything."

Humphrey shrugged and lowered his eyes modestly, but his smile was almost equal to Ximena's as he belatedly shook the hand Adam offered.

"Thank you, Humphrey. It's good to see you."

"And you, Sir Adam. Welcome home. If you'd like to wait in the car, I'll collect the luggage and meet you there. I've brought the Range Rover, since I didn't know how much you'd have. Also, the weather looks uncertain."

"Good thinking," Adam replied, handing Humphrey the claim checks. "There are five pieces. Is the car at the curb?"

"It is, sir. Being looked after by one of Inspector McLeod's lads."

Grinning, Adam took the keys Humphrey offered. "See you there, then."

Ten minutes later, with the luggage stowed in the back, Humphrey was easing the blue Range Rover onto the slip road that led to the dual carriageway back toward Edinburgh. The verges were lined with patchy snow, and the sky was leaden, threatening fresh snow to come.

"I'm instructed to tell you that there's been a change of plan from what you were probably expecting, sir," Humphrey announced, glancing at Adam apologetically in the rearview mirror. "Lady Sinclair accepted an invitation on behalf of both of you to attend a Hogmanay party this evening at the home of Sir Matthew and Lady Fraser. She said it was a social obligation, sir," he added, at the chorused groan from Adam and Ximena.

"No, she's absolutely right," Adam said, glancing at Ximena in apology. "I'm sorry, darling. The Frasers have been my friends since all of us were children, and their Hogmanay party is one of the social fixtures of the season. If they knew we were back and we didn't come, Janet would never let me hear the end of it. Good God, Humphrey, the logistics on this are going to be dreadful.''

"Hopefully not, sir,'' Humphrey replied with a smile. "Because of the weather, and to save to-ing and fro-ing, Lady Sinclair has booked you a suite at the Carlton Highland. I dropped her there on the way to the airport, and we brought up your Highland kit for this evening. She assured me that Dr. Lockhart would have brought something suitable. She'll have tea waiting for you, and after that you'll have time to catch a few hours' sleep before dressing for the evening.''

Chuckling resignedly, Adam shook his head. "It seems we're to be shown no mercy,'' he said to Ximena. "When Philippa gets something in her head, there's no stopping her. *Do* you have something suitable for a black-tie party? There'll be country dancing, but you don't have to take part if you don't want to. We can at least plead exhaustion on *that* count.''

"I'll manage to find something to wear,'' Ximena replied good-naturedly. "And so long as we do get even a few hours' sleep, I should be all right. This isn't any worse than when I was an intern, or the nights when I've had to pull a double shift.''

"Well, that's something, at least,'' Adam said. "Why don't you close your eyes until we get to the hotel?''

The manager of the Carlton was waiting to greet them in the lobby and, obviously briefed by Philippa, whisked them upstairs with all the aplomb of an accomplished social conspirator.

"I'm told that I mustn't make any reference to your good news until after the official announcement,'' he drawled, when they had reached the relative privacy of the elevator, "but I gather that we won't be kept waiting for too long.''

Smiling, Adam tucked Ximena's hand into his arm. "Philippa seems to have things well in hand,'' he said enigmatically. "For now, let's simply say that the new year promises to bring some welcome changes at Strathmourne.''

"Delightful!'' the manager declared, as the elevator doors opened. "This way, please.''

Philippa was waiting in the suite, which was filled with

more flowers. A simple but hearty tea was laid out on a table in the sitting room.

"You two look positively exhausted," Philippa exclaimed, as she hugged first Ximena and then Adam. "Thank you for bringing them up, David. Everything is perfect!"

"You're very welcome, Lady Sinclair. Just let me know if there's anything else I can do for you. The luggage will be up shortly."

When the manager had gone, Philippa chivvied Adam and Ximena over to the settee and began fussing with the tea things.

"I hope you don't mind about tonight," she said, as she poured tea for the three of them. "When I rang Janet to let her know I was back in the country—and that you two would return in time for Hogmanay—she insisted that we come to her party. I know you're both exhausted, but it would be the ideal opportunity to announce your engagement. We'll never hear the end of it if she doesn't get to share in the excitement. There's a note from her, there on the mantel."

Smiling indulgently, Adam retrieved the cream-colored envelope from the mantel and extracted the contents, skimming Janet's note as Philippa began distributing plates for sandwiches and scones. It had been penned on the back of an engraved at-home card giving the details of the Frasers' annual Hogmanay party, and was addressed to him in a distinctive copperplate hand.

*Adam darling, If you don't feel equal to being sociable tonight, please don't hesitate to decline,* Janet had written. *But if you can possibly manage it, we'd love to see you—* especially *since your dear mother gives me to understand that you and Ximena have an important announcement to make."*

Adam repressed a chuckle. Even in their childhood, Janet had been an inveterate romantic and matchmaker. Over the years since her own marriage, her determination to see him happily wed had never flagged. It was only fitting that she be among the first to learn that her efforts had finally borne fruit, if only by pressuring Adam to keep considering what she regarded as suitable women.

"Well, she appears to have guessed what's going on, unless you told her,'' he said to his mother with a grin, as he handed the note to Ximena. "But Philippa's right, darling. This is a tailor-made opportunity to make our announcement. We can leave it for a few weeks, though, if you prefer.''

Ximena chewed on a sandwich while she read over Janet Fraser's note, smiling as she shook her head. ''No, no, we ought to go,'' she said. ''I like the Frasers. Besides, Janet's been very patient with you all these years. She deserves to hear our news from your own lips.''

The luggage arrived very shortly. Once Adam had seen it deposited in the bedroom, Ximena declared herself sufficiently fed, and retired. After seeing her settled, Adam returned to the sitting room, where Philippa was lingering over her tea. He closed the door behind him before reclaiming his seat on the settee.

''Before I turn in too,'' he said to his mother, ''is there anything I should be told?''

Philippa levelled her dark gaze at him. ''I wish I could say no, but that wouldn't be true. Something *did* crop up while you were away. And since you've asked, I suppose now's as good a time as any to fill you in.''

She refilled his teacup before commencing her account of the incident at Callanish. Adam listened attentively and with growing interest, all travel weariness temporarily banished.

''Initially, Noel expected there'd be a relatively simple explanation,'' Philippa concluded by way of summation. ''You know—college students playing at being Druids, that sort of thing. Even after he and Peregrine went out to the site for a look around, and then consulted with Julian, the three of them were of the opinion that it could keep until you got back.

''Since then, however, two men Noel now believes to have been participants in the bull-slaying have been found dead under circumstances that appear more and more suspicious. It's probably a good thing you decided to come back when you did.''

''I'll want to see Peregrine's sketches,'' Adam said.

''Yes, I thought you would.'' His mother reached behind her chair to produce a large brown envelope. ''There isn't a great deal we can do in the next few days, with you exhausted and the holidays demanding time of everyone else involved. But it wouldn't hurt to give the information to your unconscious, to work on in the background.''

Adam took the envelope and removed the stack of sketches, nodding as he shuffled through them superficially.

''I won't argue that,'' he agreed. ''In the meantime, my compliments to the rest of the team for their efforts so far. They appear to have performed admirably in my absence. We'll hope something turns up on this Taliere person. It's occurred to me that Taliere might be a craft name of some sort. Whoever he is, I suspect he may prove the key to understanding this entire operation. If I'm right about that, the sooner we locate him, the better.''

Philippa smiled. ''If you're right about that, we'll owe a significant debt of gratitude to the inestimable Harry Nimmo.''

''We'll owe him more than mere thanks,'' Adam said with a fleeting smile. ''Someone with psychometric talent would be a valuable asset to our resources. I met him briefly during the Cairngorm operation, but Noel hadn't yet taken him on as a student at that time. I'll have a word and see if he can arrange a proper introduction.''

''But not tonight,'' Philippa said archly. ''If you're going to see the new year in, you'd better get yourself some sleep.''

Smiling, Adam returned the sketches to their envelope, handed it to his mother, and rose.

''I'm on my way without need of a second reminder,'' he said, bending to press a kiss to her forehead. ''Wake me at about half past seven, will you?''

The Frasers' party was scheduled to begin at eight. By a little after nine, when Humphrey drove the Sinclairs through the gates, the affair was already in full swing. The house was ablaze with lights, and both sides of the long driveway were flanked with parked cars, including a dark green Alvis drophead coupe tucked in just before the crescent that led to the house's entrance. Ximena gave it an admiring glance as Humphrey nosed the Range Rover in behind a Mercedes limousine just disgorging its passengers.

''Very nice!'' she commented.

"Which, the Merc or the Alvis?" Adam said over his shoulder, from beside Humphrey.

"The Alvis, of course!" she replied. "I'll take a classic car any day. It reminds me that I'll want to get my Morgan out of mothballs."

"Well, it's waiting for you in the stable, under a dust sheet," he replied, as Humphrey eased the Range Rover forward a few feet, to the foot of the steps. "And if you'd like to drive the Alvis, I'm sure I can arrange that. It belongs to some young friends of mine. You remember Peregrine Lovat?"

"The portrait artist?"

"The very same. The Alvis was a bequest from his wife's godmother. I think you'll like Julia," he added. "She's the perfect match for Peregrine."

Cold air and the lively strains of country dance music assailed Adam as he left the car and opened Ximena's door to hand her out. With Humphrey's assistance, Philippa had already alighted from the other side of the car, regally cloaked in dark blue velvet over a floor-length tartan gown of silk taffeta that rustled as she moved.

Adam himself was no less resplendent, in a kilt of Sinclair tartan, wing-collared shirt, and a regulation doublet of black silk barathea, with hose also in Sinclair tartan. Light glinted from his shoe buckles and the silver mountings of the small dagger called a *skean dubh*, stuck in the top of his left stocking, and was echoed more subtly in the antique silver buttons of his doublet and the chains of a silver pocket watch swagged between the two pockets of his white waistcoat.

By contrast, Ximena's slim black velvet gown provided subtle counterpoint to the two Sinclairs' Highland finery—long-sleeved and demure in front, but slit from ankle to knee on one side and cut low in back under her short evening cape. The latter was an Edwardian confection of black silk faille and braid with fine jet beading, quite in keeping with her recent bereavement but also an exquisite fashion statement. Her only jewellery was her engagement ring and a pair of diamond ear studs lent her by Philippa for the evening, just visible beneath the wings of dark hair swept back at the sides and French-braided down the back, the tail tied with a bit of black velvet ribbon. A few hours' sleep and the careful application of makeup had all but erased any signs of undue fatigue.

"Darling, you look wonderful!" Adam murmured, pressing her palm to his lips before tucking her arm in his. "I shall be the envy of every man in the house."

"And I expect *I* shall have to fight off all the other women, when they see you in your kilt," she said, smiling as she pretended to adjust his white tie. "Do you realize I've never seen you in a kilt before? I think it may be even sexier than those riding breeches you were wearing, that second time I came up to your house. Did you think me very bold?"

"Certainly not!" he declared in mock indignation. "I was delighted to have found a physician who still makes house calls."

The sound of throat-clearing suddenly reminded him that Philippa was still waiting on the other side of the car with Humphrey.

"Sorry, we're coming," he said, containing a boyish grin as he led Ximena around to join them. "Philippa, do you know if provisions have been made for the drivers?"

"Yes, and I've already given Humphrey the details," she said indulgently. "Janet's laid on supper for them in the breakfast room. Humphrey, I don't expect we'll be very late—probably not much past one. Enjoy yourself until then."

"Very good, milady. And may I wish you all a happy new year."

"And the same to you, Humphrey," Adam said. "We'll see you in a few hours."

As Humphrey set off to park the car, Adam escorted Ximena and his mother up the steps and into the convivial warmth of the Frasers' entry hall, where their host was directing arriving guests into the drawing room. Sir Matthew Fraser, KBE, was a renowned surgeon and patron of the arts, in addition to being a childhood friend of Adam's. Tall, lean, and prematurely grey, the inspiration of many a wistful sigh among his female patients, he cut an indelibly romantic figure in his blue velvet doublet and kilt of red and blue Fraser tartan as he saw the Sinclairs and came rushing over.

"Philippa, you *did* persuade them to come!" he said, kissing her on both cheeks and then embracing Adam as he pumped his hand. "Adam, I'm delighted to see you. And Ximena—welcome back to Scotland!" he went on, sweeping a courtly bow over her hand.

As he and Adam helped the ladies out of their wraps, handing them off to one of Fraser's teenaged daughters, Adam was aware of heads turning in their direction. A waiter emerged from the drawing room bearing a silver tray laden with glasses of champagne, and at Matthew's hail in that direction, his wife materialized in the doorway—a vivacious, dark-haired vision in midnight-blue chiffon, diamonds at her throat and a red and blue silk Fraser sash brooched to her right shoulder. With a barely suppressed squeal of delight, she dashed across the hall to greet the new arrivals, enthusiastically hugging first Adam, then Philippa, and then taking Ximena's hand in both of hers to shake her head in grinning wonderment.

"Ximena, my dear, I am *so* glad you could join us tonight. And Adam darling, your timing couldn't have been more perfect—the dancing's just picking up momentum. I won't spoil your surprise by saying anything else just now—I'll let you choose your time and place—but do have some champagne and come in and mingle."

As the front door opened behind them to admit another couple, she reluctantly excused herself and went with her husband to greet them, leaving Adam and his ladies to help themselves to champagne and head on into the crowded drawing room. The music was coming from a large conservatory beyond, turned into a ballroom for the occasion, and they could see couples whirling in the patterns of a boisterous reel.

Heading vaguely in that direction, and waylaid several times by friends and professional colleagues come to be introduced to his striking companion, Adam managed to spot the Lovats early on, chatting amiably with one of Peregrine's recent clients near the doorway to the conservatory. Meanwhile, Philippa's attentions were claimed by an emeritus lecturer in neurology, likewise a former student of Jung, with whom she'd enjoyed a long-standing and comfortable flirtation.

As the neurologist whisked Philippa off to catch up on old times, Adam continued to work his way through the crowded room, Ximena at his side, caught up in the festive atmosphere. Eventually Peregrine noticed them and wound up his conversation, steering his wife over to join the new arrivals. Lovat being a sept of Clan Fraser, he was wearing a kilt in the brown hunting sett of his Fraser tartan, topped off by a bottle-green Montrose doublet. Julia's gown was a softer shade of moss-green, its scooped neckline and skirt flounced with double tiers of creamy lace—a stunning foil to her fair skin and red-gold hair.

"Hello, Julia," Adam said, kissing her on both cheeks. "You're looking radiant tonight. I'd like you to meet Ximena Lockhart. Peregrine, I believe you and Ximena met when she was last in Scotland."

"We did, indeed," Peregrine replied, as his wife smiled and extended her hand.

"Hello, Ximena," Julia said. "I'm very pleased to meet you at last. Would it be terribly trite of me to say that Peregrine has told me so much about you?"

"It was all gross exaggeration, I can assure you—both the good and the bad," Ximena replied with a smile. "Hello, Peregrine. It's good to see you again."

"And you," Peregrine said, bending over her hand with a grin and a courtly bow. "A usually reliable source tells me you may be here to stay."

An answering smile touched Ximena's lips as she drew Peregrine closer to kiss him on the cheek. "Knowing your source," she whispered, with a sidelong glance at Adam, "I'd say he's impeccably reliable. But please don't quote me on that until later tonight."

"My lips are sealed until you say otherwise," Peregrine promised. "Cross my heart." He made a crossing motion on the breast of his doublet. "Just don't make us wait too long," he added plaintively.

Laughing, the four of them drifted toward the conservatory, where the bandleader was inviting couples to take their places for Gay Gordons. As Julia seized Peregrine's hand

and drew him toward the dance floor, assuring Ximena that the dance was not hard to follow, the wife of one of Adam's fellow opera supporters came bustling up to kiss him on both cheeks.

"Adam, my dear, I thought it was you! You Perthshire men always manage to cut such a dash, in your white waistcoats and white ties! What a splendid affectation! Come dance Gay Gordons with us! We need more couples. Don't worry, my dear, this one's easy," she added to Ximena, at her look of bewilderment. "Adam's a fine dancer. He'll talk you through it."

Chuckling his agreement, Adam led Ximena onto the dance floor, murmuring a quick sketch of the form of the dance as they took a place behind Peregrine and Julia, their left hands joined and right hands clasped behind Ximena's right shoulder. Perhaps twenty couples had lined up in a counterclockwise circle around the room by the time the music started.

After the opening chord, with its attendant bows and curtsies, the dance began with eight marching steps forward, turning after the first four to continue backward, then eight steps back, again with the pivot halfway through. Then Adam turned Ximena under his left arm for four bars while he executed a Highland setting step—and swept her into his arms for four bars of polka before they began the process all over again.

Ximena caught on quickly, and soon was executing her part of the dance with as much style as anyone else, laughing breathlessly by the time she and Adam exchanged bows at the closing chord. Beside them, a flushed and somewhat perturbed Julia drew up to inspect a rip in the hem of her lace flounce, where she had caught her heel toward the end of the dance.

"Oh, dear!" she murmured. "I was afraid I felt that tear. I knew I should have brought proper ghillies for dancing."

"I'm sorry, darling," Peregrine murmured. "Can it be fixed?"

"Oh, I expect so; but I don't know that I dare risk any more dancing tonight, in case it catches again and gets worse," Julia replied, disappointment in her voice.

"Now, now, let's not be rash," Ximena said, bending down for a closer look. "If all Scottish dancing is this much fun, you mustn't think of missing it! Lace is easy to fix—certainly within the skill of these surgeon's hands." Grinning, she twiddled her fingers in the air between them. "Do you know if there's somewhere we can retreat to make repairs?"

An appeal to Janet resulted in a three-woman expedition to an upstairs bedroom, where Ximena delved into her evening bag and produced a miniature sewing kit before Janet could even find a spool of thread.

"Now I *am* impressed!" Janet exclaimed. "Not only is she beautiful and witty, but she comes prepared!"

Smiling impishly, Ximena shrugged the compliment aside and reeled off a length of ivory thread. "It's always seemed to me that a surgeon should keep a needle and thread handy at all times."

"Tell that to my husband," Janet said archly. "He won't even sew on a button in a pinch!"

"Ah, but he's used to having his surgeries nicely scheduled," Ximena said with a rueful chuckle, threading up a needle. "When you work in trauma, you have to be ready for anything, any time. And I have to say, my own state of preparedness in this regard goes back to long before I became a doctor. In my younger days, I used to do quite a bit of rock-scrambling—archaeology field trips and the like. That sort of thing can be really hard on your clothes."

Her tone implied a whole range of sartorial mishaps, and Julia laughed as Ximena bent to begin mending the lace flounce.

"Adam never mentioned you had an interest in historical monuments. Have you had much chance to go out hillwalking here in Scotland? You could do a whole tour of the West organized around castle ruins and standing stones."

"So I hear," Ximena agreed. "No, I'm afraid I haven't done much exploring at all. The last time I was here, I let work rule my life. That's one mistake I don't intend to make again."

"There's a certain baronet who could stand to learn that

lesson,'' Janet remarked. ''I'm glad he's found you, Ximena.''

''So am I,'' Ximena said with a tiny smile, keeping her gaze firmly on her work.

When the repairs to Julia's hem had been completed, the three women made their way back down to the conservatory, still chatting companionably. The dancing continued for a while longer before the band adjourned to take a break. During the interval, while a pair of waiters topped up champagne glasses, the Frasers' two daughters began circulating among the guests with trays of savories—smoked salmon on buttered brown bread, thin slices of toast spread with wild venison pâté, and oatcakes topped with haggis, prelude to the buffet that would follow shortly after midnight.

When everyone's glass had been charged, a dapper and handsome Matthew Fraser moved to the center of the room and tapped resoundingly on the side of a glass. As all eyes turned toward him and conversation subsided, Janet came to slip her arm through his, beaming with secret delight.

''My lords, ladies, and gentlemen,'' Matthew announced, ''first of all, Janet and I should like to take this opportunity to thank you for joining us this evening. Initially, this little party of ours was intended simply to celebrate the coming of the new year, which is still about half an hour away. However, it has come to my attention that we have another reason to celebrate tonight. Having no wish to keep you in suspense, I now call upon my dear friend and most respected colleague, Sir Adam Sinclair. He has a very important announcement to make—one which a good many of us have been awaiting for a very long time. Adam?''

The ensuing announcement, transmitted by way of a listening device planted earlier that day by a woman posing as one of the caterers, was picked up by a surveillance team operating out of a panel van parked beyond the Frasers' garden wall. The black-clad man listening at the receiving console pressed one hand to his earpiece as he turned to his companion and grinned.

''Well, well, Sinclair is announcing his engagement. This should add some spice to our report. Must be that black-haired bit of stuff we saw him walk in with.''

He adjusted the tuning and listened a moment longer.

"Name's Ximena Lockhart," he dictated over his shoulder to his assistant. "*Doctor* Lockhart. Who'd have thought a package like that would come equipped with brains? American, too, judging by the accent. Sinclair must have been a very busy boy while he was away."

"I'll say," his companion agreed. "Well, the boss is going to be very interested when he hears about this. Just think of the possibilities!"

# CHAPTER SIXTEEN

THAT same night, while Adam Sinclair and his friends prepared to usher in the new year with time-honored pledges of good fellowship, Francis Raeburn and a small number of handpicked associates were converging on one of Scotland's less well known National Trust properties, now closed for the winter—the bleak and desolate border fortress of Hermitage Castle.

The ruined castle was an apt location for what Raeburn had in mind. Sited just north of the Cheviot Hills that marked the age-old boundary between Scotland and England, Hermitage squatted ponderous and forbidding, even on the brightest of days. A shallow streamlet called Hermitage Water bordered it to the south, joined half a mile to the southeast by a lesser tributary called Whitrope Burn.

A narrow B-road ran parallel to the burn and then beside the confluence of the two streams, meandering from Hawick, twelve miles to the north, then southwestward through a sparse string of border villages to Gretna Green and Carlisle. Even in summer, Hermitage was well off the beaten tourist track; and in the dead of winter, as the year turned, it was populated only by rooks and shadows. Popular legend asserted that the sorcerous depravities of one of its former masters, William Lord Soulis, had caused the castle to sink into the ground for very shame.

Raeburn's associates had made careful preparations for the night's work. As his white Land Rover eased into the lesser road that skirted Hermitage Water, Barclay at the wheel, a figure in white snow-camouflage fatigues materialized out of the shadows beside the road and flagged them down. Barclay simultaneously eased the vehicle to a halt and reached for the Luger under the dashboard, but the figure stripped off its mottled grey ski mask to reveal the pale, ascetic features of Klaus Richter.

Barclay relaxed. Raeburn rolled down the window on the passenger side of the car and waited for Richter to join them.

"Everything is ready, *Lynxmeister*," the German reported crisply. "We may proceed as planned."

"Good," said Raeburn. "Get in."

Richter made for the rear passenger seat. Angela Fitzgerald moved over to make room for him as Barclay set the Land Rover in motion again.

"Any problems?" Raeburn queried over his shoulder.

"None," Richter replied. "My men are stationed as you directed. Nothing has been left to chance."

"Let's hope not," Raeburn murmured. "I cannot overstress the delicate nature of this night's work. Every detail must be correctly executed, or the operation could well prove our undoing."

As he spoke, his long fingers tightened possessively around the polished ash-wood casket he was carrying on his knees. Though the Soulis dagger was locked inside the casket, its resonances damped down by spells of containment, Raeburn could sense the added potency it had gained merely from being used in the bull-slaying ritual of a fortnight before.

His lean face bore a wolfish expression as he peered out to the right, searching the dark landscape just beyond Hermitage Water. He caught his breath as the castle suddenly materialized, its massive bulk heavy and almost menacing against the starless blackness of the sky.

"Slow down," Richter ordered Barclay. "The turnoff to the bridge is just beyond that house on the left."

Raeburn eyed the house suspiciously as Barclay slowed to a crawl, for lights showed behind closed curtains in two of the windows on the upper floor.

"The house is unoccupied tonight," Richter said, following Raeburn's sharp gaze. "Its residents have gone up to Hawick for a party. The lights have been left on as a precaution against burglars—as if that would stop *me*, if I wished to gain access. Look right! There's the bridge.''

A flat wood-and-metal bridge spanned Hermitage Water just where the shoulder of the road widened slightly to permit tourist parking. Two of Richter's operatives were on hand to open the gates that secured both ends of the bridge, and Barclay dimmed the Land Rover's headlamps before easing the big vehicle almost noiselessly across the bridge, following Richter's directions around to the right, then into the shelter of the castle's blind side.

A second Land Rover equipped with a rooftop compartment was already in place, along with the sleek bulk of two powerful motorcycles parked close to the castle wall. Dim light streamed from the inside of the second Land Rover, barely illuminating a standing figure in a homburg and a voluminous scarf, just outside an open rear door. Seated in the car was a figure muffled under a dark blanket. Two more of Richter's henchmen were standing by in the background near the motorcycles, indistinguishable from one another in their snow-camouflage gear, and almost invisible.

The hatted figure turned as Barclay pulled in next to the other Land Rover and killed the engine, Mallory's handsome, dissipated features just discernible in the dim light. Raeburn alighted from the passenger side and approached, his casket under one arm, summoning the young physician with a curt gesture.

''How's our patient?'' he inquired in a low voice.

Mallory glanced back at the figure slumped under the blanket, now just recognizable as Taliere.

''He's had his medicine. He won't give you any trouble.''

''You'd better hope he doesn't,'' Angela muttered, as Barclay handed her out of the rear passenger seat. ''We're only going to get one shot at this, so everything had better go as planned.''

''If it doesn't, it won't be *my* fault!'' Mallory retorted.

''Quiet, you two!'' Raeburn snapped.

Gathering valises of personal gear from the back of the Land Rover, Raeburn and his associates made their way around the base of the walls to the postern entrance on the east side. The entryway gave access to the castle courtyard,

its broken cobbles overshadowed by frowning walls of dull
red stone. A makeshift canvas roof had been contrived to
contain the murky light of a handful of hi-tech mini-spots
set at strategic locations all around, their filtered glow washing the enclosure with a smoky amber that mimicked torchlight.

At the center of the courtyard, surrounding a large brazen
cauldron, staves of rowan wood had been woven together to
create a ritual facsimile of an execution pyre. Other necessities for the night's work had been assembled on the ground
nearby, including a coiled length of heavy iron chain, a large
jerrycan of oil, a roll of lead sheeting the height of a man,
and several large suitcases.

Raeburn took stock of the assembled accoutrements, Angela ticking off items from a written list, then curtly nodded
his approval. In the course of his brief inventory, Mallory
and one of Richter's men brought in a glassy-eyed and stumbling Taliere, his blanket now trailing from his shoulders like
a cloak over the flowing white Druid robes he had worn at
Callanish. Raeburn fell silent as the old man was chivvied
over to the cauldron and allowed to sink to his knees, turning
then to the waiting Richter.

"Everything seems to be in order," he murmured. "You
and your men can take your stations outside. Keep a close
watch. I'll send for you when we're finished."

Richter and his men withdrew. The courtyard was as dank
and frigid as the bottom of a frozen well, but Raeburn
seemed hardly aware of the cold as he shed his outer gar-
ments to pull on a full-length hooded robe of black wool
which Barclay produced from one of the suitcases. His trio
of assistants likewise effected a change of attire, their robes
embroidered on the left shoulder, like Raeburn's, with the
silver-limned emblem of a snarling lynx head. In addition,
betokening his status as senior of the group, Raeburn donned
a disk-shaped medallion of beaten silver upon which the device of the lynx head had been executed in bold relief.

Once robed, Barclay and Angela made their way over to
Taliere and pulled him unceremoniously to his feet. His wits
dulled by narcotics, the old Druid offered no resistance as
Angela whipped the blanket from his shoulders and replaced

it with the feathered mantle he had worn at Callanish. Her features took on a vulpine sharpness as she lifted the bird-feather headdress from its carrying case and set it firmly on Taliere's salt-white head.

"*Ecce homo,*" she sneered aside to Barclay, as they sat the Druid on a nearby block of stone. "The perfect offering for this momentous occasion."

Raeburn and Mallory, meanwhile, had retreated to the recess of a closed doorway, where Mallory was laying out items from his medical bag, by the light of an electric torch. Crouching down to sit on the doorsill beside Mallory, his back braced against the door frame, Raeburn cradled the casket in his lap, then bared his left arm and offered it to the physician. He paid little attention as Mallory applied a tourniquet above his elbow, mechanically clenching and unclenching his fist to pump up the vein as he mentally rehearsed the sequence of events to come.

A sharp whiff of alcohol quickly recalled him, punctuated by the cold caress of the sterile wipe Mallory scrubbed over the inside of his bare arm—and then the bite of the needle. A faint smile lifted one corner of Raeburn's mouth as he watched his own blood begin to creep down the flexible length of clear plastic tubing attached to the needle, halted by a metal clamp midway along the tube until Mallory could apply a strip of tape to stabilize the needle. That done, Mallory set a small leaden bowl in his chief's free hand, retrieved the free end of the tube and directed it into the bowl—threaded under Raeburn's thumb to secure it—then loosed the tourniquet and thumbed the metal clamp.

Immediately Raeburn's blood began to race along the tube, pooling in the bowl, steaming in the cold. Raeburn watched for a moment, stony-faced, then closed his eyes and leaned his head against the doorjamb, content to let Mallory monitor the procedure.

While he bled, Angela Fitzgerald made her way to the castle's well in the northeast tower, taking with her a metal flask attached to a long cord. The protective grid of iron bars overlaying the well-top was coarse enough to let her lower the flask to draw up a measure of dark, evil-smelling water, which she held at arm's length as she took it back to the courtyard.

Mallory was taping a wad of sterile cotton to Raeburn's arm as she returned; the leaden bowl in Raeburn's other hand was three-quarters filled with his blood. Raeburn lurched to his feet when Mallory had taken the bowl from him, steadying himself against the doorjamb while Mallory stowed the debris from the blood-letting operation in his black bag. When the physician rose, he had the bowl of blood in one hand and a brush made from swine's bristles in the other.

"You're on," he murmured, glancing over Raeburn with a physician's eye. "Any lightheadedness?"

Shaking his head, Raeburn motioned for Mallory to follow him into the center of the courtyard, where he set the casket on the ground beside the cauldron. Taking the bowl and brush from Mallory, he then proceeded to paint a large equilateral triangle on the stone flagging around the cauldron, big enough to also contain a recumbent man. While he worked, Mallory retrieved his medical bag and returned to where Taliere sat, head slumped forward on his chest and with Barclay and Angela supporting him.

Raeburn finished the triangle and went to the north of the cauldron, where he began inscribing a large circle to contain their working area. Angela moved to stand just inside the western quarter of the circle he traced, watching as Mallory crouched at Taliere's feet and filled an earthen cup from a flask in his medical bag. The physician gestured to Barclay as he rose, setting his free hand on the old Druid's shoulder.

"Tilt his head back, so I can give him this," he said.

Barclay complied, watching as Mallory tipped the contents of the cup down the old man's throat.

"Is that what he made me drink, after we did the bull?" he asked in a low voice.

"Aye, from his own supply. It's a draught of mistletoe."

Meanwhile, using all the blood that remained in the bowl, Raeburn completed his circle, set the empty bowl and brush outside, then took took the Pictish dagger from its casket. The corroded blade had been honed to razor-sharpness along one edge, so that the silvery line shimmered in the murky light as he moved back to the northern quadrant of the boundary circle and raised the blade skyward in salute. A muttered invocation stirred power in the circle, focused through the blade as he touched its tip to the line of blood with a sibilant Word of command.

Eldritch energies seared upward where metal kissed blood, like a tinder brand bursting into flames. Raeburn recoiled from its brilliance, one hand upheld to shield his eyes as, hissing, the charge raced widdershins around the circle like a spark devouring a fuse, leaving behind a ghostly afterimage of flickering motes. When the sparks faded out, the wall of force remained in place, impenetrable as a curtain of lead.

Raeburn allowed himself a tiny sigh of relief, his pale eyes gone dark like adamant. Shifting the dagger to his left hand, he moved back beside the cauldron and lifted both arms above his head in an attitude of summoning.

"Glorious is the Night, womb of eternal Darkness!" he cried. "Glorious are the Ancient Ones who refuse to be hallowed by the Light! Glorious are the Rebellious Ones who scorn the sovereignty of Heaven! Glorious are the Mighty Ones who delight in the counsels of Shadow! Shield us, we pray, from the sight of those who profess Enlightenment! Glorify Yourselves, we beseech You, in concealing the work of our hands!"

With these words he reverted to one of the arcane tongues of command to which his occult studies had long ago given him access, swaying on his feet with closed eyes as Barclay moved forward to break open the jerrycan of oil and empty it into the cauldron. With Mallory assisting, he next wrapped the length of iron chain around the roll of lead sheeting and locked it in place with a heavy, old-fashioned padlock. Then the two of them lifted the roll into the cauldron, bracing it up on one end in grotesque parody of a gallows victim.

Angela Fitzgerald, meanwhile, was standing by with the flask of well-water, watching Raeburn for her cue. His chanting had not changed while his two male associates made their preparations; but as he suddenly directed the point of the dagger in Angela's direction, eyes still closed, she gave a slight involuntary gasp, her lips parting in an instant of near-sexual arousal. Only belatedly did she move forward, as if in trance, to empty the vessel of water into the cauldron. The oil broke and swirled, the water sinking out of sight as she dropped the empty flask amid the kindling of rowan wood and raised her hands in invocation.

"By the power of this water, drawn from this unhallowed ground, I summon to this time and place William de Soulis, Lord of Hermitage! As he is named, so let him appear!"

Her voice reverberated hollowly around the courtyard. As the echoes died away and she stepped back, eyes still lit with the power stirring in the circle, Barclay moved to the fore. From a pouch at his side the pilot took out a handful of earth which had been gathered earlier that day from the hill at Nine Stane Rig, the place of Soulis's execution, and cast it into the cauldron's mouth.

"By the power of the earth that received his ashes," he declared, "I summon to this time and place William de Soulis, Lord of Hermitage. As he is named, so let him appear!"

The earth sank sluggishly beneath the glistening slick of oil floating upon the water. Barclay yielded precedence in turn to Mallory, who was standing by with a lighted black taper.

Deadly focused, the young physician circled the cauldron once widdershins, touching flame to the kindling laid about the base, then set alight the oil lying on the surface of the cauldron's contents. It had been laced with something more combustible than mere oil, and a harsh yellow flame licked upward around the roll of chain-bound lead as Mallory drew back a pace to raise both hands in invocation.

"By the power of fire which devoured his flesh and left his spirit anchorless," he cried, "I summon to this time and place William de Soulis, Lord of Hermitage. As he is named, so let him appear!"

Raeburn came last, with a handful of sulphur and saltpetre which he cast into the flaming cauldron. As yellow fumes roiled upward, he breathed deeply of their fetid perfume before raising hand and dagger in further exhortation.

"By all infernal powers of the air and all the many works of Darkness, I summon to this time and place William de Soulis, Lord of Hermitage! As he is named, so let him appear!"

The power being summoned had increased exponentially

with each elemental invocation. Prevented from dissipating by the confines of the circle, the power hung crackling in the air like the build-up of a static electrical charge. Raeburn could feel it beating about him like a strong wind, stirring the hackles at the back of his neck as his pulse rate quickened to match its rhythm.

Half-intoxicated, he seized hold of the power with his right hand and began channelling it into the dagger in his left, molding it by the force of his will, pointing the dagger at the cauldron. The dagger-hilt began to quiver in his grasp like a live thing, aglow with arcane energies.

The metal grew hot to the touch, but Raeburn, his face contorted in ecstatic endurance, continued to hold the power in check until it threatened to scorch his palms. Then, abruptly, he released it like a psychic probe, launching it with single-minded intent into the abyss of the Inner Planes, whose physical focus now was the cauldron.

Eternity seemed to hang suspended before his far-ranging senses registered a response. So faint was the signature that at first he found it difficult to distinguish from the background shimmer of so many overlapping realms.

But the locus of movement grew progressively stronger, homing in on its summoners with a speed outside normal time. No physical manifestation heralded its arrival, but Raeburn became abruptly aware of a sentient presence focused on the cauldron, malignant and hungry—Soulis, beyond any doubt, and too hungry to manifest without sustenance.

''Bring him!'' Raeburn rasped, jerking his chin toward Taliere.

Immediately Mallory yanked the old man to his feet and hustled him forward, forcing him to his knees before the cauldron and then snapping a capsule of ammonia under his nose. The old man recoiled with a jerk of his head, animating the ceremonial bird headdress he wore, but Barclay had already sidled into position behind him, armed with a stream-smoothed stone the size of two fists. The blow he dealt to the back of the old Druid's head sent the bird headdress flying; and as Mallory caught the victim's wrists to keep him from crumpling, Barclay tossed his stone aside and whipped a length of knotted rawhide around Taliere's throat.

This new assault cut off the old man's anguished moan, its force snapping his head back against Barclay's chest, eyes bulging and tongue protruding in a silent rictus of distress as one hand wrenched free of Mallory's grasp to claw ineffectually at the garrote choking out his life.

But even as his struggles began to weaken, Raeburn was moving in with grim determination, somewhat regretting the need to sacrifice Taliere in this manner—but what better to summon and bind a magician than the blood of another magician, and especially one of Taliere's calibre? And only the threefold death would satisfy Taranis, in whose service this night's work was being performed.

The Soulis dagger in one hand, Raeburn seized a handful of the old Druid's long white hair in the other and bade Barclay release the garrote, then wrenched Taliere's head sharply to the right and struck deep at the base of the left ear to sever both the jugular and the carotid artery. Blood gushed from the wound, bespattering Raeburn and Barclay and almost instantly dyeing the front of the white Druid robes with gore.

Any outcry Taliere might have made by this time ended in a liquid gurgle, drowning in his own blood as he was held face-down over the mouth of the cauldron so that his life's blood might bathe the dagger further and mingle with the burning oil and water below. As the stench of burnt blood reinforced the brimstone reek of the sulphur, and the victim's struggles slowly subsided, Raeburn cast his gaze searchingly above the cauldron, still well aware of the entity not yet manifest but drawn by the blood and the sacrifice.

"Yes, come and drink," he whispered, sharpening the focus of his will through the dagger and inviting Soulis to feast—for he had no doubt that the entity summoned by the treble link of dagger, blood, and cauldron, was, indeed, the essence of William Lord Soulis. "Come and feast, dark spirit. But know that if you do, I bind you to these elements of your demise, by debt of blood and power of this blade. I wish you no ill, but I have a proposition for you. If you do not wish to hear it, I can send you back; or if you hear it and refuse, I still can send you back."

Heart pounding, he waited, sensing the angry energy roiling above the cauldron, held back by the potency of the blade in his hand from feasting on Taliere's waning life energy, yet lured by the blood and the promise of blood. Barclay and Mallory had stiffened as he addressed the empty air, and glanced at him in alarm as an invisible force seemed to wrench suddenly at the blade.

"You shall not have him save by my leave!" Raeburn said sharply, pulling the dagger from under the waning stream of Taliere's blood, but stabbing it more forcefully at the contents of the cauldron. "If you will have his life's essence, bind yourself to the discipline of this blade. If you do not, I shall send you back whence you came. Long centuries may pass before another gives you even temporary respite from what you have endured these seven hundred years!"

He could sense the angry surge of power over the cauldron, brooding and malevolent, but it could not manifest without his assent. There ensued a brief, fierce struggle of opposing wills as the entity struggled for ascendancy; but centuries of dark confinement had robbed the banished soul of the strength to prolong the contest. Quick to sense weakness, Raeburn brought further force to bear and had the exquisite satisfaction of feeling his opponent capitulate, shrinking into still-disembodied focus in and around the dagger in his hand.

But until compliance came of compulsion, not coercion, Raeburn could not be sure of even a temporary bargain. Slowly, cautiously, he touched his blade to Taliere's bowed head and bade his reluctant visitor to feed, well aware how the other battened greedily on the old man's last life energies and then descended into the cauldron itself to revel in the blood—and allowed itself to be bound.

And once forged, the binding could not be broken save as Raeburn allowed. Grimly triumphant, he signalled his confederates to lay Taliere's now lifeless body on the ground within the triangle that encompassed the cauldron, himself moving outside the triangle. When Barclay and Mallory had withdrawn to stand flanking Angela, far on the other side of the circle, Raeburn pointed the dagger into the cauldron once more, directing the force of his will toward the entity contained therein.

"William de Soulis, know me for your summoner," he declared, utterly focused on his intent. "I called you by name, and you came. I offered you blood, and you fed. By these two articles, you are compelled to recognize my authority. In token of my mastery, I charge you to show yourself, by taking the place that has been prepared for you."

He directed the dagger toward the roll of lead sheeting in the cauldron. There followed another brief flurry of token resistance, but then, abruptly, the roll of chain-wrapped sheeting took on a hectic shimmer, as if it were about to liquefy. In the same moment, the lead bulged outward, defining the spectral outline of a human form wrapped within.

A face took shape at the top of the column, a lean, bearded visage that might have been dissolutely handsome had it not been contorted in an expression of mingled anguish and loathing. The image writhed and wavered, but Soulis himself was demonstrably unable to escape. Satisfied thus far, Raeburn drew himself up and again pointed the dagger at his quarry.

"William de Soulis, I require that you answer certain questions," he declared, never wavering in his intent. "To this end, I have provided you with a host body. I hereby charge you to take possession of it. Attempt to defy me, and I shall send you back to the infernal regions whence you have come."

Using the dagger as a pointer, he indicated Taliere's cooling corpse. The gesture carried the weight of compulsion. Sluggishly, with obvious reluctance, Soulis's presence coalesced briefly in a shimmer of malignant glitter above the cauldron, then brimmed over the edge and downward like an evil mist to engulf and permeate Taliere's body.

A shudder racked the old Druid's abandoned frame. Moving like a damaged marionette, it raised its head and then elbowed itself to its feet in a series of spasmodic jerks. The glazed eyes focused on Raeburn's face in combined hatred and fury. Then the slack mouth moved, emitting a voice that was rough as a file, and utterly unlike Taliere's.

"Who are you, and why have you conjured me?"

The language was an antique variant of Scots, but Raeburn's linguistic abilities were more than adequate to enable him to answer in the same mode.

"I am the Lynx-Master, and your master," he informed Soulis. "Beyond that, my name need not concern you. As for my purpose, I require knowledge that you possess."

"What knowledge might that be?"

"The secret," Raeburn said, "of conjuring and binding elemental spirits."

A malignant sneer contorted the corpse's face.

"What makes you think you are in any way worthy to wield a secret of such magnitude?"

"Have I not brought you here and commanded your obedience?" Raeburn countered. "Surely that bespeaks some hint of the scope of my abilities."

The corpse's lips curled in contemptuous defiance. "All the more reason to keep my knowledge to myself."

"When you hear what I have to offer," Raeburn retorted, "you may be more than willing to bargain. Or does it not interest you to contemplate release from your long banishment?"

"Speak, mortal," the corpse replied in a low, deadly tone.

Raeburn inclined his head. "By dint of my own resources, I have been able to gain access to the operative magical keys by which your adversaries were able to condemn you to banishment amid the Inner Planes. It may interest you to learn that I've devised a way to nullify them. What I therefore propose is a simple exchange of favors: You give me the information that I want—teach me to conjure and bind elemental spirits—and I, in return, will set you free."

After a deathly pause, Soulis spoke slowly, the voice flat and emotionless.

"There is nothing I would not do to regain my liberty," he said, "but it is not within my power to pay your bargaining price."

"Indeed?" Raeburn's one word spoke a world of disbelief. "And why not?"

"For the reason that half the knowledge you demand was never in my keeping," came the response. "It was supplied independently by my spirit familiar."

"By Robin Redcap?"

A look of uneasiness flickered across the face that was no longer Taliere's. "Aye, the same."

"And what, exactly, was Redcap's contribution? Answer me!"

There was another moment's hesitation before Soulis reluctantly replied.

"The required ritual demands the interweaving of two complementary sequences of spells. The first derives from the material realm. The second, however, derives from the realm of Faerie. The language in which these Faerie spells are couched is one which no mortal tongue can pronounce and no mortal mind can retain. Without Redcap's aid, I could not have performed the binding ritual—and neither can you."

"Then I suggest you find me a way to secure the services of Redcap or some other Faerie ally," Raeburn replied, undaunted.

"You have no idea what you are asking," Soulis said flatly. "Redcap was one of the few denizens of Faerie strong enough to empower the incantations."

"Then you will have to persuade him to act as *my* ally," Raeburn said. "Unless, of course, you have found your former mode of existence so agreeable that you would rather not exert yourself in that regard."

An angry snarl greeted this suggestion. "I do not know if the former link between us yet abides," Soulis rasped.

"Then we shall have to summon him and find out."

"You had better be prepared to satisfy his bloodlust. It is his nature to violate his victims before he eats them."

"Then we shall find him a subject fit for his pleasure," Raeburn retorted. "But understand that I shall expect his full cooperation in return, or you will find yourself once again relegated to the Void, never again to reincarnate."

"I should kill you now," Soulis muttered, "and eat your soul!"

Raeburn drew himself up defiantly, again pointing with the dagger. "I advise you not to make threats you cannot carry out. This is the one and only time I intend to make this offer. Do we have a bargain, or shall I abandon you to your fate?"

A shudder racked Taliere's lifeless corpse from head to foot, but the white head lifted boldly.

"I have told you Redcap's price for this favor; I have not yet named my own."

"Is your freedom not enough?"

"It is not. I shall require physical form, else freedom means little."

"Then I shall provide a second oblation for your own delectation," Raeburn said softly. "Do we have a bargain?"

"We have a bargain," Soulis grated.

Raeburn's lips framed a thin smile. "Excellent. We shall meet again when I have made all the necessary arrangements. I promise you," he added, "that it will not be long."

# CHAPTER SEVENTEEN

**A**DAM woke with a start in the twilight hours before the dawn of the new year, the previous night's sense of well-being shattered by a potent and troubling dream that fled as soon as he opened his eyes.

It was far too early to rise—perhaps as early as seven, by the light—but the Frasers' Hogmanay party had still been in full swing at two, when Philippa finally had pleaded jet lag for Adam and his newly declared fiancée and begun trying to engineer their escape. Three o'clock had come and gone by the time the three of them crept home, the patient Humphrey at the wheel of the Range Rover, and the clock in the downstairs hall had just begun striking four as all of them retired to their respective beds.

Now Ximena lay curled at Adam's side, her dark hair spilling like silk on the pillow, looking happy but still exhausted; he would not think of disturbing her much-needed rest.

But the dream that had shattered his own sleep continued to haunt him, even as he tried to recapture some of its sense—more a residual of foreboding than anything specific, but he seemed to recall snatches of imagery featuring standing stones, and smoke writhing among the stones like tentacles.

Moving carefully to avoid waking Ximena, he rolled over and stole a glance at the clock on the bedside table. The discovery that it was barely six o'clock made him groan inwardly. He lay awake for a while, pondering the possible significance of the dream, but when no ready explanations presented themselves, he did his best to push his speculations out of mind, at least for the time being, and willed himself back to sleep.

Even when he woke again, however, the emotional impact of the dream remained curiously memorable in contrast to the vagueness of its imagery—so much so that he found himself unable to dismiss the experience out of hand. Over a solitary brunch of bacon, eggs, and tattie scones in the breakfast room—for Ximena and Philippa were still abed—he went searching through the newspapers for some clue that might shed light on the mystery. Finding nothing there, he reached behind him for the phone and tapped out McLeod's number.

The inspector was on duty at police headquarters, having volunteered for holiday duty so that some of the junior officers in his division could take the time off to be with their families.

"Adam! Welcome back—and congratulations."

"Thanks very much. Listen, Noel, I've got a question for you," Adam said, when the two men had exchanged New Year's greetings. "Did anything unusual happen last night?"

McLeod gave a snort of derisive laughter. "Do you want the whole catalogue of events, or just my personal favorites?"

Adam found himself smiling, for New Year's Eve in Scotland was probably the most riotous holiday on the calendar.

"Actually," he said, "I was thinking in terms of historic landmarks. Were there any incidents having to do with any of the national monuments hereabouts?"

"Well," McLeod offered, "some lads on leave from the naval base at Rosyth got themselves arrested for trying to hang a life-sized blowup model of Madonna from the chimney of John Knox's house."

At any other time, Adam might have been amused by what was obviously nothing more than a high-spirited prank.

"Actually, I had in mind something of a more serious nature," he told McLeod. "Not necessarily in this jurisdiction."

"Ah. I gather that Philippa's briefed you about Callanish."

"She did. I've no notion that this is necessarily related."

"Well. I'm not aware of anything," McLeod said, after a taut pause. "Give me a minute, though, and I'll run a check for incidents elsewhere."

"Thanks. I'll hold on."

McLeod was gone only briefly. "No, there's nothing on the books. Anything I should know about?"

"Oh, it's probably nothing," Adam said lightly. "I had some odd dreams last night—nothing I can put my finger on. It could well have been a bit of a hangover from the Frasers' Hogmanay party, coupled with jet lag. Thanks anyway for checking."

After Ximena and Philippa had come down for lunch, Adam took Ximena out to the stables to inspect her Morgan. The battery was dead, or they would have taken it out for a spin. They settled for a drive in Adam's Jaguar instead, and spent part of the afternoon deciding on what would be necessary to get the Morgan back on the road. When they returned, in time for tea with Philippa, a message was waiting for Adam to ring McLeod at the office.

"Hello, it's Adam," he said, when McLeod had picked up his direct line. "You rang?"

"Ah." The word conveyed a world of expectation. "There's been an interesting wrinkle on your 'hangover' theory this morning."

"Oh?"

"Yes. Shortly after you rang, I had a call from young Iolo MacFarlane, out on Lewis. He's the chap who was first on the scene at Callanish. It seems he also had some unsettling dreams last night. He said he hoped I wouldn't think he was crazy, but he could best describe it as 'a disturbance in the Force.' He says he thinks something terrible happened last night. He doesn't know what or where, but it was somehow connected with what happened at Callanish."

"I see." The information tended to confirm what Adam himself had picked up, but was no more helpful. "Do you intend to talk to him again?"

"I don't intend to go back to Lewis, if that's what you mean. Unfortunately, 'a disturbance in the Force' isn't very specific, and you aren't much more help. We'll just have to wait and see what else develops. I thought you'd want to know, though.''

"Thanks, Noel. I appreciate it. Keep me posted.''

Following the long New Year's weekend, Ximena took up her new appointment at the Royal Infirmary and Adam plunged into catching up on professional commitments put on hold while he was in America. Taking over management of the domestic concerns of Strathmourne House, Philippa focused her primary energies on helping the couple make plans for their formal nuptials, which were officially scheduled for the first Saturday in February.

Meanwhile, the news that Sir Adam Sinclair was shortly to marry Dr. Ximena Lockhart was given pride of place in the society supplements of every newspaper in Scotland, and was the cause for disappointed sighs by many an Edinburgh matron who had hoped her daughter might catch the eye of one of Scotland's most eligible bachelors. Following the public announcement, a flood of notes and letters of congratulation began to pour in to Strathmourne, as Adam's many friends and associates, contacts, and colleagues from far and wide took the occasion to express their heartiest good wishes.

''You have an amazing variety of friends,'' Ximena marvelled, casting a wondering eye at the array of correspondence strewn across the breakfast table between them. ''As near as I can tell, you seem to be on a first-name basis with everyone from the senior curator of manuscripts at the British Museum to the governor of Edinburgh Castle to the head lama in charge of the Buddhist Retreat Center on Holy Isle. How on earth did you get to be so well-acquainted with so many different people in so many walks of life?''

Adam chuckled. ''Some of the connections I owe to my family, of course. As for the rest—'' He shrugged. ''I *am* a Jungian analyst. Cultivating an attitude of cultural eclecticism is one of the hallmarks of Jung's approach.''

''That still doesn't explain where you get the time,'' Ximena said. ''One of these days, you're going to have to let me in on the true secret of your manifold successes.''

Though obviously playful in spirit, her choice of words cost Adam a faint twinge of conscience, for it reminded him, however indirectly, that there were still truths about himself that he had not shared with his new wife.

"Are you sure you *really* want to know?" he replied, trying to keep his tone equally light.

Ximena looked up from pouring herself a fresh cup of tea, something a little forced about her air of innocence.

"Of course I want to know," she told him. "After all, we did vow a mutual sharing of worldly goods—hardly a week ago, as I recall. I believe that includes any and all skeletons lurking in the closets around here."

Adam managed a rueful smile. "You don't scare easily, do you?"

"Not as a general rule. But I do get concerned now and then for your safety—and not without cause, I think."

"Psychiatry is not generally regarded as a high-risk specialty," he said, hoping to divert the conversation.

"No, but most psychiatrists confine their professional activities to the nice, safe environs of the consultation room," she retorted. "You don't talk about it much—and I haven't pushed—but I know you donate no small portion of your time to helping out the police whenever they have a case that smacks of the bizarre. I gather that you regard this kind of work in the light of a special vocation—but I also know that it can be potentially very dangerous. When we both nearly got blown up on our very first date, that became abundantly clear.

"I'm not going to ask you to explain about that," she added, holding up a hand to silence any interruption. "I respect the fact that you can't talk about a lot of what you do. That being the case, I'd like to propose a bargain."

"What kind of bargain?" Adam asked cautiously.

"A sort of exchange of courtesies. It works like this. I won't make any attempt to interfere with your enforcement work, if you'll promise to keep me informed about what you're doing."

"Within limits, I'm certainly willing to do my best," Adam agreed.

"I'm not asking that you tell me everything," she reiterated. "I expect that, in its way, the issue of confidentiality is just as sacrosanct for law-enforcement people as it is for physicians—or priests, even. What I do ask is that you tell me as much as you can. That car bomb at Melrose was planted by someone you were chasing on behalf of the police. I don't even want to know the details, at this remove,'' she added, shaking her head and holding up her hand again. ''But if this is a regular feature of your lifestyle, I'd at least like to be given fair warning.''

Adam stared at her for a long moment.

''My life usually isn't that physically dramatic,'' he said at last. ''But there *is* a lot more to the truth than you realize.''

''How much more?''

Adam chose his words carefully, well aware that this conversation could make or break their future relationship.

''The crimes that demand my talents as an investigator aren't simply those involving some degree of psychological abnormality on the part of the perpetrators,'' he said tentatively. ''Every now and then a case comes to light which can only be explained in terms of—let's call it the paranormal.''

When she only cocked her head in question, Adam went on.

''When that happens, a solution can only be found by utilizing extraordinary methods of investigation. And that means calling in a special investigator—someone equipped with more than the usual range of investigative talents.''

Ximena's eyes widened slightly. ''You mean someone gifted with extrasensory perception?'' She paused a beat. ''Are we talking about Noel McLeod—or *you*?''

Adam gave a noncommital shrug, declining to answer the question directly.

''I know it has a sensationalist ring to it, but let me assure you that such faculties do exist. And wherever they manifest themselves, they provide us with valid information concerning the nature of experience.''

Ximena was studying him closely. ''What exactly are you trying to tell me? That you're some kind of psychic?''

''I suppose that's as accurate a term as any,'' Adam conceded, ''though we both know what that could mean in professional terms, if it were ever to become public knowledge. The fact is, I owe a great deal of my success in treating the mental illnesses of my patients to these special talents.

"But that's only part of the story," he went on. "You've already noted how often I work with the police on a consultancy basis. What you don't know is that I have certain . . . obligations as an enforcer in my own right."

A furrow appeared between Ximena's winged eyebrows. "I'm not sure I follow you."

"Bear with me, darling. This isn't easy for me either," Adam said quietly. "Let's just say that the possession of special perceptive abilities automatically carries with it a certain burden of responsibility."

"And?" she said, when he did not immediately go on.

He drew a breath, steeling himself for further disclosures.

"I'm by no means the only one to wield unusual talents of this sort. Unfortunately, not all those who possess such talents are also possessed of a sense of ethics. On the contrary, there are more than a few exceptional individuals out there who are prepared to use their gifts for wholly selfish purposes, often to the extreme detriment of others. And that cannot be permitted, if the balance of enlightenment in the universe is to be maintained."

"Balance of enlightenment?"

Adam groped for the words to explain, heartened by her reaction thus far.

"There is such a thing as a Higher Law in the universe— a code of spiritual morality which is, itself, a reflection of the Divine Will which instituted it. This Higher Law is the foundation upon which all other moral and ethical codes of human conduct are based, whether consciously or unconsciously. When human laws are broken, it's up to human authority to seek out the perpetrator and render justice. Police and judicial agencies carry out that function.

"Similarly," he went on, "when someone transgresses against the Higher Law, that infraction demands a response from a higher authority, if the balance of the cosmos is to be maintained and restored to harmony. Conventional detection methods usually fall short when investigating such crimes—and those who operate in contempt of the Higher Law are often quite adept at covering their tracks. Dealing with such offenders requires the intervention of individuals wielding comparable gifts. In other words,'' he finished bleakly, ''it's up to me and those like me to find them, stop them, and require them to make whatever restitution is owed to re-establish the balance of order.''

''*Me and those like me*,'' Ximena repeated softly, her eyes wide with wonder. ''Does that mean you actually work within an organization?''

''It does,'' Adam admitted. ''That's one of our greatest safeguards. As long as you work with a team, you reduce the temptation to become a law unto yourself.''

Ximena was silent for a long moment as she assimilated this. Then abruptly she asked, ''Does Philippa know anything about all this?''

Adam could not restrain a smile. ''Philippa is the one who trained me.''

This disclosure startled Ximena as nothing else had done.

''My God!'' she exclaimed. ''Who else is involved in this work? No, don't tell me—let me guess: Noel McLeod, certainly. And Peregrine Lovat as well?''

Adam nodded. ''Correct on both counts. But please don't ask me to tell you anything more. It isn't that I don't trust you to keep a secret. But we do have our share of enemies.''

''Like the ones who blew up your car at Melrose?''

''Among others,'' Adam said bluntly. ''Their methods don't stop there. There are many forms of violence, not all of them physical. If it's all the same to you, I'd rather keep the risks to a minimum, for the sake of all concerned.''

A long silence fell between them. Then, at last, Ximena spoke, her face a little strained.

''I seem to have gotten far more than I bargained for.''

''I know,'' Adam said, ''and I'm sorry. I should have told you sooner.''

''Yes, you should have,'' Ximena agreed, a faint smile curving her lips. ''But now that I think of it, you've been feeding me hints about this for quite some time now, haven't you? It isn't your fault it's taken me this long to really hear what you were saying.''

''If it's more than you're prepared to take on,'' he said, ''you're still free to back out.''

''Do you want me to?'' she replied.

Slowly he shook his head, his eyes never leaving hers.

"No," he said softly.

"Then I'll stay," she whispered—and sealed the declaration with a kiss.

# CHAPTER EIGHTEEN

"SO you've told Ximena about your secret life," Philippa said.

She was looking not at her son, but at the wintry landscape streaming past on either hand as they sped along the snow-banked ribbon of the M90 toward Edinburgh, Adam at the wheel of the Range Rover.

"I have," Adam acknowledged. "I won't say that it was an easy confession to make, but I felt it was both just and necessary. I can't very well ask Ximena to share my life, while at the same time withholding significant truths about my work. She deserves better of me than that."

"Indeed." Philippa's tone was noncommittal. "And how much did you feel obliged to tell her?"

"Enough to give her some idea of the shape of things to come," Adam replied, slowing for traffic ahead. "Ximena's no fool. For the most part, all I did was confirm guesses she'd already made for herself."

A blue route sign loomed ahead, relaying the information that they were some fifteen miles out of Edinburgh. Adam checked the road in front and behind before whipping the Rover around the slow-moving bulk of an articulated lorry. A dark green Granada traveling several cars back, attempted to copy the maneuver, but was forced to tuck back in when an ambulance came up fast from behind, blue lights flashing, and overtook them.

Philippa dismissed both vehicles with a casual glance before focusing her attention on her son's patrician profile. "Your wife certainly has more brains than most," she observed, "but this isn't necessarily a matter for intellect. If you don't mind my asking, how did she take your revelations?"

"She didn't immediately question my sanity, if that's what you mean," Adam said wryly. "Perhaps between us, her father and I have succeeded in demonstrating that the world is more full of mystery than is commonly believed, in these materialistic latter days. In any event, she's prepared to take a great deal on trust."

"Even the fact that there are going to be times in your life when you can't explain yourself or your actions?"

"Ximena knows that I have certain—special abilities," he replied. "She understands that there are limits to what I can tell her without compromising the interests of others besides myself. She accepts that keeping the peace occasionally necessitates keeping secrets, if justice is to be served. She knows the value that I set upon my vocation—and my honor."

Glancing sidelong at Philippa, he went on.

"You must have confronted these same questions when you married my father. Is this more than a marriage-partner is entitled to know?"

Philippa smiled. "Not if the partner is worthy. But that burden of knowledge is not always easy to bear."

Conversation subsided momentarily, as a flurry of snow forced Adam to give his attention to minding the road. When the air cleared again, he was ready to pose some questions of his own.

"Just how much *did* my father know about your work as a Huntsman?" he asked, his eyes still on the road.

He heard her draw a deep breath before replying.

"I told him as much of the truth as I could," she said. "As much as I dared without risking his safety. Of course, there are aspects to the work we do that can never be adequately explained to someone who hasn't experienced the revelations of the Inner Planes."

She turned to smile at Adam.

"I was very much in love, though, just as you are," she went on. "And like you, I couldn't see the sense, let alone the virtue, in keeping my spouse wholly in the dark when my actions were bound to affect our relationship. The war was on then, and he was on active service. So was I, though in a capacity he never guessed at the time—though I did tell him more in later years, when we'd got to know one another better.

"But there was a very real possibility that one or the other of us might not survive the war. Your father needed—deserved—to know what to expect from me, just as I needed to know what to expect from him. I never had cause to regret my decision. I hope you never will either."

His mother's words left Adam feeling obscurely relieved, as if he had been delivered of a weight he had not previously realized he was carrying.

A companionable silence prevailed for the next several miles, born of mutual understanding and contentment. When Philippa spoke again, it was to redirect the conversation toward the less sensitive, if no less pressing, topic of her son's wedding plans, which were proceeding apace, with the date now less than four weeks away.

The invitations had gone out the previous Saturday, as soon as a date and location had been secured for the ceremony and the order could come back from the engraver. In the days immediately preceding, Julia had helped Philippa with the happy task of addressing the invitations, so that they could be posted the socially correct four weeks before the wedding date. Several times, the two of them had dragged Ximena off in search of the perfect gown—thus far, without any decision being reached.

"While we're talking about marriages, my dear, I need to run a few wedding details past you," Philippa said, with an arch glance in his direction. "I know that with your professional commitments, you and Ximena don't have time to sit down together very often right now, but I do need a few decisions, if I'm to take the planning burden off the two of you. I *adore* being able to do it for you, but I can't operate in a vacuum."

Smiling contentedly, Adam gave her a fond side glance.

"Philippa darling, your taste is impeccable and we're doing this partially for you, so anything you decide will be fine with us. I know it isn't easy doing this on such short notice, but we're extremely grateful.'' He paused a beat. ''What do you need a decision on?''

''Well, the menu, for one thing,'' she replied, with an exasperated sigh. ''If this is to be done right, the caterers really do need a few weeks' notice. And flowers for the reception.''

''How about ringing the florist who did the flowers for Peregrine and Julia's reception?'' Adam asked. ''I liked those, and they know what the house needs.''

Philippa gave another exasperated sigh. ''Adam. This is a February wedding. You cannot get June flowers in February.''

''Then you decide!'' Adam said with a chuckle. ''Honestly, I don't care. Or rather, it isn't that I don't care—it's that it doesn't matter to *me*, so long as Ximena is happy.'' He glanced at her again. ''Does that make it any easier?''

Laughing, she gave a helpless shrug and went on to the next item on her list. By the time they pulled into the car park at the Royal Edinburgh Hospital, where Adam worked, amicable agreement had been reached on several thorny points.

''Well, I'm glad we managed to resolve a few things, while you had me captive for this drive into town,'' Adam said, as he pulled into his assigned parking space. ''And I'm even more appreciative that you agreed to come in with me today. This Gerard case has reached something of an impasse, and you're the only one I know who can deal with its—ah—'unusual' aspects. I really could use a second opinion.''

''Unusual'' was a vast understatement. Adam's involvement in the case went back well over a year when, at his own request, the patient in question had been assigned to his public case load. While Henri Gerard might be formally categorized as a catatonic schizophrenic, what the medical records did not reveal was that his malady was the direct consequence of a misguided attempt to appropriate forbidden esoteric knowledge. Already well briefed on the hidden aspects of the case, Philippa pulled a slight grimace.

''You've already made more progress with him than anyone probably has a right to hope,'' she said. ''Just getting him to recognize you without going into fits of hysteria was a major achievement in itself. But you're welcome to my opinion, for whatever it may be worth.''

Their dash across the car park to the lobby entrance was punctuated by a biting wind and flurries of snow that whirled across the tarmac like miniature dervishes. After checking in with the receptionist, the two Sinclairs made their way to Adam's office and exchanged overcoats for starched, hospital-issue lab coats before moving on to the cozy comfort of one of the consultation rooms on the same floor. Shortly thereafter, one of the charge nurses ushered Gerard into the room, conducting him to the chair provided.

The patient was a slight, dark-haired man in his middle forties, with furtive, haggard eyes and the shuffling gait of a man many years his senior. As the nurse departed, closing the door behind him, Adam summoned a welcoming smile and greeted his patient in French.

*"Bon jour, Monsieur Gerard. Comment allez vous aujourd'hui?"*

*"Assez bien, Monsieur le Docteur,"* Gerard responded dully. *"Assez bien . . ."*

As his voice trailed off, the dark eyes went unfocused.

"This lady here is also a doctor," Adam continued in French. "I have invited her here to meet you so that we may both have the benefit of her experience in seeking a cure for your distress."

The session which followed lasted over an hour. Once the nurse had come to escort Gerard back to his ward, Philippa turned to Adam and raised a winged eyebrow.

"I can't say I'm surprised that Mr. Gerard doesn't want to re-enter the real world, Adam. As far as he's concerned, there may be demons lurking under every rock, waiting to gobble him up—which, in his experience, is a well-founded fear. It seems to me that you're already doing everything that can be done. When you consider that this illness is deeply rooted in Gerard's historic past, you may have to accept the possibility that a cure may not be achievable in this lifetime."

Mother and son continued to exchange observations as they walked back to Adam's office, albeit in less specific terms, for the sake of would-be listeners. Arriving, they were greeted by a familiar, burly figure pacing up and down outside the door.

"Hullo, Noel!" Adam exclaimed in surprise. "What brings you here?"

Looking grimly animated, the inspector glanced in both directions up and down the corridor.

"Humphrey said I'd probably be able to catch both of you here," he said in a gravelly undertone, after returning the Sinclairs' greeting. "We may have had a breakthrough, on the Callanish front."

"Come into the office," Adam immediately replied, unlocking the door and standing aside to let McLeod and Philippa enter.

As soon as the door closed behind them, the inspector pulled a folded sheaf of fax flimsies from the inside breast pocket of his overcoat, opening them on Adam's desk as Philippa took a chair and Adam went around behind.

"You remember the sketches Peregrine did up at Callanish?" McLeod began. "Well, the name Taliere didn't seem to be producing any results, so I went back to the sketches and singled out those that showed our elderly bloke in Druid's vestments. I picked out the one that seemed to give the clearest likeness and faxed it to every department up and down the country, along with a note to say that Lothian and Borders Police are seeking to identify this man, and would like to interview him in connection with a case currently under investigation here in Scotland.

"To make a long story short," he went on, "I've had a response from a colleague down in North Wales. It seems this man in Peregrine's drawing is no stranger to the police down there. I've brought a Xerox of the reply. I thought you'd like to read it for yourself."

He presented Adam with a folded sheet of paper. Opening it, Adam saw that the message had been forwarded to McLeod from a Detective Inspector Emrys Davies, of Conwy, in North Wales.

*I believe I know this man,* Davies had written. *The artist's likeness you sent us looks very like a fellow in our bailiwick, name of Griffith Evans. I myself arrested Evans two years ago, for causing a disturbance at a local summer solstice festival. Wiltshire Police are also aware of him in conjunction with disruptions at Stonehenge. At the time of his arrest, Evans owned property in the Conwy Valley. Per a check of local council records, taxes are current, indicative that Evans probably is still resident at that address.*

*Please advise if we can be of any further assistance,* the message continued. *If you still wish to interview Evans, suggest you inform me of proposed arrival, and I will make certain someone is available to collect you and take you out to the site; it doesn't show on maps. Regards, Davies, Det. Insp.*

Adam passed the message over for Philippa to read, then returned his attention to McLeod.

"Well done, indeed," he said. "Your instincts certainly appear to have been solid on this one. Are you going to take Inspector Davies up on his offer?"

"Aye, as soon as I make the necessary arrangements at my end," McLeod replied. "This is early on, so I don't think you need to try to fit this into your schedule. At this point, I'd ordinarily just take the train down, maybe take Donald Cochrane along; but I was thinking it might not be a bad idea to see if I could get Harry Nimmo to fly me down instead. Who knows what he might pick up?"

His faint emphasis on the last two words elicited a faint smile from Adam.

"I agree. It's going to be very interesting to see how Mr. Nimmo continues to develop. By all means, see if he can provide you with air transport. But in case Evans *is* our man, do make sure that both of you take adequate precautions, *on all levels*. We don't know what Callanish was all about. But whoever was responsible apparently has something to hide—and might go to unpleasant lengths to keep it that way."

# CHAPTER NINETEEN

"**N**OEL, why do I have the feeling I'm being set up?" Harry Nimmo asked bluntly, the following morning.

His voice sounded tinny and slightly distanced through the Cessna's headphones. Carlisle lay behind them, and the sprawl and smokestacks of Merseyside smudged the horizon off their port wing as they headed across Liverpool Bay, making for the Cumbrian coast. It was just past ten in the morning.

McLeod cast aside a droll glance at the leather-jacketed man in the pilot's seat.

"Feeling paranoid this morning, Harry?"

"Well, you haven't really told me why you seconded my services for this jaunt," Harry replied. His gaze continued to rove ahead and to the sides for other air traffic, this close to the busy air corridors around Liverpool. "I'm glad to do it— but you could've taken the train down and back in a day, or even flown commercially in and out of Chester and hired a car, or had someone meet you from Conwy. Is this something to do with what happened at Callanish?"

"Now I know how you earned your silk," McLeod quipped. "This is what I get for trying to fool a wily Crown barrister."

"That doesn't answer my question."

McLeod had the grace to grin.

"Fair comment, Counsellor. This does have to do with the Callanish incident. We think we may have located the chap Peregrine sketched at the site. And to answer your next question, yes, I'm hoping you may be able to render similar service, when we go out to where he lives.''

Harry's capable hands tightened on the steering yoke, though his eyes did not cease sweeping the skies before them.

''I was afraid of that.''

''Afraid of what? That it will happen again? I'd think you'd be almighty curious.''

This comment elicited a darting side-glance.

''I suppose I am,'' Harry conceded. ''At least if it happened again, I might be more sure of my ground.''

''In what way?'' McLeod asked.

Harry's forehead furrowed between sunglasses and *Starship Enterprise* baseball cap.

''I suppose I'm concerned because up until recently, I'd never considered myself to be particularly impressionable— quite the reverse, in fact. So maybe you can appreciate how strange it seemed, suddenly to find myself having a—a visionary experience, I suppose I have to call it. It's something I never expected to happen. I'm still not quite sure what to make of it.''

''What do your instincts say?''

''I'm not sure I dare trust my instincts anymore,'' Harry said frankly. ''They've always stood me in good stead— that's part of what makes me good at what I do—but I keep asking myself, Did that really happen, or was it just my imagination playing tricks on me?''

''Which are you more inclined to believe?''

Harry allowed himself a short, mirthless laugh. ''I wish I knew. Oh, I've never had any trouble accepting that there's more to reality than meets the eye. If I've learned nothing else, working with you these last couple of years, it's the fact that, as the bard says, 'There are more things in heaven and earth, Horatio, than are dreamt of in your philosophy.' ''

''There are, indeed,'' McLeod agreed.

''But up until Callanish, all my experiences with paranormal matters had been secondhand, purely supportive,'' Harry protested. ''And I'd been willing to accept all of that on faith. *Since* Callanish, I can't help but wonder, *Why now?*''

"Well, people develop their potentials in different ways, and at different rates," McLeod ventured. "It could simply be that you're a late-bloomer. Or it could be that these talents of yours have been lying dormant until such time as they were needed."

"Implying that I'm going to need them now?" Harry retorted. "I'm not sure I like the sound of that."

McLeod chuckled, shaking his head. "All part of the game, Counsellor. Just keep reminding yourself that psychic talents are merely another aspect of human nature, and subject to development like everything else about being human."

"Right," Harry muttered. "I'll tell myself that, the next time I pick up something and it gives me a psychic bite!"

They touched down soon after at an airstrip near Conwy. Inspector Davies was waiting there to give them cordial welcome, leaning on the open door of a police Land Rover as they buttoned up the plane and came crunching across the new snow of the parking apron. Davies in person was dark and energetic, with a firm handshake, humor in his blue eyes, sharply defined features, and the spare, wide-shouldered stature that had made his forebears masters of the longbow in ages past.

"Good to meet you in person at last, Inspector McLeod." The lilting accents of the Welsh valleys sang in his pleasant tenor. "Mr. Nimmo, I hope you won't be bored coming along on our little outing."

"Nary a chance," Harry replied, with a glance at McLeod. "Working with the inspector is *never* boring."

Davies chuckled as his sweeping gesture invited them to pile into the Land Rover.

"So I gather. His reputation goes before him—all of it good, I hasten to add!"

McLeod took the seat beside Davies, Harry installing himself behind McLeod, both of them buckling up as the Welsh inspector started the engine.

"As you can't have missed as you came in, we've had a fair amount of snow in the last few days," Davies informed his visitors, as he set the car in gear and eased it off the parking apron. "Half of Gwynedd is under snow right now.

Since the cottage your man Evans calls home is deep in the country, I thought I'd better drive you there myself. You'll see what I mean when we get there. Mr. Nimmo, there's a file folder on the seat beside you. Would you hand it up to the inspector, please? That's what we've got on your Griffith Evans.''

With a muttered "Thank you," McLeod took the file Harry passed forward and opened it on his lap, adjusting his aviator spectacles with an absent gesture as he bent to inspect a booking photo of Griffith Evans. Davies said nothing as he negotiated the slip roads leading back to the highway; but as soon as they had joined the A470, tires hissing on the wet pavement, he glanced over at McLeod—now deeply immersed in perusing the rest of the contents of the file folder—then at Harry in the rearview mirror.

"You're lucky the weather held this morning," he said to Harry, making congenial small talk. "Flying can be nasty, this time of year. Now me, I'm a bit of an angler so. Never had much of a head for heights, do you see? One day I mean to venture up to Scotland and try my hand at salmon fishing. But in the meantime, our own Lake Bala *gwyniad* are nothing to complain about, for all they're not so large as their Scottish cousins. I think you call them Powan, elsewhere."

"I've never fished in Wales," Harry allowed, "though I did come here on holiday once, when I was a lad. Is there good fishing around here?"

"Aye, you can get the odd fighter. . . ."

The late morning sky wore a steely shade of blue as Davies drove them south along the wintry wildness of the Conwy Valley, wittering away about Welsh fishing, with the hoary crags of the Cambrian mountains barricading the sky to the west. Leaving his companions to their piscatorial discussion, McLeod gave his full attention to the file in his lap.

There wasn't much to it: besides the booking forms and a computer-generated rap sheet, just a sparse handwritten account of the disturbance which had led to Evans' arrest two years before. He had later been released, the charges dropped.

The facts surrounding the case, however, were sufficient to pique McLeod's interest, for the police photograph was a close match to Peregrine's sketches. To begin with, the incident had taken place at an ancient ring of standing stones known as Druids' Circle, located a few miles to the west of Conwy itself. A local group of latter-day Druids had obtained permission to hold an assembly there in honor of the summer solstice—not a New Age festival cum rock concert such as periodically marred similar gatherings at Stonehenge, but a solemn and dignified attempt to re-create aspects of ancient Druidic practice, in conjunction with a traditional bardic *eisteddfod.*

The celebration had been proceeding harmoniously until Griffith Evans intruded on the scene. His scathing denunciation of the group and their practices had provoked a confrontation that might have ended in a brawl had the police not stepped in—a new wrinkle on an old theme, for the disruption of non-mainstream religious gatherings usually sprang from the self-righteous objections of those outside such traditions. Evans' objections came from within.

"I gather that this Evans presented himself as some kind of arch-Druid in his own right," McLeod remarked, continuing to skim the report. "Claimed he was empowered to make judgements on the validity of what was being done. According to this, he didn't take exception to what your local folk were doing because they were pagans, but because they weren't pagan *enough!*"

"Aye, queer, isn't it?" Davies returned with a wry grimace. "But you get nutters at both ends of the spectrum. Still, the incident was unusual enough to stick in my mind—and Evans is a distinctive-looking old bird. Then, when your fax came through, and I saw the artist's sketch . . ."

"I really do appreciate your passing on the word," McLeod said. "Do you know if Evans had any followers?"

"None that we were able to trace," Davies replied, turning off onto a B-road. "Frankly, I'm inclined to believe he was acting entirely on his own. But that didn't stop him from trying to demonstrate his authority."

"By wringing the necks off a pair of pigeons as a blood sacrifice to the old gods?"

Davies gave a shrug. "Don't ask me to explain; I just report as I find. The fracas broke out when some of the members of the other group tried to stop him. At that point, it seemed a good idea to take Mr. Evans into custody, for the benefit of all concerned.'' Davies shook his head. ''I've seen fundamentalist Christians and Jews, and fundamentalist Muslims and Hindus, but the one thing I don't think I ever expected to see was a fundamentalist Druid!''

''Fanatics come in all varieties, I suppose,'' McLeod said neutrally.

''Was this the only incident of its kind that Evans was involved in?'' Harry asked from the back seat.

''This and that Stonehenge arrest that's listed on the rap sheet,'' Davies returned, ''and to the best of our knowledge, he hasn't caused any trouble since. Since I wasn't sure this is the man you're after, I only ran him through our local records; but what he might have been getting up to outside our jurisdiction is something else again.''

After another mile or two they slowed almost to a halt before an un-signposted break in the trees that flanked the west side of the road. Shifting into four-wheel drive, Davies swung the Land Rover ponderously off the tarmac onto what proved to be a snow-covered, tree-flanked track scarcely wider than the vehicle, showing no sign of recent passage save for deer and rabbit spoor.

A silence born of more than snow seemed to muffle the vehicle as they penetrated deeper into the wood. Harry released his seat harness and leaned forward to peer between the two front seats as the rutted trail plunged them along an overgrown obstacle course of thickets and boulders, with here and there a haphazard bridge of planks laid down across a shallow gully. The temperature seemed to drop, even though Davies had not touched the thermostat control on the vehicle's heater.

''Watch the deer!'' Harry warned, bracing himself as Davies braked hard for a five-point stag that suddenly bolted across their path and bounded from sight among the trees. ''Wow, what a beauty! But I see what you mean about this Evans character not wanting anything much to do with the rest of the world.''

''Aye, how'd you like to be the postman in charge of delivering *his* mail?'' Davies quipped.

McLeod was too preoccupied to do more than shake his head. The density of the surrounding woods, even in winter, seemed to absorb the rumble and crunch of the Land Rover's tires on the icy ground, leaving behind a lurking hush pregnant with hostility. The atmosphere became more oppressive, the further they proceeded. Convinced that more was at work here than the forces of nature, McLeod surreptitiously reached into the inner pocket of his jacket and slipped on his Adept ring.

"How much farther?" he murmured.

"Not far," Davies replied.

The trail carried on in a succession of zigzags, darker and darker as they meandered through increasingly dense stands of bare, ice-laden trees. When they rounded yet another left-hand bend in the track, they emerged without warning into a brighter patch of broad, snow-covered clearing. Only at second glance did McLeod and Harry spot the freestone cottage set far at the other side, overshadowed by a glowering ridge of high ground.

Squat and graceless, the cottage might have been rough-hewn from the rock of the valley wall, even remaining a part of it. Its window recesses were small and skewed, and seemed to brood like so many deep-set eyes from beneath the low slate roof. The chimney canted slightly, suggesting that the house itself had fallen victim to subsidence in the past.

"Not exactly a stately home, is it?" McLeod murmured.

"*I* certainly wouldn't want to live here," Davies said. "Evans has got his own electrical generator—it's housed in that shed you can see from here—but that would seem to be his sole concession to twentieth-century living. The phone company won't run a line all the way out here, and I'm not even sure he has indoor plumbing."

They parked the Land Rover at the edge of the clearing and got out.

"There's no smoke rising from the chimney," Harry observed, "and no noise coming from the generator. Call me a pessimist, but I don't think there's anybody home."

"Then nobody's going to mind if we take a look around,"

Davies said, blowing on gloved hands. "We'll announce ourselves first, for the sake of form."

The air seemed unnaturally still as they approached the cottage. Though the cold was bitter, and McLeod was three-quarters convinced that the place was unoccupied, he found himself unbuttoning his overcoat to allow access to the Browning Hi-Power he had clipped inside his waistband before alighting from the plane. Harry kept looking around suspiciously. Davies apparently was experiencing a similar case of nerves, for he gave McLeod a thumbs-up sign as he spotted the butt of the Browning, though he himself appeared to be unarmed.

"Mr. Evans, are you there?" he called, hammering a gloved fist on the door. "Mr. Evans, it's Inspector Davies and Inspector McLeod from the police. We'd like to have a word with you."

There was no response from inside. Davies raised his voice and shouted again, with no better results. Turning to McLeod, he cocked an eyebrow. "Well, what do you think?"

"I think," McLeod said pointedly, "that after coming all this way, I would hate to leave without at least checking to make sure Mr. Evans isn't lying dead of a heart attack on his own kitchen floor. Or he could have perished from the cold. After all, as Harry pointed out, I don't see any sign of chimney smoke, do you?"

"How very right you are," Davies concurred with aplomb. "I wonder whether he might have left a spare key under the mat."

# CHAPTER TWENTY

THERE was no key—not that any of them expected to find one—but with the aid of a bit of wire and a lock-pick Davies produced from his wallet, they managed to get the door open without damaging the lock. Entering, they found themselves in a narrow vestibule flanked by doors to either side, with a cobwebby gasolier hanging from the ceiling. Directly ahead of them, a solidly built flight of stairs led to the floor above.

"Hello?" Davies called, sweeping the beam of a powerful torch around the room. "Police officers, Mr. Evans. Anyone home?"

Still receiving no response, Davies tried the door leading off to the left. The toilet and tiny sink beyond were antiquated, but functional.

"I guess that answers your question about the plumbing, anyway," McLeod said to Davies, producing a smaller torch from a side coat pocket. "Let's see what else we can find."

Davies elected to take a look around upstairs, leaving McLeod and Harry to finish surveying the ground floor. Still not quite convinced that the house was empty, McLeod drew his coat back from the butt of his Browning before cautiously opening the door to the right of the stairs.

The doorway gave access to a dim, musty sitting room, with two deeply recessed windows piercing the east wall. Through gaps in the threadbare curtains, enough light filtered into the room to make out a high-backed black oak settle opposite the grey stone fireplace and hearth, flanked by a pair of rush-bottomed chairs. The wall adjoining the windows was dominated by a ponderous oaken sideboard laden with dusty blue and white china and a few pewter serving pieces. At some point in the decades long past, the gaslight wall sconces to either end of the sideboard had been electrified, but the overall appearance of the room suggested that little else might have changed for a century or more.

Harry drew a deep breath and saw his exhalation turn into a plume of white steam.

"I think it's even colder in here than it is outside!" he muttered. "If the temperature's anything to go by, this room hasn't been used for quite some time."

"Probably not for the last fortnight, if not longer," McLeod hazarded, as he swept his torch around the room, thinking back to Callanish. "Wherever this Evans may have gone, I have an uncomfortable notion that he isn't planning to come back."

A secondary door in the west wall led along a short corridor to a large kitchen running the entire length of the back of the house. The plaster overlaying the stone walls had been given a coat of whitewash that now was dingy with age. Harry fished a mini-Maglite out of a pocket of his leather jacket as McLeod swept his light across a tarnished array of copper pans and outmoded cooking utensils displayed on hooks above an old-fashioned coal-burning cookstove.

"I've feel like I've stepped through a time portal," Harry murmured as he and McLeod examined the age-stained porcelain sinks and wooden countertops. "I shouldn't think this place has been refurbished since the reign of Queen Victoria."

"I've seen cheerier morgues in my day," McLeod said with unsparing candor. "Let's move on."

A large walk-in pantry lay at the far end of the kitchen. After probing it with his light, McLeod entered to find himself confronted by an array of shelves running from floor to ceiling on all three sides. The boards underfoot had been overlaid with a worn sheet of linoleum that stopped several inches short of the skirting boards all around. The air was thick with the smell of mildew and mouse-droppings. Coming in behind McLeod, Harry took a sniff and curled his lip.

"Whew, not up to even my bachelor standards of housekeeping. D'you suppose he really lives this way? It has to be a health hazard.''

"It isn't physical health hazards I'm worried about," McLeod muttered.

Together the two men inspected the contents of the pantry. The storage space to the left of the doorway held a spartan range of food staples. All the sacks and tins were generically packaged.

"Flour . . . salt . . . sugar . . . lard," McLeod read aloud, moving along the shelves. "Whatever else he may be, this Evans stocks his kitchen like a survivalist."

"Maybe he still thinks there's a war on," Harry offered with a sardonic lift of one eyebrow.

"Candles . . . matches . . . kerosene lamps," McLeod continued, carrying on with his survey. "Either our man is expecting a siege, or he doesn't have much faith in privatized utilities."

He took a step backward, hoping to get a better view of the upper shelves. As he did so, he felt the floor give way slightly beneath one heel. His muttered exclamation of surprise alerted Harry, who had started to light one of the kerosene lamps.

"What is it?"

"I'm not sure," McLeod said, bending to look at the floor. "Bring that light down here. Yes, indeed." He shone his own light along the edge of the linoleum, now revealed as a crack that went right around the square.

"Right," McLeod murmured, running his fingers under the area where his heel had pressed. "I think we've found the way into the cellar. Help me lift this trapdoor."

Though the two of them braced themselves to tug, the trapdoor lifted with unexpected ease. A dark cavity yawned below, with a wooden ladder extending downwards into the shadows.

"This is beginning to get interesting," Harry said, as McLeod shone his torch down into the opening. "Should we give Davies a shout?"

"Not before we've had a chance to reconnoiter," McLeod said, testing the first rung of the ladder. "I shouldn't want to frighten our good inspector. Bring that lantern, and let's see what's lurking in the cellar.''

The cellar proved to be a cramped, rectangular chamber perhaps six feet by ten, with a trestle table under the angle of the ladder and wooden tea chests stacked untidily at one end. The other end was screened behind upright stacks of old timber and worm-eaten planking, the floor in between littered with half-open boxes and burst packing cases, like the flotsam washed up from a wrecked cargo ship. Looking around him by the flickering glow of the kerosene lamp, Harry gave a disparaging grunt.

''I'm not sure what you're looking for,'' he muttered, ''but this looks like mostly storage to me.''

''Maybe more than that,'' McLeod replied. ''Have a look down at that end, and I'll look over here. But don't touch anything unless I tell you it's all right.''

''Roger that.''

After hanging the lantern on a central hook, Harry turned his cautious attention to the indicated boards and packing cases. McLeod had not said as much to Harry, but the atmosphere in the cellar was tainted with subliminal resonances of a kind that bespoke unwholesome occult activity. Pivoting around in a circle, he tried to home in on the source of the disturbance, but to no avail. He sighed inwardly as he abandoned his efforts and resigned himself to the prospect of a more laborious search.

Near at hand was a stout wooden table lying across trestles, its work surface scarred by what seemed to be saw-cuts, and stained with a hodgepodge of tinctures. Sagging shelves at one side of the table supported a bewildering jumble of crocks, bottles, and jars, all of them so covered in dust that their labels were indecipherable, even when McLeod shone the full light of his torch upon them.

Keeping casual note of Harry's whereabouts, McLeod sidled past an overturned stool to gain closer access to the shelves. Selecting a jar at random, he took it down and blew away enough dust to read the handwritten label.

''*Conium maculatum*,'' he murmured under his breath. His knowledge of herbalism was limited, but he knew enough about toxicology to recognize the Latin name for hemlock.

Not unexpectedly, in a Druid's workbench, the jar next to it was half-filled with waxy white berries that looked to McLeod like mistletoe. The label confirmed his identification: *Viscum album.*

Further search brought to light a wide assortment of vegetable and mineral compounds. Some of the mixtures were clearly medicinal; others were more suspect. McLeod was just considering taking away a few samples for analysis when a sudden gasp from Harry made him look sharply around.

The counsellor was standing frozen over by the far wall, his back to McLeod, gripping a length of loose planking with both hands, as if arrested in the act of lifting it.

Instantly McLeod darted toward him. Simultaneously, Harry snatched his hands away and jerked backwards, colliding hard with McLeod.

"Jesus, what's the matter, Harry?" McLeod demanded, as Harry caught his balance. "I told you not to touch anything!"

Nodding, Harry took a gulp of air and pointed to the timber-lined wall in front of them.

"I didn't think you meant scrap wood," he said huskily. "There's another room beyond this one, behind that timber façade. I didn't exactly . . . *see* it—not with my eyes—but I know it's there. The entrance is behind these boards."

McLeod made haste to clear the boards away, Harry craning his neck to see what lay beyond, for McLeod made him stand well back. The labor exposed an irregular opening in the wall, more like the entrance to a cave than a doorway, with a crudely painted succession of runic symbols surmounting the arch. Playing his torch across them, and motioning Harry closer with the lantern, McLeod recognized several Druidic symbols of warding—and a few of them looked familiar.

Tight-lipped, he whipped out his notebook and flipped to the pages carrying the transcriptions he had made at the Callanish stone circle. Many of the symbols were identical, with even their combinations in common. If this was not proof that the owner of the house had been an active participant in the events at Callanish, it was certainly suggestive—and there was no doubting the malignancy of the present wards.

Fortunately, the initial power invested in these runes had largely dissipated, though their hostile influence was still palpable at close range. Handing his torch to Harry, McLeod groped in his pocket for a pencil, then copied down the newly discovered inscriptions on a separate page before returning notebook and pencil to his pocket. Then he took back his torch and shone its beam through the opening—a brighter light than that of Harry's lantern.

But he would not allow Harry to follow him inside. Touching his Adept ring to his lips, McLeod commended himself to the protection of the Light, concluding that prayer with a gesture of personal warding before moving forward.

The chamber he entered gave the appearance of having been quarried out of solid rock, its sloping walls roughly finished and surmounted by a low vaulted roof. The shape and size of the chamber suggested the interior of a burial mound. His probing torch-beam revealed no other entrance or exit, but it soon caught the design painted on the cavern's stone floor—a red-brown circle quartered by two intersecting lines. He preferred not to think of what had gone into the paint, though he sensed that the blood was animal, not human.

At the center of the circle, where the two lines crossed, a stunted pillar of dark stone bore traces of more blood along its length. Eight lesser stones made a Faerie ring around the circle's perimeter. Squinting against the reflected glare of the torch, McLeod saw that the dark-stained tops of all the standing stones had been hollowed out, like offertory bowls.

There was no mistaking the ritualistic character of the layout. Equally apparent to McLeod's deeper senses was the chaotic nature of the forces that this place was intended to honor and invoke.

"Don't come in," he called to his companion. "Go and fetch me one of those big bags of salt, and then go upstairs and see what Davies is doing. Try not to let him come down here. I have to do something."

To his relief, Harry gave no argument, receding footsteps telling of his obedience. McLeod moved forward, but soon encountered a field of resistance that set his nerves jangling with sudden inimical dissonance.

Gritting his teeth, he thrust forward the stiffened blade of his hand in a determined push until he felt the field collapse, falling in tatters behind him as he, too, passed into the circle. Here his cautious torch-beam discovered evidence of animal sacrifice in the form of scattered small bones still bearing shreds of fur and feathers—perhaps the source of the blood that had stained the stones. The standing stone at the center of the ring bore a string of runic symbols executed in the same gory medium.

As far as McLeod was concerned, no clearer evidence was needed to forge a connection between the owner of this house and the arch-Druid whose likeness Peregrine had captured at Callanish. But this in turn led to further questions. The atmosphere within the chamber was saturated with unclean resonances, bespeaking years of secretive use. What could have prompted Evans to emerge so suddenly from obscurity two years ago, only to retire again until the present, Callanish incident?

He had the feeling that the answer was hovering elusively just out of reach. Just now, however, he had neither the privacy nor the time to spare for introspection. There were no clues to indicate when or if Evans intended to return here. But McLeod's own duty clearly dictated that this underground sanctuary must be rendered untenable to those shadowy forces it was meant to serve. He had scuffed out the painted circle and was kicking over the outer stones when Harry called to him from the entrance to the place.

''Noel, I've got your salt.''

''Thanks,'' McLeod replied. ''Now, go upstairs with Davies. I'll explain later.''

Harry gave a nod and disappeared a second time, and McLeod returned to his work, ripping open the bag of salt and murmuring a litany of purification as he scattered the bag's contents around the room by the handful. Within the space of less than a minute, the floor was covered with a glistening carpet of white powder. For good measure, McLeod set one booted foot against the central pillar and pushed. When it toppled over, it made more of a thump than the smaller ones had done, but hopefully Davis would not have heard it.

Breathing a final prayer of exorcism, McLeod headed back for the exit from the place. Adam, no doubt, would know who to send at a later date to finish the demolition work he had started.

In the meantime, however, satisfied that this chapel of shadows could not readily be put to its former use, McLeod quickly made to replace the boards concealing the cavern's entrance before ascending the ladder to the floor above. There he found Harry and his lantern, both perched on the edge of the kitchen table. The counsellor was alone.

"What's happened to Davies?" McLeod asked.

"He's been going through some personal papers he found in a box under Evans's bed," Harry replied. "I told him you were still poking around, and that we'd be up to join him directly."

"That's true enough," McLeod agreed, as they closed the trapdoor and left the pantry. "I don't think we need to say anything about the cellar, do you?"

Harry gave him a sly, conspiratorial glance. "I gather there's nothing down there that would be of any material help to Inspector Davies," he said.

"It could be awkward," McLeod agreed.

"And that's part of your job—to keep awkward questions from being asked." Harry shook his head resignedly. "Well, far be it from me to interfere. I didn't see a thing. But you did say you'd explain later. Maybe on the way home, once we're safely aloft?"

"Maybe," McLeod said noncommittally.

# CHAPTER TWENTY-ONE

"I should have insisted that they let Humphrey drive them into town," Adam said, eyeing the winter sky from a library window at Strathmourne. "It looks like snow. I hate to think of them stalling out on the side of the road somewhere between here and the Forth Road Bridge."

"Then *don't* think of it, darling. Or why not worry about them stalling *on* the Forth Road Bridge, if you're determined to worry about them?" Philippa said over the top of the needlework she was stitching, ensconced in a wing chair beside the library fire. The "them" under discussion were Ximena and Julia, who had taken the Morgan into Edinburgh for a consultation with a dressmaker. "Your mechanic gave the car a thorough going-over. It was purring like a kitten when they left."

"Adam's learning a new way to worry, now that he's settling into a married frame of mind," Peregrine said with a grin, from a vantage point in one of the window seats that overlooked the approach to the house. "Why do you think Julia and I got a mobile phone, Adam? Fortunately, she's got it with her today. If anything goes wrong, they can summon the cavalry at the touch of a button. Ah, here comes Noel now."

He set a mug of tea aside and rose expectantly as McLeod's black BMW appeared at the head of the snow-bordered drive and made brisk passage toward the house, pulling up in front of the steps. The inspector had telephoned Adam with a brief account of his trip to Wales the night before, but sensitive details were to be rendered in person this afternoon. Prior commitments had prevented Julian and the Houstons from attending the impromptu briefing session called by Adam, but Peregrine was as eager as Adam and Philippa to hear what McLeod had learned.

Humphrey admitted the inspector very shortly. McLeod looked frazzled, and carried a manila envelope under one arm. As Humphrey closed the door behind him, Philippa said, "Hello, Noel. Cup of tea? You look like you could use one."

McLeod quirked a grim smile and inclined his head in acceptance as he came to collapse in a chair beside her.

"Aye, that would be grand. Sorry if I'm a bit later than I'd planned. I got waylaid by a public prosecutor just as I was leaving the office, and he wanted to talk about a case that's pending. I thought I'd never get rid of him."

Philippa set a mug of tea in front of him, adding a splash of milk. "The main thing is that you're here now," she said. "Adam, Peregrine, do you want anything else?"

"Not just now," Adam said, as Peregrine also declined. "So, tell us about Griffith Evans."

The envelope McLeod had brought with him contained a copy of Evans' police file, complete with the fingerprint record. While the others examined the documents enclosed, the inspector embarked on an uncompromising report of his findings. Adam noted Harry Nimmo's part in the operation with particular interest.

"Our Mr. Nimmo's psychometric talents are clearly blossoming," Adam observed thoughtfully. "One almost has to wonder whether something about this case has triggered their development."

"Aye," McLeod agreed. "I was thinking much the same thing myself. Don't get me wrong," he amended. "Harry's a good man—and if he's meant to take on a more active role, I'd be the first to welcome him. At the same time, if the Powers That Be have arranged to send us reinforcements, it makes me wonder if there may be bigger trouble ahead than we realize."

Pulling out his notebook, he showed them the two sets of symbols he had copied down, one made at Callanish and the other in the cellar at Conwy.

"As you can see, most of the same symbols appear in both locations," he pointed out. "And the chamber we found was set up to mimic more traditional stone circles—though with a decidedly nasty edge, given all the evidence of blood sacrifices. I'm not yet prepared to state categorically that Evans and the mastermind at Callanish are one and the same. But whatever else turns out to be true about him, this Evans character appears to have an intimate knowledge of Druidic ceremonies and rituals—perhaps more than anyone could hope to acquire in a single lifetime. Furthermore, I think there's little question that he's using that knowledge to foster contact with one or another of the Patrons of Shadow—'the dark side of the Force,' as young Iolo MacFarlane might put it."

Adam raised an eyebrow. "Isn't that how he described what he felt on New Year's Eve? A 'disturbance in the Force'?"

McLeod blinked. "I suppose he did."

Peregrine sat forward avidly, his hazel gaze darting from one to the other of them. "Noel, did you pick that phrase for a reason?" he asked.

"Or did it kick in from your subconscious?" Philippa joined in. "That isn't a phrase you'd be likely to use, Noel. Could it be that, on some level, you *have* made the connection between Evans and what happened at Callanish?"

"It's possible," McLeod conceded.

"Well, whether or not the two perpetrators are one and the same," Adam said, "we appear to have a situation that needs nipping in the bud. Noel, how long would you estimate this underground hallow has been in use?"

McLeod grimaced. "Difficult to judge. The atmosphere was so thick in there, you could almost cut it with a knife. I'd say a long, long time—maybe even decades."

"Decades?" Peregrine murmured. "How could that be? I mean, isn't there some equivalent to our own Hunting Lodge down in Wales? Wouldn't someone have noticed?"

"The English have a loose confederation of several groups that perform some of the same functions we do," Philippa said. "But unless Evans had done something to draw attention to himself, it's quite possible he could have gone unnoticed—particularly since he seems to have gone to considerable lengths to keep a low profile.''

''There *was* that incident at Druids' Circle, two years ago,'' McLeod pointed out.

''That hardly counts,'' Philippa said, shaking her head. ''I very much doubt much serious energy was raised on that occasion. 'A mere ripple in the Force,' as your young Iolo might say.''

''Perhaps you're right,'' Adam agreed. ''But the episode does tell us one thing of value. It tells us that Evans apparently has nothing but a deep and withering contempt for all modern interpreters of Druid tradition—which suggests that his own esoteric roots go back to very ancient sources.''

''How so?'' Peregrine asked.

''Well, leaving the Callanish incident aside for the moment, everything else Noel has been able to discover about Evans makes him out to be a solitary recluse who, for whatever reason, shuns contact with the rest of the world. He has, as far as we can tell, no family, no friends, and no known associates. His whole life would seem to be centered in his work as an occultist—and up till now, that is something he has pursued alone and in secret, never seriously venturing outside the hidden hallow he has created for his own private use.

''Callanish, on the other hand, was a large-scale operation. It simply could not have been carried out by one man on his own. We know from Peregrine's drawings that Evans was there, in full ceremonial regalia, presumably as the director of the ritual. But there were a number of others present as well—a fact which raises several important questions.''

He began ticking off items on his fingers. ''To begin with, what could have motivated Evans to come out hiding after all these years spent in apparently deliberate obscurity? Next, why Callanish, rather than someplace closer to home? And finally, was Evans himself the instigator, summoning outside support for a venture of his own devising, or was he himself recruited as figurehead for an operation conceived by someone else?''

''That's a lot of questions,'' Peregrine said. ''So far, we're not even sure if Evans is this fellow's real name.''

"True," Philippa agreed. "But your comment about other Hunting Lodges has made me think of someone who might be able to give us some answers. He himself doesn't work in a Druid tradition, but he'll know who does—both the legitimate ones and those who skate closer to the Abyss." Her dark eyes shifted to meet Adam's. "Do you want to phone him, or shall I?"

"I will," Adam said.

"Phone who?" Peregrine asked.

But Adam was already moving toward the telephone on the desk. A quick flick through his desktop Rolodex gave him the number he wanted. After three rings, he got a response.

"Oakwood," said a discreet male voice.

"Hello, Linton. This is Adam Sinclair, ringing from Scotland. If he's available, I'd like a word with Sir John."

He glanced back at them as he waited for the call to be relayed to Gen. Sir John Graham.

"Adam! This is a delightful surprise! What can I do for you?"

"Hello, Gray. I wish I could say that this was purely a social call, but the truth of the matter is, I'm hoping you can give me some information."

"Ah, looking to put the old warhorse back into harness, are you?" Graham said equably. "I'll do my best to oblige. What kind of information are you after?"

"I'm trying to locate a man who calls himself Griffith Evans."

"Griffith Evans." Graham paused a beat. "No, I can't say that the name rings any bells. Could it be a pseudonym?"

"How about Taliere?" Adam ventured.

"Now, that sounds a bit more familiar. Welsh, maybe—but so is Griffith Evans. What's the context?"

"We have reason to believe that this Evans may have been involved in an incident that took place up here in the Hebrides about a week before the new year," Adam said. "It may not have made the papers down in London, but it caused quite a stir up here. There were certain—ah—Druidic aspects," he added carefully.

"I see," Graham replied, in a tone that conveyed full understanding and attention. "Please go on."

"Well, we haven't been able to establish for certain that Taliere and this Evans are one and the same," Adam said, "but two of my colleagues were able to trace Evans as far as a cottage in North Wales. Unfortunately, Mr. Evans himself was nowhere to be found, so the trail peters out there. We do have a set of his fingerprints, courtesy of the police in Conwy, and we can connect him to a couple of very minor incidents in the last ten years, but the usual police sources run dry beyond that point."

"So you're hoping for alternative sources of information," Graham said.

"I am," Adam replied, smiling to himself. "I seem to recall that you have or had access to certain sources that—ah—are not available to the civilian authorities. That being so, I was hoping I might prevail upon you to do some checking on our behalf."

"I'll be more than happy to assist," came Graham's response, "though I can't guarantee success, with so little to go on."

"There is one more item that may help," Adam said. "We have a mug shot of Evans, and also an artist's impression of what Taliere looks like, done up at Callanish by Peregrine Lovat."

"Ah, young Lovat. From what I recall of your young artist-friend's abilities, that ought to be as good as a photograph. Yes, those and a set of fingerprints should suffice to get me started. Do you have access to a fax machine?"

"I can send through the material within the hour," Adam promised. "Is it the same number?"

"One digit after."

"Right. Thank you, Gray. I appreciate your help, as always."

"Happy to oblige. Incidentally, I don't suppose your mother is there, by any chance? I've been meaning to ring you since the new year. I had a very vivid dream about her."

Adam turned to grin at Philippa, who had risen expectantly from her chair.

"She's here with me now, Gray. I'll put her on."

✦ ✦ ✦

After handing the phone to Philippa, Adam took McLeod and Peregrine off to the kitchen to fetch fresh tea and to give his mother privacy. She was back at her needlework by the time they returned with the new pot of tea and a tray of fresh scones and sandwiches, but she offered no details of her conversation with John Graham. While she distributed the tea, Adam assembled the documents to be faxed through to Graham and sent them. Ximena and Julia returned shortly thereafter, effectively ending the morning's business; but until Graham came up with a new direction for their investigations, further speculation was unlikely to produce any useful results.

No inspiration came during sleep to change Adam's estimation of the situation. Aware that it might well take time for Sir John to complete his research, Adam drove in to work the following morning with no expectation of any immediate breakthroughs. After teaching rounds, he saw patients for the rest of the day, with hardly a break for lunch, and by four o'clock had finally retreated to his office to update his case notes for the day. He answered the buzz of his phone somewhat distractedly, but immediately shifted focus on hearing the voice at the other end of the line.

"Hello, Adam, it's Gray. Are you alone?"

"I am," Adam replied, "but you know this line."

"Yes, I do." A note of suppressed tension clipped the voice of Sir John Graham. "I have some information for you, but I'd rather not relay it by telephone. Could we meet up face to face to discuss it?"

"Certainly," Adam said, turning the page of his desk calendar. "I've got two therapy sessions scheduled for tomorrow morning, but I could probably catch the noon shuttle and be with you for tea tomorrow afternoon."

"I'd rather discuss it sooner than that," Graham said. "If you were to call upon me tonight, you would find the door open."

Adam caught his breath slightly as he realized that the senior Adept was not proposing a physical meeting, but one on the astral plane, as one Adept to another.

"I am entirely at your disposal," he said carefully. "Just tell me when and where to seek you out."

"Let's say ten o'clock, in the gazebo," Graham said. "I believe you already know the way through the maze."

As Adam rang off, he reflected that it was perhaps just as well that Ximena was working the evening shift at Edinburgh Royal Infirmary, for that meant she was unlikely to be getting home much before half-past eleven. He would have to forego dinner—fasting was a desirable preparation for any form of serious occult endeavor—but Philippa certainly understood that; and Ximena's absence simplified the situation for everyone concerned.

Returning home shortly after six, Adam retired to his room for a shower and change of clothes, then a brief rest until it was time to work. His mind had been restless and unfocused all the way home, turning this way and that in troubled speculation about the nature of the information Graham had promised to impart. He put on his Adept ring before lying down in shirtsleeves and his dressing gown, also pulling a light blanket over himself. Only after putting himself through a short breathing exercise was he able to drift off into a light sleep.

He roused some hours later to the distant chime of the grandfather clock in the downstairs hall. A glance at his bedside clock told him that the appointed hour was fast approaching. Casting aside his blanket, he thrust his stockinged feet into the crested slippers waiting on the floor by the bedside and headed down to the library.

Humphrey had already seen to it that a fire was burning on the hearth and the drapes were tightly drawn. Closing the door behind him, Adam turned the key in the lock, then went over to the house phone on his desk.

"Hello, Humphrey. I'll be unavailable for the next hour or so. Divert all calls until further notice. Philippa will deal with anything that needs urgent attention."

"Very good, sir."

Knowing that his valet could be trusted to uphold those instructions, Adam doused the room's electric lights and made his way back to the hearth by firelight alone, pausing to toss an incense stick into the flames before settling into his favorite fireside chair. The mingled fragrance of cinnamon and myrrh teased at his nostrils as he put his feet up on a footstool, and he inhaled deeply of their perfume while he briefly closed his eyes, testing the security of the wards around the house. Then, after taking a long moment to center himself, he fixed his gaze on the heart of the flames.

The shimmer of light and shadow was like a dance, drawing him slowly downward in a spiral toward his soul's center point, as his eyelids drifted closed. Sinking past the threshold between waking and trance, Adam became aware of a complementary resonance permeating the air around him, pulsing with the rhythm of his heartbeat. Gradually the resonance grew more articulate, assuming a formal pattern of repetition. Hearkening to the summons, Adam was reminded of the beating of a great drum.

The drumbeat became a wall of sound. The wall became an onrushing tidal wave, sweeping him off his feet to carry him away. As he rode the crest of the wave, content to ride it out, a distant shore loomed ahead, its dark tree line surmounted by a firmament of stars.

The shoreline converged with breathtaking speed. A sudden, shadowy plunge left him lying slightly breathless on a smooth stretch of turf before the maze gateway at Oakwood, shining silvery in the moonlight.

In the waking world it was winter and the moon was waning. Here, by contrast, the night was balmy and the full moon shone with a radiance almost as bright as day.

Rising to his feet, Adam approached the gateway, now robed in the formal soutane of sapphire-blue symbolic of his office and calling. The gate itself was standing ajar, in token of John Graham's invitation, glimmering like silver filigree in the light of the moon as Adam slipped fearlessly through the gap, mindful of Graham's parting words. Beyond lay the shadowy convolutions of a boxwood maze. Looking down, Adam found himself standing at the head of a white-pebbled path.

As he paused, more in preparation than from any apprehension, the drumbeat took up its rhythm once more, soft but compelling, again precisely on the rhythm of his heartbeat. Obedient to its summons, Adam set out for the heart of the maze, paying no mind to the alternative pathways that branched occasionally to left or right, bathed in the radiance of the moonlight as he followed the intended path and suddenly found himself at the center point, before the fairy-tale arches and cupola of a Victorian gazebo.

The moonlight silvered the roses threading the gazebo's trellised walls, which filtered patterned moonlight onto the wooden floor. A tall, dark-robed figure stood waiting in the arched doorway at the top of the wooden steps, a cowl obscuring his features, a shining sword cocked over one shoulder. As Adam advanced, the blade came down to bar his way, fire rippling along its length, but he did not hesitate to mount the four steps, halting at the threshold with the blade at his throat as a deep voice proclaimed the ritual challenge.

''*Who comes?*''

The question was part of a time-honored formula, Adam's response unhesitating.

''Adam, Master of the Hunt and servant of the Light, duly sworn.''

His challenger's head inclined and the sword was lowered, its fire dying to a mere glow.

''Enter and be welcome, Adam, Master of the Hunt and servant of the Light,'' the challenger said, sweeping back his cowl as he stepped aside in invitation.

As time was reckoned in the material, the man Adam had come here to meet was nearly twice his own age. Here, however, Adam needed no second glance to recognize John Graham in the individual who stood before him now, strong and vigorous as Adam himself, with flashing hazel eyes and dark hair untouched by time. Nor was this appearance of vitality any mere trick of the eye—rather, a vision of Graham in his immortal semblance, revealed by the timeless moonlight of this consecrated place as a very senior Adept of the Inner Planes.

When Adam had joined him within the confines of the gazebo, Graham briskly drew the tip of the sword three times across the threshold. Adam could feel the protective barriers strengthen with each stroke. As final warding, Graham laid the blade itself across the opening before gesturing toward a round table set at the center of the floor, where three lighted candles—black, white, and red—made a flickering triangle on the white-draped surface. The table was flanked by two waiting chairs.

With a smile, Graham invited Adam to be seated. Sinking into the chair opposite, he said, "I see you had no trouble finding the way. Thank you for coming."

"It is I who should be thanking *you*," Adam answered. "It was very generous of you to bear a hand in this inquiry."

A more sober look clouded Graham's lean face. "As it happens, this inquiry concerns me as much as it does you—though the evidence linking our interests dates back to a time before you were born. Your instincts in coming to me were entirely correct. I doubt if anyone else now alive could have made the connections necessary to link this man who now calls himself Evans with his own buried past."

This cryptic statement gave Adam a prickling sensation at the base of his skull, for John Graham was not prone to exaggeration.

"What, exactly, have you learned?" he asked.

"Enough to give me cause for grave concern," Graham replied. "To begin with, it isn't Taliere that's the pseudonym—it's *Evans*. The name Jasper Taliere occupies a curious place in the classified annals of military intelligence. And for the past fifty years, he's been on file as missing, presumed dead."

At the mention of military intelligence, Adam raised an eyebrow. Mentally performing a quick mathematical calculation, he said, "That would make him active during the Second World War. Am I to understand that he was some kind of spy?"

"Not a spy," Graham corrected. "A terrorist—though the term had not yet been coined in those days."

At Adam's look of inquiry, he continued. "As you well know, when Hitler came to power, the Nazi regime was not without its sympathizers here in this country. From the very outset of the war, there were some who actively collaborated with the enemy, seeing the threatened invasion of England as an opportunity to further their own schemes for aggrandizement.

"Jasper Taliere was hardly more than a boy at the time,

but he was old enough to harbor a host of resentful ambitions. Spurred on by dreams of power, he was among those who took part in a well-orchestrated campaign to bring havoc to our cities—a campaign all the more terrible and effective because it was carried out with the aid of supernatural powers.''

Adam was well aware of whispered tales concerning the existence of certain black lodges operating within the Third Reich, whose members had utilized their esoteric talents in support of their patron's designs for world conquest. Aware of a sudden chill creeping into his bones, he asked, ''What, exactly, was Taliere doing?''

Graham's jaw hardened. ''Committing very specialized acts of sabotage—some directed at destroying national monuments, others aimed at wiping out key individuals associated with the wartime government. To this day, I doubt we'll ever know the full extent of the damage that was done. But one thing I *am* sure of: By the time certain of my colleagues were able to bring the situation under control, these sabotage operations had cost the lives of hundreds—possibly even thousands.''

As Adam shook his head in horrified wonderment, Graham went on.

''It started in the early days of the Blitz. When the air strikes first began, the devastation seemed as random as it was widespread. As the raids continued, however, it came to our attention that the number of direct hits on politically significant targets was disproportionately high. We thought at first that the Germans had perfected some kind of highly sophisticated internal guidance system for their bombs. Then one of my own special agents in the field managed to intercept information which enabled us to piece together the truth.

''Taliere and his fellow-collaborators were using the bombing raids as convenient camouflage under which to carry out a parallel campaign of attack. The damage they were wreaking was caused not by explosives, but by lightning. This lightning was no natural phenomenon, but an emanation from the realms of chaos. The giver of the lightning was none other than one of the storm gods of old.''

Adam caught his breath. All at once, this was beginning to have an eerily familiar ring.

"How did they determine where the lightning was to strike?" he asked.

"By leaving a votive object at the site to draw down the lightning charge," Graham replied. "Those few we were able to recover and neutralize took the form of disk-shaped bronze medallions bearing a symbol that my people dubbed the lightning rune. It was not unlike the double-S *sigrunen* insignia adopted by the SS. Even at the time, it was suggested that this symbol might be part of a secret Pictish alphabet reserved for ceremonial use. But in those days, all that seemed certain was that the rune was intended to invoke the destructive power of Taranis, the ancient lightning god of pagan times."

"Taranis," Adam repeated softly. If Taliere was a votary of Taranis, the incident at Callanish suddenly began to take on a new dimension—and to connect with an old adversary. Taranis had been the dark Patron invoked in the slaying of Randall Stewart, and in a series of lightning strikes directed against prominent Freemasons—and Francis Raeburn had been at the heart of the operation, allied with another black magician whose former allegiances apparently paralleled Taliere's. The targeting principle in both instances had been a medallion.

"You're certain we're talking about the same man?" Adam asked.

"You supplied the name. And the fingerprint records you provided, no less than your photograph and Mr. Lovat's excellent sketch, match up with the fingerprints and photos contained in our files. I'd say there's little question that the Callanish affair was Taliere's work."

"That doesn't explain his motive, especially after so long. Have you any idea what made this Taliere turn traitor in the first place?"

"From what we could piece together at the time, he apparently saw himself as acting to revive the beliefs and practices of the ancient Druids—of whom he claimed to be a direct descendant."

Adam frowned. "That tallies with what we've been told of Evans. But the various forms of Druid worship were the very heart and soul of Britain from ancient times. Why would a Druid want to see the British government overthrown in favor of an invader from the Continent?''

Graham smiled thinly. ''Don't forget that Taliere's a Welshman. By his reckoning, the House of Windsor is a dynasty of usurpers. By contrast, the Welsh-descended Tudors were the last legitimate rulers of this sceptered isle—and by extension, the last keepers and users of our native shamanic traditions in the line of sacred kings. Taliere was collaborating with the Germans in the fond expectation of seeing a Tudor monarch restored to the throne under Hitler's aegis.''

Adam's frown deepened. ''That makes no sense. The direct Tudor line of succession came to an end when Elizabeth the First died without issue.''

''So say the history books,'' Graham agreed. ''But Taliere was convinced otherwise by a man claiming to be a direct descendant of her father, Henry the Eighth—this, by virtue of a clandestine dalliance between Henry and a Welsh princess who secretly bore him a son. Whether or not the story was true—and I think it unlikely—this pretender was going to assume the crown in the wake of the Nazi conquest. And between them, he and Taliere were going to reinstate the old religion—or rather, Taliere's warped vision of it.''

Adam was gripped by a sudden premonition. ''This pretender—what was his name?''

His tone earned him a curious glance from Graham. ''He called himself Tudor-Jones. Why do you ask?''

''*David* Tudor-Jones?'' Adam said.

''Then you've heard of him,'' Graham replied.

''Aye, and crossed paths more than once with a man who would seem to be his son.''

It was Graham's turn to look startled. ''I never knew Tudor-Jones had a son!''

''That's not surprising, since the son himself doesn't advertise the connection,'' Adam said. ''He uses his mother's maiden name. We know him as as *Francis Raeburn.*''

# CHAPTER TWENTY-TWO

WHEN Adam returned to the world of the outer senses, it was nearly midnight. His whole body felt chilled to the bone, as was only to be expected after so long a journey on the astral. Even more chilling were the implications of what he had learned.

Pulling his dressing gown more tightly around him, he got up and heaped fresh wood on the fire before turning on the lights. A call on the in-house telephone let Humphrey know that he was finished for the night and very much in need of refreshment, after which he returned to his fireside chair to contemplate what he had learned from John Graham.

In bringing to light the hitherto secret connections between Taliere/Evans and Raeburn, Graham had clarified aspects of the present situation, which had seemed insolubly murky two days earlier. Taliere's mysteriously brief emergence from obscurity two years ago—so baffling when viewed as an isolated incident—could now be seen to coincide roughly with Raeburn's attempt to reactivate the ancient and malignant powers of the Soulis torc under the auspices of the Head-Master. There now seemed little need for further speculation as to who had organized the elaborate ritual at Callanish. Raeburn, it would appear, was renewing his efforts to court the power and favor of the old gods, with Taliere drafted to play a supporting role.

Quite obviously, the Callanish sacrifice now emerged as an elaborate prelude to something far more ambitious and far-ranging—for Raeburn was not given to modest undertakings. The question was, What? Unable to provide an answer as yet, Adam was nevertheless prepared to make one grim and certain prediction: Whatever Raeburn's ultimate objective might be, his pursuit of it was certain to exact a high price from someone.

It went without saying that he had to be stopped. But in order to stop Raeburn, the Hunting Lodge first had to find him. The Taliere connection was a beginning—but only a beginning. Adam was just considering where to take his inquiries next when there was a light knock at the door.

He rose to answer the summons, expecting to see Humphrey standing on the threshold with a tray in his hands. Instead, he was more than a little surprised to be confronted by Ximena.

She had exchanged her working clothes for a quilted-silk dressing gown and Oriental slippers in a matching shade of opulent jade-green. Her long dark hair, still slightly damp from her shower, was hanging loose about her shoulders, and her oval face was clear as apple-blossom. In her hands she bore a silver-and-enamel tray upon which reposed a plateful of toasted sandwiches and a Limoges chocolate service for two. Lifting her eyes to meet his, she gave him a demure smile and a mock curtsy.

"Good evening, sir! I believe you ordered a collation?"

Adam covered his surprise with a chuckle. "Yes, I did—but I wasn't expecting service from the mistress of the house herself."

"So it would appear," Ximena noted drily. "Are you complaining?"

"Not in the least!" Adam assured her. With a gallant sweep of his arm, he added, "Please, won't you come in?"

"I thought you'd never ask!" she said with a twinkle.

Slipping past him in a whisper of silk, she made her way gracefully over to the hearthside and began arranging the contents of the tray on a side table. Adam closed the door and came to join her.

"I didn't hear you arrive," he remarked with attempted lightness. "How long have you been home?"

"About half an hour," she returned. "I phoned earlier to let you know I was on my way, but Humphrey said you were busy, so I told him not to bother you. Since all the signs indicated you were still ensconced when I got in, I took the opportunity to slip into something more comfortable and grab myself a snack from the kitchen. When I caught Humphrey in the act of making you a midnight feast, it seemed a pity not to make a social occasion of it.''

''I'm very glad you did,'' Adam told her, as she straightened up and turned around.

Ximena cocked her head slightly. ''Well, that's a relief. From the blank look on your face when you first opened the door, I thought perhaps I might have made a tactical blunder.''

''A thousand apologies. I was still gnawing over the problem I've been working at all evening.''

''Then it's time to put the matter behind you,'' Ximena said firmly.

She reached out and took his hands. The next instant her eyes widened in concern.

''Good Lord, Adam, is anything wrong? Your hands are like ice!''

''No, no,'' Adam made haste to reassure her. ''It's nothing of any consequence. I've just been sitting in one place for a little too long—too idle and distracted to heave another log on the fire.''

Even as he spoke, he couldn't quite repress a shiver. Ximena frowned and peered at him more closely.

''Adam, your lips are almost blue! *And* your fingernails. To look at you, one would almost think you'd been out in a blizzard!''

''On the contrary,'' Adam protested mildly, ''I've been right here in this room all evening.''

Ximena's gaze narrowed to a searching glare. ''That doesn't make sense. The room's not that cold—in fact, it isn't cold at all. Even if you say you're not ill, there's certainly something amiss. Adam, just what *have* you been doing?''

There was to be, Adam sensed, no avoiding the issue. Taking care to choose his words, he said, ''I've been engaging in what you might call a 'spiritual exercise.' ''

Ximena's frown turned puzzled. ''You mean, praying?''

''That's certainly a part of it.''

"Hypothermia," Ximena pointed out, "is not generally acknowledged to be a side effect of prayer."

"Perhaps it would be more accurate to say that I was meditating," Adam amended. "Some deep meditative states are accompanied by a decrease in heart rate and respiration. Any time the metabolism slows down, the body temperature is naturally going to drop. I've had this happen to me any number of times, and I promise you I'll take no harm by it. All I need is a little time to warm up again. That's why I ordered hot sandwiches and hot chocolate."

"If you say so," Ximena said dubiously, then added, on a more bracing note, "Well, the sooner you get some food inside you, the better! Come and have a sandwich while I pour us some chocolate."

Adam allowed himself to be chivvied over to the settee, where Ximena tucked a tartan rug around his shoulders and then presented him with a filled plate. The sandwiches Humphrey had provided were still warm from the grill, and their fragrance seemed ambrosial. Adam devoured his first helping with grateful abandon, and started in on his second. Only then did he become aware that Ximena was watching him over the rim of her cup, monitoring his progress with a thoughtful eye.

"Sorry," he apologized. "I didn't realize how hungry I was."

Amusement tugged at Ximena's lips. "Think nothing of it. I'm just happy to see you getting some color back in your face." She watched him a moment longer, then asked abruptly, "Why do you do this to yourself?"

Adam paused in the act of taking a sip of chocolate. "I beg your pardon?"

"Why do you do this to yourself?" Ximena repeated. "I mean—it can't be a very enjoyable experience, putting yourself through this kind of rigor. Even if you're not aware of what's happening to your body while your mind and spirit are occupied with higher things, sooner or later you're going to have to reckon with the physical consequences. And so I'm curious to know, Why do you do it?"

"The reasons vary," Adam said. After a brief hesitation, he added, "On this occasion, the impetus was work-related."

Ximena lifted an eyebrow. "I—see," she acknowledged. "One of those special cases you mentioned. Are we talking about a crime?"

"Not in the conventional sense," Adam said. "Not yet, at any rate." When Ximena continued to wait expectantly, he added, "I was hoping to gain some insight into the problem through meditation."

"Were you successful?"

"Up to a point. I've now been able to work out who's responsible. And I have some idea as to his motives. The challenge now will be to find him before he can attain his desired objective."

"Which is?"

"To become a law unto himself. To dictate and control the lives and fortunes of others who are weaker than he is."

"In other words," she said, "he wants more than his share of personal power. What makes this character any different from your average politician?"

"The fact that he is prepared to resort to occult means to gain what he seeks."

Ximena's reaction was incredulous. "Black magic?"

"That's as good a term for it as any," he replied, watching her carefully. "Never mind whether or not *you* believe in the efficacy of such things. The point is, our subject does— and behaves accordingly, and gets results."

A thoughtful silence descended momentarily while Ximena digested this, after which she asked, "Assuming that you find him, what will you do?"

"Hand him over to the proper authorities," Adam said. Which was nothing more or less than the simple truth. "At the moment," he continued, "our man probably doesn't suspect we're onto him. If we're careful, he won't realize what we're doing until it's too late to resist."

"Will he give himself up without a fight?"

"I doubt it."

"I see." There was another silence. "Am I to infer from this that there's an element of danger?"

"Some," Adam admitted. "But I don't take unnecessary chances."

"Well, that's a relief," Ximena said with a fillip of forced levity. "Am I allowed to know who this man is, or is that another secret?"

"Secret or not, his name wouldn't mean anything to you."

"His name *would* mean something to me, if he were to do you any harm."

"Nothing is going to happen to me," Adam said firmly. "I'm not in this alone. And the people who are with me can be trusted to look after my safety, just as I look after theirs."

Ximena gave him a narrow look, then broke it off with a shrug and a smile.

"That had the right ring of confidence," she conceded. "All right, let's not argue the point. It's getting late, and it occurs to me that we've got better things to do at this hour than sitting here debating the ethics of this branch of your profession."

Rising, she offered him her hand. As he cast off his rug and followed his wife upstairs, Adam could only hope that future events would not betray her trust.

Ximena slept in the following morning. Going downstairs alone, Adam found Philippa already at the breakfast table. His account of Graham's revelations left them both in a sober frame of mind.

"This is worse than anything I might have expected," Philippa declared, moodily poking at the grapefruit-half in front of her. "What's our next step?"

"I wish I knew," Adam said with a sigh.

McLeod and Peregrine received a similar briefing later in the day, over lunch. The news that Raeburn was almost certainly the instigator behind the Callanish affair drew predictably strong reactions.

"Raeburn? It figures," McLeod muttered. "He's like a bad penny—just keeps coming back."

"How the devil did he manage to sneak back into the country without anyone becoming aware of him?" Peregrine wondered aloud. "Aren't there all kinds of warrants out for his arrest?"

"Obviously, he still has his share of resources," Adam replied. "Those diamonds must have bought him a lot of credit in a number of circles."

"That doesn't explain why he'd want to come back to Scotland," Peregrine retorted. "Isn't that taking an awfully big risk, given his past record around here?"

"Scotland has always been his power base," Adam reminded Peregrine. "Besides that, he probably feels he has unfinished business here—scores to settle, at the very least. Furthermore, I expect he's a man in withdrawal. Drug addiction is nothing compared to the addiction that can come of tasting and craving the kind and intensity of power delegated to him by the Head-Master—and we cut off his supply when we overturned the Head-Master's operation. I shouldn't be surprised if he's attempting to reforge that link with the old Pictish pantheon of elemental gods."

"The link with Taranis," McLeod muttered. "Bloody hell!"

"Adam, are you serious?" Peregrine murmured.

When Adam only nodded, Peregrine shook his head in horrified protest. "But—how could he do that? The torc was destroyed. Wouldn't he need some kind of power-focus to replace it?"

"Not necessarily. Not if a ritual means can be found to accomplish the same end," Adam replied. "That might explain why he's gone to the trouble of enlisting Taliere. As a Druid priest with an ancient pedigree, Taliere would have resources at his disposal that Raeburn lacks himself—as well as a signature of power strong enough to mask any other occult presence in the area."

"Aye, he would," McLeod grumbled. "I just wish we'd known about the Raeburn connection when we were up at Callanish. Maybe we'd have picked up a few more clues to go on."

"I doubt it," Adam said heavily. "Raeburn knew exactly what he was doing. The fact that he left the Callanish site uncleansed was a calculated diversion. We were *meant* to pick up Taliere's trail and squander our time chasing it. Meanwhile, Raeburn has been free to pursue his plans unmolested."

"So Taliere was nothing more than a red herring," Peregrine said. The reflection made him squirm inwardly. Putting his resentment behind him with difficulty, he asked, "How do we get back on the right track?"

"By consolidating our gains, such as they are," Adam replied. "At least we now know who we're up against, which is more than we knew yesterday. I suggest we open up a new line of inquiry by revisiting some of Raeburn's old haunts. If he's been anywhere near any of them, we may be able to pick up residuals from his presence."

"I see what you're saying," Peregrine said. "But if we do that, won't Raeburn realize that his ruse has run its course, and change his tactics accordingly?"

"Probably," Adam said with uncompromising candor, "but under the circumstances, I don't see that we have any other option."

"There's that country house Raeburn used to have on the other side of Stirling," McLeod offered, after a thoughtful silence. "That might be a starting place. I'll drive over there and have a look, see if anyone's living there now. If there's been a change of ownership, the paper trail may turn up a clue or two as to Raeburn's movements and associations."

"That's not a bad idea," Adam replied, "though I'd recommend you take someone with you. Donald, maybe. As we all know, accidents have been known to happen in this line of work."

"If it doesn't have to be a police backup, I'll go," Peregrine volunteered.

"Sounds fine to me," McLeod said. "I doubt Raeburn will be there."

"Fair enough. At least it's a starting point," Adam agreed. "In the meantime, since we can be reasonably sure that Raeburn and Taliere were together at Callanish, I suggest we go back and review Peregrine's sketches. Now that we know what we're looking for, something new may yet come to light."

"It's certainly worth a try," Peregrine said. "I'll get copies made up this afternoon and we can each go over them this evening."

Anything more he might have said was interrupted by a shrill electronic chirrup from the inside pocket of McLeod's jacket. The inspector rolled his eyes apologetically and pulled out a tiny mobile phone.

"McLeod . . . Oh. Right. Yes, I'll be there as soon as I can . . . Right. Bye."

He closed down the antenna with a wistful lift of his eyebrows and got to his feet.

"Sorry about that. Domestic crisis disrupts esoteric investigative efforts. Jane's had a plumbing disaster. There's water all over the kitchen floor. I think we're about through here anyway. I'll come by and pick up those photocopies tomorrow."

He took himself off, leaving Adam and Peregrine to finish their coffee. Adam was about to set his empty cup aside when he became aware that Peregrine was toying absentmindedly with his coffee spoon, a look of baffled preoccupation on his face.

"Something bothering you, Peregrine?" Adam asked.

Peregrine looked up at the sound of his name, momentarily startled.

"No, not—*bothering*, exactly."

"Something to do with the Callanish case?"

"In a manner of speaking, I suppose so," Peregrine allowed. After a brief hesitation he continued. "I always had the impression that Sir John and the other folk at Oakwood all follow a mystical tradition derived, at least in part, from the ancient Druids."

"Essentially correct."

"Well," Peregrine said, still frowning, "assuming that *they* are the legitimate heirs to Britain's pagan heritage, how is it that someone like Taliere can use those same beliefs and practices as the basis for invoking the powers of evil?"

"In other words," Adam said, "you want to know how Graham and Taliere can be opposed to one another while appearing to venerate the same things."

Peregrine nodded.

"A fair question," Adam replied. "I would say that the explanation probably lies in the human capacity for self-delusion—and in the equally human capacity for endowing those delusions with power. It's quite literally true that evil men have it in them to create their own demons. And these demons are no less demonic for being given sacred names—quite the reverse, in fact. This confusion of identity extends even to the Great Ones who preside over the enlightened realms of the Inner Planes.''

At Peregrine's look of question, he went on.

''Think of the four great entities we call Gabriel, Michael, Raphael, and Uriel. Theologians will tell you that these beings we call archangels sprang forth from the mind of God in the same instant of Divine Thought which created the universe itself. As messengers of God and viceroys of the elements, they have been given many names down through the ages.

''Some cultures, in the absence of direct revelation, came to venerate these messengers as gods in their own right, projecting onto them a whole range of human errors and frailties. In time, fuelled by the power of belief, those projections developed a shadowy half-life of their own, so that it has become difficult for a great many people to distinguish the true Powers from their manufactured counterparts.

''Taliere probably *thinks* he's venerating the old gods of ancient Britain,'' he concluded, ''but in fact I suspect he's worshipping only an autonomous projection of his forebears' inner darkness. It's a common misconception—and not one confined to latter-day pagans.''

Peregrine rubbed the end of his nose reflectively. ''Are you saying that this ancient deity Taranis, whom Taliere purports to serve, exists only as a shadowy analogue to one of the archangels?''

''That doesn't make him or it any less real,'' Adam replied. ''Never forget that. And the more people who embrace the illusion, the stronger it becomes—until eventually, it can take on physical substance. That's why we have to stop Raeburn. And to do that, we have to find him—the sooner, the better.''

# CHAPTER TWENTY-THREE

"I think this is going to be one of the best portraits you've ever done, darling," Julia remarked admiringly as she peered over her husband's shoulder. "I can't wait to see what it will look like when you get the dress fully painted in."

Peregrine smiled and turned his head to plant a kiss on her hand where it rested on his shoulder, pausing to take more paint onto his brush before returning his attention to the canvas. Thereon was limned the first sketchy outline of a bridal portrait of Ximena, only the face approaching completion. The gossamer suggestion of a veil of Spanish lace fell softly about her head and shoulders, supported by a sparkling diamond tiara, as delicate as frost. The dress, as yet, was little more than a sketchy hint of ivory satin and lace, but the face taking shape in the portrait was already a faithful reflection of Ximena herself, dark eyes brimming with warmth and excitement, lips trembling on the brink of a smile.

"Where's that hot chocolate, woman?" Peregrine asked with mock ferocity. "How do you expect a man to paint on a night like this without fuel?"

The Lovats were together in the kitchen of the gate lodge at Strathmourne, where Julia had just set a pan of milk to warm on the top of the Aga. Though Peregrine rarely painted downstairs, preferring his upstairs studio where he could work by natural daylight, the shortness of the Scottish winter day, coupled with a recent increase in commissions, had prompted him to experiment with a new high-intensity light bulb designed to simulate a daylight effect. As luck would have it, the only light fixture able to accommodate the wattage was located in the kitchen, which had recently been rewired. The initial results had proved satisfactory, however, and Peregrine had since discovered that working in the kitchen had compensations other than being able to work on past nightfall.

Laughing, Julia drifted away to add cocoa and sugar to the warming milk, before returning to her husband's side.

"The tiara really is lovely," she commented. "Is it true that it's been in the Sinclair family since the reign of Queen Victoria?"

"So Philippa says," Peregrine returned, with a fleeting smile. "Apparently most of the diamonds were presented to Adam's great-grandfather by an Indian maharajah, in gratitude for military and diplomatic services rendered. He had them made into a tiara for his wife, and since then every Sinclair wife and daughter has worn it to the altar, including Philippa herself."

Julia cocked her head to one side while she studied the overall effect. "Well, it goes remarkably well with the mantilla. You'd almost think the two had been made to go together."

"You would, wouldn't you?" Peregrine agreed, his attention on his work. "I just hope that Ximena doesn't decide to change the hair style you two discussed, between now and the wedding day. It's tricky enough having to do this on the sly, without any major last-minute changes."

The portrait was intended as a surprise wedding gift for the bridal couple. Confident that the painting would be joyfully received, Julia was taking advantage of her new-found friendship with Ximena to gather every possible detail regarding the future Lady Sinclair's bridal ensemble. Her efforts were being ably seconded by Philippa, who had provided a Polaroid snapshot of the Sinclair tiara. Teresa Lockhart had likewise participated in the conspiracy by supplying photographs of the antique lace mantilla which was to be her daughter's bridal veil.

Peregrine added a minute flourish of detail to the veil's diaphanous hem, then set his fine sable brush aside as he contemplated his work with a critical eye, stretching backwards to relieve a crick in his back.

''I think that's going to have to be it for tonight. I can't really carry on without the particulars of the gown. When does Ximena have her next fitting?''

''In a couple of days,'' Julia said. ''I've already volunteered to go along and keep her company. I don't *think* there are going to be any major changes, but if there are, I'll try to find out in plenty of time for you to incorporate them into the final painting.''

Grinning, Peregrine lowered a protective drop-sheet over the half-finished painting, then switched off the bright light overhead, leaving on the work-lights under the hanging cupboards.

''If only the government were half as well-served by its intelligence-gathering services!'' he said to his wife. ''Have you considered giving up music for a career in international espionage?''

''Certainly not,'' Julia replied. ''I have my hands full enough, just keeping abreast of what's going on in my own household. You haven't exactly been overflowing with information about that house call you made today with Noel McLeod.''

She had gone to stir the hot chocolate, but was turned so she could see him. In a slight delaying action, Peregrine set about the cleaning of his brushes. Earlier that afternoon, McLeod had spirited him away for their planned visit to Nether Leckie, Raeburn's former residence. While McLeod had offered a partial truth for Julia's benefit—that he was hoping Peregrine's talents might be put to use in locating a missing person—he had precipitated their departure before she could inquire too closely about the individual they were seeking—for which Peregrine was grateful. The truth about Raeburn was not something he felt ready to share.

Fortunately—or perhaps unfortunately—there was no need to dissemble here and now, regarding at least part of the truth.

''There really isn't much to tell,'' he said, chucking the first of the brushes into a jar, bristles up. ''For all the good

we accomplished, Noel and I might as well have saved ourselves the trip.''

Which was true. The house had been shut up tight; and
any resonances of Raeburn's presence had dissipated long
ago—or else had been selectively erased. What remained
was a sullen aura of malevolence, but not enough to provide
any leads. Hoping to change the subject, Peregrine asked,
''Did you and Ximena manage to get the music sorted out
for the reception?''

''I think so—my bit of the programme, anyway,'' Julia
said. ''I'm glad Philippa was there to help. Whenever she's
around, things seem to have a way of getting done.''

At that moment, a plump black and white ball of fur came
shooting around the door frame in hot pursuit of one of Peregrine's art gum erasers. The chase ended abruptly when the
eraser rolled out of paw-reach under the refrigerator.

''Hero, you bandit!'' Peregrine said, laughing. ''No wonder I can never find an art gum when I need one!''

''If you'd keep them in your art satchel where they belong,
he wouldn't be able to get at them,'' Julia pointed out with
a chuckle, coming to scoop up kitten and eraser.

Hero promptly transferred his attack to a random lock of
his mistress's hair. Disregarding the assault, Julia went back
to the Aga to give the saucepan another stir with her free
hand.

''The hot chocolate's ready,'' she announced over her
shoulder. ''Want me to pour you a cup?''

''Not just yet, thanks. The smell of turpentine tends to
interfere with the taste. If you leave it standing in the pan,
I'll get it myself once I'm done cleaning my brushes.''

''Mind if I take mine up to bed with me, then? Ximena's
given me some music for a saraband she's picked out, and I
want to make some notations before I start practicing it.''

''No, go ahead. I'll be up to join you as soon as I've put
things to rights down here.''

With a companionable nod, Julia picked up her mug and
made for the stairs, the now-purring kitten cradled on her
shoulder. Outside the house, hostile eyes took note when the
light came on in the upstairs bedroom. From far at the back
of the garden, the watcher carefully scanned the house and

its environs through high-powered infrared binoculars, all but invisible in snow-camouflage coveralls and balaclava helmet. After a moment, he lifted a wrist-mounted comlink to his lips, still watching through the binoculars.

"At least one of the subjects has gone upstairs," he reported in an undertone. "The main light in the kitchen has gone out, and the bedroom light came on a minute or two later. What's left downstairs is probably a night-light. Otherwise the coast is clear."

The message was picked up by two more men sitting in a black panel van parked a hundred yards down from the gateway.

"Acknowledged," returned the driver. "Continue to observe and await further instructions."

He severed communications with a click, glancing at the clock in the dash before folding his arms on his chest and leaning his head against the headrest.

"We'll give them another half-hour," he said.

The man sitting next to him gave a huff of annoyance and shifted restively in his seat.

"This is stupid!" he declared. "It's like the bloody North Pole. What the hell are we hanging around for?"

"You know why," the driver said bluntly. "If we move in prematurely, while the targets are still awake, there may be some resistance. If we hold off until they're asleep, our success is virtually guaranteed."

"They're newlyweds; they may not go to sleep for hours. As far as I can see, the longer we sit here, the more likely it is that somebody's going to spot us and give the alarm. This whole damned thing is more complicated anyway than it needs to be. Why the hell can't we simply break in and put the bag on these people, without going through this occult rigmarole?"

"Because the boss wants it done this way," the driver snapped. "He's already had one piece of work go wrong because the offering was blemished. *I* don't want to be the one on the carpet if things don't go right this time around."

"You whine like an old woman," the man in the passenger seat muttered. "Well, I don't propose to spend the rest of the night freezing my arse off out here on the side of the road. It's quiet as the grave out there. I say let's move now.''

Flinging open the passenger door, he slid to the ground and started toward the back of the van.

"Wait, you bloody fool!" the driver snapped. But his companion had already flung open the back hatch and was pulling out something wrapped up in a burlap sack.

"Tell Otto I'm coming," he tossed over his shoulder, "and stand by to pick us up."

Once Julia had gone upstairs, Peregrine's thoughts reverted almost at once to the unwelcome subject of Francis Raeburn, his movements becoming more emphatic as he cleaned another brush against a paint-stained cloth. Only now that the visit to Nether Leckie was behind him did he realize how confident he had been that they surely must find some promising sign of Raeburn's whereabouts.

Dogged by a feeling of anticlimax, he went through the motions of putting his palette and brushes away while he tried to imagine what might be going on in the mind of their adversary. So lost in thought was he that he failed to notice that someone or something outside the kitchen door was scuffling at the cat-flap.

The odor of linseed oil and turpentine was strong in his nostrils as he gathered up his paint-rags and tossed them in the rubbish bin under the kitchen sink. Only belatedly did he become aware that there was another odor creeping into the kitchen under the covering ambience of pine—as if someone had set a match to a tub of rancid lard.

As he turned sharply away from the sink, this new and acrid reek seemed to hit him in the face like a physical blow. The stench made him gag and brought tears to his eyes.

Instinctively clapping a hand over his mouth and nose, he looked around for its source, recoiling as he spied something out of place on the floor just inside the kitchen door, its identity masked under a rising cloud of greasy black smoke. As he tried to see what it might be, all his senses suddenly blurred and he found himself folding helplessly to his knees.

Upstairs in the bedroom, Julia had just finished the last of her hot chocolate when she heard a subdued thump and clatter from the direction of the kitchen. The noise was loud enough to make her lift her head from the music score in front of her.

To her musically trained ear, there was something odd about the silence that followed. Shifting her music to the bed beside her, she slipped to her feet and made for the doorway, tightening the belt of her robe around her waist. In that same instant, Hero, who had been sleeping among the pillows, roused with a sudden hiss and start.

Julia whirled around in time to see the kitten disappear under the bed in a bristling flash. Her own heart beating faster, she grabbed the hockey stick that Peregrine kept behind the bedroom door and tiptoed out onto the landing. At once she became aware of the smell of something burning.

"Peregrine?" she called anxiously.

There was no response from below. Tight-lipped with sudden fright, Julia hurried down the stairs and darted across the hall into the kitchen.

The first sight to meet her eyes was her husband, slumped in a heap on the floor within arm's reach of some strange foreign object that smoked and smoldered like a damp Roman candle. Her second glance registered the fact that there was a gloved hand and arm reaching up through the cat-flap toward the latch on the kitchen door.

Without hesitation, Julia raised the hockey stick and swung it like a cricket bat, landing a heavy blow on the intruder's groping fingers. The resultant dull crack was accompanied by a howl of pain from outside. Before she could strike again, the arm whisked itself back through the cat-flap like a wounded rat.

A breathless string of curses punctuated the hasty rustle of retreating feet. Beating the smoke away with one hand, and staggering a little dizzily, Julia started toward Peregrine, glancing down at the outlandish object left behind. Recognition eluded her for a moment. Then, with a shock of pure horror, she realized it was a severed and mummified human hand, its skeletal fingers clenched around a dirty yellow candle that gave off a stinking flare of sickly yellow flame. The fingertips were also lit, burning with a bluer light.

Her scream pierced through the heavy fog that was smothering Peregrine's mind and senses. The realization that Julia must be in danger roused him as little else could have done. Clawing his way back to consciousness, he heaved himself up onto his elbows and forced his eyes to open. Through a stupefying haze, he glimpsed Julia pressed flat against the adjacent wall, her face blanched white with revulsion.

Her dilated eyes were fixed on the noisome object that lay burning on the floor between them. Dragging himself to his feet with the help of a chair, Peregrine nearly recoiled himself when he saw what it was. Even semi-drugged, he could have little doubt that the mummified hand was an occult weapon of attack.

"Go phone Adam!" he rasped hoarsely. "I'll try to neutralize this thing."

Julia fled to the sitting room. Fighting the sickening drag on his senses, trying not to breathe any more than he had to, Peregrine lurched over to the sink and drenched a tea towel under the tap. As he flung it over the gruesome object on the floor, it began smoking even more, but he also heard the hiss of flames hopefully being quenched.

Julia thrust her head through the doorway that connected with the hall, hanging onto the jamb, her eyes wide with fright. She was swaying on her feet, as if she was having trouble keeping her balance.

"The phone's dead," she gasped. "I can't get a dial tone."

"They must have cut the line," Peregrine muttered, backing out into the hall.

Julia bit back a sob and knuckled her eyes as she fought off the soporific effects of the fumes.

"We've got to get out!" she managed to whisper.

"No! That's what they want!"

"Then what'll we do?" she wailed.

Peregrine was cudgeling his own befogged brain, and dimly seized upon their only hope.

"The cell phone!" he mumbled thickly. "It's in my art case."

Clamping his lips firmly closed, and holding his breath, he went back into the kitchen, advancing only far enough to grab the handle of the black leather satchel lying on the floor by the kitchen table. Dragging it into the sitting room, he threw it open and rummaged inside until he located the object he was looking for. His fingers felt thick and clumsy. Concentrating hard, he began to punch in Adam's number.

# CHAPTER TWENTY-FOUR

ADAM was reading in the library when the house phone rang. Ximena had gone up to bed, as had Philippa. Setting a finger in his book to mark his place, he went over to the desk to answer the summons.

"Sir, I'm putting Mr. Lovat through!" Humphrey informed him without preamble. "Hold the line."

The uncharacteristically preemptory tone put Adam instantly on alert, even as Peregrine came on the line, sounding breathless and distraught.

"Trouble, Adam!" he gasped. "We've just had an attempted break-in, down here at the gate lodge."

"Good Lord!" Adam exclaimed. "Are you and Julia all right?"

"More or less," came the reply, "but this wasn't any ordinary burglary. There's something awful in the kitchen, and I'm not sure I've—Jesus, the lights just went out!"

"Peregrine, are you all right? Humphrey, get in here!" Adam bellowed, when Peregrine did not immediately respond. "Peregrine, answer me!"

"—got to get out of the house, but I know they're out there . . ." Peregrine's answer came through a crackle of static. ". . . kind of drugged smoke."

"What's that?" Adam demanded.

"House phone's dead," Peregrine's voice went on, through crackles of more static. "Cell phone keeps breaking up—"

"Peregrine?" Adam shouted, as the interference continued, gesturing urgently as Humphrey appeared in the library doorway. "Peregrine, hang on! We'll be there as fast as we can! Humphrey, bring the Rover around. Peregrine, don't even try to leave the house. If you can hear me, just stay put and keep your heads down!"

A scant five minutes later, Adam and the faithful Humphrey were barrelling down the drive in the Range Rover, Humphrey at the wheel and Adam beside him with a pair of loaded shotguns braced purposefully across his knees. Neither man spoke as they approached the final bend in the road, but Adam slipped his Adept ring onto his hand.

The dark bulk of the gate lodge hove into view ahead, no lights showing upstairs or down. Humphrey pulled up short by the front door in a shower of gravel and a blaze of head-lamps as a dark-colored panel van with its lights out accelerated away from the gates in the direction of the motorway and quickly disappeared from sight. Flinging his door wide, Adam shoved one of the shotguns into Humphrey's hands and snatched up a powerful torch before vaulting out of the cab with his own weapon at the ready, praying that the Lovats were not in the departing vehicle.

"Peregrine?" he shouted, pounding up the steps two at a time to hammer on the door. "Peregrine, it's Adam! Humphrey and I are here with shotguns. Philippa's calling the police."

Deathly silence suddenly gave way to the thud of hurrying footbeats on the stair within, followed by a scraping noise and the sharp click of a snib-lock being drawn. When the door swung partly open, Peregrine's drawn face appeared at the gap, squinting in the light of Humphrey's torch.

"Oh, thank God!" he exclaimed. "Quick, come inside."

He threw the door wide to allow them to enter and closed it swiftly behind them.

"Julia's upstairs," he informed them, as he replaced the chair he had wedged under the doorknob and Adam anxiously swept his torch around the room. "The air's clearer up there."

A foul carrion stench permeated the ground floor, along with a faintly dizzying narcotic residue and a more disturbing ripple of soul-chilling menace. Adam was hardly surprised to see that Peregrine looked decidedly queasy.

"We'd better deal with whatever's in the kitchen," he said, shining his torch in that direction. "You want to show me? Humphrey, stay here and guard the door—and see if you can get some windows open."

Mutely the young artist led the way into the kitchen, where the noisome bundle still lay on the floor by the kitchen door. The accompanying emanation of evil, as they approached, was nearly as palpable as the physical smell.

Laying his shotgun aside and tucking his torch under one arm, Adam used his handkerchief to mask his nose and mouth with one hand while he gingerly lifted a corner of the tea towel with the other. One glance was enough to make him drop the towel and sketch a sign of warding in the air above it.

"There's nothing I can do about this here and now," he told Peregrine. "We'll have to bring it up to the main house to deal with it properly. You go fetch Julia, but stay in the sitting room with Humphrey. I'll get this thing shielded for transport."

As Peregrine disappeared up the stairs, Adam cast his torch-beam around the kitchen until he spotted a square metal biscuit tin with a tight-fitting lid. Emptying its contents into the sink, he set it on the floor beside his bundled-up quarry and used a pair of wooden spoons to lift the offending item into the box. It was still smoldering inside the tea towel. As he set the lid in place and pressed it closed, Peregrine came down the stairs with Julia, the latter cradling their black and white kitten protectively in the front of her robe.

"Let's get out of here," Adam said, tucking the biscuit tin under one arm and grabbing up his shotgun.

With Humphrey warily covering their departure, they piled into the Range Rover, Adam stashing the biscuit tin in the back before he took the wheel. Philippa was waiting at the front door when they arrived at the house, bundled in a warm woollen robe.

"The police are on their way," she informed Adam as he alighted from the car. In a lower tone, she added, "Is there anything in particular we need to confer about before they arrive?"

"You could say that," Adam replied, handing her the shotguns.

Peregrine helped Julia from the car, with Humphrey taking charge of the frightened kitten, and Adam herded everyone toward the front door, himself lingering to retrieve the biscuit tin from the back of the car.

"The intruders planted a Hand of Glory in the kitchen," he said to his mother, carrying the tin somewhat gingerly. "Don't worry—I've got it safe in here for the time being. But you and I are going to have some work to do before the night is out."

As he pulled the door shut behind them and bolted it, Philippa setting the shotguns in a corner of the entry hall, they were joined by Ximena, who cast a questioning eye on the now sobbing Julia.

"Is everyone all right?" she inquired anxiously.

"Yes, but Julia's pretty shaken up," Adam said, ushering them both farther inside. "I've suggested a sedative or a tranquillizer, but she isn't keen on the idea—though sleep would be the best medicine, right about now. Could you look after her while Peregrine and I deal with the police?"

"Consider it done," Ximena said. "I assume she and Peregrine will be staying the night?"

"Absolutely. You can put them in the blue room."

Once Ximena had shepherded Julia upstairs, Humphrey retiring to the kitchen with the kitten, Peregrine slumped back against the newel post in the grip of a sudden faintness. Strong hands eased him to a sitting position on the bottommost step.

"Steady on," said Adam's voice in his ear. "Your wife's not the only one to have had a shock tonight."

Peregrine took off his spectacles and knuckled his eyes. "I'm sorry about this," he murmured. "I can't seem to think straight. My head's pounding like a drum."

"The police won't be here for a little while yet," Philippa said. "Why don't I go and get you a couple of extra-strength paracetamol?"

Peregrine nodded numbly, burying his face in one hand while Philippa disappeared upstairs and Adam retreated to stash the biscuit tin in the house safe. It occurred to Adam that McLeod ought to be notified about the gate lodge incident directly, rather than learning about it from a police report, but the inspector and his wife were away overnight for a christening. After considering, Adam rang the number for McLeod's home answering machine and left a terse but informative message. When he returned to the hall, Peregrine was draining a tumbler of water while Philippa massaged the back of his neck.

"Peregrine's just been telling me about what happened," Philippa informed her son. "Just offhand, I'd say that he and Julia had a very narrow escape."

"Just offhand, I'd say you're probably right. Peregrine, how are you feeling?"

Peregrine made a game attempt at a nonchalant smile, but it came out more of a grimace.

"Do you want the truth or a polite fiction?"

"The *truth*," Philippa said, "is that you've taken quite a hammering—probably worse than you realize. It's a good thing Julia was upstairs when the Hand was introduced into the house. If the fumes hadn't taken that bit longer to reach her, heaven only knows what might be happening to the pair of you just now."

Peregrine had gone several shades paler as she spoke, and turned frightened eyes on Adam.

"Adam, is that true?" he whispered.

Adam nodded soberly. "I'm afraid so. Under the circumstances, I think we'd better agree not to say anything about the Hand to the police, when they get here. I don't want them taking it away as evidence before I've had a chance to examine it."

"Indeed not," Philippa agreed. "When it comes to determining who was behind this attack, that particular piece of evidence is likely to be far more useful to us than it would be to the police."

"I understand, of course," Peregrine murmured. "But what do we tell them?"

"Just that you were working in the kitchen when a hand reached up through the cat-flap and tried to unlock the door. It withdrew when you walloped it with a hockey stick."

The police arrived shortly thereafter. After giving suitably edited statements concerning the attempted break-in, Adam and Peregrine accompanied the investigative team back to the gate lodge to view the crime scene. Philippa waited until they were safely gone, then returned to the safe and removed the tin, carrying it into the library to set on Adam's desk.

Gingerly she eased the lid off. The rank smell from within made her wrinkle her nose in disgust. After sketching a warding sign above the towel-wrapped contents, she picked the wrapping apart with the aid of a couple of pencils and peered inside. A sullen glow and a rising whiff of noxious smoke verified that the candle was extinguished, but the fingertips were still smoldering—and likely to continue doing so unless she took active measures to quench them.

Adam's medical bag lay on a chair beside the library door, where he had set it upon returning home earlier in the day. Thumbing it open, Philippa sought out an alcohol swab and a disposable needle in a sealed plastic sheath and brought them back to the desk. After consideration, she slipped the sterile needle into a vein in the back of her left hand and let blood drip from its nub onto each of the glowing fingertips in turn. The blood sizzled as it hit the smoldering flesh, and the reek of burnt blood briefly overlaid the ranker stench of the Hand itself; but she had the satisfaction of seeing all five grisly brands gutter and go dark.

She was wiping the blood off the back of her hand with the alcohol swab, still focused on what she had been obliged to do, when a knock at the door jolted her concentration. Before she could make any attempt to conceal what lay before her, the door swung open to admit Ximena, a look of consternation on her face.

"Philippa, have you got a moment?" she asked, coming into the room. "Julia agreed to let me give her a sedative, but while we were waiting for it to take effect, she told me that the people who tried to break into the gate lodge tonight pushed a *severed human hand* through the cat . . . flap . . ."

Her voice trailed off as her gaze fell upon the object in the tin. "Oh my God, Julia wasn't just imagining things," she said weakly. "That's *it*, isn't it?"

Philippa nodded matter-of-factly. "It's an occult charm of the type known as a Hand of Glory," she explained. "Any encyclopaedia of witchcraft will tell you that such items are traditionally made from the hand of a gibbeted criminal. After the blood is squeezed out, the hand itself must be embalmed for two weeks in a solution of saltpetre, pepper, and salt, then dried in the sun. The candle is compounded of the victim's fat, wax, and several other unsavory ingredients which I won't go into.''

Ximena's wide-eyed gaze fell upon Philippa's own hand, where she was pressing a bloody alcohol wipe to the back. ''What—what're you doing?'' she asked in a slightly constricted voice.

''I was putting the candle out,'' Philippa said blandly. ''As illogical as it might sound, this kind of flame can only be quenched by blood or by skimmed milk. Since we only use low-fat and whole milk in this household, I was obliged to resort to the other option.''

Aware that Ximena was staring at her in shrinking amazement, Philippa briefly inspected the back of her hand, then gave the puncture site a final wipe with the alcohol swab and tossed it into a wastebasket.

''I assure you, I'm not some kind of ghoul, my dear,'' she said, smiling gently. ''My son must have told you that there are individuals out there who have a serious interest in black magic, and who practice it with genuinely malignant intent. It follows that in order to stop these people, we need to be familiar with their tools and how they operate.''

Ximena recovered herself with a slight shake. ''I'm sorry. I didn't mean to imply any disrespect. Adam *has* told me some things about his work as a special investigator, but he's stopped short of going into detail about the cases themselves. You'll have to excuse me if I'm finding my first direct exposure a little unnerving.''

''Actually,'' Philippa said drily, ''you're bearing up remarkably well.''

With an incredulous snort, Ximena glanced briefly at the Hand, then looked away again with a grimace of revulsion. ''I hate to think of the state I'd be in if I *weren't* bearing up well,'' she murmured. ''You said a minute ago that this thing was a charm. What's it supposed to do?''

''The lore of such things tells us that in pre-industrial

times, such charms were highly esteemed by robbers and housebreakers" Philippa replied, "as a means by which one could immobilize an entire household before breaking in and entering. The candle fumes are said to induce a drugged stupor in anyone who has the misfortune to inhale them. Hence the attempt to plant one in the Lovats' house tonight."

Ximena's dark eyes narrowed. "And you say this thing actually *works*?"

"Oh, indeed," Philippa said grimly. "It works all too well, when prepared by someone with genuine occult abilities. In fact," she added thoughtfully, "given the trouble involved in making a charm of this type—after all, gibbeted criminals are not exactly easy to find these days—I think that on this occasion we may safely infer that we're dealing with an occultist of singular dedication—and power."

"You make it sound as if you've been dealing with this kind of thing all your life," Ximena said with some astonishment.

Philippa permitted herself a mirthless smile. "That's because I have. You get experienced at dealing with crimes like these—but you never get used to them."

Ximena stole another glance at the hand in the tin and suppressed an eloquent shudder. "Assuming that everything you've said is true," she murmured, "that doesn't explain why anyone would want to attack the Lovats with something like this."

"Ah," Philippa said. "In case you haven't guessed it already, Peregrine—is an extremely gifted psychic. Like Adam, he often places his talents at the service of the Law. That kind of work can make enemies in dark places. I expect there are lots of folk out there who think they have a score to settle."

Ximena took a moment to assimilate this. "What have you told the police?"

"About the Hand? Nothing. And we don't intend to tell them anything. They'd only want to take it away with them as evidence—and frankly, that could be tantamount to handing a child a loaded gun. They don't have either the knowledge or the resources to deal with a thing like this. No, everyone is better off if we keep it here until Adam has time to examine it properly, and possibly determine where it came from.''

# CHAPTER TWENTY-FIVE

**D**OWN at the gate lodge, the police had completed their survey of the crime scene and were now gathered in the sitting room by the light of candle and lantern, taking stock of their findings over steaming mugs of tea. Across the hall, the kitchen door was standing open to encourage dissipation of the residual fumes from the Hand. Peregrine had explained the lingering smell to the police as being the product of the glue sizing he used to prepare his canvases. He had been relieved when the two policemen appeared to take his word for it.

"I'm afraid your would-be burglars left precious little behind in the way of evidence," said the senior officer, whose name was McLachlan. "When they wear gloves, they don't leave prints. Footprints can be useful, but the snow's been well trampled round about the back door. The few clear footprints we found aren't likely to tell us much."

"Any idea how many intruders there were?" Adam asked.

McLachlan pursed his lips. "I'd say at least two, plus one driving the getaway van. The tracks converge on the house from two different directions. But that's about all I can say for certain."

He transferred his attention to Peregrine. "You don't happen to keep anything of significant worth or value on the premises here, do you, Mr. Lovat? Something that might interest a collector of art or antiquities?"

"No, nothing," Peregrine said with a shake of his head.

"That's strange, then," McLachlan grunted. "Most burglars try to avoid breaking into a house where they know there are people at home—unless they're after something specific, that they know is in the house. Cat burglars will sneak into a house when the occupants are sleeping—they almost regard it as a challenge—but they don't usually cut phone lines.''

''What about power lines?'' Peregrine demanded. ''Was that just to frighten us?''

''And to help them get away,'' McLachlan replied, ''though it sounds like the arrival of Sir Adam and his man was what really scared them off.''

''That still doesn't explain what they were after,'' Adam said, though he had a fair idea it was not *what* but *who*.

McLachlan shrugged. ''I don't suppose they could have mistakenly thought that you lived here, Sir Adam? After all, you're a physician. Maybe they thought there were drugs in the house.''

''If they were sophisticated enough to cut the phone lines—and then the power lines—they'd have known better than that,'' Adam pointed out.

''Well, whatever the case, you and your wife were damned lucky, Mr. Lovat,'' McLachlan said, turning to Peregrine. ''This far out in the country, you're isolated enough to present an inviting target to anyone looking for trouble. If I were you, I'd maybe reconsider that cat flap. And get secondary locks fitted to your doors and make sure your windows are securely shut after dark.''

''For that matter,'' Adam said, ''it's probably time we had the security arrangements upgraded all over the estate. You can be certain I'll start making the necessary phone calls first thing in the morning. In the meantime, thank you both for coming so promptly.''

''Glad to be of service, Sir Adam,'' McLachlan said. ''I guess that about wraps things up for tonight. Mr. Lovat, you have my card and telephone number, if anything else crops up that you think we ought to know about. Meanwhile, we'll get an advisory bulletin on the wire and let you know if and when there are any further developments.''

Following the departure of the police, Peregrine sank gratefully into the nearest armchair.

''Whew! I'm glad that's over,'' he muttered fervently. ''I feel as if I've been hit by a lorry.''

"You do look as if you could use a breather," Adam said. "Just stay put for a few minutes and recollect yourself. I'll tidy up the tea things."

He carried the tea mugs into the kitchen and rinsed them under the hot water tap by candlelight, crouching down to inspect the cat-flap again before closing and locking the kitchen door and then returning to the sitting room. Peregrine had taken off his spectacles and was knuckling his eyes like a tired child. He started at the sound of Adam's footfalls, shaking his head as he put his spectacles back on.

"I don't know what's wrong with me," he fretted. "Ever since we came back here, I've been attempting on and off to see if I could pick up some visionary impression of whoever was attempting to gain entry. But it's no use. However hard I try, I just can't seem to get focused."

"That's hardly surprising," Adam said. "The fumes given off by a Hand of Glory are intended to incapacitate the victim not only physically, but psychically as well."

Peregrine's red-rimmed eyes widened slightly. "Really?"

"Really," Adam said. "And that's one of the things about this incident that gives me serious cause for concern. If the intruders had simply wanted you unconscious, they could have used any one of a number of knockout gases available to the medical profession. The fact that they resorted to using a Hand of Glory argues that they know something of your talents and wanted to put you out of action on more than one level."

"Well, they succeeded in that," Peregrine muttered, briefly pushing his spectacles up to rub at the bridge of his nose. "I've still got a thumping headache."

"Fortunately, the headache and the nullifying effects are only temporary," Adam said. "Once you've had a chance to get some sleep, you should be back in full possession of your faculties. But, for the moment, I'm afraid you'll have to resign yourself to sitting on the sidelines while the rest of us try to piece the facts together."

"I'd certainly be grateful for an explanation," Peregrine said. "From what you've told me, the Hand of Glory is not an easy charm to manufacture. What were these people after, that they were prepared to go to such extravagant lengths to procure it?''

''I've been thinking about that,'' Adam said grimly, ''and I don't like the answer that keeps turning up. This was never intended as a burglary; it was meant to be a kidnapping.''

''A kidnapping?'' Peregrine blanched. ''Good God! Why would anyone want to kidnap Julia and me?''

''I don't know the *why*,'' Adam said, ''and I would rather not speculate too closely. Especially since the most likely *who* is Francis Raeburn.''

''Surely not!'' Peregrine blurted. When Adam merely gazed at him in silence, he said protestingly, ''But that would mean that he's been keeping *us* under surveillance at the same time we've been out looking for him.''

Adam nodded. ''Not a very reassuring thought, is it? I think we're going to have to tread very carefully from here on out.''

When they returned to the main house, Humphrey met them with the news that Julia was resting comfortably in her room.

''And where is my mother?'' Adam asked, as he and Peregrine shrugged out of their coats.

''She's in the library, sir.''

Nodding his thanks, Adam led the way to the library, and was somewhat taken aback to discover that his wife was there ahead of him. But if Philippa was in any way perturbed, she gave no sign of it.

''I'm glad you're back,'' she told the two men. ''Julia's in bed and should sleep through till morning. In the interim, Ximena and I have just been discussing how best to dispose of this repellent object.''

She indicated the tin on the desktop, the lid now replaced. Swift to take in the situation, Adam inferred that Ximena had been given at least a partial briefing with respect to the Hand.

''I'm not sure we're ready to dispose of it just yet,'' he said cautiously, uncertain how much or how little Philippa had been moved to say in his absence. ''The police didn't find much evidence to go on during their part of the investigation. That means that, as loathsome as it is, the Hand is our only tangible link with the perpetrators. It's probably in our best interest to keep it intact—at least until we've had a chance to examine it more carefully.''

He went over to the desk and started riffling through his desktop Rdodex.

''Who are you thinking of phoning at this hour?'' Peregrine asked.

''The estimable Harry Nimmo,'' Adam replied. ''With you temporarily *hors de combat*, it occurs to me that we could do with some reinforcements—and Noel is out of town until tomorrow. Actually, perhaps you'd care to do the honors. Since I know him mainly by reputation, a request for assistance is bound to seem less of an imposition, coming from you.''

With a nod, Peregrine came and took the phone, then hesitated with his finger poised above the keypad. ''How soon were you thinking of asking him to join us?''

''Tonight, if he can possibly manage it,'' Adam said. ''I know it's late, but the sooner we get our investigation under way, the sooner we'll have the answers we need.''

While Peregrine was making the call, Ximena looked to her husband for enlightenment. ''Who is this Harry Nimmo?''

''A friend of Noel McLeod's,'' Adam replied, ''who's helped us out in the past. His gifts are not unlike Peregrine's, but he's only beginning to explore his potential. This would seem to be a good time for him to get some experience in the field.''

Peregrine rejoined them a moment later, looking somewhat relieved.

''Harry's agreed to lend a hand,'' he informed Adam. ''He was a little anxious when he heard that Noel isn't available, but he's on his way.''

''Did he give you an ETA?'' Adam asked.

''About half an hour.''

Nodding, Adam glanced at his watch, then turned to the two women with an air of apology.

''It appears we *will* be working further tonight. I wonder if I might beg your indulgence and ask you both to leave us? Harry is Noel McLeod's student, not mine. I've met him once before, but only superficially. Given the fact that he's still very new at this kind of thing, it's going to be difficult enough for us to work together without the added complication of an audience.''

"Too true!'' Philippa agreed briskly. "Come along, Ximena. Let's take ourselves off and spare the poor man the discomfort of being asked to perform in front of a roomful of strangers.''

"Thank you,'' Adam said, accompanying them to the door. "I'm sorry if this seems a bit cavalier,'' he said to Ximena as he kissed her good night, "but it really wouldn't be practical for you to stay. I'll let you know how we've made out in the morning. In the meantime, try and get some sleep. I'll join you as soon as I can.''

In preparation for what lay ahead, he locked the Hand away in the safe again and called Humphrey into the library to build up the fire while he and Peregrine made a quick trip back to the gate lodge to collect Peregrine's sketch box. En route he had Peregrine brief him regarding everything he could remember about working with Harry over the last month. Upon returning to the main house, they had settled into two chairs before a now respectable fire, the biscuit tin containing the Hand now set on a small table beside Adam's chair, when the sound of a car approaching up the drive made them prick up their ears. Very shortly after, there came a deferential knock at the door.

"Mr. Nimmo has arrived, sir,'' Humphrey said.

As he ushered the newcomer into the room, Peregrine sprang to his feet, followed by Adam.

"Harry!'' Peregrine said, coming to shake the counsellor's hand. "You must have flown, instead of driving.''

"You did say it was urgent,'' Harry replied. "Sir Adam, I'm pleased to meet you again.''

"And I, you,'' Adam said, shaking the other man's hand. "Thank you for coming, so late and on such short notice. And please call me Adam. I've already put you in an awkward position by going over Noel's head to ask for you.''

Harry shrugged, pulling an unexpectedly boyish grin. "Well, I certainly never expected that he wouldn't be here, the first time I worked with you, but Peregrine seems to think

I might be able to help. This is all still pretty new to me, but I'll certainly give it my best shot. I never could resist the lure of a good mystery.''

''Well, we certainly have *that*,'' Adam said with an answering smile. ''Please, come and sit down. I'm afraid it may well seem like jumping right in at the deep end—but Peregrine has had a little—ah—setback this evening, and I'd rather not wait until he's recovered.''

He left it to Peregrine to render an account of the evening's events, watching Harry's reactions as the counsellor listened closely, his initial bewilderment abating as his interest grew.

''You say this thing is made out of a human *hand*?'' he asked at the conclusion of the artist's narrative.

Adam nodded.

''And you want me to touch it?''

Again Adam nodded.

''And did Peregrine tell you what happened when I only touched a scrap of bull hide?''

''Yes, he did,'' Adam said. ''And given the impressions you got from that, I have hopes that you might pick up similar impressions from the Hand. It would be extremely useful if we could find out who prepared the thing.''

Harry pulled a wry face. ''I can't say this is my first choice in late-night entertainment.''

''I can appreciate that,'' Adam said on a note of sincere regret. ''If we had any other immediate recourse, I wouldn't be asking you to do this. But anyone capable of making and using as grisly a weapon as a Hand of Glory is not someone to be trifled with. No lasting harm was done tonight, but future victims might not be so lucky.''

''Put like that, it makes a pretty incontestable argument,'' Harry said drily. ''Aye, I'll do it—God knows I've seen worse things than dead hands in my soldiering days. I'd better warn you, though, that I don't have much control over these psychometric flashes I've been having.''

''Experience may well change that,'' Adam said with a faint smile. ''And Peregrine will tell you that I do have experience helping people learn control over such abilities. Just now, anything you can come up with is likely to be helpful.

Even if you don't pick up on any names, a visual impression of one or more of the perpetrators would give us something to start on."

"If images are all I get," Harry said, "how are you going to know what I see?"

"That's easy," Peregrine said. "Just describe it, and I'll draw it."

Harry frowned. "I thought you said this Hand knocked you out of action."

"So it did," Adam agreed, "but only with respect to the psychic aspects of his talent. He's still one of the best forensic artists I've ever worked with. If you can provide him with a description, I promise you he'll turn it into an accurate likeness."

Harry made a gesture of mock surrender. "I can see you've thought this whole thing through pretty thoroughly. Well, I did come here to try to help. All right, let's get on with it."

While Peregrine retrieved pencils and a pad from his sketch box, Adam moved the tin from the table beside him to a smaller one he set in front of Harry. As he took off the lid and set it aside, Harry leaned closer to take a cautious look inside, recoiling briefly from the smell.

"Whew! But I guess it *is* a dead hand, isn't it?" he remarked with a grimace. He looked at it again, but his reluctance to touch the Hand was manifest.

"Take all the time you want," Adam said quietly. "Peregrine and I will be ready when you are."

"Easy for you to say," Harry muttered darkly. "Very well, here goes."

He drew a deep breath and extended his right hand over the tin, flexing his fingers and then reaching downward. The instant of contact brought a gasp to his lips as his hand jerked back almost of its own volition. With a muttered imprecation, he gave it a violent shake, as if he'd been stung by a scorpion.

"Did you see anything?" Adam asked.

Harry shook his head.

"But you *felt* something," Adam said.

"Aye, but I may just have been scaring myself," Harry allowed. "I'll try again."

While Adam and Peregrine looked on, he reached into the tin a second time, only to recoil even more violently. A third attempt provoked an equally strong reaction, and left him trembling.

"If you aren't seeing anything, what are you *feeling*?" Adam prompted quietly. "Focus on it, Harry. Tell me what you feel."

The response from Harry was a shiver, and his eyes had gone a little glazed.

"C-cold . . . icy cold . . ." he mumbled thickly. "Can't . . . seem . . . to breathe—"

As Harry gasped—a choked, strangled sound—Adam suddenly realized that he must be fastening on some residual resonance, not from those who had prepared the Hand but from the hand's owner, who would have died by hanging. Swiftly he reached out and gripped the counsellor firmly by the arm.

"Stop, Harry! Let it go!" he ordered.

Harry breathed out explosively and shuddered, then looked up shakily at Adam. Sucking in a lungful of air, he passed his free hand across his eyes.

"Whew. Thanks. I—ah—don't know what that was all about, but it doesn't seem to be getting us anywhere. Any suggestions?"

"Yes," Adam said thoughtfully. It had not occurred to him that Harry's sensibilities would be acute enough to penetrate past the veil of dark empowerments which had been used to make the Hand what it was. Impressed by this evidence of Harry's potential, he said, "I think we might get better results if you'll consent to let me put you into a trance."

Harry blinked. "That's right, you're a shrink. You want to hypnotize me?"

"I do," Adam said. "Does that prospect frighten you?"

"No, no," Harry murmured, stabbing a finger at the Hand. "*That* frightens me. I know Noel was using a bit of hypnosis when he worked with me—and it did help." He managed a pallid grin. "I suppose he learned it from you."

"I suppose he did," Adam agreed, smiling faintly.

"Let's do it, then," Harry said. "We sure aren't getting anywhere with what we've been doing so far."

"Very well," Adam replied. "Then, suppose you close your eyes and settle back. Make yourself comfortable. Let yourself relax, and take a deep breath. . . ."

The counsellor proved an apt subject, sinking into trance with the ease of a child falling asleep. Adam spent a few minutes deepening the trance, observing his subject's reactions and reinforcing a series of suggestions he layered into place, then set fingertips to the pulse in Harry's wrist.

"I think he's probably already captured what he needs," Adam murmured aside to Peregrine. "It may be that all we need to do now is help him get at it and sort the imagery. Harry, you're doing very well indeed. Do you feel ready for another go?"

Harry's head bobbed up and down.

"Very good. Now, listen closely to my voice and do exactly as I tell you to do. Visualize the Hand. See it in your mind's eye. If you think back, you'll remember that I asked you earlier to touch it. I won't ask you to do that again, but I want you to call to mind the impressions you experienced during those brief moments of contact. Cast your mind back, and feel yourself touching the Hand again. Hold those impressions in your mind's eye and tell me what you see."

Harry's face tightened. "Shadows," he mumbled. "I see a dirty ball of shadows."

"That's a good image," Adam said. "Think of that ball as an onion. Think of the shadows as layers of onion skin. Imagine yourself peeling away the outermost layer. If you hold that layer up to the light, you'll find that you can look through it like a windowpane. On the other side of the pane are the ones who made the shadows, the ones you're trying to discern."

For a long moment, Harry did not respond. Watching him closely, Adam could see rapid eye movements beneath the veil of his closed eyelids. Then his lips twitched.

"I see them!" he breathed.

"That's good, Harry. How many are there?"

"Three."

"We'll start with the one who's clearest," Adam said quietly. "I want you to describe each one in turn, as fully and accurately as you can manage."

Peregrine was already leaning forward, his pencil poised at the ready. For the next half hour he hung on Harry's every word, laboring to translate the counsellor's words into images, perfecting the images that were taking shape on the paper in front of him. It was harder work than when he could rely on his own psychic talents to help fill in the gaps, especially with a headache, but by the time Harry had wound down, Peregrine had managed to capture three distinct likenesses. At his nod to Adam that he had finished, Adam reached over and lightly clasped Harry's wrist.

"You've done very well, Harry," he told him softly. "Now I want you to rest for a while. You'll hear nothing until I touch your wrist again and call you by name. Just rest and float. Will that be all right?"

Harry's head bobbed in assent.

"Good man," Adam whispered. "Rest now. I'll touch your wrist when it's time to awaken."

As Adam withdrew his hand, Harry's head lolled back against the headrest and he exhaled with a sigh. Adam watched him for a moment, and softly whispered his name, but Harry made no response. Satisfied, Adam turned his attention to Peregrine, who was leafing through the drawings he had just done.

"All right, let's see what you've got," Adam murmured, scooting his chair closer.

The first sketch was of a middle-aged man with the disproportionately muscular build of a weight-lifter.

"I don't recognize that man at all," Peregrine observed, turning to the next sketch. "I was beginning to think I'd lost my touch, or that Harry was way off base. This second fellow, on the other hand, seems vaguely familiar—though that might only be because he looks like a Nazi. I kept wanting to sketch him in a Luftwaffe uniform, complete with a Blue Max at his throat."

Adam studied the second drawing, of a compact blond man with a military crewcut and steel-rimmed aviator spectacles.

"I see what you mean," he said, "but I've seen this man before!" He tapped lightly on the drawing with a fingernail while he concentrated a moment, mentally reviewing the gallery of faces he recalled from prior encounters with the Lodge of the Lynx—and came up with a match.

"I have him," he said, on a grim note of triumph. "You and I have both seen him before. That's the man in the dinghy, who came off the seaplane that snatched away Raeburn and his Nazi diamonds. He must be more highly placed in the Lynx organization than we realized at the time."

"And the best is yet to come," Peregrine said archly, revealing the third drawing.

Grimly intent, Adam cast his gaze over the next page Peregrine presented. Of the three drawings, this was by far the most nebulous—little more than a suggestion of fair hair and slender height.

Even so, there could be no doubt about the subject's identity—especially in light of all the other evidence he and his fellow Huntsmen had so far been able to assemble. The ghostly image looking out at them from the page could only be Francis Raeburn himself.

"Yes, indeed," Adam murmured, raising his eyes to meet Peregrine's. "An old adversary. I don't suppose you have any doubts on that account?"

The artist only shook his head wordlessly.

"Right, then," Adam said. "It seems our Mr. Nimmo has come through for us yet again. And whether or not he's aware of it, he's done this plenty of times before. I think, before we bring him back, it's high time his contributions were brought to the attention of a higher authority."

# CHAPTER TWENTY-SIX

T HE authority Adam had in mind was not to be sought on any earthly plane. While Peregrine made ready to keep watch between the worlds, Adam settled comfortably in the chair beside Harry, touching his Adept ring to his lips and invoking the guidance and protection of the Light as he closed his eyes and took a moment to ground and center himself. With his next breath, he let himself sink into the light trance that was his gateway to the deeper, more profound verities of the Inner Planes.

His inner image of the library seemed to expand around him like a soap bubble, its receding walls becoming thin and translucent as gauze before melting away altogether, leaving him suspended in an opalescent sea. Momentarily, a familiar pang of disorientation tugged at his inner equilibrium. Then the surrounding firmament began to re-form itself around him, gathering substance until all at once he felt solid ground beneath his feet.

A shining portal manifested itself before him, its panels iridescent as pearl. Above and beyond it, Adam could sense the towering presence of a great temple not made by human hands. Gathering his intent about him like a garment, he set his outward aspect on this plane in the guise of a supplicant priest, approaching bareheaded and barefooted to the foot of the great portal, where he pronounced the Word that would gain him entrance.

His utterance reverberated throughout the sanctum. As the echoes subsided, the portal swung open. Beyond the threshold lay an aery vault so vast that its proportions could only be guessed. Near at hand, however, beneath a soaring canopy of arches whose depths receded into infinity, a scintillating pillar of rainbow radiance took visible form: the astral emanation of the powerful intellectual Presence that Adam had come to recognize as the Master.

He bowed low in token of profound respect. As he did so, he was greeted by a voice in which many musical textures were combined in a single melodic strand.

*The enemy hides in Shadow, Master of the Hunt. Therefore, be as wise as a serpent, having seen the face of the Adversary.*

Adam lifted his head, surprised by the directness of the warning—and chilled by the confirmation that it was, indeed, Raeburn who had been responsible for the kidnap attempt just foiled.

"It is of another that I came seeking counsel, Master," he said. "The Hunt has taken up the scent, but into our protection has come a Hunt Follower who could be more."

*The Hunter must know himself as he seeks to know his quarry, swift to discern where weakness lies. Being wise, he will not set forth on the scent without first making provision against the storm.*

*Any companion who follows him must go armed against the perils that lurk in the shadows. But if the Follower's heart is set upon the Chase, then the Hunt itself will prove him.*

The rainbow pillar swirled to engulf Adam in a timeless instant of benison, then dissolved away. Bowing, Adam gave wordless thanks for the guidance offered, then withdrew to settle back into his body with a sigh. As he stirred, Peregrine sat forward eagerly, hurrying to lay a fresh log on the fire when Adam shivered and hugged his arms close to his chest, rubbing his upper arms.

"How did you make out?" Peregrine asked. "Did you find the answers you were looking for?"

Adam gave a blink and ran a hand over the back of his neck. "As much a warning as any guidance, I think. It does appear we're dead-on regarding Raeburn. As you're probably coming to realize, however, such guidance as we receive from the Inner Planes can be frustratingly oblique. If we hope to profit by it, we have to be prepared to work for the meaning. Give me a minute while I see how much I can sort into concrete terms at short notice.''

Peregrine subsided. Sitting forward to stretch out his hands to the warmth of the fire, Adam bent his gaze upon the leaping flames while he reviewed the Master's instruction from beginning to end. The warning about Raeburn seemed clear. The Biblical reference to serpents and the next two lines likewise had the vaguely ominous ring of a personal caution as well as sage advice for any would-be newcomer. But the rest seemed to offer guarded assent for Harry Nimmo to try his hand at the Hunt.

''I'm going to have to give this further thought,'' Adam said, looking up at Peregrine and sitting back in his chair. ''Perhaps it's simply too soon to receive an active mandate for Harry to join us. But I've no impression that we should discourage him, either. The gist of what seems applicable to him simply warns that any prospective candidate must be made aware of the risks involved, and must be equipped to look after his own safety.''

Peregrine glanced over at the sleeping Harry.

''He does still require some looking-after, doesn't he?'' he murmured. ''He's certainly game, though—and he's already helped us out more than once, in an auxiliary capacity. I don't know him nearly as well as Noel does, of course, but he certainly doesn't strike me as a man inclined to run away from danger. If you were to offer him the opportunity to serve on the front line, I don't think he'd turn you down.''

''No, but I think it might be unfair to Harry, to send him into the front lines before he's acquired adequate defenses. According to the Master, any companion who follows the Hunt must go 'armed against the perils that lurk in the shadows.' Harry is learning to *see* some of the perils; now he needs to learn what to *do* about what he sees—and not to pull back simply because what he sees looks new and frightening. I believe you'll recall the learning of that lesson, not so very long ago.''

Peregrine smiled, lowering his eyes.

''You were very patient with me.''

"My patience has been amply rewarded," Adam said gently. "Shall we talk to Harry?"

The counsellor emerged from his trance with the air of one refreshed by the experience, and apparently without conscious memory of any of it.

"That was certainly painless enough," he said, his slightly fuddled expression conveying a trace of lingering bewilderment. "Was I any help at all?"

"You were, indeed," Adam said. "Have a look, Counsellor."

He held out a hand to Peregrine for the sketches he had made, passing them across to Harry. Harry's brow furrowed as he shuffled through them.

"*These* are the blokes behind tonight's little episode?" he asked, a note of scorn in his voice. "I was expecting something far more exotic. This one looks like a stevedore, and this wispy one could be an accountant, or a school teacher." He tapped the sketch of Raeburn, cocking his head for another angle. "Or maybe a banker. Yes, I suppose he could be a cutthroat banker."

"Don't be deceived by appearances," Adam said. "That man is one of the most dangerous black Adepts I've ever come across."

"You're joking." Harry arched an eyebrow. "What's his name?"

"I'd rather not say."

"Why not?"

"Because names have power," Adam said bluntly, "and once you start to find out more about him, you'll be party to knowledge that could become extremely dangerous to you. Peregrine and I, among others, are committed to going ahead with this investigation. If you involve yourself in it too, you become partner to the same responsibilities—and subject to the same dangers."

"Do you take me for a coward?" Harry demanded, bridling slightly.

"Certainly not. But courage should always be tempered by caution and common sense. The fact that your talents are beginning to manifest at this point in time suggests that you've come to a turning point in your life. And the more often you use these talents, the more likely it is that you'll be noticed by others with similar talents. Not all of them are on our side, and some of them are *very* dangerous.''

''What do you mean, I'll be *noticed*?'' Harry murmured, suddenly subdued.

''Simply this,'' Adam said. ''Beginning to use psychic talents is a bit like sending up flares on the astral. Those who can see them tend to investigate, the opposition included. You can learn to shield those flares, conceal them from those not meant to see them; but until you do, or until you can defend yourself against those who come investigating, you'd be putting yourself in immortal danger if you join us. And you could put us at risk, trying to protect you.''

''In—*im*mortal danger?'' Harry murmured, a little white about the lips. ''Are you trying to frighten me off?''

''No, but I *am* asking you to think about what I've said. When you've had a chance to digest it—maybe in a few days—we'll talk again. Meanwhile, we should probably let you get home. It's late. I want to thank you again for your help tonight. We'll deal with this for now.''

The following morning, in a Victorian house on the outskirts of Paisley, those responsible for the previous night's events—and failures—were preparing to answer before an inquisition which had all the more sinister earmarks of a military tribunal. Seated behind the desk in the library, flanked by two of Richter's hard-eyed mercenaries, Angela Fitzgerald took a moment to rake her gaze over the three men arraigned before her. Her dark eyes were hard and glittering as marcasites as they came to rest upon the youngest of the trio, who might have been handsome had he not been green with apprehension. He was nursing a bandaged right hand.

''So, *you're* the idiot who decided to rush things,'' she observed dispassionately. ''I suppose that makes you responsible for this fiasco.''

Her tone was conversationally mild, but the man to whom the statement was addressed cringed as if struck. Swallowing hard, he opened his mouth as if to offer some excuse, but no sound came out. Beside him, the driver on the ill-fated mission spared his colleague a scathing side-glance before venturing his own excuse.

"I reminded him of orders and told him to wait, but he got impatient. I didn't think he'd bolt with the Hand—and then I didn't want to risk a commotion—"

"Oh, shut up!" Angela said in a voice that would have cut glass. "You didn't *think*! And you, Mr. Zoller," she glared at the third man, "if Summers couldn't stop him, why didn't you? You must have known Lovat was still downstairs."

Before Zoller could summon any reply, she returned her basilisk glare to the first victim of her anger.

"Hoping to make a name for yourself, were you, Mr. Fenton? It's a dangerous thing to have ideas above your station. Ambition is no bad thing, but you shouldn't have allowed yourself to forget that failure has its price."

The man Fenton flinched away from her gaze, almost on the brink of tears, his brow beaded with cold sweat.

"Give me another chance," he begged in a strangled voice. "I swear it won't happen again!"

"Indeed it will not!"

Angela transferred her attention to Klaus Richter, who was standing against the door behind the men, arms folded across his chest, as if to place himself at one remove from the proceedings.

"You're the one who recruited this nitwit," she pointed out acidly. "Are you prepared to overlook his insubordination?"

Richter shook his head minutely, his blue gaze hard as steel.

"You may do with him as you wish," he stated flatly.

This bald disavowal drew a strangled whimper from the principal culprit. Angela ignored it.

"The two of you, get out of my sight!" she told Fenton's companions.

As Richter stood aside to permit their hasty retreat, Angela turned to Fenton himself with a thin, cold smile.

"So, Mr. Fenton, what are we going to do with *you*?" she asked. "I dislike wasting resources, so I'm not going to have you killed—yet," she informed him. "It's just possible that you may be able to redeem yourself. That will be for Mr. Raeburn to decide, when he returns. But until then, I don't want to look at your stupid face. Krankauer, take him somewhere and put him on ice for now,'' she said over her shoulder to the larger of her two attendants.

Fenton blanched at these words, knees visibly trembling as he made a broken attempt to plead for mercy, but Krankauer and his partner turned deaf ears as they came to take him away, as did Angela. When the door had closed behind them, she shifted her acid gaze to the waiting Richter.

''And what's *your* excuse? I thought your people were supposed to be good.''

Richter shrugged, refusing to be intimidated. ''Most of them are. Every so often one encounters disappointment.''

''*Disappointment?* That's hardly an adequate word for *this* fiasco. Having planted the Hand of Glory, the least the silly fools could have done was to retrieve it before letting themselves be driven off!''

''I agree,'' Richter said mildly.

''Well, this mess is yours, so you can clean it up,'' Angela replied, somewhat deflated. ''Find out what's become of the Hand, and try and get it back—preferably before Mr. Raeburn emerges from his retreat. What he's going to say when he learns that all his preparations have been wasted, I leave to your speculation.''

She sat fuming behind the desk for several minutes after Richter had left. It had been Raeburn's plan to seal his pact with Soulis at the next dark of the moon, now three days hence. To that end, he had absented himself the day before for a three-day period of fasting and preparation. Another time, Angela might have taken spiteful pleasure in knowing that Raeburn was squandering his energies to no good purpose. On this occasion, she sent for Barclay.

''I need to get in touch with Francis,'' she informed him when he arrived. ''After last night's disaster, the reasons should be obvious. Do you know where he is?''

Barclay shook his head. ''No, ma'am, I don't. Last I saw of him was when he had me let him off at the railway station. Where he was planning to go from there, he didn't say.''

Angela tapped her foot in vexed frustration, biting back a

comment inappropriate in front of an underling. "This really is too much," she muttered darkly. "Being circumspect is one thing, but this is verging on paranoia!"

When Barclay made no comment, she rose and began pacing the carpet with an impetuosity born of growing anger.

"If you can't tell me where Francis is," she flung over her shoulder, "maybe you can explain what he thought he was doing when he ordered Richter's people to go in after the Lovats. For pity's sake, that wretched artist is a Huntsman. It would have been dangerous enough if the attempt had succeeded. As matters stand at the moment, we're going to have Sinclair and company hounding us with every breath we take, and us with nothing to show for it!"

Barclay said nothing, and after a moment, Angela sighed and returned to the desk. Learning both hands against it, she considered her options until Raeburn should return.

"All right," she murmured. "I'll make yet another attempt at damage control. See if you can find him. He needs to be aware that we won't be going forward on the twenty-second."

After a beat, Barclay said quietly, "Do you care about him, Miz Fitzgerald?"

The question brought her up short. After the briefest of hesitations, she shook her head emphatically.

"Don't be impertinent."

Barclay shrugged. "He does take risks, Miz Fitzgerald," he said. "But Mr. Raeburn thinks the rewards will be worth the risks."

"Mr. Raeburn is riding straight for a fall," Angela said. "I don't intend to go down with him. Anyone else who feels the same way had better start making plans for the future."

Their eyes met and locked.

"I'll certainly give the matter some thought, Miz Fitzgerald," Barclay said. Shifting his gaze to the window, he added, "You never know when the wind may change."

Two days later, Raeburn returned from his self-imposed exile looking haggard, drawn, and underslept. The pallor brought on by three days of fasting yielded to the hectic flush of a towering rage when he learned how his orders had miscarried. The ensuing display of temper was as explosive as any his henchmen had ever witnessed. Nor did the storm die down after he had dismissed everyone but Angela from the library.

"Really, Francis, you're starting to rant like a lunatic," she said petulantly, when he had finally wound down. "This kidnap scheme was ill-conceived from the very outset. If you hadn't insisted on muddying the waters with a Hand of Glory, it could have been a straight snatch, with no hiccups. It would be far more becoming of you to admit as much, and stop blaming the hired help for your mistake."

Her words brought Raeburn up short in the midst of pacing the floor. Rounding on her, he snapped, "What would you know about it, you stupid cow? If they'd followed instructions, everything would have gone according to plan—and in a fitting manner to please our Patron. If you can't comprehend that, you have even less imagination than I gave you credit for!"

He sank into the nearest chair, his pale, glittering eyes fixed moodily at some distant vanishing point. "That wretched artist and his wife were a perfect choice of offerings: an Adept's body for Soulis, a tender morsel of flesh for his familiar. The combination would have bought us everything we wanted, and more. Not only would we have succeeded in harnessing the power of Taranis, we could have sent Soulis back into the bosom of the Hunting Lodge, wearing Lovat's guise, and gained access to their innermost secrets."

" 'If, if, would have'—but it didn't happen, Francis!" she cut in brutally. "Before you interrupt again, with your lofty aspirations, let me acquaint you with the realities of the current situation. Richter's contacts have been able to establish that the Hand of Glory is *not* in the custody of the police. There's no official police record of it. We must therefore assume that it has been secretly retained by the Hunting Lodge, undoubtedly at Strathmourne—which is the best-defended of any of the residences known to be connected with Sinclair and his friends.

"Furthermore, Sinclair has beefed up the security arrangements for the entire estate, and has men patrolling at night. That makes the prospect of stealing back the Hand rather infeasible. I suggest we might better utilize our energies to scramble the psychic backtrail so that the preparation of the Hand can't be traced back to us.''

Raeburn seemed to be only half-attending. His pale eyes were abstracted, their gaze roving the room like a fly seeking a place to light.

"You would do well to listen to me," Angela said acidly. "You know, I think all this trafficking with discarnate spirits and chaotic elementals is beginning to unbalance your mind. You're starting to remind me more and more of the Head-Master—and he was barking mad by the end of his career. If you don't get a grip on yourself and start listening to reason, the same thing could well happen to you."

"I'm touched by your concern," Raeburn said coldly, casting a scathing glance up and down her form. "Is that the reason why you're looking so wan and wasted, worrying about me?"

Angela glanced instinctively at the mirror above the fire-place, which reflected an image almost as haggard as Rae-burn's own. Even the careful application of makeup could not entirely conceal the dark circles underscoring her eyes, nor compensate for the pinched pallor of her cheeks.

"Don't flatter yourself," she retorted. "As it happens, I've been working hard while you were off playing mystic—engaged in damage-control and seeking ways to compensate for this setback. Since the bid to capture the Lovats failed, it's clear you're going to need new victims for the Soulis sacrifice—if, indeed, you're set upon this folly. Well, allow me to submit my personal nominations."

Retrieving her tooled leather briefcase from a nearby alcove, she returned to set it on the edge of Raeburn's desk while she extracted a slender file folder. When she handed this across to him, her sleeve drew back enough to reveal a line of puncture marks and shallow cuts disappearing up her arm.

Raeburn took the folder without commenting on this evidence of repeated and extensive bloodletting, sitting back in his chair as he flipped the folder open. On top of several single-spaced resume sheets within were two glossy black-

and-white eight-by-ten photographs, both of the same male subject from different angles.

Raeburn arched a supercilious eyebrow before lifting the photos to read the first few lines of the resume.

"Surely you're jesting," he said.

"There's more. The family history will bear out what I propose. Just read it before you say anything else."

Lips pressed together in a prim, poisonous smirk, Raeburn set the photos aside and began to read. As he scanned subsequent pages, his brow cleared, his expression slowly shifting from sour indulgence to surprised but increasingly avid concurrence, then changing to startled rejection which, after further reading, gave way to thoughtful deliberation.

"How did you come by this information?" he finally asked, leafing back through the previous pages.

"My methods are my own affair," she said with a tight smile. "Suffice it to say that I went to considerable trouble and personal expense to obtain what's in that folder. Don't squander it."

The feral smile he finally lifted to her held a gleam of cunning far more malevolent than any earlier outburst of anger.

"Angela, my darling," he purred. "Sometimes I almost think I do love you."

# CHAPTER TWENTY-SEVEN

"I was brought up in the Episcopal church," Julia said. "I've read the Bible more than once, and *thought* I understood its teachings concerning the conflicts of good and evil. But I see now what a naive assumption that was. Up until the other night, I simply had no idea what *real* evil was like—or how terrifying it could be."

These observations were directed at Philippa. The two of them were taking tea together in the little upstairs parlor known as the Rose Room. Philippa poured herself another cup of her favorite Earl Grey tea from the hand-painted Sèvres teapot which she liked to use for intimate occasions, glancing at Julia as she stirred in milk and sugar.

"You don't have to be ashamed of yourself for being unprepared," she said pragmatically, after taking a sip of the fragrant blend. "No sane person wants to know any more about evil than he or she has to. And don't make the mistake of confusing innocence with weakness. However frightened you might have been at the time, you acquitted yourself bravely when it counted—and have continued to do so, ever since."

Three days had passed since the sinister incident involving the Hand of Glory. Once the initial shock had worn off, Julia had insisted on returning to the gate lodge, firmly vetoing Peregrine's suggestion that she take up temporary residence with her uncle in Dunfermline.

Seeing that his wife was resolved to stand her ground, Peregrine had revised his schedule to enable him work at home as much of the time as possible. When his absence was unavoidable—as today, when he was doing a live sitting with a client up in Perth—Julia had consented to repair to the greater security of the main house, where she could count on having Philippa and the staff for company.

Declining Philippa's unspoken offer of a scone, Julia pulled a rueful grimace. "It's this sense of being completely out of my depth that bothers me," she sighed. "I don't know when I've ever felt smaller or more insignificant."

"Why is that?" Philippa asked.

Julia struggled for the words to express herself. "I suppose it's the realization that Creation itself is a lot more complicated than I ever previously imagined. The malice that went into making that *thing* you called the Hand of Glory was more than human—it was positively devilish. I know Scripture warns about there being forces of evil at work in the world, but I guess it never occurred to me to take those warnings literally in the context of the present day."

"On the contrary, those warnings were never more applicable than they are at present," Philippa said quite seriously. "It's one of the unfortunate side effects of modern-day materialism that a great many people have gotten complacent and allowed their spiritual defenses to slip. Certainly, we have legitimate cause to be afraid; the forces of evil are real, and they attack under many different guises. On the other hand, if you allow your judgement to be clouded by panic, you end up blaming all the wrong people."

"How does anyone tell the difference?" Julia wondered.

"Through an effort of discernment," Philippa replied. "Why else do you think we're commanded to love God with all our heart, with all our soul, with all our mind, and with all our strength, if we weren't intended to use all these faculties in seeking enlightenment?

"As for combating evil," she continued, "take comfort from the knowledge that we are not alone in the struggle. Where there are devils, there are also angels. And help is always available to those who aren't too proud to ask for it."

She put as much conviction as she could into this assertion, for she had an uneasy premonition that all of them were going to have to do their best to protect themselves and one another in the days to come.

Adam had already made good on his intentions to upgrade the estate's security system, installing new window locks and deadbolts at the gate lodge, lights activated by motion-sensors outside, and a secure telephone line that connected directly with the main house. The old cat-flap was replaced by a more sophisticated device requiring an electronic chip in the collar of the flap's one authorized user, and was temporarily closed off altogether.

As a further measure, until the present threat should be resolved, Adam had recruited the two stalwart sons of one of his tenant farmers to assist John, his trusty stableman, in patrolling the grounds at night, adding to the increased police drive-bys that now were making a point to watch for anything amiss at the somewhat isolated gate lodge. During the darkest hours of the night, when Peregrine and Julia were asleep, someone was always on duty downstairs in the Lovats' kitchen or sitting room, armed with a shotgun and mobile phone.

On less obvious levels, Adam and Philippa had spent an entire evening strengthening the esoteric defenses protecting the house and its immediate environs, doing their best to ensure that they and their associates could rely on finding a safe working haven within the confines of Strathmourne itself.

Once off the estate, however, security considerations became more problematical. No stranger to taking risks on his own account, Adam was more worried about Ximena's personal safety than he liked to admit, especially after the attack on the Lovats. Sometimes working double shifts, in the run-up to the wedding, and often obliged to return home late at night, Ximena presented all too tempting a target to the operatives who had tried and failed to snatch the Lovats—and those operatives undoubtedly answered to Francis Raeburn.

But Ximena's personal and professional commitments were every bit as weighty as Adam's own, making it impracticable for either of them to remain at home, even if Adam had been willing to let himself be intimidated by fear of what *might* happen. Not to venture forth in pursuit of the

Hunt would render him just as impotent as if Raeburn had already won. Accordingly, Adam was obliged to search out a workable compromise that allowed Ximena's life, at least, to go on with some semblance of normalcy.

After some initial objections, Ximena agreed to let Humphrey act as her personal escort and chauffeur, whenever her schedule conflicted with Adam's own or required late-night travel. For backup, McLeod volunteered the services of his aide, Donald Cochrane, as a substitute driver. Those members of the Hunting Lodge who had dealt with Raeburn in the past could only hope that these measures would prove sufficient to offset whatever shadowy scheme their adversary might be formulating.

Some inkling of the scope of Raeburn's ambition began to take shape only a few days later. When Adam returned to his office after a particularly difficult session with a longtime patient, McLeod was pacing outside the door.

"I take it this is not a social call," Adam said, unlocking his office, when McLeod only growled a perfunctory greeting.

As the door closed behind them, the inspector handed Adam a newspaper cutting paper-clipped to a fax flimsy. The cutting was from the previous day's *Glasgow Herald*, and the headline read: MURDER INQUIRY AFTER BODY FOUND.

"We think it's Taliere," McLeod said, as Adam lifted the article to glance at the faxed photograph underneath, clearly that of a corpse. "Donald spotted the article this morning, and followed up with a couple of phone calls. Strathclyde Police are listing him as a John Doe, but I'd bet my pension that this is our man. Compare that photo with the mug shot Evans sent us from Wales, and Peregrine's sketch on the next page."

Adam did so, then flipped back to the news clipping, skimming down its contents as he walked around to sit behind his desk.

"*Strathclyde Police are carrying out a murder investigation after the body of an elderly man was found in a wooded area of Strathclyde Park near Motherwell yesterday,*" he read aloud. "*A police spokesman declined to give details, but confirmed that the so-far unidentified victim had suffered horrific injuries. . . .*

"What *kind* of horrific injuries?" Adam asked, glancing up at McLeod.

The inspector gave a grimace, sinking down in the chair opposite.

"His throat had been cut—and not where the body was dumped. No blood anywhere in the vicinity. You want to know what else?"

"Probably not—but go on."

"I don't want to even think this, but the case seems to bear some startling similarities to Randall Stewart's murder."

"Tell me," Adam said evenly, laying the pages on his desk.

Sighing, McLeod proceeded to outline what he knew so far.

"A hill-walker and his dog stumbled on the body. Police surgeon estimates he could have been dead anywhere from a couple of days to a couple of weeks. The body was half-covered with snow."

"But not," Adam said, "in any kind of ritual setting, or you would have said so. What makes you compare it to Randall's murder?"

"Because the left jugular and carotid artery had been slashed through," McLeod said, his blue gaze not shifting from Adam's. "Because he had also been garrotted first—and hit over the head."

Adam closed his eyes briefly, trying to keep at bay the memory of Randall Stewart lying in the snow in his own blood—victim of a ritual slaying involving the so-called "triple-death" favored by certain elder gods of the past. Francis Raeburn had been responsible for that atrocity and several other deaths of equal abhorrence—and had eluded apprehension the one time Adam actually had met him face to face.

"There's something else," McLeod said, cutting short the flashback. "Postmortem analysis of the victim's stomach contents revealed significant amounts of a substance derived from *miscum album*. That's mistletoe, in case you'd forgotten. When Harry and I checked out Taliere's cottage, I found a jar of mistletoe berries among the herbals in his larder. As you doubtless recall, a decoction of mistletoe was a favored elixir among the ancient Druids, thought to enhance psychic susceptibility.''

Adam sighed heavily, suddenly feeling years older than when he had walked into the room.

''I shouldn't think there's any doubt that we need to look at that body,'' he said, glancing up at McLeod. ''How soon can you arrange it?''

''I've already rung Motherwell,'' McLeod replied. ''The body's being held in Carluke. They're expecting us in a couple of hours, if you can get away. I've got Harry lined up as well. Since we haven't yet got a location to pin down the slaying, it seemed to me that Harry's talents might be more appropriate than Peregrine's.''

''They may well be,'' Adam agreed, standing to shuck off his lab coat. ''Besides that, Peregrine's heavily booked with live sittings for most of this week. It would be awkward for him to break away.''

Two hours later, Adam and McLeod were following a Strathclyde Police sergeant along a back corridor of Law Hospital in Carluke, Harry Nimmo trailing in their wake. Though scheduled for court that afternoon, the redoubtable Q.C. had seconded one of his junior associates to appear in his place, so that he could come along. En route, the three men had reviewed the aspects of the present case as they might apply to Callanish, where Harry had been, but no mention had been made of a possible connection with Randall Stewart's murder.

''The police surgeon who did the postmortem wasn't available on such short notice,'' the sergeant told them, as he opened the door to the hospital morgue, ''but I asked today's duty surgeon to go over the report, after you rang. Dr. Singh, here are your visitors from Edinburgh.''

Dr. Robert Singh proved to be an amiable Pakistani, veteran of nearly thirty years' service as a consultant to the Strathclyde Police. When courtesies had been exchanged, he wasted no time in getting down to the business at hand.

"I tell you, Dr. Sinclair, this is a strange one," he said, as he rolled out the metal drawer housing the remains of the deceased. "Never have I seen such violence done to a frail old man. He looks like someone's grand-papa."

The face of the corpse on the stainless-steel table showed signs that death had not been easy or peaceful, with a deep gash in the left side of the scrawny neck. Across the broad chest, still surprisingly muscled for a man of this age, faded blue tattoos defined a series of ancient Pictish symbols, some familiar and some not, many of them of darkling import. Bending closer, Adam noted ligature marks across the throat and along the sides of the neck, confirming a ruthless throttling of the victim during the killing process.

Noting Harry's tight-jawed focus on the body, Adam shot a speaking glance at McLeod and drew the other physician aside to discuss details of the autopsy report, leaving the inspector and Harry to carry out less conventional inquiries.

"Come around here, so our backs are to them," McLeod murmured, drawing Harry around to his side of the metal table. "Adam will get him out of here, if he can, but I think we can manage this without raising any alarm, if you take it slowly."

Harry nodded, swallowing visibly as he set his hands with care on the edge of the table.

"I hope I don't disappoint you, Noel," he whispered. "Now that I've worked with Adam, I know a bit more what to expect, but I'm not sure I'm up to this."

"You'll do fine," McLeod reassured him. "I'll talk you down. I believe Adam set you some posthypnotic triggers, to help you settle?"

"Aye."

"We'll assume they're the usual ones for our mob, then. Close your eyes and take a deep breath, Harry, and let it all the way out," he said, setting his hand on the counsellor's wrist as he complied. "That's it. Let go and relax, let yourself center and focus."

He paused as Harry took another deep breath and softly exhaled.

"How're you doing?" he asked.

"All right," Harry said with a faint nod.

"Good. Now reach out with your right hand and touch his shoulder."

Harry obeyed, his hand immediately recoiling as if stung, his eyes popping open.

"Jesus!" he whispered under his breath.

"You okay?"

"Yeah, but there's some nasty stuff here," came the whispered reply. "I don't know if I can do this, Noel—not and have to worry about our friend back there."

McLeod glanced over his shoulder, then back at Harry.

"All right. There's a way to do this that might offend your dignity, but it should get the job done. Do you trust me?"

"Aye, you know I do."

"All right, we're going to shift to advanced student mode," McLeod replied, reaching into his pocket for his Adept ring, which he slipped onto his finger with the stone turned inward. "I'll try to buffer some of this for you. I want you to close your eyes again and settle back deeper into trance. When this is over, you're not going to remember any of this until I tell you to," he added, as Harry's eyes closed obediently. "There's going to be some backlash, by taking the information this way, but it's going to look like you just got queasy from being so close to a dead body, and passed out. Don't back out on me now, Harry. Are you willing to do this?"

Harry's head dipped minutely in assent, clearly deep in trance.

"All right, when I take your wrist, you're going to go twice as deep as you are now; and when I lift your hand and touch it to the body, I want you to imagine a door opening— and it won't close until I lift your hand again. What comes into your mind while the door is open may be shocking, even horrifying, but it can't touch your essence. You're perfectly safe." He glanced again at Singh, who was bent over the autopsy report with Adam. "Nod when you're ready to do it."

Harry drew another deep breath and slowly let it out, then gave a faint nod. Without hesitation, McLeod seized his wrist, making certain his ring made contact with bare flesh, and lifted Harry's hand to touch the corpse's shoulder.

Harry stiffened, a faint gasp escaping his lips. McLeod let him tremble for a count of five, then lifted Harry's hand from the contact, shifting to catch him under the elbow as he reeled and buckled at the knees.

"*Sleep now, Harry,*" McLeod whispered, "and lose this until I tell you otherwise." And then, in a louder voice, "Jesus, Harry, haven't you ever seen a dead body before?"

The inspector's cry, plus the flurry of motion as he caught Harry under the arms and began hustling him to a nearby chair, brought Adam and Singh at once.

"I expect it's the smells," Adam said to Singh, improvising as he came to bend over Harry with McLeod. "He said on the way here that he was feeling a little fragile today. Something about a friend's bachelor party last night, I believe." He patted his pockets, then turned to Singh in appeal. "I don't suppose you've got some smelling salts around here somewhere? I should imagine this happens all the time."

Singh snorted and went over to a desk to rummage in a drawer.

"Yes, but it's usually young police officers, fresh out of training."

He returned to bend beside Adam, snapping an ammonia capsule between thumb and forefinger and passing it under Harry's nose.

"Steady, Harry," Adam murmured, laying his hand across the counsellor's brow as the dark head jerked back in reflex from the pungent smell, eyelids flickering on the edge of consciousness. "This happens sometimes. Take a deep breath. You'll be fine."

Singh made another pass with his ammonia, and Harry came fully awake, though his eyes had a vague, unfocused quality about them.

"Jesus, I'm sorry, Adam," he murmured. "I don't know what came over me. Noel and I were talking about the case, and suddenly everything began to spin."

"No matter," Adam said. "I think we're about finished here anyway, aren't we, Noel? Dr. Singh is letting me take away a copy of the forensic report."

"Aye, I'm done," McLeod replied. "And I don't think you'll get any argument from Mr. Nimmo."

Out in the car park, Harry collapsed into the back seat with a bewildered sigh, still rubbing at his temples from time to time, making room for Adam to sit beside him as McLeod turned to face them from the driver's seat. They were parked well over toward the side of the car park, and not apt to be disturbed.

"We might as well retrieve this now," McLeod said, with a speaking glance at Adam. "It's clear he got an almighty wallop in there. We did an open-door capture, Adam. You want to handle it, or shall I?"

Smiling faintly, Adam reached up to brush a hand downward over Harry's eyes, which closed as his head lolled forward.

"Go back to sleep, Harry," he murmured, though Harry had already done that. "Lay your head against the seat-back." His hand pressed Harry's head back to a reclining position. "In a moment, when I touch your wrist, you're going to remember what you saw and felt when you touched the body, but you'll find yourself able to keep a distance from it, no matter how intense the memory might get. These weren't *your* experiences; they belonged to someone else. I'll be your anchor; you've nothing to fear. Remember—now."

His hand clasped Harry's wrist on the final word, and the counsellor's eyes stirred beneath closed eyelids, lips parting slightly.

"What do you see, Harry?" came Adam's quiet prompt.

"Stone walls all around . . ."

"Go on."

"They—give me to drink from the divine elixir . . . the wine of vision and sacrifice. By—by water and earth, by fire and air, they summon one—best left sleeping . . . He comes . . . but the blood is required . . . And it is mine. . . ."

Harry's breathing was coming faster now, his heart rate increasing, and Adam stroked his free hand across Harry's brow to deepen his trance.

"Step back and observe, Harry," he murmured. "Do not feel—only see."

"They—they force me to my knees. I *know* what is to come! The triple-death! A blow to my head, profaning my office—the cord drawn tight around my throat!"

As his mouth started to gape in obvious distress, his free hand lifting vaguely, Adam barred it with his own.

"Only *see*, Harry. Only see."

"Aye. Only . . . see . . . I see the blade above me in the torchlight . . . the flash of iron like lightning, just before the coup. The kiss of darkness as the blade strikes here!" Harry's hand lifted again toward the side of his throat, but he had now managed to distance himself from his reporting. "Blood—blood gushes into the cauldron . . . to feed *him*. . . ."

"To feed *who*, Harry?" McLeod whispered.

"Dark presence . . . long discarnate . . ."

"His name, Harry . . ." Adam breathed.

Slowly the dark head shook. "I don't know. He *has* no name where he now dwells. His touch corrupts. Feeding, he besmirches souls . . . And he will walk again, if Francis be not stopped. . . ."

Blanching, McLeod darted his gaze to Adam, mouthing the surname, *Raeburn*?

"Francis who, Harry?" Adam whispered. "Francis Raeburn?"

"Aye. The great Betrayer . . . He betrayed the Head-Master . . . and now he has betrayed me. Death—is welcome, to escape him. . . ."

Harry shuddered then, anguish rippling across his face, and Adam pressed his wrist harder.

"Harry, withdraw from the memory now," he ordered. "You've done very well. Go deep asleep now, and hear nothing until I touch you on the wrist again."

As he released Harry's wrist, he turned his gaze to McLeod in wordless invitation for comment.

"Bloody hell," McLeod murmured. "Raeburn sacrificed his own man. And what was this shit about a presence with 'no name where he now dwells,' who feeds on blood and besmirches souls and is about to walk again?"

"I really don't think I want to know," Adam replied, "though we're going to have to find out. Do you think it's time we levelled with Harry?"

"Aye," McLeod replied. "I think it is."

Before bringing the counsellor around, Adam gave him

access to the memory of that night at Strathmourne when he had helped deal with the Hand of Glory—for that was information Harry needed, in order to make an informed decision regarding his future with the Hunting Lodge. Emerging from trance, Harry sat silently for several minutes, hardly looking up as McLeod started the engine and set them on the road back to Edinburgh. Adam remained in the back seat beside him, watching him closely, imagining he could almost hear the thought processes as Harry's nimble legal mind turned over all the permutations available from the information presented thus far.

"I think I need to know more about the Randall Stewart murder," Harry said at last, turning to look Adam fearlessly in the eyes. "The parts the papers didn't talk about at the time. And then I think I'd better hear about this Francis Raeburn."

They gave him a thorough briefing during the hour it took to drive back to Edinburgh. By the time they were approaching the Gogar interchange, Harry appeared anything but daunted. On the contrary, the gleam in his eye bespoke a keen commitment to the challenge offered.

"I appreciate your candor in trying to warn me off," he told his two listeners, "but now that I've heard you out, I don't really think I have the right *not* to take up this gauntlet, even if I may be stepping in over my depth—at least in the beginning. Somebody's got to stop this Raeburn and his ilk. If I have the wherewithal to help—and it appears I do have something to offer—not to lend a hand would be criminally irresponsible of me."

"Thank you, Harry," Adam said with real warmth. "We'll be speaking more about all of this, as you surely realize. Your help has already made a difference, and may well become critical before this is over. Just remember that the more often you use your talents, the more likely it is that you'll be noticed on the astral. So from here on out, be careful and watch your back. We already know that Raeburn has stepped up his efforts against us, and that he won't scruple to eliminate anyone who stands in his way."

✦ ✦ ✦

The timeliness of that warning was brought home the very next day, though not against Harry himself. While driving home late from a synod meeting in Dunkeld, Christopher Houston was run off the road, saved from serious injury or death only by the heavy safety features of the family Volvo, which was totalled. Though the police attributed the accident to black ice, Christopher had seen the black van that came up fast from behind and forced him to choose between a ditch and a bridge abutment. The next day, on McLeod's recommendation, Christopher and Victoria took the precaution of sending their two daughters to stay with their grandmother, in Dundee. In the girls' absence, Victoria moved in with Lady Julian, for strength in numbers, and Christopher took up nighttime residence at Strathmourne.

"I think we've probably made the right decision, where the girls are concerned," Christopher told Adam, over brandy in the library with McLeod and Peregrine. "But I'm not entirely convinced that the accident connects to Raeburn. There are lots of crazy drivers in black vans. It could be just coincidence."

"It was no coincidence when he had Adam run off the road two years ago," Peregrine pointed out. "Why should we assume that Raeburn will only use occult methods to get at us? If we're standing in his way, what's to stop him from simply hiring a professional hit man? One shot from a high-powered rifle—or one well-placed car bomb—could save him a lot of time and trouble."

McLeod shook his head. "There's no glory or profit in that kind of crude execution. I doubt he'd delegate the job to a contract killer when the deed, done properly, could buy him a lot of credit among the Patrons of Shadow."

"I agree," Adam said. "We mustn't forget the mind of the man we're dealing with. Whatever else is going on, Raeburn is out for a measure of revenge. That undoubtedly was part of the motive in going after Peregrine and Julia. The fact that he tried to have them kidnapped rather than killed suggests that he had an even worse fate in mind than mere death. We have only to remember Randall's fate—and Taliere's—to imagine what he may be planning. When he strikes again, you may be certain it will be with the intention of making an occasion of it.''

Christopher shuddered, his hand going to the cross around his neck.

''How do we stop him?'' he whispered.

''I don't know,'' Adam replied. ''First we have to find him.''

''Or he finds *us*,'' Peregrine murmured.

''You can stop that kind of thinking right now!'' McLeod retorted. ''Whatever we do, we can't let ourselves be driven into inactivity for fear of what he *might* do.''

''He didn't try to kidnap your wife, Noel,'' Peregrine said plaintively.

''No,'' Adam said, ''but we aren't in this business to keep ourselves safe at the cost of abandoning our greater directive to uphold the Law. Sometimes there are casualties; we all know that. And we'll do the best we can to protect those we hold dear, while still doing our jobs. But if we hobble ourselves through too much caution, Raeburn has already won. Whatever the personal risks involved, we have to press on with the Hunt. I doubt we've ever had a more dangerous quarry.''

Having Christopher Houston take up residence at Strathmourne only underlined the tension that had been building over the previous week and more. Sandwiched in with her heavy work schedule, Ximena had continued trying to carry on with wedding preparations as if nothing were amiss, but she could sense that there were things Adam either would not or could not tell her. Remembering the promise she had given him shortly after their arrival, she kept a tight rein on her curiosity and refrained from questioning him. But by Monday afternoon, arriving home before Adam, she went in search of Philippa.

Adam's mother was ensconced in the library with a book and a cup of tea, and laid her book aside as Ximena entered. The younger woman lost no time in getting to the point.

''Philippa,'' she announced grimly, ''there's something I have to ask you. It's bad enough to have everyone around me walking about under a cloud, without knowing what there is to be afraid of. I know I promised not to pry, but if I have to put up with being guarded day and night, surely that entitles me to a few explanations. How dark is this whole thing likely to get? How much danger is Adam in?''

"Enough," Philippa said.

"Enough to cost him his life?"

"I hope not," Philippa said. "But there may not be much room for error."

Ximena sank down in the nearest chair and gnawed moodily at her lower lip. "Why does it have to be Adam?" she wondered aloud bitterly. "Why can't somebody else see about bringing this malefactor to justice?"

"Because Adam is the one appointed for the task," Philippa said. "These things don't happen by chance. On the contrary, Adam's responsibilities, like his talents, are his by birthright. He was born to them, and he couldn't turn his back on them without betraying his own nature.

"Ximena," she went on, at the younger woman's crestfallen expression, "believe me when I tell you that your husband is no novice when it comes to dealing with the servants of Darkness. This isn't the first time he's crossed paths with this particular adversary. He knows what he's up against. If he goes into danger, it will be with his eyes wide open."

"I'd feel better if there was something constructive I could do," Ximena said. "I've never been a pacifist. I'm not used to sitting on the sidelines. I wish I had some psychic talent of my own—something that would be of some use!"

"Count yourself lucky to be what you are," Philippa retorted, smiling. "Being psychically gifted is a mixed blessing. You can't just turn your perceptions on and off, like a tap. On the contrary, the psychic must teach himself to handle the pain that comes with unwelcome knowledge. If he doesn't, his mind can crack under the strain."

"That's all hypothetical," Ximena insisted, spreading her hands before her in frustrated appeal. "What good am I to Adam if I can't see what he sees?"

Philippa found herself thinking back to her own long and happy marriage with Adam's father. "You are an island of quiet in his life," she told the younger woman. "You are a place of refuge from the tumult of the outside world. Without you, he would have nowhere to go to escape, even for a little while, from the constant noise that surrounds him every waking minute of the day. You are the rock of his repose.''

''I'm also something else for him to worry about,'' Ximena said, shaking her head. ''Especially in a situation like this, where I don't have the means to defend myself.''

''Your defenses are different from Adam's. In one sense, they're stronger,'' Philippa told her. ''If psychics are more open to the subtler impressions from the world around them, they're also more susceptible to forms of attack that would have little or no effect on an ordinary person. It's no accident that Julia proved more resistant than Peregrine to the effects of the Hand of Glory.

''Let me put it this way,'' she went on, constructing a medical analogy as she saw that Ximena still looked uncertain. ''Individuals who are psychically impressionable are like people whose immune system has broken down. Lacking the usual natural defenses, they have to create defense systems of their own, building them up from scratch. And that, I can assure you, is bloody hard work. Be glad you've been spared the effort.''

''All the same,'' Ximena said, ''I feel as if I've blundered unwittingly into a war zone. How do you live with the possibility that your life could be blown apart in an instant by some danger lurking unseen just around a corner?''

''How do you live with it?'' Philippa asked. ''The same way policemen's wives and soldiers' wives live with it: by taking each day as it comes.

''No, listen to what I'm saying,'' she went on, as Ximena started to shake her head. ''Adam's father was a serving officer during the Second World War. There were three things I learned during the hours I sat up waiting to find out if he was going to come back to me. The first rule is, Don't poison your life by speculating vainly about what *might* happen. The second rule is, Make each day together count as a celebration. And the third rule is, Never forget that whatever befalls the body, the spirit itself is imperishable.''

''You're talking about faith,'' Ximena declared.

''Yes, I am,'' Philippa agreed. ''And hope. And love.

'Now abideth these three—faith, hope, and love. But the greatest of these is love.' Just love him, Ximena. That's the greatest gift you can give him, and one of the most powerful weapons he will ever have at his command.''

# CHAPTER TWENTY-EIGHT

WHEN Adam returned later that evening, Philippa found occasion to draw her son aside and tell him of her conversation with his bride; and later still, when Ximena came to his bed, their lovemaking could leave no doubt in her mind how much he had come to cherish her love.

Yet even at the height of their passion, a part of him remained detached and on guard, haunted by grave forebodings regarding Raeburn's intentions. The Lynx-Master would strike again; that much Adam knew. And now he was striking closer to home.

But where and when and why the next attack might come remained unanswered questions, as did the question of how to stop Raeburn. Astral scanning had commenced as soon as Raeburn's involvement was confirmed; yet despite Herculean efforts by all the members of the Hunting Lodge, no trace of a pattern had yet emerged that might enable them to predict their adversary's next move. Given Raeburn's skill at cloaking his activities, they had little choice but to wait until he surfaced again—and hope that it would not be too late to thwart his ultimate plan.

Meanwhile, Adam did his best to maintain some semblance of normalcy, if primarily for Ximena's sake, keeping his professional schedule as best he could and savoring the time the two of them were able to share while sorting out last-minute details relating to the wedding, which was now less than two weeks away. But these small romantic concerns, which might otherwise have been a pleasure to contemplate, seemed only to heighten by contrast the ominous darkness hanging over them, and to increase his sense of vulnerability.

Tuesday came amid wintry gales of alternating sun and snow. After teaching rounds in the morning, Adam watched these unpredictable fluctuations in the weather from his office window, conscious, as never before, of his own limitations and the potential danger to those around him. The reason, he came to see, was because he had never before had so much to lose. He was still pondering this sobering revelation over a mug of tea long gone cold when the telephone rang. He picked it up on the first ring.

"There's been a new development," McLeod said, his normally gruff voice sounding flintier than usual. "You might want to come down to my office to hear the details in person."

His tone left Adam in no doubt that the "development" was one of significance. He glanced at his watch.

"I've got a patient in ten minutes," he told his Second, "but I could arrange to join you in about two hours' time. Or is it more urgent than that?"

"That'll do," McLeod said. "See you then."

Adam found it difficult to keep his mind on his work for the next hour. The session with his patient went reasonably well, thanks to a determined effort of concentration on his part, but he was more relieved than usual to bring it to a close. He gave his progress notes to his secretary to be typed up and filed, then headed back to his office to retrieve his overcoat. Knotting a cashmere scarf around his neck, he set out for the stairs leading down to the lobby and the front door.

He was overtaken on the next landing by a younger man in a lab coat over surgical scrubs, with full, dark hair and a smoothly handsome face that Adam had seen once or twice before. As the two of them exchanged vague nods of acknowledgement in passing, a glimpse of the name Mallory on the other man's name tag enabled Adam to place him as one of the newer members of the Department of Anaesthesia. Staff gossip held Mallory to be very much a ladies' man, but less flattering rumors hinted that Mallory's interest in his female co-workers might be motivated more by personal vanity than by any impulse of gallantry.

First to reach the lobby, Mallory made his way over to the desk, where his appearance was greeted with flattering enthusiasm by the pretty young receptionist. Bypassing the two of them on his way to the outer door, Adam couldn't avoid overhearing snatches of flirtatious conversation. Mallory's compliments had a false ring to them that gave Adam a twinge of misgiving on the receptionist's behalf as the door closed behind him, but as he braced himself against the sudden blast of cold outside, a host of more pressing concerns replaced any further thought about the hospital's newest Lothario.

He took a taxi across town to police headquarters rather than driving. McLeod was in the outer office, reviewing details of a house break-in with one of the younger detectives in his division, but as soon as he caught sight of Adam, he cut the conversation short and came over to meet him. Following the inspector into his private office, Adam waited until McLeod had closed the door before asking in a lowered voice, "Now then, what's up?"

The question caught McLeod on his way to the desk, which was shoved against one wall. Gesturing an invitation for Adam to take an adjoining seat, he lowered himself into his office chair and leaned back with his elbows propped on the chairarms.

"You remember that young Druid from Stornoway I told you about?" he queried softly. "The one I interviewed when Peregrine and Harry and I went up to view the scene at Callanish?"

Adam experienced a qualm of foreboding. "McFarlane? The one who later phoned you up about 'a disturbance in the Force'?"

"That's him," McLeod agreed heavily. "I've never been able to connect that feeling of his to anything we knew was going on at the time, but now it appears there *was* a connection. It looks very much as if he's been kidnapped."

Adam controlled a start. "Good Lord!" he exclaimed. "When did this happen?"

"Last night, apparently some time between five and ten," McLeod said. "His girlfriend came home from work to find their flat had been trashed, and no sign of McFarlane. Chisholm was off duty when the call came in, and didn't find out about it till this morning. When he saw that the latest production up-date still had McFarlane listed as missing and unaccounted for, he decided the situation rated a phone call to me.''

He took a file folder out of a desk drawer and handed it to Adam. ''Here are copies of the preliminary incident reports, along with a photo of McFarlane, courtesy of his girlfriend. I had Chisholm fax 'em to me so we could look them over. His men are still trying to piece the evidence together, but it seems pretty obvious that the lad didn't leave the flat of his own free will.

''The Stornoway police are postulating some kind of drug involvement as a possible motive, but I don't buy that for a minute,'' McLeod went on, as Adam glanced at the photo. ''McFarlane may not figure as a pillar of the establishment, but if he takes his vocation as a shaman as seriously as I think he does, the last thing he'd do is upset his body's natural equilibrium through substance abuse, let alone mess around with the people who peddle the stuff.''

''I'm inclined to go along with your assessment,'' Adam said thoughtfully. ''You know, two weeks ago, if anyone had asked me, I would have categorized McFarlane's involvement in the Callanish incident as largely coincidental. Now I'm not so sure. I wonder whether there may not be a hidden connection there, something that we've somehow overlooked. And if we find that connection,'' he finished grimly, ''I wonder if it might not lead us straight back to Raeburn.''

McLeod soberly nodded his agreement. ''If Raeburn *is* at the back of this, I don't hold out much hope for this boy's chances. That's why I wanted to confer with you. He may well be the replacement for whatever Raeburn had planned for Peregrine.

''Chisholm's already said he'd welcome any assistance I could spare him. What say I ring Harry Nimmo, and see if he can force a gap in his schedule to fly me up to Stornoway in the next day or two, to look over the evidence for myself?''

''With one minor adjustment, I'd say that's an excellent

idea," Adam agreed. "Under the circumstances, I think Peregrine and I ought to come along as well."

"Can you spare the time?" McLeod asked.

"I'll make the time," Adam replied. "If I don't, and this goes the direction it *could* go, given what's already happened to Taliere, Iolo McFarlane may not have *any* time."

The flight up to Lewis was attended by blustery squalls, but with Harry at the controls, the little Cessna touched down at Stornoway more or less on schedule. Hugh Chisholm was on hand to meet the plane, as arranged, and eyed Adam with some interest as he shook McLeod's hand in greeting.

"Morning, Inspector," he said to McLeod. "Sorry to impose on you a second time, but things seem to be getting murkier than ever."

"I agree," McLeod replied. "That's why I've taken the liberty of bringing along Dr. Sinclair here, by way of reinforcements. Adam, this is Detective Sergeant Hugh Chisholm. Dr. Sinclair is a psychiatric consultant with expertise in cult behavior—one of the regulars we call upon from time to time to assist in police investigations. If anybody can shed some light on what's been going on around here, he's the one."

Chisholm accepted this explanation without demur, offering Adam a strong handshake, then greeting Harry and Peregrine. During the ensuing drive across town to the flat McFarlane had shared with a young woman called Rhiannon Cummins, the sergeant brought them up to date on how the case was progressing—or failing to progress.

"Some of my colleagues are postulating some kind of drug deal gone wrong, but I don't buy that for a minute," Chisholm confided with a scowl. "I think it's far more likely that this has something to do with that bunch of crazies who defaced the Callanish Ring. After all, our missing laddie *was* the one who called the police. What if one of the perpetrators took offense at his action?"

It was clear from his tone that he was merely thinking out loud. Sitting in the back seat, Adam offered no comment. Chisholm's guesses merely served to remind him how far they still had to go to reach the heart of the matter.

McFarlane's erstwhile residence turned out to be one of a row of stone cottages clumped together at the side of the road, half a mile beyond the outskirts of Stornoway itself. The property to the left had a For Sale sign hanging out in front, and looked unoccupied.

Once the party had alighted from the car, Chisholm led the way up to the front door and knocked. A moment later it was opened by a freckled young woman with red hair plaited in a long braid over one shoulder. Her face was pale under its freckles, and her eyes were red from crying.

"Sergeant Chisholm," she murmured, anxiously searching his face. "Have you found him? Is he dead?"

"There's been no new information, Miss Cummins. I'm sorry," Chisholm replied. "May we come in? These gentlemen have just flown in from Edinburgh. They're here at my request to help out with this case."

She gave a grudging nod and stepped back to allow the party to enter, eyeing McLeod half in recognition.

"Were you at Callanish?" she asked.

"That's right," McLeod replied. "Detective Chief Inspector McLeod. I gave Mr. McFarlane my card."

He introduced Adam and the others. Smoothly taking his cue from McLeod, Adam said, "With your permission, we'd like to take a look around the premises. I know this must seem like a further imposition, but I assure you that we're only doing our best to help."

Rhiannon looked taken aback. "When I phoned the station this morning, they told me it was all right for me to start tidying up."

"And it is," Adam said reassuringly. "The kinds of clues we'll be looking for are the ones most likely to turn up in odd places."

"Oh. All right, then," she said, clearly nonplussed. "I'd better warn you, though, the place is in an awful state."

Beckoning, she led them through to the sitting room. Prior to the break-in, it had been brightly decorated with art posters and Indian print hangings, its shelves, tables, and window ledges cluttered with a typical assortment of New Age accoutrements: crystals and candles, books, house plants, and amateur bits of sculpture done in pottery and bronze. Some of the hangings had been either pulled down or torn down, and many of the ornaments were now lying smashed on the floor. A black plastic bin-bag stood open in the middle of the carpet, half-full of sad, leftover debris.

Elsewhere there were other less obvious signs of the room being set to rights. A stag's head, one antler now slightly askew, had been reverently gathered up and placed on the mantelpiece until it could be returned to its place of honor on the wall above the hearth. Clusters of dried rowan berries had been tacked over the window and the door, and a hint of incense hung on the air—evidence that Rhiannon had at least made an attempt to ritually purify the room of any baneful influences left behind by the intruders.

At any other time, Adam would have heartily approved of these measures. Now, ironically, he could only hope that Rhiannon had not inadvertently dispelled the very resonances that might have supplied them with the clues they were looking for. Catching McLeod's eye from across the room, he could tell that the inspector was thinking much the same thing. But they were still committed to trying their luck, in the hope that they were not too late.

McLeod undertook to distract Rhiannon and Chisholm, drawing them aside on the pretext of checking over various points in her written statement. Knowing he could depend on his Second to keep their attention diverted, Adam channelled his own energies into boosting the performance of the other two members of the party, keeping a particular eye on Harry. Peregrine drew off to one side, sketchbook at the ready, his hazel-green eyes taking on the telltale dreaminess that invariably betokened a shift in perception. Harry, for his part, made a wandering tour of the room, pausing every few steps to pick up objects at random.

But several minutes of this activity only left the barrister looking mildly frustrated. Peregrine, likewise, had made only a few token passes with his pencil. Abandoning his efforts, he drew himself up with a shake of his head and moved closer beside Adam.

"It's no use," he muttered regretfully. "I'm not getting anything. Any signs that might have been here yesterday have been all but—"

Before he could finish, they were interrupted by a sudden gasp from Rhiannon. Breaking away from McLeod, she darted across the room and pounced on a leather thong protruding from under an overturned futon. The thong had some kind of medallion attached to it. When the medallion caught the light, Adam saw that it was a Druidic lunula of beaten, polished brass.

"No," she whispered, tears standing out in her eyes. "Now I know something terrible has happened to him. This is Iolo's!" she informed them, as she displayed the lunula on her palm. "He's always worn it! I've never seen him take it off—"

Her voice broke. While Chisholm and McLeod attempted to calm her, Adam came over for a closer look at the lunula. It was finely made, overlaid with hair-thin traceries of runic inscription.

"May I?" he asked.

When Rhiannon nodded, too tearful to speak, he lifted the lunula by its leather thong and carried it over to the window. Beckoning Harry and Peregrine over to join him, he murmured softly, "Gentlemen, our luck may be on the mend. Harry, would you mind handling this? Not until Peregrine and I block you from Chisholm and the girl," he added, shifting Harry to stand between them.

"I'll give it my best shot," Harry murmured. "I don't see how it could possibly be worse than working with that goddammed Hand."

"Probably not," Adam agreed, glancing back at McLeod, who had re-engaged Chisholm and Rhiannon in conversation. "Do try not to react too dramatically."

Nodding, his back to the others, Harry braced himself against the window frame and held out his hand, drawing a deep breath as he did so. Adam tapped him lightly on the wrist in posthypnotic cue, and Harry's eyes closed, even as his hand closed on the lunula which Adam laid in his palm.

After a delay of no more than a heartbeat, Harry stiffened and then began to twitch. His respiration changed, becoming shallow and gasping as he swayed slightly forward, almost dropping the lunula.

Adam and Peregrine braced him before he could stumble.

"Steady," Adam cautioned in a calm undertone. "You're in no real danger. Just relax and let these impressions wash over you as if they were no more than a breath of air."

Harry recovered his balance. Satisfied that the counsellor was back in control, Adam dropped his voice still lower.

"Think of this moment as a time capsule," he instructed. "Put these impressions you've just experienced into the capsule and shut the lid. That's where they're going to stay for the time being. When you decide to open the capsule again, you'll find these impressions are as fresh and detailed as they were when you first captured them."

Harry signified his understanding with a nod. Satisfied that the counsellor would be able to reserve his impressions for retrieval at a more convenient moment, Adam guided him back from trance, taking the lunula and passing it to Peregrine to return to Rhiannon.

"This is very handsome workmanship," Peregrine said with a smile, as he handed it back to the girl. "Thank you for letting us look at it. Did Iolo make it himself?"

Rhiannon nodded, wiping away a fresh surge of tears, scarcely heeding the compliment.

"He *knew* something like this was going to happen," she said brokenly. "He's been having bad dreams ever since the start of the year—nightmares, even. He had a terrible one the night before he—" She had to stop and swallow before adding, in a shaky voice, "When he woke up, he was white as a sheet."

This disclosure made Adam prick up his ears. Coming over to join them, he said quietly, "Tell me more about the nightmare, if you can. Do you know what it was about?"

Snuffling noisily, Rhiannon shook her head.

"No. He wouldn't tell me. He might have written it down in his dream journal, though."

"Iolo kept a dream journal?"

Nodding, Rhiannon paused to pull a tissue from her pocket and blow her nose. "We Druids believe that dreams are messages sent to us by the spirit world. The shaman always takes them seriously."

Adam hardly needed such an explanation, but Rhiannon was not to know that.

"I see," he said. "Do you think we might take a look at this journal?"

Rhiannon frowned dubiously. "I don't know. It's very personal. Iolo never even let me read it."

"I can appreciate that," Adam said, "and normally I wouldn't make such a request. But what's in that journal might help us find out who kidnapped him and why. It's possible that he met someone or saw something that has a bearing on his kidnapping, and found its way into his dreams. They might contain clues that will help us."

Rhiannon stared at him for a long moment, deliberating, then said, "All right. I'll go and fetch it."

She left the room and came back a moment later with a small black-marbled hard-backed notebook. This she presented solemnly to Adam.

Crossing over to the settee, he sat down and placed the book carefully in front of him on the coffee table. The others gathered round, watching over his shoulder as he opened the book and began paging through its contents.

The earliest entries went several months back into the previous year. It required only the briefest of scans to determine that the dreams which followed the Callanish incident were conspicuously different from those which had preceded it. The imagery at that point became suddenly turbulent and strange, dominated by motifs of storm and darkness. The final entry was even more striking: a blank page with a string of letters scrawled across the middle of it in untidy block capitals.

Adam turned to McLeod, lifting the open page in his direction and indicating the inscription.

"What do you make of that?" he asked.

McLeod adjusted his aviator spectacles and leaned down. "S-O-U-L-something-S—is that a *G*?—S-T-R-I-G," he read aloud.

"That one fuzzy character between the *L* and the *S* doesn't come all the way down to the line," Harry chipped in. "Could it maybe be an apostrophe?"

Peregrine frowned. "Soul's gstrig," he pronounced. "Assuming that's right, what's it supposed to mean?"

Adam was shaking his head. "I have no idea. It could be

a mythological reference. It could be a place name. It could be something drawn from Iolo's personal dream lexicon. Whatever it means, he clearly considered it important enough to stand on its own. And that suggests *we* ought to take it seriously.''

He turned to Rhiannon. ''I'd really like to study this journal more closely. As a psychiatrist, I find dream analysis a useful tool—and it really could give us some clues. May I take it away with me? It's just possible that Iolo had some premonition that might be linked to his kidnapping. I can't promise anything, but I'd like to try.''

Having come so far already, Rhiannon did not raise any further objections now.

''All right,'' she sighed. ''If it will help you find Iolo, it'll be worth it.''

''Is this all right by you?'' Adam asked Chisholm.

The Stornoway detective shrugged. ''Our forensics boys are all finished here. If they didn't see fit to classify that book as evidence, I don't see why I should take exception. No, this is obviously your speciality. Best let you get on with it.''

# CHAPTER TWENTY-NINE

"WELL, here's where we part company," Chisholm said, pulling up outside the fence beside the parking apron where the Cessna lay waiting. "Dr. Sinclair, do you really think that dream journal might help us find Mc-Farlane?"

"It's possible," Adam allowed. "It may at least give me some insight into his psychology, suggest the kinds of things he might have been involved in, that would make someone want to kidnap him."

Which was only partially true, but it seemed to satisfy Chisholm.

"Fair enough," he said. "Thanks again for coming. You'll let me know, won't you, if anything useful turns up?"

"You can count on it," McLeod said, speaking for all of them.

As Chisholm drove off and Harry began his pre-flight inspection of the plane, the rest of them got in, Adam taking the co-pilot's seat that McLeod had occupied on the incoming flight.

"I figured you might be waiting for me," Harry said with a grin, as he got in beside Adam and closed his door.

"I'd like to retrieve those impressions you picked up off McFarlane's medallion," Adam said. "That way, we can discuss the case on the way back."

"You seem pretty sure I got something," Harry said, buckling up his seat harness. "I don't remember a thing."

"You will," Adam said with a smile. "You're really getting rather good at this. Are you ready?"

"Ready as I'll ever be," Harry said, closing his eyes. As he drew breath, Adam touched his wrist in posthypnotic trigger.

"That's right. Take a deep breath in . . . and out . . . Settle in. That's right. Peregrine, are you standing by?" he added, with a glance over his shoulder at the artist.

Peregrine nodded, sketchbook and pencil already in hand.

"Ready whenever you two are," he announced softly.

"Good." Adam returned his attention to his subject. "All right, Harry, remember that time capsule you've been carrying around with you for the last hour? I want you to take it out and open it up, and tell me what comes to mind."

There was a momentary pause, then Harry began to narrate. "Reading . . . in the sitting room . . . I hear a noise from the kitchen . . . I get up and go to the door, but three men in black burst in—"

Harry broke off, his breathing becoming more rapid, his voice going hoarse.

"Backing off, shouting for help . . . trying to escape, but I'm caught and pinned. No! Let me go! One's got my medallion, choking me! Frantic to get away, but I can't! Something wet clapped over my face—can't breathe! Chemical smell—cloying . . . dizzy . . . falling . . ."

"That's enough, Harry," Adam ordered, his hand tightening on the counselor's wrist. "That part is pretty clear. Let go of it now, and backtrack for me. Run the film in reverse and freeze-frame on the men in black. Do you have them?"

Slowly Harry's head nodded.

"Good. Now look at them carefully, and tell me everything you can about them."

Slowly, haltingly, Harry complied, now able to render a more dispassionate description of the images fixed before his inner vision. Adam and McLeod watched silently as three faces emerged from under Peregrine's pencil, shaped by Harry's narrative; but when McLeod opened his mouth to comment, Adam shook his head and held up a restraining hand.

Not until he had brought both Harry and Peregrine back to normal waking consciousness did he take the sketchbook and turn to the second of Peregrine's sketch portraits: that of a hard-faced man with Nordic features and a crewcut. It was a visage that all of them recognized, though Harry had seen only sketches.

"Him again," McLeod muttered. "Whoever he is, Raeburn's got him working overtime."

Harry ran the back of his hand across the lower half of his face, still looking a little haggard.

"I wouldn't know about that," he said, "but it was chloroform they used to nail him with. I recognized the smell."

"That would be in character," Adam said, nodding. "It's a favorite M.O. with the Lodge of the Lynx."

"Aye," McLeod agreed. "What I can't figure out is what Raeburn would want with somebody like McFarlane. The boy's sincere enough in his higher aspirations, but he's not had enough experience to count for much, either as a threat or as an offering. So what makes him worth Raeburn's trouble?"

"I've been wondering the same thing," Adam said. "Harry, let's get us in the air. I want to get back home and do some further research. For all we know, the answer might be right under our noses."

It was well after dark by the time Adam and Peregrine arrived back at Strathmourne. Ximena was working the evening shift, and Christopher had gone on a pastoral call, but Philippa and Julia were on hand to inquire about their progress. Fortunately, Iolo McFarlane's dream diary was evidence of a sort that could be discussed in Julia's presence.

"I won't know until I've gone through it, whether it's going to be of any help," Adam told them, over a supper of steak and kidney pie which Humphrey served up in the morning room. "I should think I've got a full evening's reading ahead of me. It's probably a good thing Ximena's working."

"And we'd better get back to the gate lodge," Peregrine said, drawing his wife to her feet. "We have a cat to feed, and I need to work on a project I'm behind on. Being away today didn't help the backlog."

Adam shrugged and smiled, the only one of them unaware that Peregrine was referring to the wedding portrait of Ximena.

"Sorry to have taken you from your work," he said. "I hope you have an understanding client."

"Oh, I don't think he'll mind," Peregrine replied. "Talk to you tomorrow. Good night, Philippa."

When they had gone, Philippa retired upstairs for a hot bath, and Adam took the journal into the library, where he lit a fire and settled into his favorite fireside chair to read. To help align himself with McFarlane's frame of mind, he had tossed a stick of incense on the fire, and he let its aroma help him focus as he bent to his work.

He had skimmed through the bulk of the entries on the flight home. The impressions he had gathered in that earlier, cursory examination were borne out by this more detailed study. The Callanish incident did indeed signal a marked change in tone and imagery from the entries which preceded it.

Fetching a pad and pencil from his desk, Adam noted down the key images to be found in each of these later entries. He very soon saw that they formed a recurrent pattern.

In each dream, the landscape was dominated by a high hill crowned with a ragged diadem of stones. The sky was invariably dark and stormy, the clouds shot through with branched lightnings.

*I'm afraid of the storm, but feel compelled to climb the hill,* McFarlane had written. *As I start making my way to the top, I see a figure coming down the hill to meet me.*

Initially, Adam noted, this figure appeared as a mere blur. But with each successive dream, the figure drew closer, becoming more distinct, until at last McFarlane was able to provide a description.

*I can see now that it's a knight of some kind, wearing a shirt of mail under a white surcoat. He's armed with a sword and wears a cross-shaped medallion around his neck. Urgently, he beckons and shouts, but I can't understand the words. I shake my head. He repeats the message, but it's drowned out in a sudden roar of thunder, so loud that it wakes me up.*

McFarlane's own frustration was evident from his closing remarks. *I'm sure this knight is trying to tell me something important,* he had written. *I have the oddest notion that if I could only make out what he's saying, I would know who's been defacing our ancient shrines.*

The only entry after that was the scrawl of letters. He was staring at the letters, trying to make some connection take shape, when Philippa joined him with two mugs of hot chocolate.

"Getting anywhere?" she asked.

"Not really," he said, "though some of the images are interesting." He tossed the journal on the table beside his yellow notepad. "Have a look for yourself. Maybe something will occur to you that I've missed."

Philippa read through the journal entries, then Adam's notes, while he rested his eyes and both of them sipped companionably at their hot chocolate.

"The symbolism is remarkably consistent," she commented, when she finally put the notes aside. "Too consistent to be mere coincidence. I find the figure of the knight particularly interesting. Is he merely some submerged aspect of McFarlane's own personality, I wonder, or is he an autonomous emissary from the Inner Planes?"

"A good question," Adam replied. "My next move is to start checking into McFarlane's background."

He rubbed the back of his neck and sighed, and Philippa clucked her tongue reprovingly.

"I hope you aren't thinking to start in on that tonight, dear. You've already put in more than your share of work today, and you should know better than anyone how fatigue can hamper performance. Ximena will be home very soon. My advice to you is to put this problem on the shelf for the time being, and go get some R and R. God knows you've earned it."

Adam caught himself stifling a yawn, and let it turn into a weary smile.

"Yes, Mother. I'm going to bed now, Mother." He set down his empty mug. "I'll defer the rest of this inquiry until tomorrow," he conceded.

The following day was packed with activities. After putting in a full morning at the clinic, Adam spent the afternoon junketing around Edinburgh on wedding business. He managed to get home to Strathmourne with half an hour to spare before Ximena was due to leave for her evening shift in the casualty department.

They held a brief tête-à-tête in the bedroom while Ximena finished getting dressed, after which Adam walked her down to the front door, where Humphrey was waiting beside the Bentley. Philippa was sitting composedly in the back seat.

"I didn't know you were planning to go out this evening," Adam said.

"Neither did I, until an hour ago," said his mother. "Victoria phoned to say she's needed to sit with one of the women in the parish whose husband died in hospital this afternoon. Christopher is with her. None of us liked the idea of Julian being left on her own, so I volunteered to play the role of genteel companion. I'll spend the night in Edinburgh, and you can collect me tomorrow afternoon, on your way home."

"Ximena and I are running wedding errands tomorrow, and picking up our rings," Adam said, slipping an arm around his wife's waist. "I can't guarantee what time we'll be able to pick you up."

"Then maybe I'll spend a second night with Julian," Philippa said lightly. "Don't worry about me. Humphrey can come and collect me, if it comes to that. Shoo, now. You've got work to do."

"I can see I'm going to be in for a rather dull evening," Adam said with a smile, as he handed his wife into the car.

"Somehow I doubt that," Ximena quipped. "If I know you, you'll be back in the library before we're out of sight. Just try not to work too hard while I'm gone. Mrs. Gilchrist has left you a snack in the kitchen, when you're ready for it."

As he watched the Bentley pull away, Adam reflected that there was more than a grain of truth in his wife's droll prediction. With the significance of McFarlane's dream journal still unresolved, he had already decided to devote the next several hours to extending his research on the astral. Returning to the warmth of the main house, he locked up and went for a shower, a fresh change of clothes, and a brief rest before embarking upon the night's work.

The grandfather clock in the hall was chiming nine by the

time he made his way back down to the library. Though he was alone in the house, he secured the library door behind him and took the additional precaution of warding the room before fetching McFarlane's journal from his briefcase. He was already wearing his Adept ring. Slipped inside the front cover of the journal was a fax photo of McFarlane himself, borrowed from McLeod's case file. He took a long look at it before moving back to his chair by the fireside.

The fire Humphrey had lit before leaving needed only a careful stoking to stir it back to active life. Taking a pinch of incense from a box on the mantelpiece, Adam cast it into the flames with a whispered prayer for guidance and protection, then settled down in his chair and made his usual preparations for entering into trance, the journal now in his lap.

The outside world faded from view, screened behind an aromatic haze of incense smoke. When Adam had reached the working level appropriate to what he had in mind, he transferred his now-undivided attention to the photo, commending the man he hoped was still alive to the awareness of the celestial Guardians of the Inner Planes. Closing his eyes on that thought, he framed his intent in an unspoken petition.

*This man McFarlane has fallen into the hands of those who serve the Patrons of Shadow,* he prayed silently. *For his own sake, and the welfare of many innocent others, I earnestly desire to discover his whereabouts in the outer world, together with the reason why the Shadow desires him.*

An answering glow enveloped him, his inner vision steadying into focus as he found himself weightlessly suspended in the celestial firmament of the Inner Planes. McFarlane's journal floated before him, against a shimmering backdrop of stars. As he gazed at it, he became aware that there were in fact two books, the second surfacing through the first like sunlight breaking through a cloud.

For a brief moment longer, they glimmered like hyacinthine reflections of one another, before a subtle attraction of light drew them together and made them one. In that selfsame instant, in a dizzying shift of imagery, Adam found himself standing in a marble-walled chamber somewhere deep within the infinitely convoluted halls of the Akashic Records.

Before him on a lectern of silver lay the chronicle of Iolo McFarlane's existence. The slenderness of the volume confirmed what Adam had surmised earlier—that the young Druid was a very new soul, with no past beyond the span of his present lifetime. A survey of the book's contents revealed that Iolo had only just begun to grow into those talents which would blossom later in the course of his maturity, perhaps not even until another lifetime. Beyond this, Adam could find nothing in the young man's record to explain Raeburn's unwelcome interest.

Which suggested an alternative possibility—that whatever had recommended him to Raeburn must lie buried not within the limited scope of Iolo's own experience, but elsewhere, among the history of his antecedents. The names of McFarlane's parents were included in the current record. Adam decided to take up the inquiry with them.

His quest took him backward in time, through the labyrinthine tangles of McFarlane's physical genealogy. The process was laborious, but out of these tangles of kinship an array of shining threads began to emerge, like fibers of gold mingled amongst the warp and weft of a greater tapestry, lost at a distance but visible at close range. As Adam pursued these threads back through the centuries, they gathered themselves together to form weightier filaments, strand joining up with strand until all at once they met and merged in a single skein of Orient splendor.

The brightness of this life-line hinted at an illustrious soul, of more than ordinary abilities. Following this golden clue, Adam arrived at the threshold of a new chamber of record. The chronicle enshrined in the chamber beyond was a dense compendium of many chapters, each one relating to a different incarnation. When Adam stepped into the room, the book fell open of its own accord to the chapter detailing events in the life of one Sir Andrew Kerr, McFarlane's physical ancestor from the fourteenth century.

Before Adam could commence to read, a sudden brightness suffused the chamber. The source of this radiance was a pillar of light that materialized before him as if out of thin air. Even as Adam instinctively warded his eyes from the brightness, the pillar coalesced into human form. Fully manifest, it took the shape of the knightly figure described in McFarlane's dreams.

And not just any knight. Sir Andrew Kerr was a Knight of the Order of the Temple.

The formal dissolution of the Order early in the fourteenth century had made it necessary for the survivors to modify their traditional livery, but there was no mistaking the significance of the medallion that hung around Sir Andrew's neck from a golden chain: a cross *formée*, of red enamel over gold. Adam had seen and handled a similar cross in the keeping of John Graham, and himself had been a Knight Templar in a previous life.

Taking on the semblance of that other lifetime, in the full panoply of his knighthood, Adam rendered appropriate salute to his fellow Templar. Even as he did so, his eye was drawn to the ring Kerr bore upon his sword-hand—of burnished gold, and set with a shallow, cabochon sapphire that glowed with an inner fire proclaiming it no ordinary gem. Seeing it, Adam realized that he was in the presence of one like himself, a Master of the Hunt—and one very senior to himself.

"I acknowledge your authority," he told the other man, "and I yield me to your instruction. Tell me what you would have me know."

Kerr's dark eyes sought and held his in wordless yearning. Then he lifted his hands in entreaty, gesturing first to his own lips, then toward Adam's. At once Adam realized what Kerr was trying to convey—that he wished to speak with Adam's voice.

But Adam was not a medium—and even if he had been, mediums only rarely retained any trace of memory of what was said through their lips while overshadowed by a spirit guest. McLeod could have circumvented the problem without hesitation; but McLeod was at home in Edinburgh.

"I'm truly sorry. I haven't the ability to do what you ask," Adam told Kerr. "Can you *show* me what this is all about?"

After cocking his head wistfully, Kerr swept one hand toward the book. As Adam shifted his gaze to look, the pages seemed to fall open like a window in time, revealing a dark hillside under a sky tattered by gathering storm. Lightning flashed blue-white through the pall of clouds, and in the afterflash, he caught sight of what seemed to be a funeral procession toiling up the rocky slope.

Kerr was leading the party with a drawn sword in his hand, cloaked and braced against a howling wind. Behind him came six more men in mail and surcoats like his own, carrying a rude bed of planks upon which lay a supine body laden down with iron chains. The grimness of their faces and the ragged haste of their progress suggested a fearful urgency of purpose. Slipping and stumbling, they pressed on toward the crest of the hill, where three more figures labored to pile more fuel on an already-blazing bonfire that lay within a circle of standing stones. A large cauldron was set within the flames.

The party gained the height and stumbled to a halt. The body was taken hastily down off the bier and bundled into the heavy folds of a waiting shroud of sheet lead. In that same instant, a ghastly shape suddenly manifested over the body, black as smoke from a burning abattoir. Eyes blazing red in the lightning's glare, the apparition swooped down on the body, as if to claim it for its own.

Kerr darted to interpose. A clear blue light flashed from the ring on his finger and the blade in his hand as he slashed at the intruder. The apparition reeled aside, snarling and slavering, clearly no mere illusion. While Kerr continued to hold it at bay, the other members of his party picked up the body and heaved it into the cauldron.

The entity went wild with spitting rage, diving down amongst Kerr's men with bared fangs and raking claws. Two defenders fell, gashed and bleeding, before Kerr drove it back again with scything sweeps of his sword. Before the evil spirit could recover itself, he raised the blade high over his head and shouted into the rising wind.

His utterance took the form of a sonorous incantation. One of the men still on his feet darted to Kerr's side and added his voice to the ritual spell. As the pair continued to chant, there appeared in the sky overhead a sudden rift, blacker and denser than any storm cloud.

The rift widened. As it did so, the light that blazed from

Kerr's ring took on the force of a mighty gale. Roaring like a hurricane, it seized the apparition and hurled it into the maw of the Void. The rift snapped shut as Kerr abruptly lowered his sword, leaving the survivors raggedly silhouetted against the flare of the bonfire.

A fresh gust of wind caused the fire to billow up. The silhouettes vanished, eclipsed by the hungry intensity of the blaze. When the flames died back again, the picture seemed subtly altered. As more details became discernible, Adam realized that the party now gathered round the bonfire was not the same one which Kerr had led to its hard-won victory.

The newcomers were clad not in chain mail and surcoats but in long, cowled robes of black wool. At least one of them was a woman, hood flung back to reveal a cruelly voluptuous profile, oddly familiar. Dark blood inscribed a restraining triangle on the ground around the fire. Where the flames burned hottest, a new cauldron seethed and bubbled.

Above the cauldron hovered a shadowy apparition with eyes of ruby flame—without doubt, Kerr's ancient spiritual adversary, conjured back from the Void. The leader of the robed cultists advanced to the edge of the triangle, brandishing an ancient dagger in his right hand with controlling intent. And when the firelight fell full upon his face, Adam recognized the sneering, patrician features of Francis Raeburn.

The shock of this discovery made him instinctively recoil, breaking his concentration. When he looked again, the images had disappeared, leaving him staring at blank space. Wrenching his gaze away, he found that the chamber of record was now empty apart from himself. Kerr's manifest presence had vanished, leaving Adam alone with a clamoring host of speculations.

Instinct warned that there was nothing more he could hope to accomplish here tonight. Breathing deeply, he closed his eyes and willed himself to rejoin his body. There came the familiar, rushing sensation of soul-flight, followed by an equally familiar jolt of vertigo as his spirit came to rest. When he opened his eyes again, it was to find himself safely anchored in the solid physical haven of his own library.

He shivered as he moved forward instinctively to stir the fire. The clock was chiming half past ten, though it seemed it should be later. Rising, he set McFarlane's journal aside and went out to the kitchen, turning on lights in his wake, for faint reverberations of what he had seen continued to chill the edges of his soul. As Adam poured himself a glass of milk and sat down with the plate of sandwiches left by Mrs. Gilchrist, he set his mind to considering the images Kerr had given him.

It was a bit like trying to assemble a jigsaw without knowing what the finished picture was meant to look like. But by the time he had finished his second sandwich, he had succeeded in putting together a working hypothesis. Many of the details were still hazy, and would remain so until he could get Noel to establish a better link with Kerr. Elsewhere, however, the information supplied by Kerr added up to a disturbing prospect.

Raeburn, it appeared, was out to secure an alliance with the evil spirit of Kerr's former adversary. Adam was aware that the binding of such a spirit would require an appropriate blood-sacrifice—which explained only too well the reason behind Iolo McFarlane's kidnapping. As Kerr's lineal descendant, the young Druid would make a pleasing oblation to his forefather's vanquished foe. A quick glance at the calendar on the kitchen wall pegged Imbolc Eve as the most likely immediate date for such a working—Imbolc Eve, the first of February, four days hence—scant margin for finding and stopping Raeburn, but at least Adam now knew what they must try to stop.

The next question concerned the identity of Kerr's ancient foe. Kerr apparently had tried over and over again to warn his distant kinsman of the impending danger. Though his attempts had failed, Adam reasoned that a further study of McFarlane's dreams might yet suggest a name to put to Raeburn's would-be ally. Returning to the library, he decided to begin with the cryptic brevity of McFarlane's final entry.

The young Druid's hand-lettering was no easier to decipher now than it had been in any of the earlier attempts. Taking Peregrine's rendering, SOUL'S GSTRIG, as his starting point, Adam began mentally experimenting with alternate readings. Rearranging the letters produced only gibberish.

Going back to the original arrangement yet again, squinting at it in the light, Adam suddenly wondered if the short stroke Harry had previously interpreted as an apostrophe might actually be an ill-formed *I*.

"SOULIS GSTRIG." he whispered aloud.

Frowning, he read the words aloud. As he did so, he realized with a sudden jolt that Soulis was, in fact a proper name: —a name, moreover, with infamous historical associations.

Memory supplied the appellation in full, along with a sickly, sinking sensation in the pit of his stomach: *William de Soulis*, reputedly the wickedest magician ever to walk abroad on Scottish soil.

Adam's hands balled themselves instinctively into fists as he confronted this discovery, for Soulis figured in the annals of Scottish folklore as a diabolically powerful black Adept, with a hideous catalogue of torture and murder to his credit. Virtually invincible, he had terrorized the countryside for many years before at last being captured and executed—wrapped in chains and lead and boiled in a cauldron of oil, just as Kerr had shown him.

But in reporting the manner of his death, legend spoke only part of the truth. For Adam's vision, facilitated by the spirit of Soulis' nemesis, another Master of the Hunt, had amply demonstrated that the destruction of Soulis' body had been only half the battle. Kerr and his Huntsmen had been charged with carrying out a higher Justice, which decreed that the spirit of William Lord Soulis should be cast into the Void between the Outer and Inner Planes. Only now it seemed that Francis Raeburn intended to commute Soulis' sentence for reasons of his own.

The banishment had required incredible focus and power, and would have entailed the weaving of a complex sequence of spells. To procure Soulis' release, Raeburn would have to pull apart and nullify the protocols involved—and fuel this labor with the blood-sacrifice of Iolo McFarlane. In order to forestall both eventualities, Adam realized that he was going to require knowledge as specific as Raeburn's. And the only way he was likely to get it was to speak directly with Kerr.

And seemingly the only way he could hope to speak directly with Kerr was through the agency of a trained and powerful medium such as McLeod.

Adam glanced at his watch. It was approaching midnight, but he realized that the sooner he could speak with his Second, the better. Setting McFarlane's journal aside, he went to the desk and picked up the phone, punching up McLeod's home number. He got the answering machine instead of McLeod himself—which probably meant that the inspector either had been called out or had shut off the phone to get a rare few hours of uninterrupted sleep.

"Noel, it's Adam," he said, quickly framing a message in suitably ambiguous terms, in case Jane picked up his messages. "I expect you've already gone to bed, so I'll make this short. I've just spent the evening going through McFarlane's dream diary, and I've come up with some important leads. I'm confident he's alive, and I don't think anything will go critical for McFarlane himself until after the weekend, but there's a special witness I want to talk to—and I'll need your help to do that.

"I'd like to meet up tomorrow and discuss the case in person. I've got to stop in at the hospital for an hour in the morning, and then I've promised Ximena we'll have lunch, but we have to drive over to Portobello in the afternoon to pick up our rings from the engraver. We'll swing by your office when we're finished, and Humphrey can take Ximena on home. Please ring Humphrey and leave a message if you can't make it. See you then."

When he had cradled the receiver, he mentally reviewed what he had said, hoping it had not sounded too lame or too obscure. He closed McFarlane's journal and put it back into his briefcase before going upstairs to bed, his mind already hard at work continuing to examine what he had learned. He had fallen asleep by the time Ximena came home and snuggled into bed beside him, and he woke several times during the night, disturbed by dreams he could not recall.

# CHAPTER THIRTY

A DAM woke the next morning with the previous night's revelations still heavy on his mind, but he did his best to maintain a cheery façade over breakfast with Ximena. With their wedding celebration now but a week away, and today the first full day the two of them had been able to spend together for most of the previous week, he was determined not to dampen the day's pleasures by interjecting any reminders of the past week's stresses. Lightly brushing off Ximena's inquiry about his progress with McFarlane's dream journal, he made casual admission that he had, indeed, found a few items of interest and planned to stop by McLeod's office briefly on their way home to pass on the information, but he would not let himself be drawn further.

It was not that Adam doubted her ability to cope with at least a superficial explanation of what was taking shape. In light of their recent experiences with the Hand of Glory, he knew Ximena was unlikely to question Raeburn's potential to wreak material havoc through supernatural means. At the same time, until he had consulted with his Second and engaged his help in communicating directly with the spirit of Andrew Kerr, there seemed little point in revealing the seriousness of Raeburn's threat until he had some idea how to deal with it. The knowledge that Imbolc was the first likely target date for Raeburn to act lent further justification for keeping silent.

They set out for the city shortly after nine o'clock, with Humphrey at the wheel of the Bentley and McFarlane's journal locked in the boot in Adam's briefcase. Then, while

Adam stopped in at the hospital for a scheduled consultation with a senior staff member, Humphrey escorted Ximena on into the city center to do some shopping in Prince's Street.

They rendezvoused for an intimate lunch at the Caledonian. Only when Ximena shrugged off her coat did Adam realize she was dressed in the same cream ensemble she had worn on Christmas Eve, a touching reminder of the commitment they had made and would be affirming publicly in only a week's time—and an indication of his own preoccupation that he had not noticed earlier. Lingering over a fine meal and a bottle of Veuve Cliquot, her hand in his, he made a special effort to set aside the tension of the past week and more, if only for a few hours.

The moment lingered as Humphrey drove them to their appointment with the engraver, a colleague of Lady Julian's who maintained a small studio and art gallery in Portobello, a quiet suburb to the east of the city itself. Though Julian herself had designed and fashioned their wedding rings, she lacked the equipment needed to do the very fine engraving required for the insides of the bands. There were no parking spaces on the road in front of the gallery, so Humphrey was obliged to pull the Bentley into a restricted zone around the corner on an adjoining side street.

"You'd better wait here with the car, just in case there's a traffic warden prowling around," Adam told Humphrey. "We shouldn't be very long."

The proprietor was expecting them, and had the rings ready for their inspection. The style Ximena had chosen for the inscription was a delicate copperplate match for the one used on the wedding invitations.

"Very nice indeed," Adam said to the engraver. "I must thank Lady Julian for referring us to you."

He settled the account and slipped the ring box into his coat pocket. They lingered a few minutes to admire some of the sculpture on display in the gallery itself before taking their leave. The number of people in the street had dwindled and the streetlights had come on, prompted by the gathering gloom of the January dusk. Ximena checked her watch and clucked her tongue.

"I still can't get over how early it gets dark in Scotland

in the wintertime,'' she said with a sigh. "It's only half past four, but it *looks* more like half past eight."

"It's these northerly latitudes—too near the Arctic Circle," Adam said with a grin. "If it's any consolation, just remember how long the days are in the summertime."

Ximena turned up her collar with an exaggerated shiver.

"Now I know why groundhogs hibernate! Sometimes I wonder if maybe we shouldn't think about deferring the wedding till June, when we can celebrate with an all-night garden party."

Adam maintained a straight face. "If that's what you really want. But I think it only fair to warn you that we shall be a scandal to polite society in the meantime."

"Perish the thought!" Ximena said with a roll of her eyes. "No, we've done enough shilly-shallying already—and I don't think I could keep up this pretext of only being engaged for much longer. Like the U.S. Postal Service, we must keep to our existing schedule, come rain, snow, sleet, hail, or any other adverse weather condition!"

"Far be it from me to contradict!" Adam retorted with a chuckle.

They carried on downhill past an array of parked cars. A stepped close opened up to ·their right, its cobbles overshadowed by the buildings flanking it on either hand. Several yards further on, Ximena paused to admire a Victorian doll house on display in the cluttered window of an antique shop. Adam was about to suggest that they should be moving on, blowing on gloved hands and shifting from foot to foot against the cold, when the street reflections on the glass in front of him registered a flash of movement rushing up on him from behind.

Before he could turn or cry out, his masked attacker rammed him hard in the back. His forehead hit the plate-glass window with stunning force, and a muscular arm simultaneously caught him round the neck in a throttling choke-hold, jerking him backward.

Ducking and throwing himself forward, Adam tried to buck his assailant over his head, but only succeeded in tightening the stranglehold. Still struggling, he managed to gasp out, "*Run, Ximena!*"

It had all happened in the space of a few heartbeats. Even as Ximena was drawing breath to scream, drawing back her arm to clout Adam's attacker with her shoulder bag, two more masked figures darted forward from between two parked cars. One of them made a lunge for Ximena; the other flung himself at Adam. As the combined weight of his two assailants crowded him against the wall, a gloved hand clapped a damp pad of cloth over his mouth and nose.

Adam recoiled, but not before he had inadvertently taken in a gulping lungful of chloroform. His stomach lurched and his eyes swam. He tried to hold his breath, making a sickly, frantic attempt to twist away, but powerful hands were locked around his wrists, and he could feel the first effects of the chloroform already eroding his coordination.

A sharp blow to his solar plexus drove the air from his lungs in a sharp *whoof!* Reflex made him draw another gasping breath, despite his determination not to, and further resistance began to drain away like water from a sieve as his captors began hustling him toward the curb.

Meanwhile, Ximena's attacker had one arm twisted behind her and was attempting the same procedure that had felled Adam. Squealing and twisting, she jammed a high heel into her adversary's instep with all the force and weight she could muster. His grip loosened and he reared back with a pungent curse. Before he could regain control of her, she wriggled loose and screamed for help, for Adam was sagging limply between his two assailants, being dragged into the street.

Her cry raised shouts of alarm from farther down the block, but her attacker lunged after her, catching her by the sleeve and whirling her around, dealing her a backhand blow to the side of the head. The force of it, plus her own efforts to escape, knocked her spinning into a puddle on the pavement and left her assailant with only a handful of overcoat to show for his labors. Even as she scrambled backwards out of reach, frantic over what was happening to Adam, an anonymous black Edinburgh taxi came swooping down on them and screeched to a halt at the curb.

The driver threw open the back door and barked an order to hurry up. Adam's assailants were already stuffing his sagging body unceremoniously onto the floor of the back seat, scrambling in behind. Abandoning Ximena, the third man ran to yank the front passenger door open, vaulting in even as the back door closed and the driver mashed the accelerator, barely managing to close his own door as the taxi roared away in a cloud of diesel smoke.

Stunned by the suddenness of it, and the blow to her head, Ximena could only insist to herself numbly that this could not possibly be happening, as the first of several would-be rescuers came running up and helped her stagger shakily to her feet. She answered the ensuing flurry of questions as best she could, but her mind seemed all at once benumbed. Only when Humphrey came rushing to join them did her focus return, and she choked back the sob rising up in her throat as she seized his arm.

"Humphrey, call Noel McLeod, before you do anything else," she said in a surprisingly calm voice. "Adam's been kidnapped."

McLeod was sitting at his computer console, working on a routine press release, when his telephone rang. Expecting word that Adam had arrived for their promised meeting, he was surprised to hear Humphrey's voice instead. Surprise yielded to shock when Adam's butler informed him of what had just occurred.

"I'm afraid I can't tell you much more, sir," Humphrey insisted, in response to McLeod's blurted demand for details. "I was waiting around the corner with the car, so I only caught a glimpse of the taxi racing by, just after I heard Dr. Lockhart scream. We've two beat officers here now, and they've called in for support, but Dr. Lockhart instructed me get in touch with you directly."

"Is she all right?"

"She took a nasty fall, and I believe she has a few bruises and abrasions, but she insists that it can wait until she's given her statement. One of the officers is with her now."

"I'll be there as soon as is humanly possible," McLeod assured him, grabbing a pen and pulling a notepad closer. "What's your location?"

Humphrey gave him the address.

"I've got it," McLeod muttered, jotting it down and then

copying it a second time onto the bottom half of the paper. "Whatever you do, don't let Dr. Lockhart out of your sight until I can get there. And tell her to try not to worry. We'll find him—no matter what it takes."

A bellow out the door of his office summoned Donald Cochrane on the run. As McLeod tore his note in two and handed half to his aide, he minced no words in acquainting Cochrane with the bare bones of the situation.

"Adam Sinclair's been kidnapped," he said bluntly, as he pulled on his coat. "That's where it happened. They'll call in bigger guns than me to handle this, as soon as the word gets out, but I want to be the one to handle the preliminary investigation. Tell anyone else who wants to know that I'm on my way to the scene."

"Do you want me to drive you, sir?"

"No, I need you to anchor for me at this end. I'll take Gilston. For starters, I want you to notify Adam's mother. She isn't at Strathmourne; she's staying with a Lady Julian Brodie, here in the city. You'll find the address and number in my files, under *B* for Brodie."

"Will do," Cochrane agreed, scribbling a notation. "Anything else?"

"Aye, get onto press relations and alert them to what's happened. This won't make the evening papers, but the TV folk will be all over us as soon as word gets out. Tell McDade I'll ring him with an official statement as soon as I know more. Then just stand by."

Knowing he could trust Cochrane to follow through, with no questions asked, McLeod grabbed up his hat and overcoat, collected P. C. Gilston from the outer office, and within minutes was striking out eastwards across the city in a raucous blare of sirens and emergency lights. Three uniformed officers were in attendance when they arrived, two of them protecting the crime scene. The third was taking a statement from one of the men who had tried to come to Ximena's rescue.

"DCI McLeod," the inspector said, displaying his warrant card to the first officer he approached. "Where's Dr. Lockhart?"

"Over in the squad car, sir."

McLeod was already headed in that direction, for he had spotted Humphrey leaning down to talk to someone sitting inside the car. At the inspector's approach, Humphrey turned, a look of profound relief on his face.

"She says she's all right, sir, but I really think she ought to be checked over," he told McLeod. "She took a couple of nasty whacks to the head."

Ximena was huddled miserably under a tartan rug that McLeod recognized as belonging in the Bentley, which was now double-parked behind the squad car. Her face was very pale, and a bruise was beginning to show on her right cheek.

"Noel, oh thank God!" she exclaimed, sitting up with a start as he opened the back door of the car. "Tell me you know who did this—or rather, tell me you *don't* know."

"I have a pretty fair idea," he acknowledged bleakly, crouching down on his hunkers. "But before I let you in on my suspicions, I'd like you to tell me everything you can about what happened."

Ximena nodded numbly, drawing the tartan rug closer around her with a shiver. "It happened so fast," she murmured. "They seemed to come out of nowhere. I think they stunned Adam when they slammed him into the plate-glass window." She gestured vaguely toward the front of the antique store. "They were dressed all in black, and wearing gloves and ski masks, so I couldn't make out anything of their faces. When they grabbed Adam, they clapped a cloth over his nose and mouth. They tried the same thing on me, but I managed to get away. It was chloroform, Noel. They had this planned."

The remainder of her account only served to confirm McLeod's worst fears.

"I expect they've been tailing him for some time, waiting for their chance," he observed grimly. "And today was a bonus, because they might have got the two of you at once—followed you to the engraver's studio, where there weren't apt to be as many people around, then set themselves up to jump you when you came out.

"After that, I'm afraid the pattern is all too familiar. I don't think there's any doubt that the man we want is an old adversary by the name of Francis Raeburn. We've been after him for some time, but by God, I intend to nail him this time.''

Philippa met them a short time later in the casualty department of Edinburgh Royal Infirmary, while they waited for Ximena's skull films to come back. She, too, was looking pale and shaken; and McLeod was not surprised to see that she was wearing the heavy scarab ring of gold and sapphire which symbolized her Adeptship.

''I suppose we should have expected something like this, after that attempt on Peregrine and Julia,'' she told Ximena grimly, ''but somehow we all must have thought Adam would be immune to such a direct attack.''

''What is that supposed to mean?'' Ximena asked.

Philippa passed a hand across her brow. All at once she looked every one of her seventy-seven years.

''It means,'' she said with bleak candor, ''that we have every reason to fear for my son's life.''

# CHAPTER THIRTY-ONE

ADAM returned groggily to his senses to find himself sprawled on his right side, cramped arms stretched upward and his head half-cradled against his shoulder. Dull pain throbbed behind his eyes, accompanied by a faint stir of nausea when he opened them and tried to focus—though he could see only the rumpled white of his shirt sleeve close beside his face.

Swallowing down bile and a moan, he tried to draw his hands to his aching forehead—and found his wrists secured above his head by a pair of handcuffs run through the white-painted frame of a narrow iron bedstead. The restraint brought back memory in a head-splitting surge of alarm and dull despair. Still reeling, he risked moving his head a few painful centimeters, trying to get some idea of his surroundings.

Harsh light from an aged ceiling fixture revealed a tightly shuttered window, four blank walls in need of paint, a grey metal bedside locker, a single straight-backed chair, and a metal-reinforced door. The blinking red eye of a closed-circuit television camera looked down from a corner. The effect suggested a prison cell crossed with a mortuary.

The analogy made him shiver, and he let his head fall back against his arm, suddenly aware of the pounding of his heart, in rhythm with the aching in his head. The dry thickness of his tongue and the erratic behavior of his pulse suggested he might have been subjected to something more potent and long-lasting than the chloroform used to subdue him initially. Trying to pull himself together, probing sluggishly at memory, he realized he had no idea how long he had been unconscious, though the state of his bladder suggested a significant time span.

The memory of his abduction was all too clear—the sudden attack, the chloroform disarming him, resistance and then awareness fading as his abductors bundled him roughly onto the floor of a taxicab, like a heap of dirty laundry. As he shifted position slightly, attempting to ease cramped muscles, the twinges he could feel attested to the likelihood that he had cost them enough trouble to warrant a kick or two. His single fragment of consolation within that final waking memory was the image of Ximena's would-be abductor abandoning his quarry in order to keep from being left behind.

The fact that they had been willing enough to let her go suggested that Adam himself had always been the main prize. Nor had he any doubt who was responsible for his present captivity. The method of his abduction followed an all-too familiar pattern—palpable evidence that despite repeated setbacks, Francis Raeburn retained the will and the means to exact retribution.

Adam's present situation was clearly designed to underline how very vulnerable he now was. Quite apart from being drugged and restrained, he had been stripped to trousers and shirtsleeves while unconscious, relieved of shoes and belt and tie and all personal effects. While his watch, cufflinks, and a gold fountain pen were laid out on the bedside locker beside his wallet, what gave Adam the strongest pang of misgiving was the absence of his Adept ring, along with the rings intended to seal his marriage. These were items that might well be used against him, because of their strong emotional link—a potential weapon he did not doubt Raeburn would attempt to exploit for his own profit and amusement, and to Adam's detriment.

And handcuffed as he was, Adam held little hope that his old adversary would allow him any chance to make a bid for escape. His one frail recourse in his own defense was to try and send out a call for help on the astral—if he could pierce the drug-induced lethargy dragging at his thinking.

Hoping that any observers would think that he was merely drifting back into unconsciousness, he closed his eyes and attempted to retreat into trance. But before he could adequately compose himself, his concentration was jarred by the sound of brisk footsteps outside the closed door, followed by the harsh clatter of bolts being drawn.

Queasy apprehension gripped him as the door opened. The face of the man who entered was all too familiar to Adam's bleary gaze—deceptively ordinary-looking in a navy three-piece suit. Francis Raeburn left the door ajar behind him as he advanced to Adam's bedside with a reproving cluck of his tongue, his normally pale face aglow with high color.

"That will do, Dr. Sinclair," he said briskly. "It's most uncivil of you to try and contact your associates the minute you believe my back is turned. The courteous guest should avoid causing trouble for his host—besides which, you would be wasting your efforts. These premises are quite heavily shielded, even by your discriminating standards."

Rolling onto his back to gaze up at his captor, Adam made no attempt to summon a rejoinder. Even half-drugged, he could see that Raeburn had undergone a change in the months since their previous encounter. The ascetic features were now more sharply defined, and the thinning blond hair had gone a trifle silver. The pronounced flush, the overly elaborate banter, were signs of a man only marginally in control of himself. A detached part of Adam reckoned that Raeburn had been driving himself hard since they last met— pushing himself near to the breaking point in search of the elusive touchstone of power and victory.

The result was a loss of equilibrium. Raeburn's intellect might remain as sharp as ever, but the emotional core of his personality was being systematically eroded. The process was a long-term one, the results only now becoming outwardly apparent. But Adam knew that such erosion was one of the dangers ever-present in courting the favors of the Patrons of Shadow.

As this thought moved sluggishly across his mind, he became aware that Raeburn was speaking again.

"I must apologize for the inelegance of your restraints," Raeburn said, nodding toward the handcuffs. "My men were more efficient than I dared to hope. I wasn't expecting you quite so soon. But we'll remedy this embarrassing oversight very shortly.'' He paused a beat for emphasis. ''Aren't you the least bit curious to know what I have in store for you?''

His tone was lightly edged, as if the quality of Adam's silence had vexed him. Faced with a direct question, Adam was careful in his answer.

''No doubt you'll get around to telling me in your own good time.''

Raeburn laughed. ''Well-reasoned. Just now, I think I'll let you indulge your imagination—especially since I have no wish to blunt your anticipation.''

Reaching above Adam's head, Raeburn turned on a high-intensity light clamped to the bedstead, then delved into the pocket of his suit jacket and produced the small velvet box which Adam had brought away with him from the engraver's studio. Opening it, he took out the two wedding rings and made a show of examining each of them in turn under the light.

''A. S. to X. L., X. L. to A. S.—how touchingly Victorian,'' he quipped, his Lynx ring flashing like blood on his hand as he replaced the rings in their box. ''I can't say that sentimentality much appeals to me—but then, your appetites and mine never have coincided, have they?''

Closing the box with a snap, he pocketed it and brought out Adam's Adept ring, subjecting it to the same degree of scrutiny.

''A handsome enough stone,'' he conceded, ''but it could use a bit of polish.''

Watching Adam out of the corner of his eye, he held the ring close to his lips and breathed heavily on the sapphire. As he did so, Adam felt himself swept by a sudden flush of mingled heat and cold that penetrated to the bone, so intense that it forced a hissing intake of breath.

''Yes, that's better,'' Raeburn purred. ''A significant improvement.''

With ostentatious care, he rubbed the stone gently against the lapel of his jacket and returned it to his pocket. The searing cold abated, leaving Adam drained and breathless as the door beyond swung fully open to admit the back of a black-clad blond man towing a tea trolley behind him.

Raeburn was still smiling as he nodded toward the new-comer.

"This is Herr Richter, my head of security, whose oper-atives have so amply redeemed themselves after their little mishap at your gate lodge last week," he said genially, even as Richter turned and Adam recognized the lean, bespecta-cled face and hard eyes that had figured time and again in Peregrine's drawings of recent weeks.

A darting look at the trolley Richter was rattling closer to the bed evoked a pang of more visceral dread, for the pur-pose of the paraphernalia laid out in such orderly array was all too obvious to anyone medically trained—stark declara-tion of Raeburn's ability and intention to hold Adam helpless for as long as it suited his pleasure.

Nor was Raeburn leaving anything to chance, where the handling of his prize was concerned. Though Adam could have predicted the appearance of the two hard-eyed profes-sionals who followed Richter into the room, the self-assured younger man accompanying them seemed out of place at first—pin-striped suit cut in the height of Bond Street fashion, with dark hair worn full and longish above a hand-some, self-indulgent face—and with an expensive stetho-scope draped around his neck with studied arrogance.

"I believe you already know Dr. Mallory," Raeburn said smoothly, even as Adam took a startled second look at the suave newcomer. "I have asked him to ensure that your stay with us will be as restful as possible."

Raeburn's immediate plans for him had been evident from the moment Richter arrived with the trolley. Still, a sense of queasy betrayal reinforced Adam's apprehension as he real-ized that the physician engaged to facilitate the arrangement, in violation of all medical ethics, was the slick young anaes-thetist from his own hospital.

Mallory gave him a nod in sinister parody of a pleasant bedside manner, tearing open an alcohol swab and then se-lecting a pre-loaded hypodermic syringe from the tea trolley. Simultaneously, Richter's two associates came briskly around to the other side of the bed and, at a signal from Raeburn, pinned Adam's body and legs flat to the bed. There was nothing Adam could do as Richter pushed back his left sleeve and constricted the blood-flow with a vise-like grip around the upper arm, holding the forearm steady so that Mallory could slip his needle home.

"Consider this in the light of pre-op medication," Raeburn said softly from the sidelines, as Mallory's thumb slowly tightened on the plunger. "It would be extremely inconvenient if you were to raise a hue and cry. I simply can't abide the thought of so many good plans going to waste— so I think we'll be keeping you sedated from here on out."

As Adam's Second, it fell to McLeod to convene the council of war that, even then, was getting under way in the library at Strathmourne. Peregrine had spread the word immediately upon receiving Donald Cochrane's telephone call earlier in the evening, and key members and supporters of the Hunting Lodge had converged on the house in the next several hours.

When McLeod finally arrived with Philippa and Ximena, following the latter's release from Edinburgh Royal Infirmary, they had found the assembled household huddled around a portable TV set hastily brought in by Humphrey, for the abduction of Sir Adam Sinclair, a mere week before his scheduled society wedding, had been sensational enough to rate mention on the ten o'clock news. Among the members of the Hunting Lodge anxiously awaiting a more specific update from McLeod were Peregrine, the Houstons, and Lady Julian, fetched by Humphrey directly upon leaving the crime scene. Also present, by special dispensation, were Julia Lovat and Harry Nimmo.

"The way the abduction was carried out is totally consistent with methods used in the past by Francis Raeburn and the Lodge of the Lynx," Philippa said, after Ximena had related the basic circumstances of Adam's kidnapping. "Raeburn has crossed swords with Adam more than once; and while we've always been able to short-stop him, we've never quite managed to bring him down. Quite clearly, revenge will play a large part in Raeburn's present motivations. While I cannot overstress the danger to Adam himself, however, there is little doubt in my mind that the abduction is also the prelude to something infinitely more sinister in its implications.''

A shiver of greater uneasiness rippled through the company, but the library and, indeed, the entire estate had already been rendered as secure against intrusion as was possible. PC Gilston was standing guard outside the front door of the house, to fend off further press inquiries; and with Peregrine and Julia withdrawn to the greater safety of the main house for the duration, McLeod had pulled back Adam's recent security patrols to the immediate vicinity of the house, with strict instructions to safeguard the family's privacy.

"Naturally, the regular police are prepared to do all they can," Philippa continued. "Unfortunately, I doubt they have the resources to find Raeburn—at least in time. Certainly they aren't equipped to deal with him. That means most of the burden falls upon us. I expect that, at best, we have three days to accomplish this.''

"Why three days?" Harry asked.

"Adam left a message on my answering machine late last night," McLeod said. "He was none too specific, because all of us try to avoid leaving hard evidence of what we do, but he said he'd been going through Iolo McFarlane's dream journal and had come up with some leads—that he was convinced McFarlane is still alive, but he didn't think anything would go critical until after the weekend." He paused a beat.

"Monday is Imbolc Eve, one of the most significant festivals of the old Celtic calendar, a traditional time of blood-sacrifice. Adam was concerned for McFarlane when he rang me; but now that he himself is in Raeburn's hands, I think it's highly likely that Adam will become the sacrifice instead. I kick myself now that I didn't ring him back this morning to clarify," he added, steeling himself to Ximena's appalled intake of breath.

"He also mentioned a special witness that he wanted to talk to—and that he needed my help to do this," McLeod went on, sweeping his gaze across the other members of the Hunting Lodge, who immediately realized he was not speaking of a living witness. "I have no idea who he had in mind, but I think it's important that we try to find out—and start in immediately on trying to locate Adam himself. Philippa,

I'd like to defer to your greater experience in directing this operation. You're in the best position to coordinate our efforts from here, while I continue to liaise with more conventional police efforts to find him.''

Ximena, whose face had gone progressively paler during McLeod's recitation, glanced at all their faces in something of despair.

"Am I really hearing what I think I hear?" she whispered. "Are you saying that this Raeburn is going to make a human sacrifice of Adam?"

McLeod looked at his hands, unable to meet her gaze, and Peregrine, too, averted his eyes, both of them remembering Randall Stewart. The other members of the Hunting Lodge looked away as well. Julia bit at her lips, fighting back tears, and Harry looked stunned. Only Philippa remained undaunted as she reached across to take her daughter-in-law's hand.

"I'm afraid we are, darling," she said quietly. "But that isn't until three days from now. Meanwhile, there's much we can do. Noel, I'll need you to fetch a few things for me from downstairs."

A quarter-hour later, they were ready to begin, arranging folding chairs around two card tables pushed together in the center of the room. Victoria had covered the tables with a clean white cloth, and upon it in the center was set a large sphere of rock crystal on a silver stand. The electric lights had been extinguished, so the room was lit only by the firelight and a single new beeswax candle in a silver holder, set close beside the crystal.

Signing for everyone to find a chair, Philippa took a place between McLeod and Julian and laid Adam's silver-mounted *skean dubh* on the table beside the crystal. While upstairs to fetch it, she had changed from her smart designer suit of earlier in the day to a comfortable caftan of sapphire-blue velour whose color echoed that of the gem set in the *skean dubh*'s hilt and the lesser sapphires gracing the hands of each Huntsman.

In addition, Philippa had donned an Egyptian necklace of exquisite workmanship—blue faience and enamelwork depicting a solar disk flanked by two ostrich plumes and gripped by a Horus hawk. While most of those present were aware that the necklace had belonged to Adam himself, in an earlier incarnation, she offered a modified explanation for the benefit of those who had no knowledge of such mysteries.

"This is apt to be a very long night, so I thought I'd change into something more comfortable before settling down to work," she said, adjusting the angle of the *skean dubh* more to her liking. "This will all seem very strange to a few of you, so I'll try to explain a little before we begin.

"The items we've assembled here are tools—nothing more. It's said that a good magician should be able to work high magic while naked in the middle of a desert—but the proper tools make the work far easier."

She touched the solar disk on the necklace at her breast and smiled at Ximena, in particular.

"This necklace is one of those tools. It was once the badge of office of a priest of Amun Ra—someone with whom my son has special affinities. Adam's father bought it for me, shortly after Adam was born, so it means a great deal to me as well. By wearing it while I work, I hope to put myself in harmony with my son while I attempt to locate him by means of scrying. That's what the crystal is for."

She let one hand rest on the crystal as she went on.

"Scrying is a form of self-induced clairvoyance. It's tantamount to a radio operator trying to tune in to a particular radio frequency—except that the resonances I'll be trying to home in on are psychic. For a more specific focus on Adam himself, I've brought down his *skean dubh*." She picked it up by the sheath, with the stone uppermost.

"This particular *skean dubh* is more than just an item of fancy Highland dress; it's a magical tool that Adam uses regularly in his work. Other than the ring that most of you have seen him wear—and that will be in the hands of Raeburn by now—this carries perhaps the strongest residual of his unique psychic signature that we could hope for. An affinity also exists between this stone and the one in Adam's ring, just as there's an affinity between his ring and the ones the rest of us wear. That may also work in our favor.

"In this instance, I plan to use the *skean dubh* like a tuner to help me focus on the particular signature band that I'm looking for. If I'm successful," she concluded, laying the *skean dubh* beside the crystal, "at least a few of us will be able to catch visual images in this piece of rock crystal."

So saying, she joined hands with Julian and McLeod and watched as the others joined hands as well, following her lead—Ximena between Julian and Christopher, to Philippa's left, Harry at the end opposite them, and Julia directly across from Philippa, between her husband and Victoria. When everyone had settled, Philippa drew a deep breath and began entering into trance.

One by one, the other members of the Hunting Lodge did likewise, silently linking their wills to Philippa's, Christopher bowing his head in a whispered prayer which Ximena found herself repeating. After a moment, at Philippa's silent cue, McLeod and Julian released her hands and shifted their contacts to her arms instead, maintaining the circle while Philippa took up Adam's *skean dubh* by the sheath and held it before her entranced gaze, elbows propped on her chair arms and against the table edge as she stared into the depths of the azure stone.

The hushed silence became a tranquil focus of stilled anticipation, only soft breathing and the faint crackle of the flames upon the hearth edging the stillness. Long minutes passed before Philippa slowly reached out her left hand to cup the stand of the crystal ball, her right hand bringing the pommel of the *skean dubh* to touch her bowed forehead.

A shiver passed through her body, transmitted along the circle as a frisson of certainty that *something* was happening, though no one dared break the silence. For another long moment there was no other sound—until all at once Philippa drew a sudden sharp breath, leaning slightly forward to peer into the heart of the crystal, the *skean dubh* still pressed to her forehead.

"Show me," she whispered. "Oh, please—let me see. . . ."

Hardly daring to breathe herself, Ximena leaned closer, as did Harry and Julia, hardly knowing what they might be expected to see. The others did not move.

Philippa's eyes sharpened, her gaze flickering minutely back and forth as if she were, indeed, following some moving sequence of images. Then, abruptly, she exhaled gustily and slumped back in her chair, the *skean dubh* slipping from her fingers with a dull clatter.

"You got *something*," McLeod declared, eyeing her intently, as Julian's nimble fingers shifted on Philippa's wrist to check her pulse.

The other members of the Hunting Lodge also roused themselves, all of them looking to Philippa for enlightenment.

"Nothing of substance," Philippa murmured, shaking her head as she made her eyes refocus. "Only a few fleeting images associated with the actual kidnapping. They may even have been triggered by Ximena's descriptions of what happened."

"Nothing of Adam himself?" McLeod pressed.

Philippa shook her head again, and Ximena drew herself up, clinging to Christopher's hand.

"Does that mean he's dead?" she forced herself to ask.

"No," Philippa said emphatically. "That's the one piece of good news. If he were dead, the evidence would be clearly emblazoned on the astral. My guess is that he's being kept drugged and unconscious, in addition to being magically shielded. Raeburn's already proven his effectiveness at keeping things hidden."

"Then what next?" Peregrine asked.

"With some minor modifications to allow for a sharing of the work, we repeat this exercise at regular intervals, in the hope of catching Adam in a moment of wakefulness," Philippa replied.

"Isn't that a bit hit-or-miss?" Harry asked.

"It's *very* hit-or-miss," Philippa retorted, a little more sharply than she had intended. "But until and unless I can come up with a better approach, it's better than doing nothing."

She had Humphrey set up a pair of cots in the downstairs parlor, so that Julian, Christopher, and Victoria could keep up the search through the rest of the night, taking turns as two of them trolled on the astral for traces of Adam's unique psychic resonance while the third kept watch for their physical welfare. Ximena, exhausted both physically and emotionally, was sent upstairs with orders to sleep or else face the likelihood that Philippa would insist on a sedative. She did not argue the wisdom of the order, for all of them knew that fatigue might well prove one of their worst enemies, but neither did she manage to sleep much—though Julia accompanied her upstairs and lay down beside her, and she, at least, dozed.

Once the two of them had retired, Humphrey was sent to retrieve Adam's briefcase from the Bentley, so that McLeod, Philippa, Peregrine, and Harry could examine Iolo McFarlane's dream journal. Though the four of them worked well into what remained of the night, trying to fathom what might have sparked Adam's telephone call to McLeod, no enlightenment was forthcoming. Toward morning, they, too, retreated for a few hours' sleep.

First light saw Huntsmen and Hunt Followers gathered in the library again for brunch and a morning briefing, save for Julian, who remained on astral duty in the parlor until relieved by Christopher. Philippa had phoned John Graham immediately after rising, and knew he also had his resources focused on finding Adam.

The phone started ringing shortly thereafter, and McLeod soon was embroiled in liaison functions with the official police investigation now picking up speed. Donald Cochrane arrived later in the afternoon to assist McLeod, shortly after Ximena announced with horror that she had just remembered that her mother was already en route to Scotland for a wedding that now might well never take place.

"Dear God, she left San Francisco two hours ago," Ximena said with a groan, as she looked at her watch. "I'd forgotten all about it. She'll be here first thing in the morning. What am I going to tell her?"

"We'll decide closer to the time," Philippa replied, hugging the younger woman close. "I haven't told Adam's sister yet, either, though I suppose I'd better ring her. Try not to worry, darling. We aren't beaten yet."

The rest of Saturday crept past without any definitive leads, official or private. The press had a field day with the Adam Sinclair kidnap case, positing motives that ranged through demands for ransom, the possibility of retaliation by a former mental patient or criminal Adam had helped apprehend, and even the desperation attempt of some jealous former love interest to thwart the upcoming wedding.

The police did their best to keep press speculation from becoming too outrageous, but could provide no hard news to replace it, as detectives doggedly pursued the conventional side of the investigation and kept turning up blanks. A taxi thought to have been used in the abduction was discovered overturned and burnt out in a cul-de-sac just west of Edinburgh; but even when McLeod brought Peregrine and Harry into the police impound yard where it had been taken, neither was able to pick up any residual resonances.

Meanwhile, using Iolo McFarlane's dream journal as an additional focus, Philippa directed the members of the Hunting Lodge to extend their search to McFarlane as well as Adam—for if McFarlane had also been taken by Raeburn, as increasingly seemed the case, his captors might not have felt the need to shield his whereabouts as carefully as Adam's.

The logic was sound, but the widened search yielded no better results. At the end of the first full twenty-four hours following Adam's abduction, his would-be rescuers were no closer to finding him than they had been when they started.

# CHAPTER THIRTY-TWO

THE passage of the second night brought no change in the status of the Hunt. While the rest of the house caught what sleep they could, Victoria kept the last watch of the long early morning hours, Christopher by her side. Sunday dawned cold and blustery, with a hint of snow on the air.

First light found Philippa and Ximena making their way blearily downstairs, where Harry Nimmo was already tucking into a plateful of scrambled eggs and bacon, ready to drive Ximena to the airport to collect her mother. McLeod, Peregrine, and Donald Cochrane were just finishing breakfast with Harry, and headed off to police headquarters while Philippa tried to coax Ximena to eat at least a little.

When Ximena had reluctantly downed some tea and toast, and Harry had bundled her off to the Range Rover, Philippa watched until the car disappeared up the drive before taking a mug of coffee into the library, flogging her weary brain for some new inspiration in the search for her missing son. She was momentarily startled to find Julian there ahead of her, her wheelchair parked close by the fireside, thin shoulders huddled under a paisley shawl. Julian looked up as Philippa entered, offering her a ragged smile.

"Good morning, Pippa. I hope you won't mind, but I borrowed Humphrey during the night to run an errand for me."

"Oh?"

"I couldn't get to sleep after I finished my watch last night, so I decided to meditate for a while. I had a sudden flash of inspiration around three A.M.—something that might be useful for strengthening the link between ourselves and

Adam. I wasn't exactly sure where it had gotten to, after all these years, but thankfully it was right there in my jewel case that Humphrey brought back.''

She opened her hand to display a finely engraved Victorian locket on a silver chain—the gift Philippa herself had given to Julian and Michael Brodie at Adam's christening, when the couple had pledged themselves to be his godparents. The oval locket contained a miniature photo of Adam as a baby, to which Julian had later added a curl from his first haircut.

Momentarily overwhelmed with fear for him, Philippa reached out to take it, fighting back tears as she opened the locket to gaze at the well-remembered image of her infant son, and the dark snippet of fine baby hair sealed behind fragile glass on the opposite side. When she closed it, she made herself draw a sobering breath and focus again, forcing a faint smile as she sank down on the edge of a chair beside Julian.

"He was a beautiful baby, wasn't he, Julian?" she breathed.

"Beautiful," Julian agreed. "And he grew into a beautiful man."

Philippa nodded. "He did. I wonder . . . Julian, I'm getting an idea."

"Yes?"

"We've always held that hair and blood are the two best physical links to a subject," she continued softly, as if reciting a well-rehearsed lesson. "Now we have the hair, but the blood . . . Actually, we *do* have the blood," she murmured, looking at Julian in sudden enlightenment. "In fact, we have something even better than blood."

"We do?"

"We do, indeed." Philippa handed the locket back to Julian, her smile broadening. "We have the genetic blood-link that Adam and I share. For nine months of both our lives, he and I were as one. And if we were to link that connection to his hair, and his *skean dubh*, and the Horus necklace—"

After briefly absenting herself to rouse Victoria and Christopher—and to give Humphrey instructions about diverting Julia to breakfast, if she should come downstairs before they were finished—Philippa outlined what she proposed. Christopher, in particular, had reservations.

"I'll give you that the genetic link idea may be sound," he said, to the distant ringing of church bells as he rubbed both hands across early morning stubble. "But the blood aspect of it strikes me as perilously close to the methods the opposition uses. It also leaves you more open to psychic rebound, if you do manage to make some kind of contact. You can always drop *things* out of the equation, if you start to get caught up in whatever's holding *him*; but if your body is part of the equation, extricating yourself might not be that easy."

"No one's expecting anything to be easy," she replied. "I *am* expecting that the locket will be the primary focus, though, because it's his hair that's the most direct link. I plan to use the locket as a pendulum for map scrying. Even if we can't pin down the exact location, we might at least be able to get a directional fix on him."

"Then let me put some additional protection on you before we start," Christopher insisted. "The last thing we need at this point is for you to get trapped and drawn into whatever devilry Raeburn has going."

Philippa did not protest as he blessed holy water and made a circuit of the library, refreshing the wards always resident in the room and, indeed, around the house, then coming to sprinkle each of the women in turn. When Philippa sat down at the table where Victoria was opening out a general map of Scotland, she had Adam's *skean dubh* in hand again and had donned the Horus necklace.

As Julian rolled into place at her right and Victoria sat on her left, Philippa took the locket back from Julian and looped the doubled end of its chain around the hilt of the *skean dubh*, just below the sapphire in the pommel, then held the weapon by the sheath and propped her elbow so that the locket dangled just above the Perthshire coordinates of Strathmourne. Julian and Victoria laid hands on her shoulders as Christopher sat down opposite, joining hands with him to close the circle as all of them prepared to begin the Work.

Philippa drew a deep breath and slowly let it out, settling

into trance. She could feel the others' support as she gathered herself for the attempt and began casting back for memories of her pregnancy with Adam. Calling to mind the strong, secret rhythm of his heartbeat in her womb, her remembrance of the first time she had become aware of him as a distinct presence, she visualized their two lifelines entwined within the vessel of her own body. Then she began a conscious willing to reweave each and every tie that bound her to her son, fashioning the strands into a shining net that she finally cast outward, flinging it as far as she could.

She sensed a faint resistance as she started to reel it in, but she focused the pull through the links of her body and blood, through the necklace that had been Adam's in a distant land and time, through the *skean dubh* that was working tool in his present life—and down the silvery strand to the locket holding his likeness and a curl of his hair. She could feel her hand starting to tremble under the strain of channelling so much intent, could see it trembling as she let her gaze drift toward it—but then the pendulum itself began to vibrate, of its own accord. And then it began to circle slowly clockwise—and then counterclockwise—and then clockwise again.

"What . . . ?" came Victoria's soft whisper, cut off at a nudge from Christopher.

Philippa did not move, holding her focus against increasing strain, but the locket continued to circle, refusing to take direction. At length she gave a long sigh and closed her eyes, letting the locket and *skean dubh* sink to the map and then slip from her fingers as she bowed her head in her hands.

"What happened?" Christopher asked gently. "Philippa, are you all right?"

She sighed again and lifted her head, weariness and discouragement writ stark across her face.

"He's out there," she murmured, "but I couldn't get past whatever's shielding him. They must be holding him somewhere that's incredibly well protected—quite probably Raeburn's own bolthole."

"And given how well *we* can hide psychic activity," Christopher said archly, "we have to assume that Raeburn probably has similar expertise in that regard. Clearly, he does, or we should have been able to break through by now."

"I agree. But having said that," Philippa went on, "it occurs to me to wonder whether Raeburn would risk compromising such a secure retreat by using that location to carry out whatever he has planned for Adam. In other words, would he risk fouling his own nest? Also, given the way Callanish was used, and Raeburn's known predilection for working with ancient god-forms, I can't imagine that he'd pass up the chance to enhance his working by tapping into the power of some other ancient site.

"This gives us a two-pronged possibility of attack: By compiling a list of all the likely sites in the country, we may be able to narrow down some possibilities for his physical destination tomorrow night. And if they do move Adam to one of those sites, probably in the next twelve hours or so, they'll have to bring him out from under the heavy protection of wherever he is now. They can't maintain the same kind of cloaking on a moving subject that they can while he's stationary, in a long-established safe-house."

"That assumes that they *will* move him," Victoria pointed out. "What if they don't?"

Philippa shook her head. "I don't want to think about it; I *can't* think about it."

"I think you ought to get some rest," Christopher said quietly. "You're too worn out to—"

"I'm worried about *his* rest—which may be eternal, if we don't find him!" she retorted, rounding on the clergyman with all a mother's fierce determination. "And what if it isn't merely physical death that Raeburn is threatening? I *can't* give this up, even if it costs me my life!"

"And wasting your life isn't going to help him!" Julian said sharply, at the same time slipping an arm around her friend's trembling shoulders. "Get some rest, Pippa—*please*. We have to believe it's Imbolc Eve that Raeburn is aiming for—which means we've still got close to thirty-six hours to come up with something. If you think Raeburn is apt to use another ancient site, I'll put Julia on compiling a list right away.

"Meanwhile, you'd do us all a favor if you try to sleep

for a few of those hours, so that you'll be ready to face the last ones. That's when Raeburn is most apt to slip up, most apt to get sloppy. But if you don't rest, you'll be no good to Adam.''

Philippa said nothing for several long seconds, face turned away from Julian's entreaties; but then the proud shoulders unbent and she gave a long sigh as she looked up.

''You're right,'' she whispered. ''All of you are right. I'll go upstairs and lie down for a few hours. Do have Julia start that site research, but carry on with the sweeps we've been making for the past two days. You might want to switch to pendulum dowsing, now that we've got the locket. And call Noel. Have him get back here with Peregrine. If we did make a contact, we wouldn't be able to make a timely response, physically scattered as we are right now.''

''We'll do all of that,'' Christopher reassured her. ''But you *will* get some sleep in the meantime?''

''I promise I'll try,'' she replied.

Philippa was as good as her word, and came back downstairs for tea when Ximena and Harry finally returned at midafternoon. McLeod and Peregrine had arrived a short time before, and took Harry off to the parlor to bring him up to date on police efforts.

''We've installed Mom at Harry's town house,'' Ximena told them, shaking her head as she gratefully accepted a mug of tea from Victoria. ''His housekeeper will look after her. She took the news well enough, under the circumstances, but I thought her jet lag would never kick in. That's why we're so late.''

''The poor thing,'' Julian murmured. ''Hopefully, she'll sleep through the night.''

Ximena managed a resigned shrug. ''I expect she will. She wasn't happy that I wouldn't bring her back here to the house, though. She'd thought she'd be staying here, after all. But I tried to explain how that really wouldn't be a good idea, without telling her why it *really* wouldn't be a good idea. I've given her to understand that the house is being used as a staging area for the police search—which I suppose it is, in a way. Anyway, she'll never know the difference.

She does know that cops over here don't operate like the ones back home.''

"Some of them do," Philippa said with a faint smile. The look she exchanged with McLeod made it quite clear she was not referring to conventional police agencies.

"Oh," Ximena said. "Well, anyway, she'd never understand about all of this." She gestured toward the items temporarily set aside on the map on the table. "I wish *I* understood." She sighed. "I'm almost afraid to ask whether you made any progress while we were gone." She gnawed at her lower lip, fighting back tears. "Philippa, tell me he's still alive. . . .''

"I *can* tell you that, my darling," Philippa whispered. "I only wish I could tell you more."

"Can he hear us?" a voice asked, just edging at Adam's consciousness.

"Maybe a little," another voice replied. "Give me five minutes, to be sure he's stable."

"Very well. I'll be back."

The exchange came to Adam through a faint easing of the oblivion forced upon him. A hand turned his face slightly to one side and a bright light shone momentarily in first one eye and then the other. As the light withdrew, random tiny sounds began to anchor him to hazy awareness.

That awareness was hardly reassuring. He had managed to surface this far before. Following his second descent into oblivion, his drugged and unresisting body had been stripped naked and hooked up to a panoply of medical devices designed to monitor his vital signs and ensure that he never achieved more than a twilight level of consciousness. His occasional drifting forays back across the threshold of the abyss were accompanied by the soft, measured beep of an ECG somewhere behind his head, heard as if muffled through layers of cotton wool.

More rarely, when he managed to surface enough to open his eyes, he could see an IV bag hung close by the left side of the bed, its near end disappearing under strips of adhesive taped across the top of his wrist. Close pressure around a forefinger told of a pulse oximeter clamped there to monitor blood oxygen.

The IV itself was unalarming—a drip of dextrose and saline to sustain him. More insidious was the syringe pump attached to the IV, delivering a continuous infusion of the drugs keeping him sedated and helpless.

From his inability to move, Adam vaguely supposed that one of the drugs being given him must be a deep muscle relaxant of some kind—perhaps even one of the curariform substances that paralyzed voluntary movement and, in higher doses, interfered with breathing—for at some point, Mallory had intubated him. Since Adam was not now hooked up to a ventilator, he supposed that it must have been done as a precautionary measure until Mallory got the dosage fine-tuned—which was only what one might expect of a competent anaesthetist. . . .

"Stay with me, Sinclair." Mallory's voice stopped him drifting, reinforced by the sensory stimulus of a sharp pinch to his right earlobe. "Mr. Raeburn is going to pay you a visit in a few minutes. It wouldn't be polite to go to sleep on him."

A squeezing around his right bicep told of a blood pressure reading being taken. His gaze drifted dimly to Mallory's hands, applying the cool bell of a stethoscope to the pulse at the inner elbow, and then beyond, where he was distantly amused to see a padded restraint now buckled around his wrist. He found himself idly wondering whether they really thought he was in any state to break free.

"Yes, indeed, you're doing just fine," Mallory murmured, the hiss of released pressure punctuating his brisk smile as he laid his stethoscope back around his neck and unpeeled the Velcro securing the cuff. "We certainly wouldn't want you slipping away on us prematurely. You have a very important social engagement to keep—though it won't be that posh society wedding that has all the tabloids in a twitter.

"*Wedding of the season: dashing Edinburgh psychiatrist to wed American trauma specialist,*" the taunting voice continued, still sounding faint and far away. "What a pity they'll all be disappointed.

"Still, I don't imagine that pretty fiancée of yours will

waste much time grieving, even if she *will* be cheated of a title. I might pay court to her myself, after you're gone. I expect her main regret will be that your failure to consummate the marriage means she won't inherit any of your wealth.''

The door had opened and closed on his final remark, and a brief whisper of moving air raised goose bumps along Adam's exposed arms as another presence took Mallory's place.

''Now, Derek, it isn't sporting to tease our guest.'' Raeburn's face materialized above Adam's—lean and vulpine, and looking very smug. ''A very pleasant good evening to you, Dr. Sinclair,'' he said silkily. ''How are we doing today?''

Even if Adam had wanted to reply, the endotracheal tube would have prevented it. He closed his eyes, just able to turn his face minutely away.

''Now, Dr. Sinclair, that isn't very sociable,'' Raeburn purred. ''I had hoped you would grow resigned to your situation. In case you've lost track, the Eve of Imbolc is hardly twenty-four hours away. Can you guess what that means?''

Behind his closed eyelids, Adam could guess at all manner of possibilities, none of them comforting, and knew that his captor's blatant reference to Imbolc was clearly intended to provoke a fear response—and did, especially bolstered by the drugs in his system. The beep of the ECG monitor made audible confirmation of the increase in Adam's heart rate.

Sickly dispirited at this betrayal by his body, Adam nonetheless found himself opening his eyes with a start as the sound abruptly stopped—and caught Mallory's smarmy expression at the reaction as he adjusted a knob on the monitor. Raeburn, meanwhile, did not scruple to go into more explicit detail regarding his plans, clearly relishing the opportunity to further discomfit his victim.

''Oh, I can imagine what's going through that very fine mind of yours. You've probably already concluded, and rightly, that you're to be a featured participant in a very special ritual tomorrow night. The celebration will be in honor of the lord Taranis. It promises to be the crowning achievement of my career as well as an occasion of particularly satisfying personal revenge.

"And when all is said and done, I shall have succeeded where the Head-Master failed—where *you* thwarted his ambitions. I shall have made a slave of Taranis himself, so that all the lightnings of the Realm of Storms will be mine to command."

Adam's chest rose and fell on an involuntary gasp, and he would have spoken if he could, for the megalomania displayed in Raeburn's boast was exceeded only by the immortal peril inherent in what he proposed—even more for Raeburn himself than for Adam. Nor did the Lynx-Master seem to recognize the danger. While the Lords Elemental might condescend to allow the illusion that mortal grasp could contain their favors, they were by no means subject to human authority. Even less were they inclined to tolerate human presumption. What could Raeburn be thinking?

But Raeburn apparently mistook his captive's gasp for purely personal fear, because he settled negligently on the side of Adam's bed to elaborate on his boast.

"Do you doubt my claims, Master of the Hunt?" he purred. "Perhaps I failed to mention my new ally. You shall meet him tomorrow night on what was once his home ground. His name is William Lord Soulis. You *have* heard of him, haven't you?"

Adam closed his eyes as his mind reeled into disbelieving dismay, spinning him perilously near the brink of unconsciousness again.

"Yes, indeed, I thought you might recognize the name," Raeburn went on, enjoying his captive's reaction. "Shall I tell you of our bargain? Seven centuries ago, in exchange for favors rendered, Soulis engaged the services of a spirit familiar called Robin Redcap, and induced him to share the knowledge of how to bind elementals. Soulis has pledged to share that knowledge with me, in exchange for release from limbo and freedom to walk the earth again in human form. Shall it be your form or young Iolo McFarlane's? I wonder . . ."

The sheer audacity of Raeburn's intentions bespoke an ambition that had outpaced the limits of reason, and the stark reality of Adam's own peril at last overwhelmed the fragile act of will that had kept him from sinking back down into oblivion again.

He almost managed to surface again, some unknown time later, dragged sluggishly back to the very threshold by vague queasiness and a dull, pulsing drone that buzzed to his very bones and somehow reminded him of flight. The drugs binding him to his body prevented him from dreaming, but just before the darkness pressed in on him again, a part of him disjointedly imagined that he was being carried aloft in the belly of some great saurian bird. . . .

And at Strathmourne, as the midnight hour came and went, McLeod and Julian watched as the locket fastened to the end of Adam's *skean dubh* stirred slightly in McLeod's hands.

"What's that?" Julian whispered as McLeod stiffened, bleary eyes fixed on the trembling locket.

"I don't know," he murmured. "I'm not getting any direction. It's just—vibrating."

"It isn't just you, trembling from fatigue?" Julian ventured.

"No, it's bloody well not me!" he snapped—then exhaled with a whoosh and shook his head, bending it to concentrate once more.

"Sorry, Lady J. I *am* tired, but I'm not doing this. Maybe they're moving him, as Philippa suggested. *God*, why can't we get through?" As he slammed his free hand flat against the table in frustration, Julian set a hand on his shoulder and held out the other.

"Let me take over on this, and go call the others," she said. "We'll see if we can boost the signal, as it were. I don't think this is critical yet. I can't see them making their move nearly a full twenty-four hours before optimum time."

Nodding, McLeod surrendered the *skean dubh* and locket to Julian as he pushed back his chair and stood. "Moving him in the dark. Aye, that would be in character," he muttered. "I'll get the others."

They were assembled within five minutes—Philippa and Peregrine, Christopher and Victoria, with Ximena, Harry, and Julia breathlessly looking on, lending their prayers to the venture. Though they cast their combined energies into the effort for the next several hours, and some of the participants reported a general southerly inclination, none of them could induce the pendulum to take up a more definite direction. When the effect finally ended, around two in the morning, no one had any doubt that they had made a near contact with Adam; but that was all it had been.

"I think my fear for Adam is changing into anger with Raeburn," Philippa said, when Christopher and Victoria had withdrawn to resume their previous monitoring and the others were sipping dispiritedly at mugs of hot chocolate. "As a psychiatrist, I've spent most of the afternoon and evening trying to get inside his head.

"Why is he doing this? It isn't only a lust for illicit power that drives him; vengeance has to be one of his motivations. And if Adam is going to be the object of that vengeance, Raeburn will want him well aware of what's going to happen to him and who's responsible. That dish is best served up sufficiently in advance that the victim has time to fully savor the anticipation and dread.

"That means that if they're keeping him heavily sedated—which they must be doing, or he'd have broken through by now with a call for help—they're going to have to bring him around at some point, at least enough to appreciate the helplessness of his situation, and with enough lead time to make him sweat. That could give us the window of opportunity we'll need to find him and get to him before it's too late."

"But he could be anywhere!" Ximena blurted. "Even if you can figure out where he is, how can we *ever* get to him in time?"

"Harry and I have been working on that aspect," Philippa said grimly. "If there's even an hour's lead time, we have a chance; *he* has a chance. All we need is that one, vital break. Pray God that we'll get it!"

# CHAPTER THIRTY-THREE

EARLY morning of Imbolc Eve found McLeod and Harry sheltering in the lee of Strathmourne's entry porch, McLeod with a cellular phone in one gloved hand, Harry scanning the grey skies to the south through compact Pentax binoculars. The rest of the house still slept, in varying stages of exhaustion, though pairs of Huntsmen continued to keep watch by turns in the parlor, hoping to renew the all too brief contact of the night before. Rousted from his first real sleep in the last twenty-four hours by the general's telephone call, McLeod felt like someone had poured sand in both his eyes.

"Bloody hell," Harry muttered under his breath, as a mottled grey shape with military markings materialized out of light snowfall, slightly preceded by the chuff of rotor blades. "I hope this isn't an omen."

"You hope *what* isn't an omen?" McLeod retorted, as Harry lowered his binoculars and the chopper ghosted to a gentle landing on the front lawn in a flurry of snow.

"I was expecting a Wessex," Harry replied. "That's a goddamn Lynx."

McLeod's stomach did a queasy turn, but he forced himself to move past the unfortunate name to more immediate considerations.

"I don't care if it's called a goddamned bloody Raeburn. Can you fly it? Will it do the job?"

"Hell, yes," Harry drawled, stuffing the binoculars into a pocket of his flying jacket. "Not as big a payload as a Wessex, but a damned sight faster. I'll go see who they've sent for the team. Stand by."

Harry set out across the snowy lawn as the pilot cut power, hunched against the wind of the slowing blades as the side door slid back to disgorge a lanky figure clothed in the distinctive black combat smock, paratroop boots, and body armor favored by the SAS. Close on his heels came a tall, grey-haired man neither of them had expected to see here in person, with the shoulder slides of a brigadier on the epaulets of his olive-drab pullover. As McLeod saw who it was, he headed down the steps to meet the new arrival, who nodded grimly to Harry as they passed, then jogged on toward McLeod, keeping his head down and one hand on his tan beret.

"Good morning, Gordon. Thanks for coming," McLeod said.

"Morning, Noel," said General Sir Gordon Scott-Brown, as he and McLeod exchanged handshakes. "Sorry about the Lynx, but that's what they sent up from Hereford this morning. What's the update on Adam?"

Shaking his head, McLeod set a hand under the general's elbow and urged him back toward the house. Behind him, Harry and the SAS officer had disappeared back into the helicopter.

"Not good, I'm afraid. I hope to God I haven't brought you out on a wild goose chase. Come on into the house and we'll bring you up to speed. Adam's man has laid on breakfast for the troops, so Harry's going to bring them in in shifts. We can brief them once you know the lay of the land."

"Fair enough. Incidentally, Ian Duart is your mission commander. You'll remember him from the Cairngorm operation. And a couple of the lads in the hostage rescue team were along on that one as well."

"Then they aren't likely to be flapped by what may crop up this time," McLeod said, opening the front door and standing aside to let the general enter first. "*If* we get a chance to turn them loose on the opposition, that is. How many are we talking about?"

"Duart, two pilots, and a four-man hostage rescue team. I know that doesn't sound like many, but if it can be done, they'll do it; if it can't, it wouldn't matter if I'd brought three times that number."

By mid-morning, with Duart added to the briefing, assorted members of the Hunting Lodge once again assembled in the library at Strathmourne. McLeod, Harry, and the two newcomers had been joined by Philippa, Julian, Victoria, and a taut and anxious Ximena. Closer by the fire, Peregrine was doodling in the margins of the list he and Julia had compiled of ancient sites in the southern half of Scotland. Julia herself was ensconced in the library bay window with Iolo's dream journal, still brooding over the text and the cryptic lettering. Christopher alone was absent, patrolling on the astral from the nearby parlor.

"I understand the limitations, Lady Sinclair," Duart was saying to Philippa, "but telling me you think he's in the southern half of the country isn't much help." He indicated the map spread on the twin card tables in the center of the room. "Until and unless your people can pick up something more specific, I don't see how we're going to be able to do anything. I've got a crack unit on standby out there, and we can be anywhere between here and the border in close to thirty minutes—but if tonight is as critical as you think, we've got to have some lead time. *He's* got to have the lead time."

Philippa drew a deep breath, schooling herself to forbearance, and let it out slowly. "I'm aware of that, Major," she said softly, not looking at him. "You'll just have to bear with us. Believe me, we're doing all we can."

When Adam next struggled out of the abyss, his body seemed no more responsive than it had been, but he thought his thinking might be slightly less muddled than at any time since his capture. Bright light shone against his closed eyelids, but before he risked opening his eyes, he tried to take stock of his condition.

He was still laid out flat on his back, but something warm and vaguely comforting draped his naked body from the chin down, something of a more domestic nature than the silvery mylar blanket that had covered him earlier. Under the concealment of whatever it was, he tried flexing a wrist, then an ankle—and felt restraints at both—but the slight escalation of physical restraint hardly mattered, since he clearly was still in no condition to make any physical bid for freedom.

Temporarily setting that option aside, Adam turned his attention to visual input. A furtive peek from under closed eyelids revealed that the IV line still snaked from above his head to some point beneath what he now could see was a patchwork quilt, but he seemed to have been divested of any remaining medical paraphernalia save an oxygen cannula held in place at his nostrils by an elastic band. The variety of electronic beeps that previously had punctuated his twilight sleep had been silenced; nor could he readily spot any electronic leads emerging from under his quilt. Furthermore, though his throat was parched and scratchy, the endotracheal tube had been removed.

Marginally reassured, he turned his attention beyond his immediate vicinity, hoping to maintain the fiction that he was not yet conscious. The air outside his covering was colder than he remembered. The change in temperature, coupled with a warring variety of new smells, suggested that he might have been moved from his bare holding cell to another location.

This realization caused his pulse to quicken slightly, for no matter how competent his captors might be at cloaking his psychic signature from would-be rescuers, such cloaking was difficult to maintain while on the move—which meant there was a chance that the Hunting Lodge might have been able to get a bearing on him, at least for a while. Unfortunately, the move—and the reason he was being allowed to regain consciousness—also meant that Imbolc Eve probably was fast approaching.

Even as his still fuddled mind shrank from that near-certainty, a door off to his right swung open with a stiff creak. Hard-soled footsteps approached his bedside, bringing with them a residual whiff of expensive perfume. As the footsteps halted, a female voice said acidly, ''I know you're awake by now, so you might as well stop pretending.''

Adam had heard that voice before. He opened his eyes. The light above him was momentarily dazzling, but after a blink or two, he managed to bring the woman's face into hazy focus.

Her appearance was hauntingly familiar—dark hair

smartly coifed above clear olive skin and features that might have been attractive, had they not been hardened by a predatory coldness of expression. Despite the artful application of makeup, dark circles stained the hollows of her eyes, suggesting that his captors might have shared some of the stress they had inflicted upon him.

But it was the blood-red color of her pullover that helped him make the sinking connection as to who she was. Two years before, when she had given him a lift to the hospital following a car crash near the Forth Road Bridge, she had called herself "the Christmas Samaritan." He had never learned her true name, but later events made it abundantly clear that the "accident" and its aftermath, including her convenient and timely assistance, had all been orchestrated by Raeburn.

He was too debilitated to mask the shock of recognition. She saw it, and gave him a feline smile.

"Why, Dr. Sinclair, how flattering. I see you still remember me. I don't believe I introduced myself properly before. My name is Angela. Unfortunately for you, I am not the kind of angel apt to offer you any hope whatsoever."

Still smiling, she turned away to open a large leather satchel on an adjacent bed. Now that his eyes had adjusted to the light, Adam could see they were alone in what appeared to be the bedroom of a holiday cottage. Thin curtains had been drawn across the windows, but he had the impression that it was dark outside—which meant that the Eve of Imbolc must be already upon them.

Rummaging sounds recalled his attention to Angela and the satchel, as she unpacked an assortment of items that included a cutthroat razor, a shaving mug, and a shaving brush with an ivory handle. The sight of the razor reminded Adam absurdly that he had neither bathed nor shaved for at least three days.

Still thinking somewhat sluggishly, he watched her take the mug and brush to the sink, humming tunelessly as she turned on the hot water tap. Just audible above the sound of running water, the hollow clink of ivory against china held him in dumb fascination as she began lathering up the brush.

"You really could do with a shower," she remarked over

her shoulder, smiling coldly at him in the mirror as he started at the sound of her voice, "but I doubt you could manage to stand up to take one. That means it's going to be up to me to make you presentable."

Desperate to clear his head, Adam decided to test his voice. "For what?"

Angela paused to cock her head at him in the mirror.

"Why, didn't Francis tell you?" She turned off the water and slung a towel over her shoulder before sauntering back to the other bed to pick up the razor. "You have a starring role in tonight's little drama. I'm afraid we do have a very demanding Patron, but I'm sure you'll be a great success. Unfortunately for you, the production is for one night only."

He closed his eyes and turned his head away, grateful that he could manage even that, his dry throat trying to swallow down his dread. The clatter of her implements being set on the bedside table recalled him from his drifting even as she took hold of his covering and whipped it from his body. Caught off guard, he was unable to keep from flinching at the abrupt exposure.

"You *are* a fine figure of a man, aren't you?" she murmured as she eyed him up and down. "It really is a pity you haven't had time to father a child on that pretty sloe-eyed bride of yours—or have you, you sly devil? Is *that* the reason for the rather rushed incipient nuptials?"

Laughing at his tight-jawed silence, she seated herself on the bed beside him and removed his oxygen, then set to work shaving him, taking perverse pleasure in each keen stroke of the blade against his helpless throat.

"I could do it now," she whispered, her lips close beside his ear, the corner of the blade poised against the jugular.

"But you won't," he managed to reply with some conviction. "You dare not cheat your Patron. Not if you hope to survive."

She drew back, her eyes going colder, if that were possible, and the smile faded. She finished shaving him without further comment, her gaze unreadable, then proceeded to wet a fresh towel and rub him down with brisk and impersonal efficiency, loosing his restraints only long enough to turn him when necessary, sparing no part of him. The water in the sink was icy cold by the time she finished, and he found himself shivering despite his determination not to give her that satisfaction, though the cold rubdown did seem to clear his head a little—or perhaps it was the drugs continuing to wear off.

She had just tossed her towel in the sink when the door opened again to admit Mallory, carrying a tray piled with assorted items of an obvious medical nature, pre-packaged in plastic. Adam turned his face away, determined not to give the other physician the satisfaction of a reaction.

"He isn't giving you any trouble, is he?" Mallory asked, chuckling as Angela twitched the quilt back to her victim's waist and turned her back.

"Other than talking too much, no."

"I see."

Still smiling as he set his tray on the other bed, Mallory reached across to thumb shut the clamp on Adam's IV line, then popped open the packaging on a 100 cc syringe and plugged it into a sterile needle.

"You did ask to have him conscious while you prepared him," he said, fumbling at the cannula in Adam's wrist. "That suits me as well. Francis may not think it matters, but I don't like using blood that's tainted with too many drugs— and he's had quite a cocktail. This still won't be clean—but it's better than it will be after I've taken him down again. Will this be enough for you?"

"It ought to be. What about Francis?"

"I'll take care of his order next," Mallory replied.

Adam tried not to react as the young doctor withdrew the syringe, now filled with his blood, and handed it across the bed to Angela. It was harder to ignore the rustle of plastic packaging as Mallory unreeled the line from a plastic blood-collection bag and plugged it into the port from which he had drawn the first measure of blood—a far more serious bloodletting, unfortunately quite in keeping with what Adam imagined of the impending night's work.

"So, how're you doing, Dr. Sinclair?" Mallory asked, turning Adam's face toward him to shine a pocket torch in his eyes. "Hmmm, still pretty dopey, eh?"

He grinned as Adam turned his face away again, turning

off the flash and slipping it into the breast pocket of his stylish suit.

"I'll be back to check him in about ten minutes," he said to Angela, before leaving the room.

Angela, meanwhile, had produced another towel, a sable artist's brush, and a small glass bowl from the leather satchel, setting the bowl on the sink while she removed the needle from the syringe and expelled the contents into the bowl. She was smiling a cold, hard smile as she came around to Adam's right again, the brush in one hand and the bowl of his blood in the other. She paused to pull the quilt lower on his loins before sitting again on the bed beside him.

"I *am* going to enjoy this," she said. The blood-red carnelian in her Lynx ring matched the blood she stirred with the brush. "I wonder whether you'll be able to guess what symbols I paint on your chest, to make you a fitting offering. . . ."

He turned his head away from her in denial, only to find his face mere inches from the slowly expanding bag of his blood, fed from the scarlet line snaking to the cannula in his wrist. Dismayed, he realized that watching either procedure was likely to unnerve him; but he dared not close his eyes, lest her suggestion conjure the very symbols he knew could weaken what few defenses he might yet possess.

Any semblance of choice quickly became academic, for the clink of the brush being stirred in the bowl was followed by the faint, cold tracery of the sable brush against his skin. He stiffened, determined to resist; but unbridled by the drugs in his system, his imagination began to supply ghastly form to the patterns she began tracing out across each breast, down the midline of his chest and past his navel, up the sides of his throat, the brush strokes making his skin crawl with instinctive revulsion. Though a part of him vaguely recognized that his reaction was precisely what she intended, he could not suppress a growing mental image of hideous carrion insects crawling up and down the length of his body, seeking places to nest and feed.

Nausea rose up in his throat, and a profound shudder of revulsion racked him from head to foot, damped by the restraints at wrists and ankles. His empty stomach threatened to rebel, and he had to swallow hard to keep from retching. Angela laughed to see his shrinking abhorrence.

"I guess it must be true," she observed, "that the righteous can't abide the mark of the Beast any more than the Beast can abide the trappings of holiness. So much the worse for you—and so much the better for our purposes."

He fought down another shudder and looked away again, for he knew full well how open his weakened state had left him. Absurdly he flashed on the image of the patterns tattooed on Taliere's dead body—symbols to brand the dead Druid as the property of the deities he had served. And Angela was branding him with symbols no less potent for being merely painted, preparing him as an offering to unspeakable corruption and depravity.

He tried hard to put that thought from his mind, closing his eyes against the sight of what she was doing, lamely trying to turn his thoughts to an ancient plea for deliverance: *O God, come to my assistance; O Lord, make haste to help me. . . .* A fifth-century interpreter of the Psalms had recommended the phrases as an impregnable wall for all those struggling against the onslaught of demons, an impenetrable breastplate and the sturdiest of shields. . . .

At some point Mallory returned to seal off the first bag of blood and switch to a second, giving Angela's work an appreciative nod before going out again. By the time the second bag was nearly full, Adam found himself drifting in and out of consciousness again, weaker every time he surfaced—whether from blood loss or the drugs or the effect of Angela's rune-binding, he could not tell. A recurrent if scant source of comfort, if only temporary, was the certainty that Mallory would not bleed him dry, no more than Angela had been prepared to cut his throat prematurely: they needed him for their ritual. And perhaps help still would come—though he held out little real hope.

Perhaps twenty minutes passed while Angela completed her design. As she worked, herself becoming caught up in the spell she wove, she began occasionally to pass a hand more intimately along his body, adding to his dismay. Each instance was like an electric shock, startling him back to full attention, unable to ignore the assaults—though at least they broke his concentration on the symbols and lessened their potency, little though she realized that.

When she had finally finished and set her implements aside, she trailed a teasing hand down his belly to rest on his manhood, catching his gaze with hers when his eyes popped open in startlement, smiling as she slowly bent her lips toward his—and drew back at the sound of the door opening again. Her laughter grated like broken glass as she straightened, the offending hand drawing the quilt back to his waist as she stood.

"You've come in the nick of time, Derek," she said, as Mallory entered and came to close off the second unit of blood. "I do believe I nearly had our very attractive captive convinced that I was going to ravish him on the spot."

"What, and deprive our Patron of his sport?" Mallory retorted, with a heavy-lidded leer. "But you mustn't tease, Angela dear. We wouldn't want to spoil the offering."

Still smirking, he took a blood pressure cuff from the bedside table and applied it to Adam's right arm, sobering as he took his reading and then felt for a pulse, first in Adam's wrist, then in neck and groin.

No longer smiling, Angela watched as Mallory removed the cuff and stuffed it into his pocket, then unplugged Adam's old IV and capped off the cannula in his wrist.

"Two units—that's a lot to lose, in his condition," Angela said, as Mallory picked up the two bags of blood. "Is he going to be all right for the ceremony?"

"Oh, he'll last," Mallory assured her. "I don't dare sedate him any further, but we'll give him a unit of dextran en route. That ought to improve his blood pressure a bit. Keep an eye on him. I'll be back in a minute."

When he had gone, Angela settled on the side of the bed again beside her victim, smiling again as she brushed her fingers lightly along one shaven cheek.

"Mmmm, soft as a baby's—" She broke off and laughed wickedly, showing her teeth. "Dear Adam Sinclair, I'm going to let you in on a little secret before Derek comes back to work his wicked ways on you again. I thought you might like to know what Francis has planned for you. I hope you'll appreciate the delicious irony." She gave another tinkling laugh before deigning to enlighten him further.

"In consideration of the number of times you've interfered with us in the past, we put a great deal of thought into deciding how best to incorporate your participation into our little performance tonight. You *will* die—I don't think you ever doubted that—but the actual moment of your death will be framed within the context of a Satanic Mass—with suitable adjustments, of course, since the ritual ordinarily calls for a young virgin of the female persuasion. It seemed a fitting end for a Christian Adept—to see all your holy symbols profaned, and to know that your Patron is powerless to save you.

"Of course there are—other details that needn't concern you yet," she went on, smiling again. "Let's just say that a prize like you should suffice to buy Francis exactly what he wants: Satan's own authority to command all lesser demons, including Taranis. I just thought you'd like to know," she concluded, as Mallory returned with one of Richter's mercenaries.

Already drifting perilously close to shock, Adam was also reeling with numb rejection of this revelation as Mallory and his assistant set about finishing his preparation. After releasing his restraints, the two men hauled him up into a sitting position so that Angela could pull a white robe over his head, the three of them then working his arms through the sleeves and tugging its folds into something approaching alignment.

"All right, he's ready," Mallory said. "Let's get him out of here."

Adam would have struggled if he were able, but even holding his head up was too much effort. Praying that intent would count on some level, he continued trying to visualize spiritual resistance, unable to prevent them dragging him to his feet, the two men shouldering his sagging weight between them. Angela gathered up the quilt and followed as they hustled him out the open door and along a dimly lit corridor, toward another open door and his impending fate.

# CHAPTER THIRTY-FOUR

**B**ACK at Strathmourne, the grey afternoon had merged indistinguishably into a greyer dusk by five o'clock, and full darkness by six. Earlier, Duart had brought his men into the kitchen by shifts, for a hot meal, and Philippa had insisted that members of the Hunting Lodge sleep by turns, in hopes of conserving precious energies for a last-minute breakthrough regarding Adam's whereabouts; but as seven o'clock came and went, and the standby crew fretted, an even deeper depression had begun to settle on the occupants of the house.

They had by no means given up their search, but they had yet to find a focus. In the library, Philippa had resumed attempting to scry in the crystal ball with Adam's *skean dubh* and Julian's locket, assisted by Julian and both Houstons. Harry had taken up a post to watch them, straddling a straight-backed chair and with chin resting on his folded forearms laid across the back, his distracted gaze ranging idly over the map of Scotland spread on the table beneath Philippa's crystal. McLeod was stretched out on the couch, arms folded on his chest, eyes closed behind his aviator spectacles. The general was pacing back and forth before the library window.

Ximena had retreated to a place in the window seat with Julia, gazing out dejectedly at the lights in the waiting helicopter, idly watching Donald Cochrane talk to two of the SAS men sheltering in the lee of the craft for a smoke. Having argued persuasively earlier in the day that Adam might well need emergency medical attention if they found him alive, she had gained grudging permission to go along on the rescue mission if it ever got off the ground—and had packed her medical bag with essentials that the SAS medics might not have to hand, since it was far more likely that she would have to deal with reversing the effects of heavy sedation than with battlefield-type injuries. She had also dressed in rugged outdoor wear of heavy trousers and boots and multiple layers of sweaters, similar to the way McLeod, Peregrine, and Harry were attired; but it appeared less and less likely that she or any of them would be given the chance to utilize any of their preparations.

"Peregrine," Harry said softly, lifting his head to glance over to where the artist was hunched over a sketch pad. "What ever happened to those drawings you did, that night you called me out to touch the Hand of Glory?"

Peregrine had been doodling in light trance, hoping he might pick up some impression too faint for conscious perception, that might somehow transmit itself through his drawing hand. As he surfaced at the sound of his name, looking blank, McLeod also roused, and Philippa gave a little gasp, turning to stare at Harry.

"The Hand of Glory," she murmured. "Dear God, how could we have been so blind?"

"The Hand of Glory?" Peregrine asked, still muzzy.

"That's an angle we haven't even considered," Philippa went on, as McLeod slowly sat up, comprehension lighting his blue eyes as he came fully awake. "They've got Adam hidden . . . and they'll be expecting us to focus all our energy on finding him—which is exactly what we've been doing."

"Pippa, what are you saying?" Julian asked, leaning across to touch her friend's hand.

"We have a very potent link to Raeburn himself," Philippa continued, hardly hearing her. "We know he participated in the preparation of the Hand of Glory. So if we find Raeburn, we find Adam—because whatever Raeburn has planned for Adam, he wouldn't miss it for the world! Back in a minute!"

"But—where is she going?" Peregrine asked, still at sea as Philippa dashed out the library door.

"To fetch the Hand, I should think," Julian replied, motioning for Christopher and Victoria to clear the crystal and *skean dubh* off the map, as the rest of them surged closer.

"Wait a minute," Ximena protested. "Are you telling us that she's had the Hand locked away all this time?"

"Well, of course," Julian replied. "One doesn't leave that sort of thing just lying around. Don't worry; I'm sure she had it in the safe."

"But—Julian, this is crazy," Peregrine said with a shake of his head. "What makes you think Raeburn won't be cloaked the same way Adam is?"

"He probably was, in the beginning," McLeod retorted, "but I doubt he is now. He'll be saving his energies for tonight. Besides that, he's too damned arrogant to expect we'd be looking for him instead of Adam—and he may have forgotten about the Hand; we did.

"Now, how to set this up?" he wondered aloud, pushing his spectacles onto his forehead and rubbing at his temples as he considered, scanning around the room. "Maps first, of course—and we've got those. Victoria, stand by with that stack of larger-scale ones; we'll want to scale up, once we've got a general fix on the master map. And we'll need a focus for separating Raeburn's trace from the others who helped prepare the Hand. Peregrine, fetch the sketch you did of Raeburn that night."

Peregrine was already shuffling through a stack of sketches, and flung the one of Raeburn onto the table.

"We'll also need to insert a dowsing factor into this working," McLeod went on, still thinking out loud. "A pendulum is out, because the Hand itself is too big—and I don't know about using just a piece of it—"

"Ximena," Philippa said, coming back into the room with the biscuit tin under one arm, "get me one of those fat crystal tumblers from the liquor cabinet, and let's clear everything off the big map."

"Already done," Christopher said, pulling out a chair for Philippa. The teamwork of the Hunting Lodge on the scent was astonishing, and Harry was dumbfounded at the speed at which things had suddenly taken off.

"I gather it was something I said," he murmured, as Philippa plonked the biscuit tin down on the table and took her seat, motioning all of them to gather closer. "What on earth are you going to do with that?"

McLeod shook his head and yanked out two more chairs.

"No time for explanations now, Harry. Sit down," he ordered, hauling the counsellor to the chair beside him as he sat next to Philippa and the others gathered around.

As Ximena set the requested tumbler on the table beside Philippa, Julia also drifted closer, Iolo McFarlane's dream journal tucked under one arm and a look of astonishment on her face. The general, too, came to stand behind Julian.

"All right, I'll say this only once," Philippa announced turning the glass upside down over their present location and then prying at the lid of the biscuit tin. "The sketch is our focus, and the Hand of Glory is our link to Raeburn. He helped prepare it, so his psychic signature is all over it.

"The way this works will be something like a Ouija board, except that the glass will be our planchette and we'll use the map instead of a board with letters of the alphabet. To add the Hand to the equation—and I haven't time for anyone's squeamishness right now—we'll set it on the glass and then make our link through *that* instead of the glass itself."

Despite her admonition, a collective gasp whispered among the group as she pulled the lid off the biscuit tin, to a whiff of decomposing flesh and sulphur.

"With any luck," she went on, "the glass will move on the map and zero in on Raeburn's location—which will also be Adam's location."

The silence was almost palpable as she turned back the towelling and, without hesitation, plucked the Hand out to set it with the palm on the base of the glass, the dead fingers extending all around. Though mostly mummified, it was covered with blue-green mold, and the smell was appalling.

"All right, there isn't space enough for all of us to do this," she said, holding the Hand in place with the fingertips of both hands, "so I want the following to touch it the way I'm doing: Julian, Peregrine, Noel, and Harry. Yes, you, Harry. Impressions through touch are your special gift, and I think it's definitely needed here."

Julian had complied immediately, Peregrine hardly a heartbeat after, but Harry had stiffened at the mention of his

408 ✦ *Katherine Kurtz and Deborah Turner Harris*

name, his face draining of color. McLeod glanced sideways at him, afraid that the counsellor was going to hold back— but Harry only drew a deep breath and let it out—and set his fingertips lightly beside McLeod's, drawing another breath more slowly as his eyes took on the faraway focus of trance.

"Good man, Harry," McLeod whispered under his breath.

Watching, Philippa nodded and glanced up at Sir Gordon and the Houstons.

"Gordon, I'll ask you to help Victoria and Christopher keep us on the maps," she said quietly. "The rest of you, please add your prayers to our intent." She returned her gaze to the five pairs of hands now touching fingertips to the Hand atop the tumbler, four of them with Adept rings glimmering like sapphire stars.

"Now, let's focus on the sketch of Raeburn and get started," she said. "We're looking to tune in on Raeburn's psychic residuals and use those to divine his location. Fix his image in your minds, concentrate . . . and now reach out to find him. . . ."

Nothing happened for several long minutes as the five began to concentrate, only the soft sounds of breathing intruding on the silence. But then the glass jerked sluggishly beneath its burden of hands, both alive and dead. Ximena stifled a gasp as, after a few false starts, it began inching slowly south and westward, on a straight-line heading between Edinburgh and Glasgow.

As soon as it had crossed the Firth of Forth, Victoria began flinging aside the larger-scale maps of everything northward, Christopher roughly following the progress of the glass on the section diagrams that showed each map's position on the master grid.

"You're about on Map 65," Christopher announced, as the glass crept to a halt. "Sort of midway between Edinburgh and Glasgow. Do you want to change scales? This area is awfully built up—not at all promising for the kind of site we projected."

Though she nodded faintly, Philippa did not look up, only shifting one hand to lift the glass against the Hand of Glory, holding it steady against the touch of the other four sets of fingertips as Victoria swept the large map away, Sir Gordon retaining the sketch of Raeburn so that Christopher could slip one of the larger-scale maps into its place. As he guided the glass to the spot approximately corresponding to the location indicated on the first map, and Philippa lowered the glass, it did not move for several seconds; but then it began inching very slowly southward again, gradually taking a more easterly heading.

"Something has changed," Sir Gordon murmured, after watching the glass take several minutes to creep across a six-inch span of map. "The scale is larger, but it's moving slower. I don't think you're zeroing in on a location any-more; I think your target is actually in motion—and moving fast." He grabbed a pen and paper from Julia and did some rapid calculations with inches and scales, then bent to lay a hand on Harry's shoulder.

"Harry, it's Gordon. Pull back and see if they can keep this up without you," he said.

Nodding, Harry drew a deep breath and withdrew his hands, but the glass kept inching inexorably onward.

"Harry, these are the rough figures I've used to try to figure out his speed," Sir Gordon murmured, thrusting the piece of paper in front of the counsellor. "Can this be right?"

Harry eyed the figures, glanced at the map, then gave a slow nod.

"Better'n a hundred miles per hour, if those are the right numbers," he said, "and I think they are." He drew a steadying breath. "Noel, he's flying. Light plane or maybe a hel-icopter. And if we want to catch up with him, we'd better move!"

"Go scramble the flight crew," Philippa whispered, not looking up. "Take Ximena with you. I'll send Noel and Per-egrine in a minute. We'll hold this end. I think we've got a lock on him now. Noel, pull out slowly, and Victoria, take his place."

"Switching to Map 72 before you do that," Christopher interrupted, unfolding another map with a rustle as Harry grabbed Ximena's hand and the two of them dashed from the room. "You're about to go off the edge of 65."

410 ♣ *Katherine Kurtz and Deborah Turner Harris*

Again work was suspended while maps were shifted, after which McLeod and Victoria made their switch. The glass now was moving through the region of Biggar.

"All right, Noel, go get Humphrey to come and help Gordon with map shuffling and the like," Philippa murmured, still mostly focused on the glass and the hand, "and then take Peregrine and go."

As thudding footbeats told of his compliance, Christopher smoothly changed places with Peregrine, so that when McLeod reappeared with Humphrey, the artist had already pulled on his coat and was stuffing reference books into his art satchel.

"Godspeed, Noel," Philippa whispered, as Julia began a whispered explanation to Humphrey of what was going on. "We'll ring you on one of the cell phones as soon as we've got a destination fixed. Now go! And pray God you get there in time!"

# CHAPTER THIRTY-FIVE

**H**ERMITAGE Castle brooded on its foundations like a massive gargoyle, but the castle itself was not Raeburn's destination tonight; rather, the ruined remains of a small stone chapel, several hundred yards to the west. He had considered using the nearby Nine Stane Rig, where Soulis had met defeat so many years before at the hands of his enemies—and in reversing the results of that defeat, Raeburn intended to see his own latter-day disappointments avenged and undone—but the Black Mass he had chosen as a fitting framework for his revenge on Adam Sinclair required a site consecrated according to Christian rites. The chapel ruins were somewhat more in the open than Raeburn regarded as optimal, with most of the foundations standing no more than waist-high, but on the first night of February there was even less chance of interruption than there had been on New Year's Eve.

It had been dark for more than four hours when a white Land Rover rumbled across the bridge and whispered to a halt next to a second one parked a short distance from the start of the chapel ruins, screened from the road by a stand of winter-bare trees and almost invisible against the snow. Ahead, heavy snowfall had softened the ragged outlines of the stones and lent a deceptive tranquillity to the icy gloom of the winter's night.

As Klaus Richter materialized out of the darkness beside the driver's door, clad in snow-camouflage and with the mouthpiece of a radio headset protruding from under his balaclava helmet, the driver rolled down his window.

"All secure," Richter murmured, gloved hand resting on a compact semiautomatic weapon slung around his neck as he leaned down to glance at the three passengers in the back seat. "You can bring him on out and unload the rest of the equipment."

No lights showed as the vehicle's front doors swung wide and two of Richter's mercenaries bailed out, white-clad like himself, a back door opening more slowly for Derek Mallory to emerge, wearing a cowled black robe and a bronze medallion stamped with the head of a lynx. When he had pulled out his medical bag, he stood aside to let the men haul Adam from the car. Simultaneously, Angela alighted from the other side, the two bags of Adam's blood tucked under one arm, garbed incongruously in the black habit of a nun.

Adam gasped as his bare feet touched the snow, wincing as one of his handlers grabbed his left wrist where Mallory had pulled out the IV just prior to their arrival. With his drugs discontinued and most of a unit of dextran in him by then, Adam had rallied somewhat in the preceding hour; but he still was dangerously weak, and had to fight back a swooping episode of lightheadedness as Richter and Mallory half-walked and half-carried him between them toward the chapel ruins, dragging his bare feet along the snow-covered ground. The night was still, but the cold penetrated Adam's single layer of wool almost as if he wore nothing at all. Behind him, muffled thumps and grunts told of equipment being unloaded from the Rovers' rear compartments.

The chapel's interior was open to the sky, its ruined walls conveying the impression more of a paddock than a building. Snow lay heavy within, piled in drifts against the side walls downwind, but the area around the shattered altar in the eastern end had been shovelled clear, and a series of white-painted plywood sheets had been erected along the chapel's northern side, to further screen the inside from the road.

Adam was reeling by the time his handlers dragged him over to a clean-shovelled spot to the right of the altar, where one of Richter's white-clad underlings was shaking out a thick white blanket beside a pair of folding chairs. The blanket was a welcome weight around his shoulders as he was wrapped in it and lowered to sit on one of the chairs, Mallory remaining with one hand set solicitously on his shoulder. It was all that kept Adam upright. He drifted for a little while, huddled and shivering, until awareness of movement nearer the altar brought him back to remembrance of his peril.

They were preparing for the unholy work to come. The altar was largely ruined, but two of Raeburn's men had lifted several broken slabs back into place to form a roughly horizontal surface, and were draping the altar with a heavy cloth of black velvet. Another man brought two heavy wrought-iron candlesticks, as tall as a man.

From a capacious duffel bag came a battered wooden crucifix, a brass thurible and incense boat, and a massive chalice of tarnished bronze with matching paten. These Angela arranged on the altar, while a cohort shook out a set of Satanic vestments—black wool faced with scarlet silk, emblazoned front and back with a blood-red inverted cross.

These, too, were laid out in readiness, along with the bags of Adam's blood, an aspersing pot, and an aspergillum made from black goat's hair. The totality of this assemblage of paraphernalia left no doubt in Adam's fuddled mind that Raeburn intended to extract every iota of anticipation from his intended victim, who could not fail to recognize the trappings required for the promised Black Mass.

The soft, whistling chuffle of a helicopter descending beyond the ruins behind Adam heralded the arrival of Raeburn himself shortly thereafter, wearing a cowled black robe and the silver medallion which betokened his status as Lynx-Master. He gave Adam a steely-eyed nod as he entered the chapel accompanied by Barclay, also robed, and a tall, gaunt stranger with furtive, darting eyes—by his Roman collar and greasy black soutane, surely the requisite defrocked priest required for the night's undertakings.

Behind the priest came two more anonymous henchmen supporting another drugged and drooping figure between them, white-robed and barefooted like Adam, bowed head lolling forward on his chest. When Mallory had spread a second blanket on the chair beside Adam, the two deposited their charge and supported him while Mallory turned the newcomer's face upward to shine his pocket torch in the other's eyes.

Adam had a brief, dazed impression of glassy eyes, drooping moustaches, and thick braids falling to either side of the slack face. Memory supplied a name, previously attached only to photos: the missing Iolo McFarlane. As Adam himself came briefly under Mallory's scrutiny, he found himself almost envying the young Druid, for it occurred to him that before too much longer, he might well wish to be equally insensible of what was happening around him.

The prospect became more probable as Mallory's place was taken by Raeburn, who smiled coldly as he produced a lynx medallion, near-mate to the one he was wearing, and reached out with both hands to slip the chain over Adam's head. The medallion felt heavier than stone where it fell on Adam's chest, and seemed to reverse some of the recovery he had made in the past hour, dragging him into renewed lethargy, setting him drifting. . . .

Somewhere in the vicinity of Peebles, some twenty miles due south of Edinburgh, the ringing of McLeod's portable phone made itself barely heard above the mechanical roar of the chopper's powerful rotor-blades. Thumbing the On switch, McLeod jammed the instrument to his ear as Peregrine and Ximena leaned closer from adjacent seats. The red cabin illumination lent an infernal cast to their taut faces.

"McLeod."

"Noel, they think Raeburn may have gotten wherever he's going," Julia informed him excitedly through snaps and crackles of static. "Sir Gordon says you're to head straight for Galashiels, then drop due south toward Hawick. Hand me to Peregrine while you're relaying that, and I'll give him exact map coordinates."

"Right."

Handing off the phone, McLeod scuttled forward to pass the instructions to Harry and Duart. He could feel the chopper picking up speed and slipping slightly to the right as he returned to his seat, where Peregrine was opening a map under a penlight Ximena was holding above it. Cochrane now had the phone to his ear, keeping the line open for further instructions. Behind him, the four men of the hostage rescue team checked and rechecked their equipment.

"What have we got?" McLeod demanded, crowding closer.

Peregrine shook his head, consulting the numbers he had copied onto a notepad.

"Apparently he's on Map 79, somewhere on a line due south from Hawick," he said, running a fingertip down the map and then pulling off his spectacles so he could focus closer in the dim light. "She said to allow about five miles to either side, but if we're looking for something on the scale of Callanish, I don't see much that qualifies. A couple of cairns . . . some earthworks . . . here's a wee stone circle out by someplace called Dodd, and something called the Tinlee Stone . . . the Catrail Earthwork—that's old . . . a stone circle at someplace called the Nine Stane Rig—probably with nine stones . . . and something called the Buck Stone, near Hermitage Castle . . . and—"

"Hold it!" McLeod broke in. "Did you just say Hermitage Castle?"

"Yes."

"Bloody hell," McLeod muttered, leaning back to rummage in Peregrine's art satchel. "Where's that book on Scottish castles?"

"I've got it," Ximena said, plucking it out and opening it. "What am I looking for?"

"Hermitage Castle. And Peregrine—how far is that from here?"

"About—twelve miles south of Hawick," Peregrine said, holding the place on the map with his finger as he looked up at Ximena, who was frantically paging through the book. "Why? What's special about Hermitage?"

"I've found it," Ximena said, as McLeod pulled the map around for a closer look. "Hermitage Castle . . . built in the thirteenth century by Walter Comyn, Earl of Menteith . . . cause of an invasion by Henry the Third in 1243 . . . had passed to the de Soulis family by 1306, then to the Douglasses in 1320, then the Earls of Angus, who traded it for—"

"Run that by me again?" McLeod interrupted sharply. "Did you say Soulis?"

"*De* Soulis," Ximena amended. "It says here he was a—"

"—famous Scottish sorcerer," McLeod finished for her, digging in Peregrine's art satchel again to snatch out Iolo McFarlane's dream journal. "Now, where's that page with the code or anagram or whatever it was? Here!"

Opening to the page, he thrust it under Ximena's light.

"Just what I thought. Stupid, stupid, stupid! We've been mistaking an *i* for an apostrophe. It isn't *Soul's* Gstrig—it's *Soulis*—and the other word is *Gstrig*—whatever the hell that is. Peregrine, grab that book on Scottish folklore and look up Soulis. *Gstrig*," he repeated, brainstorming aloud, as Peregrine grabbed the designated volume and began paging through it. "Maybe *Gst Rig*. A rig is a ridge or narrow hill."

"Here it is," Peregrine said. "William Lord Soulis of Hermitage Castle, notorious for his wickedness, said to consort with evil spirits, boiled in lead at the stone circle at Nine Stane Rig, a mile or so from the castle."

"That's got it!" McLeod declared, bending closer to Iolo's page. "If this first *G* in *Gst Rig* is actually the number 9, that makes it 9 *St Rig*—Nine Stane Rig. And if Raeburn is headed there, to the place of Soulis' death—Dear God, he's going for some kind of pact with Soulis, some dark alliance, and Adam—"

He closed the journal with a snap, his face deadly taut in the red cabin light. "Harry!"

He grabbed Peregrine's folklore book and scrambled forward again. "Harry, I'm taking a big gamble, but it's the only one we've got—the only one *Adam's* got. How long to get us to the Nine Stane Rig? It's about ten or twelve miles due south of Hawick, near Hermitage Castle."

"We're just coming up on Galashiels," Harry said, walking callipers across his map as Duart and one of the SAS pilots looked on. "Say, five to ten minutes down to Hawick, and maybe another ten to where you want to go. We'll have to follow the road, from Hawick, or we'll never find it in the dark. You think that's where he is?"

"God, God, God," McLeod whispered, "I hope so. Just get us there as fast as you can, Harry. We may be almost out of time!"

✦ ✦ ✦

Only snatches of Raeburn's further preparations filtered through to Adam in the next little while: Raeburn passing widdershins around the inside perimeter of the ruined chapel with a darkly glittering dagger, defining the boundary of this most unsacred space, then tracing that same boundary with one of the bags of Adam's blood, leaving a scarlet line of life marking out the limits of death . . .

A black-robed acolyte taking up the thurible and setting it alight, charging it with a noisome mixture of sulphur and saltpetre whose fumes lay reeking along the path he trod close behind Raeburn . . .

The black priest donning black vestments as Angela lifted the skirts of her habit to squat down and urinate over the aspersing bowl, which the priest then used to pollute the altar and unbless the most unwilling victims set helplessly before it. . . .

There followed an obscene parody of an ecclesiastical procession up and down the chapel, led by the thurifer and fresh clouds of noxious smoke. Raeburn followed in his wake, brandishing aloft a staff of alder-wood from which a crucifix hung by the heels, in blasphemous mockery of all the holy symbol stood for.

Two of Raeburn's black-robed subordinates came next, each bearing one of the iron candlesticks, squat black candles now alight. Barclay, Mallory, and Angela followed, preceding the black priest, who sprinkled urine left and right and led a dissonant litany in some unknown tongue, whose rhythms sent chills up Adam's spine.

By the time the band had reassembled before the altar, the incense smoke had settled to a noxious and vaguely visible carpet of mist that lay uncannily across the entire expanse of the chapel floor. Adam stifled a gasp as tendrils of that smoke snaked softly upward to lick at his bare ankles, but he could not summon the will to shift his feet. It was hard enough merely to remain sitting upright, all too aware that to overbalance and fall off his chair would be to expose his entire body to whatever animated the smoke.

"*In nomine Magni Dei Nostri Satanas, introibo ad altare Domini Inferi,*" the black priest intoned, moving behind the altar, his words snapping Adam's attention back to even more immediate concerns as he began the sequence of the Black Mass.

"*Ad eum qui laetificat meum,*" came the response of Raeburn and his associates.

"*Adjutorium nostrum in nomine Domini Inferi.*"

"*Oui regit terram . . .*"

"*Confiteor coram Principe Tenebrarum, Domino Satanas . . .*"

The perverted introit gave way to a Satanic confession of faith, praising the depravities of Darkness and importuning the intercession of ancient Evil, the corrupted Latin phrases echoing within the invisible confines of the ruined chapel. Closing his eyes, Adam tried to close his ears as well, retreating to his mantra of psalmody; but discordant fragments of the black priest's words kept breaking in on his concentration like shards of broken glass piercing vulnerable flesh.

The growing pain of it stretched him to the brink of crying out, but he set his teeth in stubborn denial, knowing that any vocal expression from him would be tantamount to participation, praying for the strength not to be swept away by the encroaching darkness. The ending of the collects brought relief of a sort—but only until someone brushed roughly past him, jarring him back to urgent awareness and the discovery that the dark ritual was moving forward.

They had come to take Iolo McFarlane. Opening his eyes, Adam saw Mallory and one of Raeburn's acolytes jerk the young Druid to his feet and hustle him, unresisting, over to the front of the altar. Raeburn was there already, kneeling down with the second bag of Adam's blood to trace a large triangle on the ground. Already drawn were two sides of a second, even larger triangle, scaled to define perhaps a two-foot border between the two.

After finishing the inner triangle, tracing it a second time to be sure there were no gaps, Raeburn handed off the bag to Mallory, who was standing by with the glassy-eyed Iolo. As Raeburn rose, he pulled Iolo to him, so that they both were standing in the open side of the outer triangle, facing the smaller one inside. Then, from the bosom of his robe, Raeburn produced an ancient and evil-looking dagger.

Its design proclaimed it to be the product of Pictish work-manship. Its aspect proclaimed it an object of power. As Adam gazed at it, he found himself suddenly remembering the torc which Raeburn's superior, the Head-Master, had worn at the height of his power, and knew the blade to be of kindred crafting and potency.

Raeburn, for the moment, was unmindful of anything out-side his own intentions. With one arm braced around the shoulders of the oblivious Iolo and the other directing the focus of his will into the dagger in his hand, he embarked upon a new chant. In contrast to the voice of the black priest, Raeburn's was deep and sibilant, a voice of subtle entrap-ment that ended on a note of command as he thrust the point of the dagger toward the heart of the inner triangle.

A mote of darkness materialized as if out of nowhere, winking once and then expanding with explosive suddenness into a pillar of smoke the height of a man. Churning, the smoke resolved at length into a shadowy humanoid figure with eyes like twin flames—a likeness that made Adam catch his breath, for he had seen the infernal spirit of William de Soulis reflected thus in the vision Andrew Kerr had shown him.

Raeburn took a step closer, holding the dagger between himself and the dark presence he had summoned.

"Welcome, Lord Soulis," he declared. "All that we agreed upon has been prepared. I bring you your new host—one I think you will approve of."

He indicated the passive, vacantly staring form of Iolo swaying beside him. Soulis' ember eyes shifted.

*This?* The query reverberated beyond mere hearing. *You deem* this *worthy? This creature has no fire in its soul.*

"Not yet," Raeburn replied. "But the tinder is there, awaiting only your spark. And he has an illustrious ances-try—one which gives testimony to his potential. By direct descent, he is blood-kin to your own most bitter foe: Sir Andrew Kerr, of the Huntsmen of the Light, who imposed your sentence of banishment—the sentence *I* can rescind."

This disclosure of Iolo's identity caused Soulis to rear up, his gaze glittering more brightly than before.

*Of Kerr's bloodline, is he? Then he is, indeed, eminently*

*acceptable. But why shows he so little regard for his fate?*

"Your new host has been drugged to suppress his resistance," Raeburn explained. "I will have the appropriate antidote administered before you take up residence. And then you will give me what *I* want, before I grant you freedom."

Fire flickered in the ember eyes as Soulis appeared to consider the matter. Then the shadowy head gave a nod.

*Very well.*

Mallory had already produced a loaded hypo. Smiling mirthlessly, Raeburn forced Iolo to his knees, twisting his neck to one side so Mallory could inject directly into the jugular.

Iolo's eyelids fluttered. Letting him sink to his hands and knees, Raeburn and Mallory stepped back, and Raeburn closed off the third side of the outer triangle with a fresh infusion of blood. Then, with the point of the dagger, Raeburn stretched across to scratch a gap in the inner triangle, giving Soulis access to his host.

With an exultant hiss, Soulis burst the bounds of the inner triangle, reverting to fiery smoke as he surged over the vaguely stirring Iolo. The young Druid shuddered from head to foot as Soulis took him, body arching backward against the violation, clawing hands clapped to his head as Soulis' essence forced access to the temple of his flesh. As the infestation was completed, Iolo gave a single, strangled cry, then sank back on his hunkers, arms falling slack at his sides, his eyes going wholly blank.

Glittering life returned to the eyes with his next breath, but the light of conscious presence was that of Soulis, not Iolo. Chuckling with lascivious delight, the black wizard drew himself to his knees, then staggered upright with feet wide-spraddled. His lips drew back in a terrible grin as he cast his burning gaze on Raeburn, speaking with Iolo's voice.

"You may proceed with your preparations," he instructed. "I shall prepare myself to petition the Dark Powers, while this body regains its full strength."

He paused for a luxurious sigh, flexing his hands before running them possessively up and down Iolo's body. Then he made an abrupt turn and dropped to both knees, abasing

himself before the black altar with a raucous shout of exultation.

His cry shivered Adam to the bone, edging him closer to
despair as, with sinking heart, he felt hard hands dragging
him to his feet, throwing off his blanket to chivvy him forward with rough force. Behind the altar stood the black priest
in his Satanic vestments, his eyes wide with mingled shock
and awed anticipation. Beside him stood Raeburn.

The two acolytes were waiting to divest Adam of his robe.
Though he tried weakly to resist, his body refused to obey
him as he was stripped and hoisted up onto the altar, his
wrists bound with cords of scarlet silk that then were drawn
hard over the sides and secured to the wrought-iron candlesticks now set to either side of the altar's base. They left his
feet unbound, but that hardly mattered, since his legs were
numb from the cold, his body debilitated from the drugs and
loss of blood; and he knew full well that escape—at least of
his own devising—was now beyond any mortal hope.

Quivering with cold and shock, he fixed his gaze on the
icy stars overhead, squinting against a light snowfall, and
tried to offer up his prayers anew—for that was the only
recourse that now remained. He tried not to hear as the black
priest launched into a twisted parody of the Latin Preface to
the Mass, turning his face away as Angela spread a square
black cloth over the symbols she had painted on his chest in
his blood, shuddering as she set chalice and paten there in
readiness. He could feel a brooding Darkness building up
around him, threatening to smother him, as the black priest
spoke the words of Consecration and lifted the Elements in
turn.

Against his will, unable to retreat into trance, Adam was
then forced to witness the savage desecration of a Host, followed by the pollution of the Cup with a mixture of urine
and his own blood—surely no valid profanation, a still de-
fiant part of him reminded the part that cringed from this
calculated sacrilege, for his higher self knew full well that
only the Holy Spirit could will the transformation that made
Sacrament of bread and wine—not any human agency. Nor
could any man compel the descent of Spirit—not even a
priest. Especially not this priest.

Trembling nonetheless—for Evil surely had been called down—Adam did his best to show no emotion as the black priest crumbled the desecrated Host above the chalice; but when the priest then turned to lift the cup toward Raeburn, an inadvertent gasp did escape his lips as the Lynx-Master produced two gold wedding bands and Adam's confiscated Adept ring, displaying them triumphantly before he dropped them one by one into the polluted cup.

That simple act underscored Adam's helplessness far more insidiously than the more lofty desecration he had already been forced to witness. As his stunned gaze dimly tracked the cup to Raeburn's lips, marking the other's elation as he drank, dull despair eroded at Adam's will to keep resisting— so that he was almost taken by surprise when Raeburn lowered the cup, dragging the back of a hand across his mouth, then gave a minute signal to his acolytes.

Hard hands upon Adam's ankles and shoulders gave but scant warning of their intent. Physical resistance was useless; nevertheless he fought them feebly, at the same time groping in sluggish memory for words of spiritual defense.

*"Accipe calicem voluptatis carnis, in nomine Domini Inferi,"* the black priest murmured, even as one of Raeburn's men seized Adam's head and held it while another forced his jaws apart and Raeburn moved in with the cup.

*I believe in God the Father of Our Lord Jesus Christ,* Adam prayed, trying to shield himself in words from the baptismal rite in the Book of Common Prayer. *I believe in the Holy Spirit, the Lord and Giver of Life. I reject Satan and all his lies, and all his works and all his empty promises—*

He started choking as Raeburn poured a goodly measure of the polluted wine down his throat. Gagging, he felt some of it start to explode through his nose, but Raeburn seized the cloth from his chest and clamped it over his mouth and nose, holding it there relentlessly until anatomic reflex forced his victim to swallow or pass out.

Adam swallowed and was released, a shudder of profound revulsion racking him from head to toe as he came up for air, gasping and coughing. Raeburn's spiteful laughter rang in his ears as a hand wiped a cloth across his mouth and nose. His heart was hammering against his ribs as he fell back, sick and faint.

*I reject Satan and all his lies, and all his works and all his empty promises,* he told himself again, eyes closed against his torturers. *The essence of what is sacred cannot be sullied by any human agency, nor can the spirit be touched by anything that the will categorically refuses.*

"Enough of fun and games, Master of the Hunt. Time now for a more potent sacrifice."

The words jolted Adam from his attempt to retreat, bringing his focus back to Raeburn with a start. Raeburn's chill smile seemed to float above him as he moved the Lynx medallion back onto Adam's chest, centering it almost gently amid the symbols painted there in Adam's blood, that spelled out his doom. As strong hands again locked on Adam's ankles, Raeburn's gaze briefly locked upon his, mocking, then shifted to the Pictish dagger now glittering in his right hand. With almost caressing slowness, as if to draw the moment out, Raeburn slid his other hand under Adam's neck and tilted his head back to present the helpless throat.

As the black priest sidled closer, the chalice ready to catch the spilling of Adam's lifeblood, Raeburn slowly raised the dagger, his face contorting in a look of fervid exultation, lips moving in an offertory invocation that seemed to deepen the silence all around. Closing his eyes, Adam commended himself once again to the Light and braced himself to render up his spirit with courage, if this was indeed how he was destined to die.

"Goddammit, visibility's getting worse," Harry muttered, night-vision goggles giving him an alien appearance as he strained to see through the perspex of the chopper's windscreen. "We must be getting close, though. We passed Hawick five minutes back."

He was sitting in the co-pilot's seat of the chopper, next to Kinsey, the senior SAS pilot. Crouching behind them, McLeod and Duart were likewise scanning the darkness. Below them, a powerful searchlight beam from the chopper was illuminating a narrow, snow-edged road meandering southward along Whitrope Burn, another sweeping the countryside off to their left. According to their maps, the Nine Stane Rig lay somewhere in that direction, perhaps half a mile off the road, just past the place where an unpaved track joined the road they were following. In the dark, following a road was the only way to find what they were looking for—and even this way seemed woefully inadequate, as half a dozen pairs of eyes continued to search ahead and to either side.

"I'm not seeing anything," Duart said, scanning with infrared binoculars. "Noel, are you sure they'll be out in the open?"

"No, I'm not," McLeod replied, braced between the two pilot seats. "And if they aren't, I doubt we have a prayer of finding them."

"Then, let's concentrate on finding what we *can* see," Duart said. "If they're outside—which follows, if they're using an ancient site like the Nine Stane Rig—there'll have to be some lights showing where there shouldn't be lights—which means just about everywhere out there that isn't on a road—and there aren't many roads out here. This isn't a highly populated area. But I sure don't see anything near where the Nine Stane Rig should be. Do you have any idea how big it is? Stonehenge size?"

"I haven't a clue," McLeod muttered.

"Could they be at Hermitage, then?" Peregrine asked. "That's certainly associated with Soulis, and it's only a mile or so further on. If it's ruined enough—no roof—lights inside might show. And we can find the castle by following the road."

"I can have you there in two or three minutes," Kinsey said over his shoulder. "Do you want to check it out? There's nothing out here."

Raeburn's satanic offertory was drawing to a close, its cadence quickening with Adam's racing pulse. But stretched helpless upon that unholy altar, all in the sinking space between one heartbeat and the next, Adam suddenly sensed another presence looming opposite Raeburn—felt icy dread clutch at his heart with paralyzing force, even as something far worse began to probe at his soul. In a vain attempt to throw off the assault, instinct arched his back in violent denial—visceral reflection of his inner revulsion as he felt what shreds of spiritual defense he yet possessed being sounded with irresistible strength.

The instant of penetration was more brutal than any physical violation—and over almost before it began. It drew a scream to his lips that could find no voice as, still quaking, he forced his lids apart to behold the soul-destroying smile of William de Soulis.

In that stunned instant of eye contact, while a shocked part of Adam noted that Soulis apparently was no longer constrained by Raeburn's triangle, a more dispassionate part of him sensed that he was in the presence of a black Adept more powerful than any he had ever encountered—far more powerful than Raeburn, though it was doubtful that Raeburn recognized as much.

And Adam was certain of one thing more, in that shivering infinity before he wrenched his gaze away. Whatever bargain Soulis and Raeburn might have struck, Soulis was merely awaiting the chance to dishonor it.

But Raeburn was finishing his offertory chant, his hand behind Adam's neck thrusting the throat upward even as his blazing eyes followed the slow, glittering descent of the ancient blade sweeping downward to deliver the coup de grâce.

Except that Soulis suddenly intervened physically, diverting the death-stroke with a decisive sweep of Iolo's forearm.

"Hold!"

The tone stopped Raeburn as much as the word or the outstretched arm. Panting with frustrated bloodlust, he glared at Soulis with hot eyes.

"Hold? Why?" he rasped.

Soulis' response was cool, but colder still was the hand he brought to rest atop the lynx medallion around Adam's neck, the fingers wide-splayed to caress the symbols painted on the chest of his chosen oblation.

"I find the body of this man better suited to my needs than the one you chose for me. I will have it—or none. Render another to the Prince of Darkness."

Adam could scarcely breathe, dared not move, darting his glance furtively between Soulis and Raeburn. Raeburn's chest heaved. Wavering, he transferred his glare to Adam, the blade in his hand still mere inches from his victim's throat. Adam could almost hear him thinking, weighing his own lust for murder against the more subtle prospect of letting Adam become possessed by Soulis, a prisoner in his own body. After a moment Raeburn exhaled heavily and lowered the blade.

"Very well," he agreed. "You may have this one—but only after you have kept your part of the bargain by empowering the dagger."

Soulis nodded agreeably. "As you wish. The blood of an unwilling victim is still required. I will appoint one myself. It shall be . . . *him!*"

He stabbed a finger at the black priest. The man gasped and recoiled, only to be seized by two acolytes, the chalice wrenched from his grasp. As Angela came to take charge of it, Barclay and Mallory joined in to help strip the priest of his unholy vestments. Smiling a secret smile, Soulis retreated to the far end of the altar to observe. Raeburn, with a calculating glance at the struggling priest, cut the cord binding Adam's right wrist and summoned Mallory to help him shift Adam far to the left side of the altar to make room.

"Well, out of the frying pan, Sinclair . . ." Mallory remarked, ducking to tighten the remaining cord binding Adam's left wrist. "Do you want me to get something for the other one?" he asked Raeburn as he straightened, jutting his chin toward the now naked priest.

"No, we'll make this quick," Raeburn replied. "Our guest doesn't seem to like drugs. Barclay, get him over here!"

The black priest moaned and twisted in his captors' hands as the lynx medallion was transferred from Adam's neck to his, bucking and pleading as they lifted him onto the altar beside Adam and held him down rather than bothering to tie him. He continued to struggle weakly as Raeburn forced him to take a draught from the chalice he himself had desecrated, Mallory holding his head and another man leaning across Adam to pin his left arm. He subsided whimpering as the chalice was handed off to Angela, tears trickling from the outer corners of his eyes as Raeburn raised the dagger and began the offertory again.

With all attention now focused on Raeburn, and one of

his minions still leaning across Adam's body to help hold
the now sobbing black priest—blocking Adam's view but
also partially shielding him from observation—Adam dared
to gather himself for one last, desperate, silent cry for help,
refusing to squander whatever time he might have left—for
when the priest died, Soulis would turn his attention to his
preferred offering.

Shrinking from the obscene power being focused right at
his side, but with his thinking somewhat cleared by the ad-
renalin-surge of the past minutes, Adam dragged himself
sluggishly downward into trance, doing his best to visualize
one of the psychic flares he had once described to Harry
Nimmo, sending it aloft with a prayer.

As the image spiralled haltingly up and outward, his exertion was rewarded with a faint but familiar flicker on the
distant edge of psychic awareness. His head was pounding
with the strain, but fuelled by hope, his psychic cry for help
surged upward again with renewed brightness. This time his
straining senses touched a familiar hint of presence.

*Noel! Peregrine!*

Pulse pounding, he concentrated on forcing a psychic
shout through the blanketing miasma of evil enveloping the
chapel. A rushing whisper began to pulse through his entire
body. It took him a few seconds to realize that the sound
was coming not from inside his head, but from somewhere
outside—the rhythmic whuff of helicopter blades descending
out of the night.

# CHAPTER THIRTY-SIX

A dazzling searchlight-beam from the chopper scythed down the chapel's length, a second raking the burial ground to the south. Raeburn ducked to a half-crouch with a short-bitten oath, warding his eyes as the first beam swept back. His henchmen likewise cowered from the light's revelation, but they did not abandon their hold on the black priest as automatic-weapons fire peppered the night and the chopper lifted slightly to the north, suddenly trailing abseiling ropes. Though Adam immediately lost sight of it, new hope surged in his breast as he heard the heavier chatter of return fire. But he knew he still could die before his rescuers reached him. And even if Raeburn did not kill him, Soulis had already marked him for his own.

In that instant, however, Soulis was no longer fixed on his chosen prize. Apparently oblivious to the implications of late twentieth-century technology, he darted closer to Raeburn and extended taut hands over the black priest's heaving chest.

"Strike here!" he cried. "Strike *now*! You must release the power by which I may destroy this demon!"

His voice cracked like a whip. Startled into obedience, Raeburn hauled himself upright, arm cocked back with the dagger in his hand, and plunged the blade downward into the black priest's heart.

The body of the sacrifice arched violently on the altar, his piercing scream momentarily masking even the gunfire. Beside him, Adam flinched from the backlash of power suddenly being channelled through the dagger, sluggishly dragging his unbound arm upward to shield his eyes. Raeburn's men likewise cringed, releasing their holds on the victim; but as the priest's body spasmed in mortal agony, Raeburn himself held firm, bearing down on the dagger white-knuckled, eyes blazing and lips drawn back in a rictus of anticipation.

A brooding rumble shook the ground as the dagger drank the last spark of life-energy from the sacrifice. In that instant, the blade became a conduit for an inrush of power so potent that its kiss all but took Raeburn's breath away. The taste of empowerment was ravishing. Still clinging to the dagger, Raeburn threw back his head in a moan of mingled pain and delight as his body was gripped by a trembling ecstasy.

The engine-roar of the helicopter had receded to a whistling, whuffing sound as it settled on the burying ground to the north of the chapel, its searchlights now stabbing horizontally across the snow, splashing against the plywood hoardings, arching over the chapel like a roof. Adam could not see it, for the hoardings blocked his view in that direction even as they blocked the view of his would-be rescuers; but as he tried to lift his head, still cringing from the body of the now dead priest, he wondered whether he had the strength to roll off the edge of the altar—though to do so would move him closer to Soulis, still inhabiting Iolo McFarlane's body; and to stay, left him within reach of Raeburn, who might yet choose to kill Adam as he had the priest, both to exact his revenge and to try augmenting his power even more.

But variables were shifting too fast for Adam to keep up, in his dazed condition. As automatic-weapons fire again shattered the night, off to the south, Soulis drew back a pace from the altar, a malicious smile contorting his lips as his hands sketched a sequence of ritual gestures too swift and intricate for Adam's eyes to follow, the while muttering a harsh incantation.

In the next instant, the body Soulis wore was overtaken by a violent convulsion. Iolo's mouth gaped, his hands groping forth blindly to catch on the edge of the altar as blue smoke poured from his lips in a vomitous stream. As the vacated body crumpled, Soulis' essence reared up in a ghostly column of flame-eyed shadow, infernal fire pulsing at its heart.

A hoarse shriek from Angela warned Raeburn's other accomplices of danger from within as well as without, for the shadow that now was Soulis surged up from the foot of the altar to blanket the still-twitching body of the black priest like a lightless shroud. Adam managed to shift his left leg off the side of the altar, cringing as far from Soulis as he could, but he had not the strength to roll all the way off. As the dead man's lips began to move in the whispered syllables of a further incantation, Adam tried again to throw himself clear. Raeburn, only now recovering from his unholy rapture, sagged dazedly against the head of the altar, with the dagger clasped to his breast, apparently oblivious to Adam, Soulis, or even another exchange of automatic-weapons fire outside the confines of the chapel—though he flinched as a thunderous *boom* rocked the ground underfoot.

Even as the echoes were still reverberating, a squat, wild-eyed creature suddenly materialized behind the altar, as if out of nowhere, wearing the form of a gnarly, bandy-legged old man with bare, sinewy arms and a gaping mouth full of carious yellow fangs. Clothed in a loincloth and mantle of ragged skins, his grizzled head was crowned with a filthy red cap—by which token Adam could have no doubt that Soulis had summoned his dreadful familiar, the cannibal-spirit known in Scottish folklore as Robin Redcap.

With a hideous gloating laugh, Redcap made a bound for Raeburn's nearest acolyte, oblivious to the several shots the man managed to get off, and ripped out his throat with a single snap of powerful jaws. Pausing only to fling the body aside, Redcap wheeled around and charged next at Raeburn, blood glistening on his hairy cheeks and down his chest.

The impact of the charge broke Raeburn's grip on the dagger. Juggling the knife in a vain attempt to retain it, he bowled backward under a heavy blow that sent him reeling to the ground on the altar's other side, even as Redcap seized the dagger's bloodied hilt in taloned fingers and held it triumphantly aloft, chuckling throatily to himself. Simultaneously, the shadow that was Soulis surged upward to wrap shadow-hands over those of Redcap.

Shrinking from this combined abomination, Adam summoned every shred of strength he could muster and at last managed to fling himself sideways off the altar-slab, his fall cast askew by the cord still binding his left wrist to the wrought-iron candlestick, which toppled with him. He landed heavily atop the crumpled form of Iolo McFarlane and tried to make himself invisible by flattening himself as much as possible, his free arm upflung to protect the back of his head as the candlestick fell across both of them.

Above him and behind the altar, Soulis and Redcap merged together in a blur of sulphur and shadow. Out of that blur two harsh voices called out as one in cacophonous invocation. Amid the ringing chaos of otherwise unintelligible syllables, Adam heard the name *Taranis*—warning that the unholy pair were uniting their powers to summon the dark Lord of Lightning.

Their voices rose to a screaming crescendo. In that instant the air above the altar was riven by a blinding bolt of blue-white lightning.

Outside the chapel, crouching low behind a snow-covered tomb stone, McLeod paused to draw breath as he shoved a fresh clip into the butt of his Browning Hi-Power. The flash and chatter of automatic-weapons fire continued to punctuate the darkness beyond the chapel, and bullets had splintered portions of the plywood hoardings ahead. He was about to hail Ian Duart, huddled a few yards to his left, when a low rumble drew his attention to an uncanny break in the clouds overhead.

In the space of a single breath, the break deepened to a fathomless rift, from which shot a sudden crackling lightning-blast that struck behind the hoardings, briefly lighting the night in an actinic glare. An accompanying backlash of wind bowled over two of Duart's men.

McLeod stared at the chapel aghast, for the bolt seemed to have struck very near to the altar area where they had spotted Adam from the air. Collecting himself, and keeping his head down, he bolted for Duart, ducking as a spatter of bullets ricocheted off a nearby tombstone.

"We've got to get in there *now!*" he rasped, gripping the major by the sleeve.

"I'm working on it," Duart replied.

A whistle and a shout from him sent members of the rescue team darting across the snow, firing as they ran, but return gunfire drove them to ground. Tracking the muzzle flashes back to a dark shape briefly silhouetted against the glare within the chapel, McLeod squeezed off three well-aimed shots and had the satisfaction of seeing his target go down with a cry.

Twenty yards behind McLeod, tightly clutching her medical bag as she sheltered behind a tree, Ximena eyed the advancing SAS men and made a move to follow, but Peregrine grabbed her arm and pulled her back.

"Not yet!" he warned. "You've got to give the experts time to clear the way. And for God's sake, keep your head down! If I let anything happen to you, Adam would never forgive me."

"And *I* will never forgive *you* if you let anything happen to *him!*" she retorted, rounding on him with suppressed ferocity. "Are you coming or aren't you?"

Before he could remonstrate, she darted away from him. With an inner groan, he sprang after her. More bullets peppered the snow around them as they caught up with McLeod in the shelter of one of the parked Land Rovers. Peregrine was just going to ask about the possibility of creating a diversion, when the clouds overhead convulsed, spitting another searing shaft of lightning into the confines of the chapel.

Lancing like a javelin at the dagger upthrust by Soulis and Redcap, the lightning of Taranis briefly lit the night like the sun at noon, boiling upward from the blade in a crackling blaze of fire-arcs. Exultantly, the shadow that was Soulis rose up to bathe in the unearthly rain of energy, taking ever more substantial form. United with his master in possession of the dagger, Redcap likewise strained upward to drink in his share of the lightning's might.

Raeburn's remaining henchmen broke and ran, preferring to face the SAS rather than what Soulis had called forth.

Shadow-head backflung in ecstasy, Soulis cried out to the heavens, demanding more power, which continued to course through the dagger sacred to Taranis.

Dazzled and deafened, still fettered to the candlestick and too weak to free himself, Adam continued to cower at the base of the altar, his body sheltering Iolo's. Above him, just visible if he strained his neck backward, he could catch only a glimpse of the tip of the upheld dagger, now glowing white-hot in the fire of Taranis' might, beginning to melt under the strain of channelling so much energy. As the metal slagged, molten gouts rained down on the altar-top and on the body of the black priest, and greasy smoke began to billow upward in earthly echo of the very hell-fires whose retribution the priest had courted by betraying his holy vows and daring to mock his office.

The heat intensified—welcome warmth to Adam's half-frozen body, but his peril was no less for that, only different. As he clawed vainly at the knots still binding his left wrist, another dull explosion bowled him over again, heralding the final destruction of the blade.

A sulphurous wind swept the chapel bounds as the shadow-form of Soulis reared ever larger, flushing the last of the defenders from their coverts. Redcap could not be seen. More daring than her male counterparts, Angela made a furtive bid to retrieve the discarded chalice, only to fling it from her with a scream as the heated metal scorched her hands.

As she, too, bolted into the darkness, Adam craned his neck after her, trying to see where she had gone. Unable to locate Raeburn either, and desperate to get as far away as possible from what was happening on the other side of the altar, he hauled himself upright enough to try picking with his teeth at the knots imprisoning his wrist, though the effort made his head reel, and he was on the verge of passing out. He could only hope that if McLeod and his other would-be rescuers did succeed in breaking through, they would not be instantly overwhelmed by the infernal forces that had been summoned here.

The glut of power had enlarged Soulis' presence until the boundaries of Raeburn's circle could no longer contain it.

Inflated to monstrous proportions, his shadow-form flexed and then burst free. Outside, crouched down behind the Land Rover, Peregrine watched in dumb astonishment as a heavy black cloud mushroomed upward and spread itself like a greasy canopy between the ground and the sky.

"What, in God's name, is *that*?" he breathed, as Ximena buried her face against his shoulder.

"I don't think God has much to do with it," McLeod muttered in reply. "Take a closer look."

Following the line of the inspector's pointing finger, Peregrine saw that the cloud had eyes—twin lamps of infernal fire that flickered hungrily this way and that, as if searching for something to devour. Even as they watched, horrified, it began drifting westward into the darkness.

"It has to be some demon of Raeburn's summoning," McLeod continued in a tight voice. "Or maybe Soulis himself, somehow transformed. Pray God it wasn't at the expense of Adam; we've got to find him! And if Raeburn called that thing, I expect we're going to have to get at Raeburn to send it back."

As he was speaking, Duart ghosted out of the shadows behind them to crouch alongside.

"I think we've got the perimeter secured," he said. "My men have several prisoners. You ready to go get Sinclair?"

Summoning Peregrine and Ximena to follow, McLeod trotted after Duart toward the end of the hoardings. They were almost abreast of a gap when a clumsy shape suddenly burst out at them, whisking past McLeod with explosive speed. The inspector had a fleeting impression of a grinning, fang-mouthed face surmounted by a red cap before the creature made a break for open ground, bowling Peregrine over in the speed of its passage.

With a startled curse, Duart dropped to one knee and fired several bursts after it, but with no apparent effect. Recovering himself, McLeod set a restraining hand on Duart's arm.

"Save your ammunition," he ordered. "Finding Adam is our first priority."

The chapel's interior was awash with firelight behind the hoardings. First to make cautious entry, McLeod was not surprised to note a line of blood traced around the perimeter of the foundations, though it had been rubbed out near at hand by the scuffle of many feet. Whatever magical containment field it once had defined, that had since been broken by those attempting to escape from the demon that Raeburn had summoned.

But power of another sort stirred with McLeod's next step, as something seemed almost to shimmer in the air about him, accompanied by a sudden thudding in his head that reverberated behind his eyes. Gasping, he nearly dropped his weapon as he caught at a wall for balance. Peregrine almost trod on his heels.

"Noel?" he cried, as Ximena glanced over in alarm.

"I'm all right," McLeod said dazedly. "There's—ah—another Presence here, wanting in."

"What?" Ximena murmured, as Peregrine gripped the inspector's shoulder in alarm.

"Well, *don't* open up to it," the artist said. "We haven't a clue who it is!"

Just then, as Duart and one of his men slipped into the chapel to secure it, weapons at the ready, Ximena stifled a cry and pointed past them, eyes wide.

"Look!" she cried. "There!"

At the base of the altar, just visible through screening fire and smoke, two bodies could be seen sprawled one atop the other in the snow, a dark-haired and naked one sheltering another, who was, partially shrouded in a filthy white robe. One arm of the naked one was stretched taut above his head, caught all too close to the flames that were eating down a black altar-cloth spilling from the ruined altar above their heads.

"Adam!" McLeod cried, breaking into a run as the others, too, dashed after him, Peregrine muttering, "Dear God!"

"You two tend to Adam and the other one!" the inspector shouted to Ximena, himself ripping at the burning altar-cloth and starting to trample out the flames.

As Peregrine grabbed up a pair of blankets discarded amid a tangle of overturned chairs nearby, Ximena threw herself down beside her husband's prostrate form, thrusting trembling fingers hard against the side of his neck.

"He's breathing, and I've got a pulse," she reported, "but only just. He's probably in shock."

"Can I move him enough to get a blanket under him?" Peregrine asked, as she shifted to check the other figure. "He's lying in the snow."

"Try to untie his hand first, until I can check whatever other injuries he may have."

McLeod meanwhile scrambled to help Ximena turn the white-robed figure Adam had been shielding.

"It's young McFarlane!" he exclaimed.

"Is he dead?" Peregrine asked, worrying at the knots at Adam's wrist.

"No, but he isn't in great shape," Ximena replied, as Duart made his way over to them, accompanied by one of his men.

"We've found our missing Druid," McLeod announced. "They're both alive, but we could use your medic to assist."

"He's on his way," Duart replied, listening to his headset. "The second pilot took a hit, but—"

As he spoke, the night was pierced by the mechanical whine of a helicopter starting up—but coming from the other side of the chapel from where the Lynx had landed.

"What the devil?" Duart muttered, as his trooper swung his MP5 in that direction and broke into a run.

Simultaneously, automatic-weapons fire chattered from the vicinity of the sound, but the engine noise strengthened even as Duart, too, swung on his heel and started toward it, only to almost collide with Harry and another SAS man.

"Sorry, boss," the trooper panted, "but a couple of these bastards managed to get to their chopper. Kinsey is cranking up ours."

As he spoke, Raeburn's helicopter rose up from the north side of the chapel in a boiling whirlwind of snow and immediately headed west. Shouting to make himself heard over the noise of the engine, Harry, said, "Want me to do something about this? Sounds like you're down one pilot."

Duart peered at him through eyes narrowed against the gale. "D'you think you're up to it?"

"Up to it?" Harry retorted with a tight grin. "Remind me to show you my Falkland medals someday, laddie. Or come and watch me put a Spit through her paces."

# CHAPTER THIRTY-SEVEN

CLOSE by the base of the altar, Adam roused sluggishly to an awareness that several people were calling him by name. Something warm was being wrapped around him, and he could feel deft fingers tugging at the cord imprisoning his wrist as someone else lifted his feet to rest on something soft.

"Oh, Adam, Adam, don't *do* this to me!" said a voice he recognized as Ximena's, as pressure constricted around the bicep of his free arm. "*Please* say something!"

As the knots at his wrist gave way, his left hand dropped limply to the ground, but the impact was enough to rouse him further. Forcing his heavy eyelids to open, he found himself squinting against the glare of a powerful torch. As it was turned quickly aside, the sight of Ximena, Peregrine, and McLeod nearly caused him to lose consciousness again, out of sheer relief.

Then he remembered what he had to tell them, and forced himself back from the abyss. Nearby, an SAS medic had started working on Iolo.

"Is this blood on his chest?" McLeod growled, as Ximena pressed the bell of a stethoscope against Adam's inner elbow.

"I'm not bleeding," he managed to whisper, his free hand groping vaguely for a handful of snow. "Blood's mine, but they painted it on me. Marks of Taranis—got to scrub 'em off . . ."

"That's the least of your worries right now," Ximena muttered between tears and fury, as she pulled the stethoscope from her ears and dashed the snow from his hand. "Oh, Adam, what have they done to you?"

"Kept me pumped full of sedatives," he mumbled dazedly. "All very slick. Took a lot of blood, too—more'n two units."

"Well, that's why your pressure is shit!" she retorted, already pulling items from her medical bag. "We've got to get you to a hospital, the sooner the better."

At any other time Adam would have agreed. But with his physical welfare now in his wife's capable hands, his overriding worry at the moment was that Soulis had somehow broken free. Even if he never returned to claim what he had marked as his own, Soulis would be poised to prey upon an unsuspecting world, freshly energized by the fire of Taranis. Until he could be brought back under control, nothing else mattered. And Adam must be clear-headed to direct the operation, no matter what it cost him.

"Can't go anywhere yet," he said, fighting back a wave of nausea. "Got work to do *here*. You've got to stabilize me. I need a plasma extender in me, if you've got it, and something to lift my blood pressure, stat."

"Will you please let *me* decide what you need?" Ximena said as she stripped the packaging off a large bore needle and plugged it into the IV line on a bag of Ringer's lactate. "You're in no condition to do anything that smacks of exertion."

"Just do what I'm telling you!" Adam rasped, as she pumped up the blood pressure cuff again, searching for a vein. "I need my head clear! Do whatever it takes. And don't worry if I seem to slip away for a bit."

"You haven't even got any decent veins, your pressure's so low," she muttered. "Do you have any idea what you're asking?"

"Ximena, he knows," McLeod whispered. "Please—help him do what he needs to do."

Her expression was mutinous, but as she rolled her eyes, she ran her fingertips along the side of Adam's neck.

"All right," she said, tearing open an alcohol swab, "but I'm doing this under protest. If you die, I'll never forgive you. Peregrine, give me some light here on his neck. Adam,

I'm going to have to go for the jugular, so bear with me.''

"I've married a vampire," he whispered weakly, his faint smile twitching as the needle slid home.

While Peregrine set about scrubbing the blood from his chest with more alcohol wipes, and McLeod righted the heavy candle-holder to improvise an IV stand, Ximena began plugging various medications into Adam's IV. As he sought a level of trance to assist his body's recovery, he could feel himself already beginning to rally. Vaguely aware of hands shifting him to wrap more blankets around his body, he embraced a brightness reaching out to him from the heart of the Inner Planes, bringing with it the promise of restoration and remedy. Extending himself in turn to meet and welcome it, Adam suddenly found himself once again in the luminous presence of Andrew Kerr.

Relief flooded through him, for here at last was the link by which Soulis might be defeated—and McLeod was at hand this time, to be Kerr's voice. Spreading astral hands in a gesture of momentary suspension, but remaining deep in trance, Adam opened his eyes to seek out McLeod, who now was kneeling at his left side.

"Noel—I have contact with someone who can help us, but he needs a vessel. I can vouch for him without question. Will you let him in?"

McLeod traded quick glances with Peregrine.

"I think he's been knocking at the door ever since we arrived," he told Adam with a faint smile. "Aye, he has my permission to enter."

"Then take my hand," Adam whispered, closing his eyes again as McLeod complied.

Still poised with Kerr on the threshold of the Inner Planes, Adam saw the other Huntsman's face transformed with relief as his image likewise came to clasp Adam's hand. As the other's likeness faded, becoming no longer discernible on the astral, Adam sensed the transfer of essence and place and opened his eyes again, though he remained in trance. The presence that looked back at him through his Second's blue eyes was recognizably that of Andrew Kerr.

"Be welcome here," Adam whispered.

Nodding, Kerr released Adam's hand and scanned swiftly around them.

"Where is Soulis?" he demanded urgently.

His voice was lighter and clearer than McLeod's own gravelly bass. The sound of it made Ximena start and stare, but Peregrine only smiled faintly and shifted closer to watch and listen in wonder. With no time for explanations, Adam gave his full attention to his historical counterpart.

"Soulis has gone, at least for the moment," he told Kerr. "His spirit was conjured here by a black Adept called Raeburn, but he broke the bounds meant to contain him and took flight into the night. Redcap is also free."

Kerr, wearing McLeod's aspect, looked visibly shaken by this disclosure.

"This bodes ill, indeed, if those two are at liberty," he muttered. "The future of many is in jeopardy."

The blue gaze clouded, focused in some other time and place, and McLeod's breathing deepened.

"Aye," Kerr continued in the same troubled voice, "the tapestry begins to reweave itself even as we speak, as that which was destined *not* to be now once again becomes possible."

"Forgive me, but I'm afraid I don't understand," Adam said.

Kerr turned back to him, the blue gaze holding him fast, willing him to comprehend.

"Soulis was no common evildoer," he explained grimly. "So monstrous were his crimes that it was decreed his existence should be cut short—not just once, in what is now your own past, but for all time to come: by denying him all future incarnations. In releasing Soulis from limbo, this man Raeburn has restored the potential to incarnate. The consequences of that act now threaten to change the whole fabric of creation, from this time forward."

Adam's mind reeled at the prospect. "Is it possible to put things right?" he asked.

"It is," Kerr responded sternly, "but it will not be enough simply to send Soulis back to the Other Side. The doors to his own future must also be closed against him."

"Do you know how to do this?" Adam asked. "For I do not."

"I do," Kerr replied. "For as far back as my memory reaches, through many lifetimes, it has been given to me to see and know the shape of things to come. That is why I was chosen to be Soulis' executioner. You know his past and I know his future. If a means can be found to lure him back to this place, then together it may be possible for us to force him back across the threshold of existence, and consign him once again to the Outer Dark."

"You need look no further for a lure to entice him," Adam said grimly. "I myself am already the lure."

Swiftly, and in as few words as possible, he related how Soulis had intervened at the very instant before Raeburn would have slain him in unholy sacrifice.

"His touch was—unspeakable," he whispered, shuddering. "He left Iolo's body to drink of the power of Taranis, but he expected to take me in Iolo's place. I doubt he's gone far. In order to experience the full pleasure of existence, he still requires a physical body—one, moreover, which is accustomed to the stresses of walking between the worlds, moving on the Inner Planes. When he sounded me, he found such a host—and marked me as his own. It's only a matter of time before he returns to claim me—especially if I offer myself, without defenses."

"Then, your stake in this is personal, as well as for the common good," Kerr said gravely, "for if Soulis takes you a second time, he will destroy you utterly."

"With your help, he will not destroy me," Adam replied, "but you must guide me."

"I will do that, right gladly," Kerr agreed. "But be warned: Even discarnate, Soulis is a powerful adversary. And having drunk from the well of Taranis, he will be all the more powerful now. Have you friends you can summon to aid in your defense?"

"Many and trusty," Adam said with a fleeting smile.

"Then call them to us," Kerr said. "You and I cannot do this thing alone. I must remain here, anchored in this body, to perform the necessary workings when the time comes.

Your other friends must be your bulwark while I keep watch between the worlds.''

McLeod's grizzled head bowed, a soft breath whispering from his lips. Only then, released from Kerr's regard, did Adam find the will to glance back at Ximena. She was reading his blood pressure again, and glanced at him sharply as she felt his gaze upon her.

"Are you done yet?" she murmured, pulling her stethoscope from her ears.

Gently he shook his head, smiling faintly as he took her hand in his and kissed it.

"Afraid not," he said softly. "Just beginning. Keep me safe while I'm away."

"Adam!"

But he only shook his head and released her hand, commending himself to the grace and protection of the Light as he bade Peregrine help him sit up slightly, reclining his head against the curve of the other's arm. As he willed himself onto the astral, unseen wings encompassed him, sweeping him up in a dizzying shimmer of flight that brought him through a sea of opal clouds to a lofty plateau canopied by stars. It was Peregrine who had carried him, and who stood ready at his side as, a moment later, they were joined on the astral by McLeod's spirit, oddly translucent for being partially constrained by the tenant now resident in his body.

Clothing himself in the celestial blue that both of them wore, Adam called out in spirit to the other members of the Hunting Lodge, soberly enjoining them to come and be present at this mustering of the Light. First to join them was Philippa, her face radiant with joy, who folded him in a swift caress before taking her place beside Peregrine, at his left hand. The others followed in swift sequence—Christopher, Victoria, Julian, together with a company of others who, from time to time, had shown themselves to be at one in spirit with Adam and his Huntsmen.

John Graham was there as well, black-robed and powerful, bearing the sword that had barred and then guarded the way to his sanctum at Oakwood, backed by half a dozen of his own Huntsmen. Present, too, were members of the Masonic fraternity who had assisted Adam in times past—Sir Gordon,

Ian Duart—and Alan Lockhart among that bright company, boldly lifting a sword that was echoed by like blades in the hands of all the others, as befitted warriors preparing to do battle in the service of the Light.

Lifting his arms to include all those present in the sweep of his embrace, Adam set the challenge before them with the winged speed of thought. Then, bidding them fall back to positions of concealment, he moved to the forefront to take his stand, casting aside all defenses to present himself in the white-robed guise of the sacrifice he nearly had been—and might yet be, if they could not stop Soulis.

A breath of sulphurous wind from the west was the first harbinger of Soulis' impending return. Trembling in body and spirit, acutely aware of the immortal danger in which he willingly placed himself, Adam offered himself for Soulis' enticement, faithfully reproducing his utter vulnerability before that other assault, when Soulis had probed so deeply into his soul. Far on the distant horizon to the west appeared a looming mass of dense black cloud, charged with venomous flickers of lightning.

Closer to the storm, a menacing rumble of thunder reverberated on the physical plane as well as the astral. The rumble was loud enough to penetrate the roar of the Lynx's powerful rotors as it streaked westward in hot pursuit of a fleeing smaller helicopter. Eyes intent on the quarry, Harry Nimmo noted the approaching storm beyond, but could see nothing else amiss.

"What the *hell* was that?" he muttered through set teeth.

Sitting next to him in the co-pilot's seat, hurriedly scanning their instrument displays, Kinsey shook his head.

"Nothing mechanical," he reported. "Must be the weather up ahead. Everything reads normal."

"I'm not sure that's weather," Harry muttered under his breath, as he bore down harder on the throttle.

Out in front, dipping in and out of the searchlight spear of the pursuing Lynx, the fleeing target skimmed dangerously close to the trees below, jinking left, then right, then left again as its pilot tried to shake off pursuit. Undaunted, Harry

kept the Lynx close-handled and steadily narrowed the gap
between himself and his airborne adversary.

"Another minute, and we've got 'em," he said aside to
Kinsey. "I'd really like to shoot 'em down, but I suppose
that would create a lot of bad press for Noel."

"Not to mention what the general would say."

"Guess we'd better force 'em down, then."

Even as he spoke, another boom of thunder spoke, heavy
enough to rattle the Lynx's armored bulkheads. Biting off an
oath, Harry made a rapid-fire adjustment to their trim and,
in that instant of diversion, heard Kinsey utter an explosive
profanity. As he glanced up in alarm, it was to see a black
wall of cloud rising up before both aircraft.

The cloud bank was heading their way with the speed of
a tidal wave. Banking sharply, the chopper in front made a
vain attempt to outflank it, only to be overtaken and engulfed. An instant later, the cloud was illuminated from
within by a stark blaze of lightning. Harry caught a fleeting
afterimage of the other craft suspended in a corona of flame
just before its fuel tank caught fire and exploded.

The thundercloud rolled on, raining burning debris from
its underside, the Lynx squarely in its path.

"Jesus, Harry! Get us the hell out of here!" Kinsey
shouted.

Harry was already taking measures. As the storm cloud
levelled out over the treetops, he punched the throttle into
overdrive and sent the chopper clawing for altitude. The engines stuttered, and for one awful moment he thought they
were going to be overwhelmed.

Then the rotors caught an updraft and lifted them clear
with only yards to spare as the uncanny cloud mass surged
past beneath them.

Back at the ruined chapel, well aware of Soulis' approach
on two levels, Adam briefly opened his eyes for a last scan
on the physical before battle was joined. He was aware of
Peregrine supporting him, of McLeod at his left side, of Donald Cochrane now crouching down by his feet, head bowed
over the Masonic ring he always wore. Behind Donald, Ian
Duart and two of his troopers were hunkered down with

heads bowed over their MP5's—further reinforcements for the Masonic support Adam had already noted on the astral. At his left, Ximena had turned to assist the SAS medic in Iolo's treatment, and was stretching to hang another IV between the two she had already started for Adam.

Commending them all to the protection of the Light, he let his eyelids close, again focused wholly on the astral as he braced himself for Soulis, bait for the trap, still offering no resistance. It was no easy thing to stand thus, as the wind of Soulis' approach was suddenly upon them.

But though a suffocating darkness accompanied the psychic gale that heralded Soulis' descent, sufficient Huntsmen rose up to just deflect it—a calculated defense to begin diminishing Soulis' power before he realized he was being drawn into a trap. The assault was still sufficient to buffet Adam to his very core; and the answering surge of Soulis' dark anger very nearly reached him before McLeod and then Philippa diverted it.

But he dared do nothing in his own defense, lest Soulis take alarm and draw back, or even escape. Adam must keep the lure of his soul dangling before Soulis, enticing him to squander his energies until it was too late to break away.

Meanwhile, Soulis rampaged, drunk with power and the promise of more. For a while, Adam felt like a bottle set adrift in the midst of a typhoon, uncertain which way was up, as the world around him was rent with catastrophic bursts of thunder and lightning and Soulis tried to get at him. The firmament beneath his feet seemed ready to burst asunder as the tempest raged around him with insensate fury.

But around him, directed by Kerr, Adam's Huntsmen and their allies prepared to close the net. With a word, McLeod/Kerr reached out a hand to take Philippa's, and she in turn reached out for Peregrine. The web of contact spread, and the firmament beneath them seemed to stabilize as, united by mind and hand, they planted themselves like so many oak trees and settled down to ride out the storm.

Gradually, though an eternity seemed to pass, the fury of the storm began to weaken. Still the Huntsmen held their net. But finally, even when Adam lifted his arms to Soulis in cautious enticement, still obviously helpless, the lightning-play died back to an exhausted flicker, the thunder subsiding to a sullen, intermittent growl.

The quarry now was run to ground. The storm-force of his malice was largely spent. Even so, Soulis was still a dangerous opponent, as insanely destructive as a rabid dog. Gratefully shedding his aspect as victim, Adam gathered back his defenses and once again clothed himself in the celestial hue of his office. As he took up his sword, he scanned the astral darkness at the edges of the Huntsmen's circle. The astral storm had yielded to the darkness of normal nighttime, but off to his right, a lingering blur of shadow crouched down in a hollow. By the sulphuric quality of its density, Adam knew it at once for the disembodied essence of Soulis.

Holding his sword at the ready, he slowly advanced on Soulis' position. Likewise arming themselves, the astral forms of his companions fanned out on either hand, as together they made to draw tight the web they had woven.

Soulis fathomed their intentions in an instant. Rising up in a vaguely humanoid pillar of fiery smoke, he made a furtive attempt to bolt, only to find the way blocked by Christopher's sword. Wheeling, he tried another route—this time blocked by Philippa and Peregrine. John Graham stood ready when he turned another way. By then the trap was unmistakable—and inescapable.

"We must return him now to the place where he first was summoned," Adam instructed those with him. "Be careful, though. He fears the swords, but he still has sufficient spite to do us harm."

With Adam and McLeod directing the endeavor, the circle of astral Huntsmen began chivvying their quarry back toward that physical counterpart of the astral door through which Soulis had made his entry into time and space. Soulis did not submit gracefully to being driven. Pulsing with rage, no longer able to hold any semblance of humanoid form, he lunged and surged in an attempt to wreak some injury, but his adversaries forced him steadily toward the astral reflection of the ruined chapel.

An echo of the chapel's physical appearance took shape on the Inner Planes. Retreating before Soulis to mark the way in, Adam became momentarily distracted by the sight of

Ximena standing up beside his own inert body, adjusting one of the IVs hanging from the wrought-iron candlestick. Peregrine was seated cross-legged against the side of the altar with Adam's head cradled in his lap, and McLeod/Kerr knelt beside him. Adam was about to return his attention to the astral, when another figure dragged itself upright from behind the wreckage of the altar slab, black-robed and fair of hair.

*Raeburn!*

And the black Adept had a pistol in the hand he was raising, his face transfixed with malice as he took careful aim at the back of Ximena's averted head.

"*No!*"

Adam's cry of horror made itself heard on both levels. Still in possession of McLeod's body, Kerr started upward but then hesitated—for if he fell, there was none to do to Soulis what must be done. But Peregrine was already in motion as well, letting Adam's head drop to the ground with stunning force as he rolled to tackle Ximena about the knees without a second thought, throwing her to the ground even as Raeburn's shot exploded. It missed both of them—and Soulis' harsh exclamation precluded a second try.

*You! Lynx-Master!* Soulis rumbled, as he surged up onto the altar in a darkly sparkling cloud like a tornado funnel. *Give me the use of your body and I will reduce these enemies of ours to ashes!*

Raeburn recoiled hard against the wall behind him, his pale eyes wild as he swung the muzzle of his pistol toward Soulis.

"No, stay back!" he shouted hoarsely. "I have no wish to join you in the Void. The worst these people can do is kill me. But you would destroy me utterly!"

The shadow that was Soulis stretched tall in its fury.

*Then, die, you miserable serf!* he howled. *And learn that there are worse things than oblivion! Redcap, he is yours!*

From out of the shadows at the chapel's edge, a misshapen goblin figure made a sudden leap. Swinging his pistol in that direction, Raeburn was still firing as Redcap seized him and bore him to the ground behind the altar. The gunfire ceased abruptly, with a crunch of shattering bone and a bubbling cry. As Redcap popped back into view with a triumphant cackle, demon eyes blazing, the taloned fingers of one hand were clutched red and dripping around the still palpitating lump of flesh that had been the Lynx-Master's heart.

He thrust it upward in gory salute to Soulis as his flaming gaze shifted to the other humans present in hungry calculation. But in that instant, Kerr heaved McLeod's body to its feet and flung up both hands in orison, crying out the opening words of a powerful incantation.

Redcap shrieked defiance, but a stabbing gesture from Kerr shrank the demon to a spitting, bristling ball of blackness that imploded with a thunderclap, sent back whence it had come. Never missing a beat, Kerr returned his focus to Soulis himself. As his chant piled note upon note and syllable upon syllable, Adam let himself be drawn back on the astral to stand at Kerr's side with his Huntsmen as an oval iris of fluctuating light opened before them out of nowhere, like a window on some distant futurity.

The oval had length and width, but no depth that Adam could see. As it turned toward the shadow that was Soulis, its surface scintillated like a mirror, with flashes of changing imagery. Looking more closely, Adam saw that the images were all changing guises of the same individual: a dark, arrogant man with cruel lips and heavy-lidded eyes. When the shadow-Soulis turned toward the window in sudden, aching yearning, Adam realized that he was seeing reflections of Soulis' future lives as well as past ones.

But all those lives bore the same stamp of depravity, and a greater Wisdom than Adam's had decreed that these were not to be, now or ever. As Adam embraced that certainty, Kerr's incantation underwent a shift, its cadence changing as his voice altered in pitch and intensity.

As the shimmering pane of light continued to revolve just beyond Soulis' yearning reach, there appeared above and behind it a jagged line of darkness that gradually widened, pulling itself apart like a self-inflicted wound. Its presence seemed to tear the fabric of the physical world in two; and beyond the gap lay a black and bottomless eternity.

With a rending shriek, Soulis attempted to dodge away.

"Keep him penned where he is!" Kerr shouted across to Adam.

Sword in hand, Adam leaped to hem Soulis in on the astral. His fellow Huntsmen did the same, hedging him about with their blades. While they held Soulis thus at bay, Kerr approached the mirror-like window in the air, where it hovered just below the mouth of the Void. With a single Word of command, he drove his clenched fist into the window's scintillating center.

The pane of light shattered like glass. Soulis' howl of despair was accompanied by a dissonant clangor of chimes. The gap yawned wider still, like a giant, sucking wound. As the shards of his broken future were engulfed by the darkness, Soulis himself was drawn inexorably after them into the Void.

Screaming, he attempted to cling to the threshold, but his shadowy essence could find no purchase there. Still clawing at empty air, he slipped backwards into the gaping rift. His eyes blazed and died as he fell, his own darkness merging with the greater darkness of the abyss. Then abruptly the rift snapped shut, leaving Adam and his companions alone in an astral chapel filled with echoes that gradually died away.

The silence that followed was like a benison. One by one, giving weary salute to Kerr and Adam, the astral company withdrew across intervening space to rejoin physical bodies, wherever they might lie. Retiring likewise from the field, Adam found himself once again on the high plateau among the clouds, where he was joined a moment later by Kerr.

"We have done good work this night," Kerr said. "Your Huntsmen are brave."

"Without your help, we could not have prevailed," Adam said.

A smile crossed Kerr's face, though his essence was already reverting to light.

"I see that the sword I once bore is in good hands, and flames as bright as ever. Go back to your friends in good hope for the future. And take my thanks and commendations with you. The Light has been well served this night."

# EPILOGUE

"WHAT would have happened if Soulis had made good his escape?" Peregrine asked McLeod as they waited for the police and ambulances to arrive.

"Best not to speculate," McLeod grunted. "There was enough havoc wreaked tonight, as it was. What the headlines are going to say when the news hounds get a sniff of the story doesn't bear thinking about."

Peregrine's gaze turned toward the two blanket-draped bodies laid at the foot of the ruined altar, awaiting transport to a police mortuary. One of them belonged to the defrocked priest who had been slain at the height of the Black Mass; the other was Francis Raeburn's. Two more lay dead from SAS gunfire, and Harry and Kinsey were bringing in two additional bodies from the helicopter crash site.

But three of Raeburn's henchmen had been rounded up and were now in military custody awaiting the arrival of the police, two of them with minor wounds—clearly hirelings with little or no grasp of what had really been going on.

Of more concern was the fact that, somewhere in the midst of the confusion, a further unspecified number of Raeburn's associates had managed to escape in one of the Land Rovers. Among those thus far unaccounted for, three were known to Adam by name: Klaus Richter, Dr. Derek Mallory, and Angela, his "Christmas Samaritan." And he had never gotten an accurate count of how many men Richter had altogether. But that was a matter which could be safely left to the conventional police—at least for the moment.

Cochrane, meanwhile, was securing the crime scene for

the inevitable police investigation, though at least three items of evidence retrieved at the scene would *not* be handed over to the police. Adam's Adept ring and the two wedding rings, rescued from the dregs of the profaned chalice, were tucked away in a secure pocket of Peregrine's duffel coat, wrapped in a silk handkerchief, to be delivered to Philippa later for appropriate cleansing and purification. The recollection of the rings brought Peregrine back to the thorny problem of how to minimize adverse publicity.

"You don't suppose the general will be able to help you put a lid on this thing, do you?" he asked McLeod as the distant whuff of helicopter blades announced the imminent return of the SAS chopper.

Chuckling, McLeod shook his head. "Certainly not directly, but he'll do what he can. He wasn't here, of course, so he doesn't have personal explaining to do, but Ian Duart is well enough placed to run some heavy-duty interference. He did mention that Gordon had gone so far as to suggest hinting at a breach of national security, if all else fails."

"And to think that I used to be a simple struggling artist," Peregrine retorted, as they turned to watch the chopper touch down. "How to you plan to square all of this with the department?"

"Oh, Duart's support will certainly help—and we did resolve two kidnappings and a whole raft of crimes involving Raeburn—not that most of them can be proven. I'll have to do a lot of fast talking to explain things back at headquarters.

"On the other hand, it could have been a whole lot worse—and very nearly was. We were all very, very lucky."

"Adam *is* going to be all right, isn't he?" Peregrine asked quietly.

"Ximena says so—and she's the one who would know. She wants to admit him to hospital for a day or two, of course, but Adam himself seems confident that they'll still be able to make their wedding date."

Duart had already arranged for Adam to be taken to a military hospital where no questions would be asked. Peregrine was just about to ask McLeod if they would be allowed to know the location when he caught sight of Harry Nimmo's neat form jogging their way.

"Duart's getting Adam and his brave lassie loaded on board the chopper," he reported when he arrived. "And that young Druid bloke, McFarlane—he's regained consciousness, but he doesn't seem to have much recollection of any of this. It could be he's the luckiest of any of us; I know *I'm* going to have nightmares. Anyway, I expect they'll check him in for observation and a thorough going-over, just to be on the safe side. Oh, and police and ambulances are on their way; we saw them a few miles up the road."

"And about time," McLeod grumbled.

Harry shrugged. "Hey, middle of the night and middle of nowhere. What do you expect? Anyway, we'll be lifting off in a few minutes now. But before I go, there's something I think I ought to give you."

"What's that?" McLeod asked.

For answer, Harry reached into the inside pocket of his flying jacket and brought out a folded handkerchief wrapped around a small object. McLeod took it and opened it up. Inside was a man's gold ring set with a blood-red carnelian. The carnelian bore the cartouche of a lynx's snarling head.

"Well, well, near mate to the one I took off Raeburn," the inspector said, grizzled eyebrows rising above his aviator spectacles.

"Oddly enough, the bodies from that downed chopper were relatively intact," Harry explained, glancing at the ring. "This came off that blond Nazi-type who's been turning up everywhere we looked since Callanish. He had one man with him, also dead, but no ring on that one. Hired help, I'd say. If there were any more, the remains have yet to be recovered. In the meantime, I thought the ring might tell you something."

"Aye, and then we'll destroy it," McLeod said. "You didn't touch this, did you?"

"Are you kidding?" Harry said with a touch of indignation. "I've learned *something* these past few weeks."

"Aye, so you have," McLeod said with a smile. Pocketing the ring, he added, "Once all the dust from this affair dies down, you and I need to have a serious talk."

"Just name the place and the time," Harry said with a

grin. "Just now, though, I've got to stand in for the flying Red Cross."

After takeoff, as the heavily laden Lynx droned across the night, Adam looked on from his stretcher bed as Ximena adjusted the flow on Iolo McFarlane's IV and then shifted farther to check on the wounded SAS pilot. Exhaustion weighed heavily upon him, but he fought it off, waiting for a chance to speak with her. He got his chance a moment later when she came back to check his blood pressure yet again.

"That's the third time you've done that in the past quarter hour," he noted gently.

Ximena looked down at him over the bridge of her nose. "You have your vocation; I have mine."

Adam captured her hand and held it. "Are you angry with me?"

"No, but humor me," Ximena said. "I'm feeling a wee bit insecure. If I can put up with being frightened out of my wits for the past three days, you can put up with being fretted over, now that the danger's past."

She mollified the briskness of this declaration by leaning down to kiss him lingeringly on the mouth. The sweetness of it gave his heart a lurch when he remembered how close they had come to losing one another.

"I really am sorry about all this," he told her, when she shifted her lips to their joined hands.

"What's to be sorry about? I can't say you didn't warn me," she replied.

"True," Adam said, "but there was more I might have told you. And if I had, this whole affair might have been resolved sooner. I shouldn't have been so close-mouthed about Iolo McFarlane's diary. And if I'd rung McLeod the very next morning—"

"Adam Sinclair, don't you dare go playing the 'if' game!" she warned. "You were doing your best to make the right decisions at the time. And I'm willing to believe that you succeeded."

Adam reached up and brushed her cheek, smiling faintly.

"Thank you," he whispered. "I wish I could promise you something like this won't ever happen again."

''I haven't asked you to,'' she replied. ''Suffice it to say that I love you too much to let anyone or anything scare me away. Now get some sleep. If you're determined to be fit enough for a wedding in five days' time, you're going to have to cooperate with your very grumpy doctor!''

Thanks to the discreet offices of friends in high places, the facts surrounding the rescue of Sir Adam Sinclair from the clutches of his kidnappers were never allowed to surface in the media. Any resentment that might have been harbored by journalists on that account, however, was soon assuaged by the newsworthy manner in which Sir Adam and his radiant bride celebrated their marriage on the following Saturday.

The features and photographs detailing the wedding and reception dominated the society pages for several days in succession. The romantic glamour surrounding the match continued to sell newspapers, prompting a number of society reporters to join the small crowd of well-wishers who gathered at Edinburgh Airport a week later to welcome the couple back from their short honeymoon abroad.

As Sir Adam and the new Lady Sinclair settled into the waiting comfort of a classic Bentley, their departure was noted at a distance by two observers in a yellow Mercedes, rendered anonymous by oversized sunglasses, deep-brimmed hats, and well-wrapped scarves. The driver was a man with a lean, wiry build. The passenger was a woman with heavily bandaged hands, whose painted lips curled in studied malice as the Bentley slipped away into traffic.